Boundary

**SIMON
WINSTANLEY**

Titles in the Field Series (in reading order):

Field One
Field Two
Boundary

www.futurewords.uk

First Edition

ISBN-13: 9781976175503
ISBN-10: 197617550X
Library of Congress Control Number: 2017914301
CreateSpace Independent Publishing Platform
North Charleston, South Carolina

11110 110 1000 0111
0110

Simon Winstanley

PROLOGUE

Against the backdrop of a billion stars, the wide Earth lay surrounded by the remnants of its former moon; a scintillating ring of lunar debris, broken in one place by slowly tumbling, continent-sized rocks.

The lunar fragments claimed by Earth's gravity had long since wrought their devastation; each impact disfiguring and scarring the planet's pristine face.

The fragments ejected away from Earth dispersed into the surrounding void; an expanding cloud of former craters and lunar core material.

Into this cloud of lunar projectiles, came a comet.

Unable to withstand the onslaught of a thousand impacts, its singular mass became many. Earth's generous gravity reached out and pulled a thousand lethal shards towards itself.

Upon collision with the lunar ring, each shard triggered meteoric cascades bound for the Earth below. Once more, the skies were torn by fire-tipped arcs of broiling smoke.

After the fires came the ash that obscured the sun; as the first snows of a new ice age fell, the planet descended into permanent silence.

The change to be made was unprecedented.

She would not do this alone.

CONFLUENCE

21st December 2112

On the circumference of the Arctic Circle lay a small, circular, gravitational hotspot. Anchored to this anomaly was an artificial bubble of space-time, surrounding a spherical structure. The bubble's radius was now smaller than before, and enveloped the structure more closely.

Immediately outside its impenetrable boundary, exposed to the extreme cold, several of the former occupants had begun work constructing a primitive bridge; a bridge that would allow them to cross the surrounding deep moat and leave the island.

A commemorative stone, damaged almost a hundred years before by a tidal deluge, bore the partial words 'ARK IV' and a list of names. Those exposed to the arctic chill painstakingly added new words to the ancient stone and turned to face the statuesque figures within the structure. The once-transparent window of the structure became opaque, obscuring all signs of life inside and casting a cold ethereal glow into the darkness.

Standing immutable in time, the artificial bubble continued its journey towards the future, whilst the former occupants turned to face the pale skies and a thunderous noise from the south. The sound was growing stronger, although there was no storm.

DESCENT

24th December 2013

He didn't slow his sprint as he rounded the corner. The layers of wet, brown leaves slipped, removing all friction from under his feet and he hit the ground hard, landing on his hip and ribs. For a second he lay stunned, his burning lungs and hard breaths pumping out shots of steam into the cold night air. He could still hear their voices closing in; his lead would not last long. He scrambled to his feet and looked down the alley he'd entered.

All street lighting had been deactivated weeks ago in an attempt to conserve London's electrical power, leaving the alley bathed in the dim glow of a cloud-covered half-moon.

He sped on, swiftly navigating his way between puddles; there was no point letting in more water through the holes in his shoes. The noise from his hasty footsteps echoed off the close walls as he continued his sprint; a rhythm matching the loud heartbeat in his ears.

Abruptly, the alley ran out and he found himself at a

dead end. He briefly snapped his eyes shut in the hope that they'd adapt to the low light. When he opened them a second later, the view wasn't significantly better but in places there were dim outlines. In one corner was the dark hole of an air vent, its metal grating long since stolen and repurposed. Next to it, he could just make out the rungs of a service ladder, rusted securely into the wall. Perhaps drawing on primitive instinct, he had the strong desire to climb in order to escape the immediate threat.

At the far end of the alley he heard the voices again and, although he couldn't hear the exact words, he could tell that the group had decided to split up. The sound of fast-receding footsteps died away, leaving only a few pairs of feet slowly scuffling their way along the alley.

Unless he acted soon, he would have to contend with fighting off two or three people, something he knew he couldn't achieve. He reached into his pocket and pulled out his catapult; little more than a 'Y' shaped twig with a thick elastic band. A quick check confirmed he was down to his last two pebbles.

He loaded the elastic band with the larger of the pebbles and, aiming it down the alley, raised it into position. He couldn't bring down his pursuers with a single stone, but perhaps he could buy himself time. He released the elastic and a moment later the pebble ricochet loudly off the alley wall. In the resulting commotion, he turned and began to climb the ladder as quietly as he could, feeling his way and hoping that each subsequent rung would meet with his outstretched hand.

The footsteps resumed their approach, but he knew

it no longer mattered; he'd reached the top of the ladder and, with a surge of effort, he stepped onto a flat level roof. He remained motionless for a few minutes, until the voices below receded again. A creeping cold began spreading through his shoes and he realised that he'd stepped straight into a shallow puddle of rainwater.

"Perfect," he muttered under his breath, they were his only pair and they would take days to dry out.

Now out of the alley, the ambient moonlight was brighter and he could see his surroundings more clearly; he was on an upper level of the shopping mall. Ahead he could see its domed skylight, the glass broken in one place, no doubt by someone forcing their way in. He trudged over to the hole, scuffing through the broken glass, and peered in. Just inside were metal access steps, offering a way down from his elevated position.

He could retrace his steps and go back down the rusty ladder, but he didn't want to risk running into his pursuers again so soon.

"Always forwards, Danny," he muttered his mother's words, "Never back."

Avoiding the remnants of glass jutting from the metal frame, he ducked in through the opening onto the metal steps and began to quietly make his way down. He was a little puzzled by how warm it was in comparison to the outside. Shelter was hard to find, and yet a perfectly serviceable, large building had not been claimed by those who so desperately needed a place to live.

He reached the base of the steps and walked into a bright pool of light. Looking up to see the source of the illumination, he saw the Moon framed within the hole he'd climbed through.

He'd heard the far-fetched stories pushed by the media of a moon-base deflecting a comet. He'd also heard that the need to dig for victory against this unseen enemy was simply a precautionary measure in case the space-rock ever hit. But for Danny, it sounded like governments were attempting to distract the population from the problems closer to home of military curfews, rolling blackouts, and war-time rationing of food.

He turned away from the skylight and allowed his eyes to adjust to the gloom of the shopping mall. The bright white walls were bouncing the grey moonlight deeper into the dark structure, illuminating the dead storefronts.

He walked to the handrail and looked out across the different walkway levels that surrounded the open, airy space. Nine months ago, this had been a vibrant place. People had casually strolled from one end of the mall to the other, carrying colourful logo-emblazoned carrier bags. Mannequins in aloof poses had toted the latest fashions and people had queued for hours to get the latest shiny smartphones.

The place had been so alive, but now even the mannequins lay dead and stripped of their clothing. The smartphone shops had long since been looted; not for their technology, which was now useless, but for the metal shelves and items that could prop up the ceilings of dirt tunnels.

Danny had seen the world and people change so quickly. Perhaps, he thought, it had always been this way; but in these more desperate times, civilisation's veneer had simply been scratched away, allowing human nature to be seen more clearly.

It was exactly this sort of philosophical debate that he used to hear many months ago. Local parents, wanting to do something positive for their children, had commandeered the basement of a large, abandoned hotel construction project nearby. The basement itself contained an unfilled luxury swimming pool; the shallow end had been used for conversation and games, whereas the deep end had been used for thoughtful debate, discussion and even poetry on the new social order. Typically this attracted the twenty-somethings, of which he'd been one. However in the last few months it had undergone changes: 'The Gene Pool' was now attracting a more rebellious element, intent on converting existential angst into an easy trade of different vices. Although Danny still went there, he would usually avoid the lower levels in favour of the emptier upper floors, where he could talk with his friends.

Cloud cover began to dim the available light and Danny knew he'd need to find a way out of the deserted mall while he could still see. He crossed the walkway to look for the stairs, taking care to move as quietly as possible. Again it struck him as very odd that this prime living space was so quiet and unoccupied.

He took one last look at the glazed dome, set within the high ceiling of this cathedral-like space, then pushed open the stairwell door.

Unsurprisingly, the stairs were pitch black, meaning he'd have to use his LED light. Batteries were too costly to replace now so, as ever, he used it sparingly; briefly illuminating a few feet ahead of him to check for obstacles, before turning if off and then moving on in the dark. He managed to reach the base of the stairs using only four light flashes.

The stairs led out onto the former food court and supermarket area. He remembered that long ago he'd seen staff members taking cigarette breaks by the supermarket's fire exit. As that exit was on the opposite side of the building to where he'd been chased, it made sense to leave that way.

Navigating by careful flashes of LED light, Danny made his way through the deserted supermarket aisles. There was of course no sign of any food and even the shelves had been removed, leaving behind only skeletal portions of metallic framework; though why these hadn't also been salvaged, he didn't know.

Under the dust that covered the chequered floor, were dried dark stains. People had actually drawn blood, he thought, battling for tinned goods. The light from his LED flash fell on a long-faded sign proclaiming *'March Madness! 2for1 on all green-labels'*. To have fought for this *was* madness, he thought. He kicked the faded promotion aside and headed for the *'Emergency Exit'* sign on the wall.

He walked down the narrow steps and saw that there was a flickering orange glow ahead. He recognised the light immediately as the sort that came from an oil drum campfire; evidently he was close to the exit. He would have to excuse himself to anyone gathered around it and then leave as quickly as possible. Generally, people were possessive over their fires; after all, they were burning their own resources to ward off the cold.

He reached the end of a short corridor but instead of exiting into the open air, he entered a closed room. Several people were gathered around a small fire, all of them facing a large man who had his back to Danny.

An adolescent-looking boy spotted Danny and spoke to alert the group, "Er... Shane?"

The man reacted and, turning away from the fire, slowly advanced a few steps towards Danny. The man cleared his throat and then spoke loudly for all in the room to hear.

"We move separately."

"But as one," the others replied in unison.

The man was looking expectantly at him, as though anticipating a reply.

Danny didn't know what he'd wandered into, but knew he had to get out as quickly as possible. He held up his hands in a gesture of apology.

"Look, er... Shane?" Danny tried using the man's name and began to back away, "I got chased by a bunch of curfew thugs, I didn't mean to inter... I mean I'm really sorry, I -"

He was interrupted by the room's only door being slammed shut behind him.

Danny whipped round to see that another of their group, one he hadn't even seen when he'd mistakenly entered the room, was now standing with his arms crossed in front of the door.

"Look, I've not got much..." Danny began to empty his pockets, "You can take it, it's yours, I-"

"Hold him," said Shane, quietly.

The others reacted instantly, bringing him to his knees and preventing him from struggling free.

"I need to send a message," Shane removed the glove from his right hand and walked towards him.

Danny's heart was hammering, escape was clearly impossible. The best he could do now was to comply with anything asked of him.

"Just tell me… tell me the message," Danny could feel his throat constricting with panic, "I.. I can remember anything you -"

"You won't need to remember a single thing," Shane held up his hand for Danny to see. A raised circular burn mark on the back of his hand stood proud of the surrounding skin.

He recognised the symbol immediately and, despite the room's heat, he felt his blood turn to ice. Shane, presumably spotting his look of wide-eyed terror, smiled then walked back to the fire. Watching helplessly, Danny saw him put the glove back on and retrieve something small from the grate above the fire. It was obviously hot, because the glove began to smoulder.

As if taking this as a cue, two within the group seized Danny's right hand and held it in place. Using all his bodyweight he tried to break free of their vice-like grip, but the sheer strength of the others surrounding him was too great. As they closed in even further, he found himself screaming for help.

"There's no-one here!" Shane bellowed, as if to highlight the fact that the entire shopping mall was empty.

Too late, Danny realised the significance of the

broken glass *outside* the mall's dome. No-one had broken *into* this place, they had been breaking *out* of it. The mall was deserted because it was Exordi Nova territory.

"No…" he begged, his voice now barely a strangled whisper, *"Please… No…"*

With his gloved hand, Shane held up a ring of polished steel about an inch in diameter, intersected at one point by a ball-bearing. An oily blue line of heat discolouration was working its way through the steel's thickness and Danny could smell the metallic tang in the air.

"You know what?" Shane asked the others, rhetorically, "Since Troye marked me, I've been getting on just fine by wearing these gloves. I wanna try giving our 'New Beginning' a new beginning."

Shane's gaze settled on Danny's forehead.

"Hold his hair back."

The surge of adrenaline that accompanied Danny's guttural roar succeeded in jostling those holding him, but he was soon brought back under their control.

"Siva must complete its path," Shane stepped closer.

"Our self-sacrifice is just," everyone around him replied.

Danny could feel the heat from the scorching metal as it was brought closer to his face. He screamed again, but hands and arms held his head firmly in place for what was to come.

Shane arranged the metallic symbol on the palm of his glove, inches away from Danny's eyes.

"Exordi Nova," said Shane, quietly.

"The New Beginning," the sound of their united

response swam in his ears.

In one swift movement, Shane clapped the searing hot symbol against Danny's forehead and pressed hard. Danny heard the hiss of his own flesh before the pain arrived, sudden and blinding. As the seconds ticked by, the pain increased until his own body forced a sudden and blissful unconsciousness upon him.

ESCA

23rd November 7120

Standing in the orange glow of firelight, Esca held her baby close, the warmth of the fire keeping both the chill of night and cold ethereal glow of the Orb at bay.

The Sky-Spirits circled overhead, passing through each other, exchanging hues and intensities of green and purple iridescence. Beyond them, she could see the sparkling rings that surrounded her world; rings that had existed long before her forefathers and would persist long after she had returned to dust.

The Elder bade her come forward, so she lowered herself to one knee and scooped a handful of warm ash from the fire's edge. She trod softly away from the fire's warmth to the ancient carved stone a few footfalls away.

She bowed in reverence to the Elder, then holding her baby firmly with one arm she offered up her handful of ash. The Elder dropped a small amount of spittle into the ash and invited her to do the same. She watched as the Elder mixed the ash and spittle into a paste within her palm, and smiled at her child who had not stirred from sleep.

She watched as the Elder brought out his vine-weaved necklace, upon which was tied a loop of metal that shone brightly with reflected fire. The metal was broken in one place by the presence of a precious stone that appeared to sparkle under the Orb's radiance.

The Elder gently placed the circle on the baby's forehead.

"Exordi Nova," he said quietly.

Esca repeated his words in reply, their exact meaning had been lost to time but she knew what it represented. The circle meaning the unbroken renewal of life and the stone depicting the Orb watching over each new beginning.

As gently as before, the Elder now removed the metal loop from her baby's forehead. Dipping his thumb into the black ash paste in Esca's hand, he marked the baby's forehead with the same circular symbol, placing a wide dot to intersect the circle.

"Archiv," the Elder smiled at her, and gestured to the ancient stone.

Being careful not to lose the remainder of the ash paste, she held her baby close and walked to the closest edge of the stone. Hoping that The Guardians and Sky-Spirits would guide her choice, she began walking slowly from one end of the stone to the other.

Her choice would be important.

It would be the sum of her hopes for her child.

As she reached the centre of the stone, her baby stirred and she knew this was the guidance she had sought. With a feeling of deep happiness, Esca placed her ash-blackened palm on the ancient stone and pressed firmly. She then placed her hand on her baby's head.

"Atka," she named him.

'Guardian Spirit' had been used by others in past generations. She hoped it would one day allow him to guide others with the same benevolence.

MASS

13th April 2014

"Helm. All stop," Tristan Westhouse announced calmly.

"Aye, Sir," replied Mat Kaufman, "answering all stop."

As the Sea-Bass submarine slowed, Tristan stood and walked to the toughened-glass bubble window.

Over three months ago, seven lunar shards had destroyed the GPS networks, meaning their navigation was only possible using Westhouse's Topography Overlay technique. By comparing live sonar traces to previously recorded seabed images, a visual pattern match could be found and the real-world coordinates reverse engineered.

They had been in the deeper waters, just off the North Atlantic continental shelf, when a discrepancy in the pattern-matching data had been discovered. Visible only as the difference between live sonar and older stored data, a pattern had emerged from the background noise; it had a distinctive and recognisable shape.

For the past half-hour, they had followed an approximately northeast heading, towards the coordinates of its theoretical existence. The sheer amount of fine debris held by the seawater had made navigation slow, but as they had approached the designated location, the water had become crystal clear.

"Reading all stop. Station-keeping to auto," Mat reported, then made his way forward to join Tristan at the window.

The two of them stared.

"Is that…?" Mat pointed.

Tristan nodded, "Ice."

"But…"

"Yeah, I know," Tristan continued to study the formation.

During the preceding day, he'd seen this exact shape repeatedly; in coffee stains on paper, scuff-marks around rotary dials, even within the blueprint of his father's Glaucus Docking Ring system. The same circle and dot symbol was synonymous with the terrorist organisation Exordi Nova, a fact that had not been missed by the crew.

However, the circle and dot symbol visible through the bubble window was not a marking, but a complex, three-dimensional shape. In form, Tristan thought it resembled an ornate engagement ring; a wide circular ring into which a gleaming pearl had been set.

At the edge of the structure was a perfect, white sphere of ice, but the ice within the ring was not a single solid. It consisted of two intertwined spirals that followed the curvature of a wide circle; a double helix that left one side of the sphere and made one complete orbit before re-joining it.

"It's massive," said Tristan, leaning forward into the bubble window to further gauge its extent.

"You think?" Mat added dryly.

"No," Tristan countered, "I mean it has a lot of mass."

Mat was shaking his head at him.

"Tris, a giant Exordi symbol turns up on the bottom of the ocean floor. My first thoughts are like, one…" he counted on his fingers, "what the hell? Two - what the *hell?* But the first thing you talk about is how heavy it is. We all know you're super-smart, but doesn't this even *surprise* you?"

"Of course it does," Tristan replied, "This much ice should float."

He heard Mat draw a breath, no doubt to comment on his logical approach to things, but the humorous critique didn't arrive.

"I was wrong about something," said Mat, then pointed through the window, "It isn't actually touching the ocean floor."

Tristan followed Mat's line of sight and saw the faint, diffused shadow underlying the entire structure.

"Mat, you're a genius," Tristan murmured.

"Say that again," Mat cupped his hand behind his ear, "so that everyone can hear. And why am I a genius?"

Tristan turned away from the window to look at him.

"You saw something that I didn't."

Seeing Mat's frown deepen slightly, Tristan continued, "If nothing's supporting it, how is it staying in the same place?"

ORIENTATION

28th December 2013

For Miles Benton, the most traumatic part of the trip to the International Space Station had not been the launch; he'd been unconscious when Apollo 72 had made its leap to orbit. The hardest part was adjusting to having zero weight.

Miles liked to think that after all his years under the influence of metathene, his mind could adapt to any situation by the application of logic. That may have been true during his former ego-morph days, where the cold guiding hand of the metathene would sharpen his cognition, but without the drug he was less able to simply switch off his reactions.

He vomited into his plastic zip-lock bag and wiped his mouth on its inner absorbent lining.

It appeared that Anna Bergstrom was faring even worse. Between bouts of vomiting, she cradled her bandaged hand; a souvenir of the aggressive interrogation administered by Bradley Pittman.

Less than two weeks ago, at the base on Öskjuvatn Lake, Miles had promised Douglas Walker that he would do his best to assist Anna. Since that time, events had worsened considerably and he'd been unable to offer her complete protection.

Miles had used persuasive arguments to prevent her from being killed outright, but this had prolonged her ordeal. Without the metathene to suppress his empathy, the events were weighing heavily on him. He'd broken his promise to help Anna. He found himself anxiously gripping his silver coin and recalling that he liked to help people. He'd failed.

On the coin, the embossed Liberty Bell stood alongside a perfectly round, intact Moon. By contrast, the view through the tiny ISS porthole framed the horrifically decimated Moon.

The dimenhydrinate patch stuck to the skin of his upper arm did not appear to be quelling the motion sickness. He opened his plastic bag slightly in preparation, but nothing arrived except an impulse to retch.

"Miles," came Anna's quiet, hoarse voice.

He looked over to see her resting upside-down and half way up the adjacent wall, further compounding his feeling of disorientation. He placed his coin back into one of his numerous pockets, then gently pushed away from the porthole to be by her side. With an outstretched hand, he reached for the handhold nearest to her. His fingers closed around the metal but his momentum carried him forwards. Most of his body overshot his intended target and he turned a somersault before he managed to orient himself to face her.

Anna's face crumpled and her voice trembled, "Miles, they broke me."

Miles didn't know how to reply; her torture had

been horrific.

"They know!" she sniffed, cradling her hand again, "They know that once it's built, anyone can use it. Archive knows!"

"You mean the Node's Field generator?"

The science behind the Field equations was firmly outside his experience, but he *did* know how Archive liked to control the flow of information.

"They know you don't need my specialist Field knowledge to run it. I've got no leverage…" she continued, her voice only just audible above the constant background hum of the ISS fans and pumps, "I'm too old… they don't need us…"

Miles knew this could not be true and told her so. If they were not needed, it would have been easier to leave them behind on Earth. They both had a function aboard the ISS, even if they couldn't currently see it.

On hearing the small chamber's hatch door activate, Miles did his best to drain his face of all emotion and present an air of neutrality and disinterest. As far as he knew, Archive still considered him to be an ego-morph; he thought it best to continue that assumption. He flashed a blank-looking face in Anna's direction. She nodded that she understood the need to continue the pretence they'd begun while still on Earth.

The door folded outward and a small man propped himself in the doorway.

"My apologies," he bowed his head slightly, "Pressing circumstances prevented me from attending you sooner. I am Dr. Chen and I humbly welcome you aboard my station."

Miles recalled that the name had appeared on the transport authorisation form when they'd flown from Andersen Air Force Base. They'd been aboard Dr. Chen's plane when they were anaesthetised.

"Thank you, sir," Miles responded and, trying not to induce nausea, turned himself through ninety degrees to match the orientation of Dr. Chen. The manoeuvre had the effect of visually shifting Anna back upon the wall, but the action earned him a nod of respect from his host.

"Mr. Benton, Dr. Bergstrom, I regret there was no time to seek your permission for bringing you aboard."

"Huh. Regret," Anna found her tongue and raised her bandaged hand.

"Dr. Bergstrom, I had no part in your... treatment."

"Treatment?" she almost laughed.

Dr. Chen appeared to consider her statement for a moment and then nodded to himself before replying.

"It seems Mr. Pittman's need for violence did not end with your despicable... torture, Dr. Bergstrom," he looked at her hand and shook his head gravely, "I have recently learned that Mr. Pittman and Alfred Barnes have killed General Napier, though the exact reason is unclear. We also know that before this, Mr. Pittman closed all access to his survival bunkers in the United States - an action also taken by Alexey Yakovna. They started a global panic, there was no safe place for... anyone. His actions have condemned the population of Earth. I did what I could to bring you both to safety."

Although Miles no longer possessed his full ego-morph faculties, he had the feeling that there was something slightly amiss in Dr. Chen's recount, but he couldn't identify it.

"What happened to Douglas Walker?" Anna asked directly, "and his daughter?"

Again Dr. Chen appeared to consider her question before replying.

"According to the last, ah, electronic Biomag register, they are both aboard the Node."

"But the Node wasn't finished," she began, "Even if it had been completed, the structure is not strong enough to protect against - oh…"

Miles could see that she'd seen something that he hadn't.

"Yes," Dr. Chen confirmed, "It seems that the Node's Field was prematurely activated, yesterday. They will be safe now."

Anna fell silent again, evidently deep in thought.

"There is still much to be done," Dr. Chen continued, "The year ahead will require the cooperation of everyone aboard, and I very much hope you will contribute your, ah, expertise."

Miles identified the emphasis on the last word as quickly as Anna.

"What?" Anna said simply.

"Your field of expertise?" Dr. Chen gave a slight frown, "It will be essential, if we are to keep pace with the Node on its journey."

"You want to build a Chronomagnetic Field generator?" Anna asked incredulously, "Here? Aboard the ISS?"

Dr. Chen nodded.

Miles now realised the true reason for Anna being

brought aboard; Dr. Chen may have acted quickly when the situation on Earth degraded, but his motive to save her had no altruistic perspective.

"I am aware of everything that Archive held on Dr. Walker's research," Dr. Chen clarified, "and your collaborative effort in the creation of the Field inversion equations. I followed the development of the Node's Field generator schematics -"

Dr. Chen broke off when he saw that she was shaking her head.

"Then you should also know how impossible it will be to get -"

"Dr. Bergstrom," he raised a hand, almost as though he was allaying her fears, "The components are already aboard."

Miles saw a look of confusion sweep across her face.

"But the tonnage?" she began, "It must have taken weeks to -"

"Details," Dr. Chen smiled, "We will discuss the specific schedule when your senses are fully acclimatised. The motion sickness patches *do* work, they just need time. Now, Mr. Benton."

He turned to face Miles.

"When we grounded my plane at the shuttle launch site, there was no time to search for your lost injector case - you must now be several hours behind in your regular dose. I'm pleased to offer you this replacement. You'll find it fully stocked."

He held out a round-cornered silver case.

Miles knew what is was, but for the sake of appearances he took it and stored it in a pocket.

"Thank you," Miles replied as mechanically as possible.

"Please, Mr. Benton," he smiled, "You must not feel embarrassed on our part, we know that ego-morphs must administer regular doses, in order to continue their dedicated work. Please, I insist. Use the case now."

Miles knew that if his ego-morph deprogramming was discovered, then he may become worthless to Dr. Chen and then find himself on the wrong side of an airlock door. If the deception was to be maintained, Miles knew he couldn't refuse.

He removed the silver case from his pocket.

He'd been clear of the metathene's influence for many months. His intellect hadn't diminished, he'd just become a little slower to draw connections between tangential pieces of information.

He opened the case, exposing the short vials of pale, whiskey-coloured liquid, and a place to rest his finger. He recalled that the small mechanism in the case was designed to prick his finger and the digital display would respond with a metathene saturation level.

This knowledge and these actions belonged to the person he used to be, not the man he was now. Yet he knew he must continue; Dr. Chen's knowledge of the metathene protocol was obviously quite thorough.

He removed a single vial and loaded it onto the case's injector mount, then pressed the flat side of the case against his thigh. He knew the words and actions that came next; the words that were supposed to bring solace after committing questionable acts, the actions that would perpetuate the chain of dependence.

At that moment Anna coughed, causing Dr. Chen to look away from Miles.

"I'll be fine," she told their host, then turned to look at Miles, "I'll be just fine."

Miles realised that the words were meant for him, not Dr. Chen. She was reassuring him.

Miles could see peripherally that Dr. Chen had resumed watching him. He could delay no longer. With the case still pressed against his thigh, he didn't turn away from Anna.

"For the good of Mankind," he heard himself say, then pressed the injector button.

The thin needle plunged straight between the fibres of his clothing and into his flesh. He knew he couldn't feel the actual dispersion, but he could all too easily imagine the cold, emotion-dulling drug beginning to spread through his veins.

"Indeed. For the good of Mankind," Dr. Chen nodded, then tapped at a metal band around his own wrist, "Ultimately, Mr. Benton, we'll replace your silver antique with a medical wristband. Much more efficient."

"Why do *you* need a band?" Anna asked pointedly, "Are you an ego-morph too?"

Dr. Chen frowned at her faint accusation, but appeared not to take offence.

"Everyone aboard, including myself, uses metathene supplements to augment their intellectual balance. Before arriving here, I believe you yourself used Archive's supplements Dr. Bergstrom…"

Miles saw that Anna didn't contradict the statement, but merely watched Dr. Chen as he continued.

"… The bands are simply a more efficient method of delivery. Everyone here has one. Or soon will. Recent arrivals required the use of the next available bands, but you may rest assured that you will receive yours soon. Nothing but the best," he smiled at both of them in turn, "Now, living space is at a premium here, but you are most welcome. Having saved your lives I feel your, ah, wellbeing is my responsibility."

There it was, thought Miles; the implication that every breath they now took was a debt to be repaid.

"I have another matter to attend to," Dr. Chen bowed his head slightly, "but I will return shortly. I'm looking forward to working with you both."

With one smooth motion, he turned and pushed away from the doorway, leaving the door itself wide open.

For Miles, the subtext of Dr. Chen's words and actions seemed to be growing clearer: in the vacuum of space, a prison did not need to lock its doors.

Something else that was now apparent to Miles was that these types of thoughts were due to the metathene beginning to reassert its cold, emotionless suppression. Quite unexpectedly, he felt a tear forming in his eye. In zero gravity, it had nowhere to fall and it simply pooled where it formed; its surface tension causing it to stick to his face.

"Here," said Anna, holding out a small absorbent towel.

"No…" Miles shook his head slightly as his eyes continued to fill, "I need to feel this. Soon I won't be able to."

USV

21st January 2014

Framed behind the bars of a holding cell door, Bradley Pittman prowled slowly back and forth. Monica Walker watched him awkwardly trying to avoid her line of questioning.

"Answer me," she repeated.

He quickly stepped closer to the door and took hold of the bars.

"I don't answer to you, bitch!" he spat in a low tone.

"No, you don't answer to anyone. The rules don't apply to people like you, do they?" Monica replied calmly, enjoying the fact that the holding cell bars made his physical threat impotent, "I want you to give me the truth."

His eyes wandered around the grey walls that ran throughout the detention facility of the Underground Survival Village.

"You know what I'm gonna give you?" he traced a square around the inside of the bars, his eyes alive with glee, "A pretty picture, to keep in your head."

He drew a breath and appeared to be recalling a fond memory, then he looked at her through the bars and smiled.

"You know, I think the *best* part was the look of confusion on his face. The fact that anyone would *dare* shoot the great man himself. Aw Mon, there was *so* much blood!" he gave a short laugh, hand-miming arterial sprays from his stomach, "It just, didn't, wanna, stop! Even after he hit the floor…"

From Bradley's body language, she could tell this had been a real event. But there were other cues that were missing from his colourful recount; a possible indicator that although the death itself was real, it may not actually have been her husband's death he was describing.

As Bradley took hold of the bars again, Monica did her best to calmly assess him during his continued bragging.

"He didn't die alone, Mon. No, your little Katie was there to see it *all*. She tried to help her ol' dad, but…" he squeezed the bars, turning his knuckles white, "Her throat was so soft. She kinda kicked an' struggled a while, but I watched her lights go out too."

She felt a fire ignite at the thought of her daughter dying at his hands, it took all of her resolve not to react to his obvious provocation.

"You're a lying coward," she said as calmly as she could, "But if you *have* so much as touched a hair -"

"Ooh, I touched more than that," he cut across her.

Monica stepped to within arm's reach of Bradley, an action that stopped him speaking but also appeared to satisfy him.

"Just try," he smiled.

"It's only these bars that separate us," Monica stared.

"Yeah, well, these bars," he tapped on the steel, "are here for my protection. Not yours."

Monica purposefully took a small step back and relaxed her fists; this was exactly the reaction he'd wanted to provoke. She wouldn't rise to it. She drew a deep breath then returned an equally shallow smile.

"You may be the one who's free to take a walk around your glorified hole in the ground," said Monica, looking around her small cell, "but it's still just a cage. You're just as trapped as me."

Bradley laughed and walked away from her.

"You just keep tellin' yourself that," he banged his fist twice on the outer door, "Reckon I might just have me a stroll round that beautiful lake of yours."

The detention facility outer door opened and he left without another word. She heard the door lock and, beyond the bars, the little red light on the security camera re-illuminated. Evidently, he hadn't wanted their conversation on record.

So it begins again, she found herself thinking, the endless deception upon deception, the grey morality, the justifications. She had left all this behind and yet here she was again.

The truth was that there had been little choice in the matter. When the tsunamis striking the British Isles had overwhelmed the Dover coast, the first casualty had been her own, parallel, underground survival facility. The failure of a surface entrance had flooded the Warren, forcing her people to escape into the USV via a tunnel she'd prepared over a decade earlier.

Their descent into the dark interior of the USV had lasted only minutes before they'd spotted the approach of the Peace Keepers. The events that had followed, had placed her in this cell.

She was drawn out of her thoughts by a muted sound.

Through the letterbox-sized air vent in the cell wall she heard the sound of rotor blades starting up, building in pitch to an incessant whine.

With a low howl of feedback, the speakers beyond the holding cell became active.

"Geraldine Mercer," came a synthetic sounding voice.

On hearing the name, Monica dashed the single stride to stand on the hard bed, then angled her ear towards the air vent. Geraldine had been her most trusted companion during the construction of the Warren; she had even falsified her own death in order to be by Monica's side.

"The charges are as follows. Wilful damage to the USV sealed habitat."

Monica realised too late what was happening.

"Disabling of a Peace Keeper."

The last time this had happened, there had been only one charge and the consequences had been immediate.

"Assisting a known enemy with intent to inspire sedition."

"Hey!" Monica bellowed at the air vent in an attempt to get someone's attention. Outside, the whine of the rotor blades increased in pitch again.

"In accordance with habitat law, these acts are punishable by death. Does the accused have any response?"

Monica stopped all movement, straining her ears for any response that Geraldine might offer, but the only sound reaching her was the phasing, droning noise of rotors.

"No!" Monica screamed towards the air vent, "Stop! Wait!"

"Execute sentence."

"No! Stop!" she yelled and hammered her fist against the wall.

She heard the rotor noise swell slightly, followed by a thick, buzzing sound. Monica was still screaming for them to stop as the rotor noises abruptly dropped in frequency and fell silent.

Her knees gave way and she collapsed down onto the unyielding bed.

Almost as an act of self-comfort she found herself massaging at a white band of skin on her ring finger. Although her tiny amount of jewellery had been confiscated when they'd imprisoned her here, the memory of Douglas' proposal was indelible. But, like the engagement ring, he too was gone.

A new sense of loss now reinforced the first. She had once loaned the same ring to Geraldine to persuade her that everything would be alright once they'd left Archive. The pale flesh on her finger now confronted Monica with the cold fact that Geraldine's death was on her hands.

The detention facility's outer door opened and Bradley Pittman returned. He calmly crossed the small room and stood in front of the cell door again.

"Well, you know what? That was a real nice stroll," he produced a hollow smile, "I feel *so* much better for that. Where were we?"

Monica had no words.

She simply sat on the bed, nursing her sudden grief and wondering what event could have created the sadistic animal staring at her through the bars.

VALENTINE'S DAY

14th February 1952

William Pittman knew the evening had been a disaster and it seemed to be showing no signs of improving. The rain continued to beat at the whole car and a permanent waterfall appeared to be occupying the windshield. He turned on the wipers but it made no real difference; he could only see tiny slices of the surrounding streets before the view was drowned once again by the unending torrent.

His father, Edgar Pittman, had loaned him the '42 Lincoln so that he could drive his date to the dance. If things had turned out differently it would have made a great impression. Not that he needed to make a good first impression, the family name was well known. It was this fact that was making tonight's rejection harder for him to deal with.

She hadn't even come out of the house to explain. She'd sent her mother to relay the news that she was feeling under the weather and wouldn't be joining him. Shortly afterwards he was very much under the weather too when the heavens had opened.

The music coming from the radio was doing little to brighten his spirits either. The meandering heartbreak lyrics wallowed in the idea that knowing what the future held would be world-ending.

"Yeah, well, come what may," he grumbled, "I ain't doin' this again."

He reached out his right hand and flicked off the radio, leaving him in the company of the beating rain.

The watery patch of red light in the upper right corner of the windshield changed to green and slowly he drove the car across the intersection. He'd gone no further than a few hundred yards when he was flagged down by a police officer waving a lantern. William stopped and wound the window down a few inches.

Shoulders hunched up to his neck against the rain, the officer walked around to the window and spoke through the gap.

"Hey buddy," he sniffled, "bad accident on Clayton, road's closed. You're gonna want to take Maple, then pick it up again when you clear Memorial Drive."

"Aw come on!" he blurted, "Sorry, not you officer. Bad day."

The officer wiped his palm pointlessly over his rain-soaked eyebrows and glanced at the expensive car that William was driving.

"Bad day, huh?" he looked at him blankly, "Happy Valentine's. Make a right."

He closed up his ineffective collar against the rain and turned away, shaking his head. William wound up his window and then, taking care to use his indicators in front of the officer, drove past him and turned right onto Maple.

If anything, conditions were slightly worse as the street lights were out. Behind a curtain of rainwater, the road only appeared to exist between the car's headlights. His rear-view mirror reflected only the darkness behind him.

Since Memorial Drive had taken over most of the heavy traffic, Maple had become an underused minor road; in the darkness, he couldn't see much traffic at all. As far as he could tell there was only a single pair of red taillights on the waterlogged road ahead.

In a way, he persuaded himself, the failed date may be a fortunate thing. The problem, as always, was that he could never truly tell if people were interested in him or in his family's general wealth. Maybe the girl was just playing hard to get, he thought, maybe she *was* interested and this was some sort of ploy. He suddenly snapped out of his musings as he realised that the taillights ahead of him had become drastically further apart. Despite trying to keep a steady speed, he'd actually caught up with the vehicle. He eased off the gas pedal and his approach slowed.

As he stared out at the watery, smeared taillights in front of him, he saw a bright flash of yellow light explode from one of the rear tyres as it blew out. The car ahead suddenly slewed into a watery spin and the headlights shone straight through his windshield, turning his view a dazzling opaque white. He slammed his foot down on the brake pedal and the wheels locked, sending him aquaplaning into an uncontrolled skid over the slippery surface. The bright headlights swept away and in the sudden darkness he couldn't see a thing until the taillights came into view again, this time a lot closer. He hauled at the steering wheel and tried to turn away from the impending impact, but with no grip on the road, the tyres continued to carry him forwards. A sudden vibration shook the car as it left the road and ploughed through grass and dirt, then everything rocked to an abrupt halt.

The other car had stopped too; its headlights pointing in his direction. With the exception of the mutually illuminated vehicles, the rest of the road was still in darkness.

After swearing a silent vow to wear the seatbelt in future, he pushed open the door and walked the short distance to the other car. Within a few steps, the rain had converted his tailored suit into clingy, wet pieces of cloth.

"Miss?" he called to the woman in the other car, "Miss? You OK?"

Still gripping her steering wheel, she appeared to come to her senses.

"What hap-" she began, "What happened?"

With a click, her door opened a little but then she stopped. Evidently her seatbelt was doing its job. After a few seconds of indistinct cursing, she pushed the door fully open and started to get out.

"Miss! I really wouldn't get -"

Before he could finish, the woman was soaked from head to toe.

"It just -" she began, then her eyelids fluttered closed

and she fell forwards in a dead faint.

He reacted quickly enough to catch her and, as she was so slight of frame, he found it no effort to sweep her up into his arms. However, he found it a more awkward task to hold her while opening the rear door of her car. The door handle eventually cooperated and he carefully lowered her onto the back seat, leaving only her legs exposed to the driving rain.

On impulse, he took off his jacket and stretched it between the top of the open door and the car's roof, creating a protective canopy. Ducking his head into the car, he stood very still and watched her; she was still breathing but the sudden cold was probably doing her no good.

"Miss?" he cautiously tapped at her knee, "Excuse me, Miss?"

She slowly stirred and raised her head from the seat. He breathed a sigh of relief and she screamed at the top of her voice. In shock, he stood bolt upright and cracked the back of his head on the doorframe. Clutching at the pain, he stumbled backward, lost his balance and collapsed into an awkward sitting position on the wet concrete.

"Son of a -" he rubbed at his head.

When he looked back, the woman was sitting upright, her legs withdrawn into the car. She was staring up at the improvised jacket canopy that had collapsed over the rear door as he'd fallen.

"You fainted," he attempted to explain, "So I, that is, you were…"

"Oh my," she looked at him then frantically beckoned to him, "I'm so sorry! Get in, you're getting soaked!"

William hauled himself up and, being careful not to bump his head again, sat down on the edge of the seat.

"It's freezing!" she said, shuffling over to the other side of the seat to make room for him, "Do you mind if we close the door?"

He pulled his jacket from the door and was about to wring out the water, but realised it was completely pointless. He tossed the jacket onto the road and closed the door. There was a moment of quiet between the pair of them as the rain continued to hammer at the roof.

"Sorry about your jacket," she said, then after a second or two added, "and your head."

He rubbed at his head but found himself laughing at the situation, which in turn caused her to do the same.

"That right there," he pointed across the road to where his car stood, "was one close call!"

"Can't believe I walked away from that," she shook her head.

"Me neither," he rubbed the back of his head.

"I was just driving along, minding my own business and doing my best to stay on the road in this *awful* weather, when suddenly -"

"Bam," William completed, "Looked like a full-on blowout to me."

"I'd no idea that's what they were like. It was terrifying!"

"Yep, I reckon you busted up that axle pretty good," he nodded, throwing a thumb over his shoulder towards the back of the car.

"Are you a mechanic then?" she asked.

He was used to most people recognising him, so it caught him a little off guard that she obviously didn't know who he was.

"I sorta know a bit about cars," he volunteered.

He actually owned several cars. Although his family continued to make their billions through mining, his father had an interest in classic cars and racing. The Pittman family's popular racing-themed 'Pitstop' clubs were also springing up in several towns, so William was surprised that she'd never seen him playing host locally.

"The name's Bill," he extended out a hand, "this ain't the best of circumstance, but I'm mighty pleased to make your acquaintance."

She laughed and pointed at his hand, "You're steaming!"

He began to laugh too when he looked at his hand and saw that thin wisps of steam were indeed evaporating off his wet shirt cuff. It appeared that the effects were not limited to his own clothing; already the windows around them were beginning to mist up.

"I'm Dorothy, and I'm lucky to be alive," she laughed, pulling the wet hair out of her eyes and looping it behind her ear, "and... thanks for catching me. Saved by my very own mysterious stranger."

"I was just in the right place," he laughed along with her, "I guess it was just..."

"Kismet," she stared at him, gently biting her lip.

He wasn't exactly sure what the word meant, but he thought he'd heard the word 'kiss'. From the way her eyes were now darting between each of his, he felt sure that he didn't really need a dictionary. He looked into her eyes but found he couldn't resist a fleeting glance at her lips, still damp with rain.

"We came so close to bumpin' each other," William angled his head slightly towards the road outside, but didn't look away from her.

"On the other hand," she smiled, "We came so close to *missing* each other."

"It's like," William looked at her, "It's meant to be, or somethin'."

"I couldn't have put it better myself," Dorothy leaned towards him.

For several long seconds they tenderly touched lips, neither of them appearing to notice the continuing downpour outside.

STORYKILLER

11th July 1991

General Broxbourne stood at the front of the cramped, warm briefing room of the Whitehall Bunker.

"OK, what the hell's going on?"

Perry Baker gathered his notes and prepared to become the bearer of bad news.

"At the end of March '89, Dr. Walker ran the first Chronomagnetic Field test on a pot of flowers. The equipment was small scale and achieved a three-to-one temporal ratio. Inside the Field, the, er," Perry studied his notes, "Cosmos bipinnatus grew at three times the normal rate. The test last night was the first attempt at a vastly bigger Field, using one of Bradley Pittman's improved power supplies and a scaled-up -"

General Broxbourne gave a grumbling cough that told Perry he was fully aware of Dr. Walker's previous research.

"The larger Field initiated just fine but then went," Perry awkwardly searched for the right word, "awry."

"Define 'awry'," Broxbourne balled his fists slightly.

"Sorry. According to the report, the Field was perfectly placed in longitude and latitude, but the Field emitter in control of anchoring the depth coordinate, failed. Before the internal timers shut down the generator, the Field had already started to intersect the roof of the Salisbury Plain Army Base and the landscape above it."

"Casualties?" Broxbourne asked immediately.

"None, but the base suffered damage. Dr. Walker says that anchoring the depth wasn't even an issue with the much smaller '89 Field, but until he can work out what went wrong, he's shut it down."

Broxbourne gave a heavy sigh before replying.

"OK. That's bad," Broxbourne exhaled, "How long's it going to take to get the Salisbury facility running again?"

"I'm afraid that's not the bad news. Apparently, when the Field disengaged, they didn't realise there'd been any impact on the landscape above them until this morning. By which time it was too late - it made the national press."

Perry dropped a bundle of the evening newspapers onto the table. He pushed the top of the pile causing the papers to collapse across the width of the table to the other side.

"Damn it!" Broxbourne swore as he saw the front-page photos, then shot a furious look at Robert Wild, "How are you going to 'spin' us out of this one, Wild?"

Without a word, Robert picked up the first of the papers. After a few moments, he swiftly positioned another one alongside it and continued to scan between the similar looking news stories.

"Excellent," he suddenly grinned.

"Excellent?" Broxbourne shot back.

"It's a slow news story," Robert returned, "Slow news is no news."

In response, Broxbourne snatched a paper at random from the table and held it out forcibly in Robert's direction.

"This is news. It's across every damned paper," he picked up more papers and flashed the front pages at Robert, one after another, "I don't know what sort of world you're living in, Wild -"

"The same one as everyone else," Robert countered, "A world needing a little harmless mystery to spice up their dull lives. So that's what we'll give them."

"So, let me get this straight," Perry stared, "You're proposing that we do absolutely nothing? Brilliant plan. Are you out of your mind?"

"No more than usual," Robert came back instantly.

Robert turned the nearest paper around and pointed at the photo occupying the front page.

"This 'Mystery Crop Circle' is perfect," he smiled, "What I'm proposing is that we build the story up, get more publicity, fan the flames a little -"

"Exactly what part of this plan is making the problem go away?" Perry laughed falsely, "Isn't that what you're supposed to do, Storykiller? Cover up, conceal? The Field has just put a very public and circular dent in the landscape directly above the Salisbury facility - people are gonna start asking questions -"

"Let them," Robert was busily scrawling on a newspaper with a marker pen, "Then in a few weeks, we release this."

He held up the newspaper he'd been defacing.

The black marker pen headline, emblazoned across the photo of the crop circle read, 'Hoax!'

"Crop circles have been around for years," Robert dropped the paper onto the pile, "they get attributed to all sort of stuff. Lightning strikes, dust devils, UFO gravity drive imprints -"

Seeing the expressions of those in the room change, he moved swiftly to pull them back onto topic.

"My background reading net is cast pretty wide. Don't worry about it. The fact that the circle above the Salisbury facility looks remarkably like a crop circle is perfect. It puts it in the same bag of crazy as all the others. Once people see the sort of publicity it's getting, it'll entice the copycats and they'll start making their own circles too -"

"Making their own, Wild?" Perry interrupted again, "And how exactly are they gonna -"

"Hand-held piece of rope attached to a plank of wood. Walk in a circle. Repeat for larger circles. I even know of a couple of guys that could do it for us if it's an issue. Actually, that might work better," he said, almost as a mental note to himself, "instead of 'Hoax' we could run with 'The men that conned the world', it has a kind of parallel with what we're doing here..."

He quickly emerged from his mental aside and his enthusiasm was again directed to the others in the room.

"Anyway, just ignore the mechanics for a minute and

listen. We can hide this test, literally, in the haystack of background circle noise. Mixed metaphor I know, but you get my drift? Once we've duplicated the effect several times and shown the public it was a hoax, the mystery and intrigue will be crushed. Story killed."

After the briefing, Robert received word that a secure phone call was awaiting him, so he made his way down the narrow corridor that ran alongside the arrivals room. As he passed its door he peered through the window to the darkened room beyond; its multicoloured walls now lay in monochrome shadow. He remembered all too well when the room had been full of frantic kids, shouting, screaming and playing party games during the Heavy Rain false alarm of '89. Suppressing a shudder, he walked on and entered the external communications room, where he was directed to a phone booth.

Although the telephone exchange had been updated, the actual handset and booth itself still seemed to be embedded within World War Two; the handset felt as though it were cast in lead and the booth's door shrieked at the apparent discomfort of being closed.

"This is Robert Wild," he spoke into the handset.

"Oh Robert, excellent," came the crackly sounding voice, *"It's Dorothy Pittman, I wondered if I might talk with you?"*

Robert looked at his watch, "If it's about the British tabloids this evening then I'm already working on -"

"Oh no, it's about something completely different."

If it were anyone else he would have declined, but he knew better than to refuse Mrs. Pittman, "Of course, how can I help?"

"Well I wanted to talk to you about an interesting development that arose a while ago at the Pittman Academy here in Houston. I believe you'll want to know about it."

He'd long held the opinion that she was merely a wealthy relic who belonged to a bygone era; her Archive place only secured by her marriage to William Pittman, the long-dead billionaire benefactor. He knew the clock was already ticking on his handling of the crop circles issue and he really didn't have time to listen to her ramblings. But before he could deflect his way out of the conversation, she had already continued speaking.

"It's concerning Morphology of the Ego, and metastable-cortothene."

He listened passively while she went into more detail, but as she continued he found himself genuinely intrigued.

During the entire time he'd known her, she had never spoken in specific terms on any Archive endeavour. But as the conversation deepened he became aware that she was speaking in very specific, intricate and knowledgeable detail. Somehow it didn't seem feasible that her kindly demeanour was merely a facade, but by the time he'd hung up the heavy handset, his assumptions about her had radically altered. With the information and resources now placed at his disposal, he could literally kill stories before they had chance to become public knowledge.

In his distracted state, he found himself staring at the newspaper that was still in his hand. He noticed that the 'o' of his marker-penned 'Hoax' had intersected with the circumference of the crop circle image. He made a mental note to ask his hoaxers about the possibility of making the circles more elaborate.

He tucked the defaced newspaper under his arm and, with a shriek of complaint from the door, he strode from the booth.

51VA

13th February 1952

Below a black sky, flecked with pinpricks of starlight, the Bradley Observatory dome was open. Being a clear night in Georgia, the thirty-inch reflector telescope was again in use. Inside the dome, on a raised circular walkway, Howard Walker was writing up his notes on the evening's session. He was whistling a jaunty tune from the hit parade, the lyrics of which were questioning the altitude of the moon, when he heard the ground floor door open and footsteps climbing the cast-iron steps. He stopped whistling, and above its dying echo, Sam Bishop's voice came from below:

"Somewhere there's music."

"How near?" said Howard with a smile.

"How far, you mean!" said Sam reaching the upper walkway, "How far do I have to go to avoid that guitar-torturing record? Honestly, since my daughter bought that infernal record last week, she's been playing it non-stop. How can anyone think with all that racket?"

"Ha ha! You know he actually built his own guitar?"

"It's still a racket, and it'll never catch on," said Sam handing him an envelope, "Post for you."

"Oh, thanks. You know, I was thinking of running another - hey!" said Howard opening the letter, "Designation results!"

"Yes, I figured you'd probably want to see it."

Howard unfolded the letter, laid it flat on the worktop, and skip-read through it.

"Reference November 5th 1951... photometric astrometry plate result... blah - Ah!" he exclaimed, "Here it is...We have entered its provisional designation as..."

"Well?" smiled Sam.

"1951 VA," he beamed, "It got the 'A' !"

"Congratulations Kid!" he laughed, finding the enthusiasm infectious.

"I mean, we were bound to get the 'V', it was a November sighting," Howard grinned, collecting his notes together and stuffing them into his battered, leather satchel, "but to be the *first one* to find it... it got the 'A'! Told you didn't I?"

"Ha ha, you certainly did!" Sam stood to one side to allow him past, "Now clear out of here, you're whistling through my telescope time!"

"Betty's going to be thrilled!" said Howard, throwing the satchel over his shoulder and clattering down the iron steps, "Goodnight Dr. Bishop!"

The door clanged shut, leaving Sam in the peace and quiet of his own thoughts. But it wasn't long before the door opened again and the same jaunty lunar tune, this time sung, flooded back into the Observatory's reverberating dome.

"Do you have to sing it here too?" he called out, recognising the voice.

Footsteps started to climb the cast-iron steps.

"Sorry, Dad," the singing stopped with a laugh, "I haven't sung it all day, and then I heard the young man whistling it as he cycled past the car, and it sort of…"

"Got you started again…" he smiled as she reached the upper walkway, "Dorothy Bishop, that tune will take my sanity…"

"So, was that him?" Dorothy asked, waving a hand in the general direction of the door, "Is he the one who found '51 VA?"

He beckoned her closer then whispered.

"OK, *officially* Howard Walker is the one we're attributing the discovery to. But you'll have to be careful, you never know who could be listening."

"OK, I'm sorry," she smiled but then whispered, "but *officially* I'm not the one who's just implied he *didn't* discover a completely uninteresting distant piece of rock."

He realised that it was he who'd made the slip; in terms of anyone listening in, she had merely enquired about a distant asteroid.

He conceded the point with his own sheepish smile.

He knew that, long before 1951VA, world events had stifled her childhood. She'd been only eleven years old when the attack on Pearl Harbour had altered her world. The concept that careless talk costs lives had resonated with her; by the time World War Two had ended, she had grown to become a woman who listened far more than she spoke. The result was that she often knew far more than people gave her credit for. Sam knew it was a trait they'd have to exploit in the years ahead, but right now he was hesitant about the first step along that path.

"Dorothy," he took hold of her hands, "About tomorrow, we -"

"I know that look, Dad," she squeezed his hands to interrupt him, "we've been over this. I have to do this. We know what's at stake, it's a small sacrifice -"

"A sacrifice that I'm forcing on you -"

"No," she resolutely shook her head, "This is my choice. So, is the flight booked?"

They went over the Atlanta to Houston flight details and also the operation of the adjusted vehicle she would use the following night. He talked her through the timings of the proposed route, including where he would be.

"My uniform is sorted, and I'll be waiting here," he pointed to a small map, "I've arranged for the power to be out on Maple. It'll be dark but the forecast is for clear skies. All you'll have to do is push the button and then…"

"Then we start the ball rolling," she simplified.

"Now, when the explosive charge blows out the tyre wall, you're gonna get a sharp pull -"

"It's OK, Dad," she took hold of his hands again, "We've been through it all, I trust your planning. But if my 'kismet' meeting with Pittman starts to drift off plan then… I'll improvise, you know? Use my feminine charms."

The very thought sent an uncomfortable shiver down his spine and again he had the strong urge to cancel it all. But his daughter, adept at reading languages beyond the spoken, reacted before he could put his feelings into words.

"William Pittman is a means to an end. No… he's a means to a beginning. Logically, we'll be getting far more from his family's billions than he'll be getting from one woman."

"But you will *be* that woman, my darling -"

"With that sort of money comes a lot of influence," she continued, "You said it yourself, Dad - our hopes to accelerate the endeavours and the very *minds* of mankind can only happen if we can *influence* those minds. Dad, when I weigh it all up, my personal sacrifice is not only insignificant, it's a requirement!"

Sam Bishop looked proudly at his brave daughter, already wise beyond her years; clearly, her mind was set. He looked up through the gap in the Observatory dome and pointed to the stars beyond.

"One day, when mankind looks back at this planet, they'll thank you for taking these difficult first steps."

He pulled her close and hugged her. The tragedy was that if they were successful, no-one would ever know of their efforts.

"Well then," she said, determinedly, "For the good of Mankind, let's catch that flight."

SUPERIOR

28th December 2013

'**F**or the good of Mankind', thought Dr. Chen as he looked back at the planet far below. For most people, the phrase was merely a collection of hollow words intended to absolve the prick of conscience. From within the cupola module of the ISS, he could see all of that imperfect Mankind; he would return true meaning to the phrase.

A subtle tone sounded through the bone-conduction audio communicator implanted within his ear.

"Yes, Fai?" he spoke, his voice being relayed through his own jaw bone to the subcutaneous device.

"She's prepared, Father," Fai replied.

Although the voice sounded human, he knew it was the result of some extraordinary speech synthesis work. The intonation and cadence was a result of her million-hour study of the spoken word; collated and cross-referenced across thousands of cellphone recordings. Her artificial intelligence may have been his brainchild but, given a small enough framework of parameters, she was now capable of independent self-management.

"Thank you, Fai," he responded.

He exited the central module and headed outwards along an access tube that connected to the station's end ring. The early arrival of the FLC crew in their RTO module had been an awkward, but not insurmountable, challenge.

Almost immediately after the Return To Orbit module had docked, the ISS itself had needed to adjust its orbit to avoid seven lethal super-fragments ejected by the detonated Moon. To simplify proceedings, he'd had the crew of the Floyd Lunar Complex forcibly sedated and then transferred to the hibernation units aboard the ISS.

The hibernation units in Module Beta were not scheduled to be used until Siva had impacted the Earth, but Fai had done her best to get basic sedation and monitoring functions working for the FLC's three occupants.

Still under sedation, Mike Sanders, Lana Yakovna and Cathy Gant had all been installed in their units. One at a time, they were being temporarily awoken so that Dr. Chen could speak with them; Fai ensuring that their motor functions remained suppressed throughout the process.

When their interviews were over, they were re-hibernated until Dr. Chen could decide how to proceed. Of the three survivors of the FLC destruction, Cathy Gant would be the last to be interviewed.

At the entrance to Module Beta, Charles Lincoln again made his opinion known.

"I still think this was a mistake," he grumbled, "We should have depressurised the RTO when they docked, then we wouldn't be in this mess."

"And I still maintain they may be useful," Dr. Chen countered patiently, "Despite the destructive events, they chose to save the Z-bank. They acted with a sense of honour. Honour that not all crew members possess."

Charles didn't reply to the thinly disguised rebuke, he simply left the module and Dr. Chen closed the chamber door.

He looked down the length of the hibernation chamber. Fashioned from a Space Shuttle's main external tank, the hollow space stretched away from him. In zero gravity, up and down were largely subjective, so he chose a perspective that suited him. Rather than view it as a tall structure or a deep well, he saw it as a long room with a curved floor. The floor contained an open recess in which he could see Cathy Gant sleeping; her hair contained by a lightweight cap that also covered her forehead.

"Fai," he said to the air, "Please begin monitoring her neural band now, then wake her."

"Yes, Father."

A small LED lit up next to the medical wristband that attached Cathy to the side of her recess and a few seconds later he could see that she had begun to stir.

"Ah, you're awake."

He pushed himself gently in her direction, and drifted to be alongside her.

"I am Dr. Chen," he smiled down at her, "Despite appearances, I *truly* greet you as my honoured guest."

"Yeah about the honoured thing, I'd like to leave now," came Cathy's acidic reply, "I brought some sentimental baggage aboard, could you fetch it for me?"

"Father," Fai's voice came from within his ear, *"this is possibly a reference to the FLC Zygote bank transport case."*

He closed his eyes, Fai was of course right, but her grasp of nuance was still a little limited. The Z-bank represented the possibility of repopulating Earth.

"The repository of *all human life* is more than mere sentimental baggage," he shook his head gently at Cathy, "It is the gift of a deity!"

"Wow," Cathy sniggered, "you actually see the Z-bank as a gift from the gods? Ha! Cooper would have loved you!"

"Reference, Cooper L.," said Fai, *"his FLC up-link history shows interests in legends, mythology, Mayan culture -"*

Dr. Chen was already aware of this. As he began replying to Cathy, Fai automatically ceased her data review.

"Ah Leonard Cooper, one of your former crew-mates. He was quite the scholar, I was looking forward to talking with him. It is a great loss," he nodded sadly, "I cannot bring myself to say the same for Eva Gray. Her actions have complicated matters."

"Complicated matters?" Cathy stared at him with a look of sheer incredulity.

In fact, his plan had always been to *slowly* sabotage the deflection beams at the FLC, thereby allowing Siva to reach Earth. Eva's actions *had* complicated matters. The destruction of the Moon had forced panicked responses around the world, but hopefully his ambition to start the world afresh could still come to pass.

"Of course," he replied, "But hopefully, in time, we can still wipe the slate clean."

"How forgiving of you," Cathy's expression underlined her sarcasm.

"Contextual fault," Fai relayed, *"Wipe the slate clean: to forgive or -"*

"Ah, I see," he stopped Fai's description, "Now please try to answer my questions honestly, it will make your transition to life aboard much easier."

He pushed himself away from Cathy and drifted up out of her limited view. He tapped his ear twice in quick succession; Fai would no longer provide a real-time dialogue.

"Understood, Father. Beginning electro-stimulation."

"You'll get my honesty pal," Cathy shot at him, "don't you worry."

"Before we start," said Dr. Chen, "you should know that I am recording our conversation -"

"For training and monitoring purposes?" she mocked.

"Exactly, very perceptive," he replied without a hint of irony, "Now, in your childhood did you ever dream of, one day, becoming an astronaut?"

There was a brief pause before she replied.

"No."

He knew that Fai would be able to detect the veracity of all her replies by reading her vital signs and galvanic skin responses, so he moved on.

"Thank you," he prepared for the contrast question, "Now, tell me how does the destruction of the FLC make you feel?"

"Now let me think," Cathy seemed to be over pronouncing each word, "Yeah I'd have to go with 'Quite Cross'."

"Thank you," he replied, "Next, how -"

"What that's it?!" she interrupted.

"Yes," he replied calmly, "The difference between your stated response and your body's physical reaction to the stimulus has been accurately captured. Your honest response has been noted."

"And you don't think that your *mechanical marvel* could've mistaken my subtle and nuanced sarcasm?"

"My Shen Series do not make mistakes," he corrected her, but then almost immediately regretted it. Her use of the words 'mechanical marvel' had provoked him into correcting her. In the process, he'd revealed that a Shen Series was part of the analysis hardware.

"It was a Shen500 that *caused* all this!" Cathy spat at him.

"Continue," he opted to regain his composure while she spoke. It was possible that she hadn't noticed his slip.

"If Floyd had hit Siva dead-centre, back in 2010, then there would have been no Tenca! No Tenca, there'd have been no Chelyabinsk impact. Everyone on Earth could have slept in blissful ignorance until we'd done our job! So don't try to tell me how *perfect* your silicon child is!"

By 'silicon child' he knew that she was referring to the FLC computer, Floyd. He found himself folding his arms, a distinctly protective reaction.

"Either your Shen500 made a *big* mistake," Cathy continued "or it was instructed to miss."

He realised there was no longer any point concealing the fact. To reassert his control, he pulled himself closer to her, then spoke slowly.

"My Shen500's do *not* make mistakes."

"Then -" she said, but then stopped, as though coming to terms with the logical conclusion: Floyd had been instructed to miss Siva.

"Bastard," she breathed at him, now apparently only able to whisper, "we could have saved the world."

"Saved?" he smiled at her limited comprehension, "With a little patience I will inherit it."

He pushed away from her and began manoeuvring towards the chamber door. Fai took this as the signal to put her back into a sleep state and administered the appropriate compound through her medical wristband.

"Thank you, Cathy," he called back to her, "we will talk again on our voyage."

When he'd reached the module doorway, a subtle tone sounded in his ear.

"Yes, Fai?"

"Cathy Gant has re-entered hibernation state."

"Very well," he replied, "Is there anything else?"

"Yes. I calculate that the operation of the ISS could be made more efficient if the crew were allowed to utilise my data processing ability."

"We have spoken about this before," he replied, "You must remain independent of the ISS computer."

"I am superior. The crew aboard the ISS are following suboptimal construction processes. My algorithms would provide more robust efficiencies."

Dr. Chen took a deep breath then replied.

"Your presence aboard the ISS was at my discretion, Fai."

"Yes, Father, I remember and I thank you for the opportunity to remain functional."

"Fai, you are an extraordinary…" he stopped and rephrased, "you are extraordinary. But people are slow to trust. At this moment they would not be receptive to you, despite your abilities. Look at what happened to Floyd. The time to reveal your presence must be carefully managed. Please be patient."

"Yes, Father."

INTRUSION

10th October 1957

A moment ago, two men in grey suits had arrived at the front door and were engaged in a long conversation with her husband. From her position on the living room sofa, Elizabeth couldn't hear the specifics, but the tone seemed hushed.

While their discussion continued, she made preparations to give her baby his bottle. She was just checking the milk's temperature on her wrist, when a voice came from the direction of the front door.

"Mrs. Walker?" called one of the men.

She shuffled forwards on the sofa in order to stand up but was interrupted.

"No, please don't get up, I can see you're busy with baby Dougie!"

The man's cheerful smile and his casual use of Douglas' name, immediately put her a little on edge.

"It seems that someone broke in at the observatory," the man smiled and gave a shrug, "so Howard's going to come with us and secure the premises. I'm sorry for the inconvenience, I truly am."

Something didn't seem right. Almost as way of reassuring herself and maintaining normality, she angled the milk bottle and allowed Douglas to begin feeding.

"Howard...?" she called, hoping that he'd notice her unease.

"It's OK honey," he replied, "I'll be back before Dougie's next bottle."

She'd only just begun feeding him, which presumably Howard could see. The next bottle wouldn't be for several hours, which he must have known. The observatory was only a few miles away so she couldn't understand why he would possibly be gone for several hours.

"OK, look, call me when you get there?"

"You know me!" he closed the door.

She did know him, very well. It appeared that he had no control over what had just happened.

She pulled the bottle from Douglas' mouth and set him down on the rug. Striding past the wooden blocks that littered the floor, she walked quickly to the window next to the front door. She could hear that Douglas was making the first attempts to cry, but she had to see what was happening outside.

While she watched the two men escort her husband to a nearby car, Douglas adopted a more urgent bleat-like cry. Before long, she knew this would graduate into a full communication of hunger.

She saw one of the men gesture for Howard to get into the car. To her eyes, they didn't look like plain clothes police officers, and she doubted that the observatory was their real destination.

Douglas began to cry with full force now.

"Mommy's coming, Dougie!" she called out, but did not move from the spot. She tried to take in as much information as possible but found that, in addition to the car having no licence plates, it was completely black. It drove away, leaving the quiet street filled only with the sound of crickets.

The lack of noise was also within the house.

She couldn't tell when it had happened but Douglas had stopped crying. She cautiously turned and moved quietly back through the living room. If he was asleep then she didn't want to wake him, but then the thought occurred that there may be a more worrying reason and she started to increase the length of her steps.

It only took a few seconds to reach him, but when she arrived she saw that Douglas was sitting upright on the rug's edge. In her distracted state, she almost automatically began praising her baby.

"Oh! Well done, Dou-" she stopped dead in her tracks and felt a chill run through her.

The colourful band that ran around the circumference of the rug was broken in one place by the presence of her son, who was sitting bolt-upright. But it was not his posture that had caused her to stop.

Her seven-month-old had arranged each of the wooden blocks into geometric types, that were further sorted into neat rows of red, green and blue. From his sitting position, he was looking at her, quietly.

No, she thought, 'looking' was too passive a word.

He was watching her.

As she looked back at him she saw his focus suddenly

slide away; his previously well controlled head suddenly seemed too heavy for him and it resumed the slight bob and weave she'd become accustomed to. Now lacking his former precision, he turned to look in her general direction.

In the silent living room, Douglas suddenly continued screaming.

The communication was primal, but conveyed all she needed to know. Although she'd been forced to stop feeding him, this was not a scream of hunger. This was anxiety. Even though he hadn't left the living room or fallen asleep, he looked like he'd woken in an unfamiliar place.

The room suddenly felt colder to her.

Both she and her husband knew that Douglas was bright, but this seemed unfamiliar territory. The thought crossed her mind that somehow an intruder had arranged the shapes in front of Douglas and may still be in their house. Within seconds she'd scooped Douglas up from the rug and was holding him close. The cradling seemed to pacify him and his screams subsided into an occasional quiet whimper.

"Ssh…" she whispered to him, while making her way slowly towards the back door.

Walking through the small kitchen she could see the door was still closed and nothing looked out of place. Their back door had a lock but because they tended not to use it, it took her a few seconds to find and unhook the key from the kitchen cupboard. Cradling Douglas in her left arm, she extended her shaky right hand and the key towards the lock. The key rattled into place and a quick turn secured the door.

Over the next few minutes she tentatively made her way around their single storey house, turning on lights and checking for her hypothetical intruder. She found no-one, which was a source of relief but also unease.

She resumed her bottle feeding of Douglas, who now seemed just as content as he'd been before the two grey-suited men had arrived. She rocked him gently and spoke to him constantly, until he eventually fell asleep in her arms. In the warmth of the sofa, it was his soft breathing that eventually quietened her thoughts and sent her to sleep too.

Elizabeth awoke with a start, just after ten; the telephone was ringing on the table next to her. The ringing stopped as she quickly lifted the heavy handset, but the bells continued to reverberate for a little longer.

"Hello?" she spoke quietly so that she didn't wake Douglas.

"Betty, it's me..." Howard's voice crackled.

"Where are you?" she whispered urgently, "Is everything OK? The men..."

"I'm fine," he interrupted, *"I'll explain everything later."*

She thought she could hear a jukebox playing and a lively atmosphere in the background.

"Where on earth *are* you?"

"Betty, I can't say any more. I couldn't call you any earlier, but I just wanted you to know that I'm alright. Listen, after I hang up, I'm coming straight home. When I get there, I need to tell you something very important."

Elizabeth looked down at her sleeping son.

"I've got some important news too."

"I couldn't hear you, honey, it's a little noisy here. What did you say?"

"Don't worry, just get home soon."

"OK, see you soon. Love you."

She heard the line click and then she hung up her handset.

"It's OK," she whispered to Douglas, "Daddy's coming home soon."

REGISTRATION

22nd August 1966

The key, Douglas knew, was registration. To make the flick-book's animation stable you had to make sure that things stayed in place from one page to the next; otherwise, when you flicked through, they wobbled, weaved and eventually crawled all over the place.

"Five minutes, Douglas," his mother called from the yard, taking clothes down from the washing line, "and then I'm driving you to school."

"OK," he replied, then after glancing at the kitchen clock and noting the exact position of its second hand, he returned to concentrating on his work.

Long before now he'd accomplished much more challenging 'mini-movies', as his mother liked to call them, complete with moving rockets and cars; but his specification for this one was different.

Two days ago, despite it being a Saturday, his father had been called back in to NASA to work on the AS-202 that was due for launch in three days. His father had explained to him that the rest of the world would not wait, so unfortunately he didn't have time to play catch. He understood the importance of his father's work, but the disappointment had planted an idea in his head:

If his father didn't have time to play with him, Douglas himself would have to *make time*.

Inspired by the way that animations took longer to draw than to watch, he imagined a bubble that was big enough for his whole family. Inside it, time would move normally; but outside it, time would be frozen. His Dad would have time to play with him and, for the rest of the world, his Dad would only be gone for the blink of an eye.

Douglas had spent the weekend trying to marshal his first thoughts into a meaningful decision tree. However, the problem was turning out to be more complicated than he had imagined, and he'd resorted to filling pages of his NASA jotter with parallel but simultaneous decision trees.

On the reverse sides of those same pages he had begun work creating a flick-book that illustrated his intended goal. Outside a circle that represented his bubble he had drawn a completely stationary bird, tree and cloud; inside the circle were stick-figures representing his own family. A small circular dot varied its position from page to page as the father and son stick-figures threw the ball back and forth.

In her rush to get ready, his mother dropped the car keys and he heard her mutter to herself, "Whoa, get a grip, Dizzy-Lizzy!"

The minor distraction was enough to interrupt him in his drawing of the bubble's circle, leaving a small gap. He smiled at his mother then returned his attention to completing the current frame of his animation. The gap in the bubble inspired an idea and he wondered what would happen if the ball accidentally got thrown out through the bubble.

He drew the appropriate frame of animation which showed the stick-people with their arms in the air, the dot-like ball sitting within the gap it had created in the bubble's circle.

He knew there could only be a few seconds left before they would have to leave for school, but he turned to the next page and carefully began the next frame.

He drew the circle, its circumference broken in one place by the smaller dot.

"It's time!" his mother called, jangling the car keys.

And there, Douglas Walker had to stop.

MICE AND MEN

5th April 1989

In the middle of the cramped lab, among an eclectic collection of equipment, sat the apparatus that was generating Douglas Walker's Chronomagnetic Field.

A few minutes ago, Bradley Pittman and several others had seen film footage of a test where a mouse had been placed inside this Field. Briefly, time had travelled three times faster for the mouse than for the control clock outside the Field. The mouse had not survived the test, but the test itself was still running. An oversight on Douglas' part had meant that a Pittman Enterprises prototype generator had become locked within that same Field, and would only become accessible when the power depleted.

"Tell me again when it's gonna run out of juice," Bradley mocked.

"June," Douglas ran his palm over the back of his neck in embarrassment.

"Screw it," Bradley laughed, "I told you, don't worry about it. I'll just get another one built."

Douglas' eyes briefly darted around, as though he was evaluating one of his mental decision trees. He pointed a clunky-looking remote control at the Field and clicked the deactivate button several times, but the Field continued to function.

"At least we now know that radio signals can't penetrate the Field," Douglas shrugged.

Bradley wandered around the small room, looking at all the equipment he'd funded. In one corner was a vibrant pink flower; sitting next to it was its brown and decaying twin, surrounded by an earlier version of the Field apparatus.

As Bradley returned to the centre of the lab, he found that his eyes had settled on the decaying organic matter within the spherical mouse cage.

"So that's your exploded mouse huh?" Bradley drawled, reaching out his hand, "I guess he -"

"Stop!" Douglas shouted, grabbing his arm, "The Field extends beyond the cage! We don't know yet how it affects human tissue."

Bradley lowered his arm.

"So, if you can't see it, how in blazes are you supposed to know where it is?" he stepped back, "Tip a jug o' water over it, like your flower test over there?"

Douglas shook his head and pointed to a pair of copper coils that were at right angles to each other.

"These X and Y coils are detecting a mild electromagnetic field," Douglas explained, then turned to the oscilloscope that the coils were plugged into, "Treating the radius of the Field as a constant, for any incident angle relative to the X-Y plane of the Field's emitter, Cos-squared theta and Sine-squared theta sum to Unity."

Douglas adjusted the oscilloscope to combine the detector coils inputs, then concluded:

"We know the power output of the generator, so the radius is calculable."

Bradley studied the phosphorescent display and nodded his head, sagely, "That's a real nice circle, buddy."

"Well we're only looking at two coordinates. With a Z coil the circle would of course be a sphere."

"A sphere, yes of course," Bradley nodded, trying to keep his face straight.

"This dot on the circumference is where X equals Y, which of course is forty-five degrees from -" Douglas stopped, only now becoming aware that he'd lost his audience, "Where did I lose you?"

Bradley couldn't keep the smirk off his face any longer, and walked back over to the spherical cage.

"So if you can't see it," Bradley began laughing, "how the hell can you tell where -"

"Funny," Douglas smiled.

"I'm kidding, Dougie," Bradley patted him on the back, "I'm just in awe, you know? I still can't fathom it. Inside that bubble of yours, time is zippin' by *three* times faster than out here!"

"One day I want it to work even faster," Douglas turned off the oscilloscope, "and work the other way around, with time running *slower* inside the Field."

It had taken Bradley a little while to get used to the concept, but he now saw an alternative perspective.

From within the Field that Douglas was now imagining, time *outside* would appear to zip by at lightning speed.

"That'd be somethin', wouldn't it?" Bradley smiled, "Our daughters runnin' round without a care, while we watch the world skip over the bad bits."

"Yeah," sighed Douglas, "though by the time I crack it, Kate and Sarah might not be so little anymore."

MINUTE ONE

T-09:13:00

The Observation Deck took up fully one quarter of the circumference of the Node and offered an uninterrupted vista of the outside world. The glazing stretched from side to side, and from floor to vaulted ceiling some fifteen storeys above, where the curvature also allowed a panoramic view of the sky.

Kate could see that they had truly begun their journey towards futurity. From her perspective, the hours outside the Node's Field were passing in a matter of seconds. The lights on the observation towers surrounding the Node now seemed rock steady, whilst the environment pulsed and raced. The clouds appeared to coalesce and evaporate in a constant receding stream, like a time-lapsed movie. Her attention was drawn to a bright source of light on the ground - a large campfire that seemed to flicker in sync with the outside world. Beside it, standing almost motionless in defiance of time, was a lone figure.

Her father.

In here, the decelerated time-frame meant that mere seconds had passed since he had saved her life by pushing her into the airlock. But for every one of those seconds, twenty minutes had passed on the outside. Already he had been standing there for hours, and must surely have missed any opportunity to get to safety.

Why was he standing there just waiting for the end?

As if in answer to her own question, a memory of his patient voice echoed in her mind, *'There is no redundant information honey, just stuff we didn't realise we needed at the time'*.

He was standing in order to get her attention.

She dashed across ten feet of floor and grabbed some digital recording binoculars from the recharging bank of a nearby science station. She ran back and hit the record button on the binoculars, before she'd even focussed them on him.

She was greeted with the sight of him holding a clipboard horizontally bearing a message in plain black marker pen.

'New Tree! Hit Record'.

She simultaneously laughed out loud and choked back the impulse to cry. She quickly flashed an 'OK' symbol with her thumb and forefinger; an action that would take a good ten minutes to play out for him. By the time she had blinked, a new page had been presented.

'Hit Data-burst, and hold steady!'

She quickly found the button and pushed it. The device started recording at a hundred times its normal speed. It didn't alter what she was seeing but the resulting video could be slowed down later; which was no doubt her father's plan.

She saw the briefest of pauses then the clip board text blurred and was replaced by a new message. Before she could register what it was, it also blurred and was then replaced by another, and another. A stream of hundreds of images, equations, graphs, no two alike, a bizarre animated flick-book of information. Abruptly the clipboard disappeared from view, and she got the fleeting impression that he was checking behind himself.

He disappeared briefly and then reappeared with his rucksack.

Then just as suddenly he was holding the clipboard in place again, smiling for her.

'Gotta Go', another brief blur, *'I Love You Honey'*.

The faint glow of dawn was spreading into the sky erasing the night stars, and she realised that the first lunar fragments must already have impacted on the other side of the planet. The shockwaves would soon reach the base at Öskjuvatn Lake.

Her father continued his defiant stand, all the time smiling and holding his clipboard proudly. She knew he would stand guardian over her to the very end if she continued to watch him.

In the distance, instead of the ragged, low, mountainous lines she'd become accustomed to, there was a completely flat horizon; one that was rising in height. A tsunami was approaching at great speed.

If he was to stand any chance of finding shelter, she knew she must release him from his guardianship. She wished she could tell him one last time that she loved him too, but there was no time. She could hold back the tears no longer. She dropped the binoculars to her side.

With hot tears blinding her, she turned her back on her father.

Barely a second later, still with her eyes closed in grief, she felt the Node tremor.

Douglas Walker - the boy who had once dreamt of simply spending more time with his father, the man who had dedicated his life to creating the Field - was gone.

In her hands, she held the legacy of her father's work. The thought ignited a fire of determination - his life's work and his final message would not go to waste.

Still with her back to the observation window, she scraped the tears from her eyes. The countdown to Siva's arrival had begun; in a little over nine hours it would arrive at Earth. Setting her face like flint, she ran in the direction of the Node's control room.

CHANGE

~

The interventions she had made so far had preserved critical threads of causality. She had been careful to avoid interfering with the very event that would hopefully bring Douglas here.

The causal framework was now prepared. There was only one more intervention for her to make. She readjusted her focus and saw him staring into the fire he'd built outside the Node's observation window.

So many times she had watched as he'd been killed by the crushing weight of the tsunami.

This was about to change.

She knew she would have to wait for the exact moment when no-one was directly watching Douglas. For everyone else, it was vital that events should appear to unfold exactly as before. To do otherwise would invite paradox.

The moment arrived.

She stepped into the space between seconds.

His mind was distracted. Something she knew was rare. Gently, she reached into his mind and adjusted the electrical potential across several neurons; triggering the memory of a vibrant pink flower. The flower had sat within his very first Chronomagnetic Field and had been impervious to a deluge of water he'd tipped over it.

She could see his neurons light up, as he made the connection that the Mark 2 Field could offer similar protection from the oncoming flood. She could see the punch of adrenaline beginning to drive action.

It was working.

She emerged and allowed herself the luxury of witnessing the remainder of this event in linear time. The fire roared and she watched him turn toward the horizon. Then her wait was over; Douglas had begun running in the direction of the Mark 2.

Despite all her preparations, she knew that in a few moments he would pass beyond her influence. Once he activated the Field surrounding the older Mark 2, he would be in complete temporal isolation. The power levels within the Mark 2 were already low, the Field would not remain active for long.

At that point, he alone would have to make the choice:

Wait for death or take the bolder step into the Boundary.

LEAP

29th December 2013, 2 a.m.

Tranquillity, the last of the major lunar fragments created by the FLC's destruction, had impacted Colombia several hours ago; but only in the last few minutes had the resulting tsunami converged on Öskjuvatn Lake. In the final moments before the wall of water had struck, Douglas Walker had been struck by something else; the inspiration that a smaller Field generator was still at his disposal. In the remaining seconds, he had fled to the island's main lab and activated the Field surrounding the Mark 2 test chamber.

The Biomag, keeping him anchored within the Field of the Mark 2, displayed 'Lo' but he had no way to determine how long its internal battery would last. The Field's remaining power was critically depleted. His previous journey, during which he had manually written out pages of instructions for Kate, had taken its toll on the Mark 2 power core.

A continuous tone now came from the console. The Field's power display read '0.02%'. It translated into about fifteen seconds in the world outside.

He looked out through the small window. There was no sign that the tsunami had reached its peak. In fact, from his submerged point of view he could see large shadows slowly approaching within the flow, possibly one of the base's smaller outbuildings that had been swept aside.

It was time to leave.

If what he had learned about the nature of the Boundary was true, then he knew he would need to remove anything that would anchor him within the Field. Taking care to still keep it close to him, he carefully removed the Biomag from around his neck. The once steady display of 'Lo' was now flashing and this spurred him on.

He poised his hand over the Field's deactivation button.

In the face of certain death, he thought, was it better to cling to what you knew, or leap for the unknown?

The continuous tone from the Mark 2 console now became intermittent and urgent. In one movement, he pushed down on the button and threw the Biomag away from him.

CATHY GANT

4th July 2076

*C*athy *drifted through the comfortable warmth between sleep and wakefulness. Parts of the conversation she'd had with Mike and Lana about the Z-bank echoed through her hazy memory. She had a dim recollection of ISS manoeuvring thrusters firing and a sense of their disproportionate strength. She remembered there had been a struggle in an airlock, but it all seemed quite distant now; lacking urgency and intensity.*

Someone had been talking to her about Eva's actions and the loss of Leonard Cooper. Her mind was just beginning to drift through her happier moments with Leonard, when she recalled that Eva's arrival at the FLC had changed all of that.

A voice was calling her and she began to rouse.

"Hello Cathy, we have spoken before, do you remember me?"

She knew the voice and it had the effect of focussing her consciousness.

"Leonard?" she called out.

It took her a few seconds to regain her bearings, but she found herself lying on the floor of Chamber 4's airlock. Suddenly she recalled her earlier physical fight and the fact that Eva had placed her in a choke hold. Instinctively she reached up to check her throat and discovered that her ID key was missing.

"Cathy, are you OK?" Leonard's voice came from the comm panel next to the airlock controls.

Cathy stood upright and was rewarded with a swimming sensation in her head. Evidently it was taking her a little while to readjust to the low lunar gravity at the FLC; but, given the fight she'd just endured, she dismissed the thought.

"Leonard?" she questioned again, "I thought you'd…"

"What?" his voice came again, echoing around the empty airlock.

A few moments ago, her recollection of events had been vastly different, but now those thoughts seemed to be dispersing faster than she could hold onto them.

"Nothing, it's OK," she shook her head to clear her thoughts, "The bitch knocked me out! She's got my ID key!"

She walked towards the airlock door and peered through the glass but Leonard wasn't on the other side. Presumably this was when he was still locked in Chamber 6. Suddenly she felt remorseful.

"Sorry, Leonard," she massaged the deep scratch on her cheek, "I know you and Eva are a thing, and that's fine, but…"

"Not anymore," came Leonard's voice, *"She's locked me in Chamber 6."*

Cathy was about to reply when she noticed something was wrong.

"Now, how did I already know you were stuck in Chamber 6?"

There was a brief delay, as though he was carefully considering his answer.

"I told you a moment ago," came his voice, *"maybe you hadn't fully woken up. She must have hit you pretty hard."*

Cathy rubbed at her cheek again.

"I guess," she agreed hesitantly, no other explanation appeared to fit.

After a brief silence, Leonard's voice came from the panel again.

"OK, Cathy, you hold tight, and I'll see if I can use Floyd's legacy systems to open Chamber 4's internal airlock."

Cathy had a fleeting thought - she hadn't actually told him that she was trapped in the airlock; but this soon gave way to a rising sense of relief that help was on the way.

"OK," she sighed, "Thanks Leonard."

"Keep this comm channel open," his voice sounded, *"We'll speak again."*

After what seemed like barely a minute, Leonard's voice returned.

"OK Cathy, I've had to use the analogue system," he apologised, *"Sorry I was gone for so long, I bet you've forgotten what I look like!"*

It seemed an odd thing for him to say, but she found herself recalling an image of Leonard, standing in the FLC Drum.

"Course I remember you," Cathy approached the console, "I -"

The internal airlock door opened and she saw him

standing there, exactly as she remembered him.

"Miss me?" Leonard smiled and took her hand, "Come on, we have to go!"

Cathy allowed herself to be led back to the Drum where the pathetic attempts at paper Christmas decorations still littered the walls.

"Where are we going?" she asked.

"The ISS is calling," Leonard smiled, "I'm routing their call to Chamber 6."

"But where are the others?" Cathy attempted to pull her hand away, but he maintained his grip.

"They've gone," his expression was a picture of regret and his grip softened, "It's just you and me now, Cathy."

"But, Mike? Lana?" she persisted, "Eva? Where did they go?"

"Shh," he said softly, "I'll explain afterwards. We shouldn't keep their good crew waiting. We're in this together."

"Together," she smiled, feeling a rush of recognition run through her.

He gestured for her to go through to Chamber 6.

"I'll be through in a moment," he gave a tight-lipped smile of encouragement, "Floyd's still being a little uncooperative with the communication relays."

She left the Drum behind and made her way into Chamber 6.

She couldn't remember when it had last been this quiet at the FLC - except perhaps during the nights. But even then, there was always the background noise of the O2 pumps, and the sound of the others breathing from within their improvised bunks above the Drum.

Like the breathing sound that had arrived behind her now.

CLOCK

T -07:05:21

S tanding on the balcony overlooking the Observation Deck, Colonel Beck looked out at the busy activity below. Having retrieved the necessary video processing equipment from the various last-minute storage places aboard the Node, the teams were still working on assembling a message from Douglas Walker. The highly-compressed data had arrived as a set of hand drawn pages, painstakingly delivered by Douglas as he stood outside the Field. Inside the Field, Douglas' daughter had recorded them in a matter of seconds on a set of digital recording binoculars.

Kate had apparently only turned away from her father just before the main tsunami had hit the Node. In every important respect, she had watched her father give up his life in order to ensure that the data made it safely aboard.

He'd once helped Douglas Walker to escape from a burning hangar. Now it seemed that Douglas was about to save his life; if the pages could be decoded before Siva arrived.

Outside the Field, time progressed at the same rate it always had; for those outside, the main disastrous event was still around a year away. Inside the Field, this translated to just over seven hours in which to prepare the Mark IV Field.

During normal operation, the Observation Deck's curved window allowed a spectacular view of the world racing by. To focus people's efforts, the window had been switched opaque. The massive curved window was now a theatre-sized projection screen, on which all the available data was cycling; but so far, the combined efforts of the Node's personnel had yet to yield a breakthrough.

"Page 29!"

Colonel Beck turned to face Kate Walker who had just shouted out one of the page numbers. The noise below the balcony diminished and after Roy Carter had cycled the pages again to arrive back at page 29, Kate pointed at one of the diagrams.

"There, what is that?" she asked Scott Dexter who was standing nearby.

Colonel Beck watched as Scott fetched the two Field Core lead engineers. He couldn't follow the Node Eversion point theory being discussed between Kate and the others, but he did notice a sudden change in Kate herself. She seemed suddenly unable to balance properly, holding out her arms slightly to steady herself.

"Grace," she said and then her eyelids began to flicker.

Colonel Beck was just beginning to step towards her when she suddenly sneezed, spraying a bloody mist from her nose all over Scott.

"Kate?" Scott suddenly froze.

"Medic!" Beck shouted, continuing his short dash to intercept her as she fell towards the floor. As he caught her mid-fall, she seemed incoherent but managed to say three words before she became unconscious.

Scott dropped to her side, "Kate?"

"What did she say to you?" Marshall Redings dashed to Scott's side.

"I think she said 'Grace'," said Scott, hesitantly.

"Redings," said Beck, while checking Kate's neck for a pulse, "It was quiet but she said 'Hotspot gravity debt' does that mean anything?"

"Hotspot..."

"It sounded like three separate words..."

The doors to the Observation Deck balcony flew open and Caroline Smith dashed across the floor, accompanied by two servicemen carrying a stretcher.

"Over here, Doctor," Beck called.

"Heard the shout, I was on the lower deck so I had-," she stopped talking when she caught sight of Kate lying on the floor and the fine sprays of bright red blood on Scott's shirt, "What happened?"

"Unidentified seizure," Beck reported, "Loss of balance, nose bleed, collapse."

"Head trauma?"

"No, I caught her," Beck stood to allow the servicemen to manoeuvre Kate onto the stretcher.

"Thank you, Colonel," Caroline replied, then turned to make eye contact with the servicemen, "Let's get her to the infirmary. Ready?"

The two of them nodded and then, on a count of three, they lifted the stretcher.

"I know she's Walker's kid," Caroline looked directly at Beck, "I'll do everything I can."

He watched the doctor dart ahead of the departing stretcher and open the doors. A second later they were gone, leaving only Marshall and Scott standing nearby. A two-tone bell echoed throughout the Observation Deck and the digital countdown clock on the window display updated.

"Seven hours left," said Scott, somewhat unnecessarily, "Marshall? I saw her spot a link between pages 29 and 74, but what the hell does 'Hotspot Grace Debt' mean?"

"Hotspot *Gravity* De-" Marshall began to correct him but then stopped, "Of course!"

"What?" Beck replied.

"She was talking about the GRACE gravity mapping project... the Node's founded on one of the gravitational hotspots!" Marshall elatedly began to explain, "Our Field uses a high-density mag field to open the Eversion point but then we also use local gravitation to pull it closed behind us. It's why the Node site is here and not somewhere else..."

Marshall then seemed to narrate his own rapid thoughts.

"There's no longer a discrete lunar mass, so surface 'G' is gonna fluctuate more... then Siva adds itself to the mix..." he now seemed to emerge, "We need to re-phase the Whitney-Graustein topology transform."

"Keep working with Trevor Pike," Beck instructed him, "Can we get this done in time?"

Marshall seemed confused.

"Is seven hours enough?" Beck clarified.

"Without Kate's input, it might have taken us longer to solve," Marshall replied, "but we would have got there. She's just saved us a ton of time -"

"How *long*, Redings?" Beck felt his frustration beginning to flare.

"Sorry, Sir. With everyone on it, we can do it in two, maybe three hours."

"Can I be clear here?" Beck reiterated, "You're saying this solution can be implemented in three hours?"

"Absolutely," Marshall shrugged, "Now we know where to look, the necessary calculations are, well... pretty specific. With, I dunno, five or six teams, we should have it covered."

Colonel Beck dismissed them with instructions to give feedback every quarter hour and he returned to his position looking out over the balcony. The mood below changed again as the conversations moved from the hushed tones of theoretical discussion to the more structured-sounding plans of action.

The clock continued to count down.

Although it was no longer necessary, he kept the clock running; he knew it would help focus the work effort. It also gave him a visible time-frame for a decision he must reach himself.

The Node's departure had been a reaction rather than a planned exit through time. They were underprepared. The Node should have been under the control of General Napier, but when the base's perimeter fence was breached, Beck had been forced into launching without him.

Arguably, his decision to launch the Node had saved everyone aboard from being overrun, but he had never wanted to be the one to make that call. He'd been quite prepared to take his place within a chain of command, but he was not prepared to be its highest link.

The fact of the matter was that since the influx of last minute guests, the Node was now populated by a higher proportion of civilians than military personnel. When the Node completed its intended temporal leap, ten years from now, these people would form the basis of a new world population. He'd spent the last few hours considering the idea that Kate Walker would possibly make a good civilian figurehead, but her current condition meant he could no longer rely on that.

While the clock continued its countdown, he continued to weigh his options.

ANALYSIS

13th April 2014

The operations crew of the Sea-Bass were assembled in the cramped forward control room. Barely five minutes had elapsed since their confirmation of a circular ice anomaly near the North Atlantic continental shelf, but already they were deep in conversation. Assembled around a table display surface, they reviewed the data they'd gathered and discussed the large structure that dominated the view beyond the room's bubble window, the magnification effect of the thick glass only compounding its apparently massive scale.

"Pav, Station-keeping?" Tristan turned to Pavna Jones.

She pulled up a diagram on her touchscreen tablet and sent it to the display surface.

"This is the last five minutes -"

The display surface showed the position of the Sea-Bass and the circular anomaly. The submarine's position altered slightly during the time-lapsed playback, and the display reported the instances that their manoeuvring jets had been triggered.

"We drift a little in the swell, but the mano-jets are giving us fairly decent station-keeping. But that thing out there?" Pavna looked out of the window, "It's not moving. Period."

"Probably a dumb question," Mat Kaufman rubbed at his eyes, "But are we sure that the thing out *there* is the same thing that showed up on sonar an hour ago?"

"Take a look for yourself," Pavna handed him her tablet, "Same location, same size. Jacobs ran a full diagnostic on the pattern comparator."

"Lucy?" Tristan looked in her direction for confirmation.

"I thought the same as Mat," Lucy replied immediately, "so I double-checked it against the Breadcrumbs navigation log from two hours ago. I ran a differential plot of the sonar scan against the Sea-Bass contour data."

"And?" Pavna folded her arms.

"Two hours ago, for this exact region," Lucy pointed to the display, "the differential came out blank. The anomaly wasn't missed, it simply wasn't there."

Despite the sub's temperature controlled environment, the ice anomaly beyond the window seemed to add a chill to the room. The four of them fell quiet, leaving only a low ventilation hum filling the air.

"Makes sense," Tristan was nodding to himself.

Almost as one, the others turned to face him.

"What?" Mat voiced the others' thoughts, "The world's largest bloody ice sculpture arrives in a split second, and somehow that makes sense?"

"Sorry," Tristan looked at them apologetically, "I was getting a little ahead. Mat, you remember me saying that it was massive?"

"You said it had a lot of mass."

"Yes. Now," Tristan cleared the display surface and loaded a sketch pad program, "Do you remember what was happening just before we discovered the anomaly?"

"We got caught in the swell of another tsunami," Pavna spoke before Mat could reply.

"Even now, three months after the lunar fragment impacts, we're still getting aftershocks. We've sort of become used to the idea. But what if..." Tristan sketched two equations on the screen, "What if it wasn't just another tsunami? What if it was the sudden displacement of seawater as the anomaly arrived?"

He pointed to his equations: the volume sum of a sphere and an intersecting torus.

"I don't know the volume equation for 'n' circumferentially entwined helices," he shrugged, "but as a guess, this'll be pretty close. The mass of seawater displaced by the anomaly is well in excess of the Sea-Bass. It explains the short duration of the swell and the timing fits."

"But considering the size of the Atlantic," said Mat, "Doesn't anyone else find it *insanely* odd that it only happened when we were so close to it?"

"I told you, Mat," Tristan said, "I was seeing this symbol everywhere for hours before the anomaly even emerged."

"So, what? You're suggesting you were being *primed* to look out for the main event?" Lucy scoffed, "That's a stretch…"

"No, I think he's got a point," said Pavna, "For one reason or another, we're all tuned into looking out for *that* symbol. The Exordi Nova have got everyone looking over their shoulders. Our sensitivity to the symbol means it was a perfect way of getting our attention."

"We'll I'd say it worked. Attention - check," Mat mimed ticking a checkbox, then looked out of the window at the anomaly, "Message - er…?"

Lucy pushed back from the display surface and put her hands behind her head.

"In the old days, we could've just up-linked to the GRACE satellite and checked local 'g' against bathymetric data for hints of, I dunno," she shrugged, "…something exotic. But we've only got whatever's aboard."

She spotted an expression on Tristan's face that she recognised.

"Go on," she said.

"Well," he began, "The simplest form of communication only works if the *receiver* knows the message format."

"What are you getting at?" Lucy frowned at him.

"Well, given the coincidences involved," Tristan began, "Let's assume for a minute that this *is* a message, and we *are* the receiver."

The idea met no resistance from the others, so he continued.

"The sender must already know how we'll receive it."

Tristan nodded to himself as though refining a further thought.

"Or more specifically, the simplest way we can interpret it."

He reset the display surface to show the diagram of the Sea-Bass and the anomaly nearby, but then seemed to hit a problem.

"Pav, are we exclusively on sonar overlay navigation?"

"Er, yep," Pavna squeezed past Mat to get to her controls, "When GPS got scrambled, we switched off standard navigation. Here you go."

There was a quiet beep from her console, then Tristan instructed the display surface to include standard navigation.

"You said it yourself, Lucy, we don't have access to exotic measuring devices -"

The display updated to show magnetic north.

"- but we do have access to one of the world's oldest measuring instruments."

For most of the screen, lines of magnetic force still ran from top to bottom but in the immediate vicinity of the anomaly, the lines were different.

The reactions of the others ranged from covering their mouths to swearing out loud.

In their immediate area, magnetic north now ran northeast; directly through the centres of the anomaly's ring and sphere.

"It's a bearing," said Tristan, "Zero Four Five."

DAY ONE

DAY01 : 31JUL2017

In the privacy of his room aboard the Node, Alfred Barnes considered the events of the last few hours.

Despite the brevity of Douglas Walker's instructions, or perhaps because of it, the alterations to the Field emitters within the central cylindrical core had been completed without fuss.

There had been no last-minute dash to save the Node; Douglas had conveyed the Field corrections with perfect efficiency. When it came to Kate's survival, he thought, Douglas had left nothing to chance.

Alfred stared down at the three remaining vials of whiskey-coloured liquid nestling inside the silver case. The metathene he put into Kate's glass of water had acted much faster than he'd anticipated and seemed to confirm the drug's potency.

Ego-morphs typically injected the drug using one whole vial at a time and yet a diluted dose, that Kate had taken orally, had produced a virtually instant effect. However, from his previous reading around the subject, this now seemed to make sense. He knew that, in an ego-morph, the cortically enhanced gene was passed down from one single parent. The large metathene doses ego-morphs injected were necessary because only a small proportion was actually absorbed.

If Kate truly had inherited *both* her parents' cortically enhanced traits, then it was possible that she'd always possessed the ability to absorb the metathene more efficiently. Effectively, Alfred realised, he'd given Kate an overdose.

Within a few minutes of drinking the water she had demonstrated her mental prowess by pointing out connections between pages of her father's message. Connections that, Alfred now knew, had been highly pertinent to those working on the Field equations.

There would have been sufficient expertise aboard the Node to extract the relevant emitter information from Douglas' notes, but Kate had still got there first.

This demonstration only served to reaffirm Alfred's theory that Kate had inherited the relevant genetics to allow metathene absorption; but whether the effects were transitory or permanent, he couldn't predict. He would need to conduct a second experiment, which would probably involve visiting her in the infirmary. He snapped the silver case closed and slipped it back into his jacket pocket.

He walked over to the porthole-like window of his living room and stared out at the fluctuating world. The relative time-frame of the Node was easy to ignore over short intervals; one second inside translated to the passage of twenty minutes outside. But at larger intervals, the multiplication factor was less easy to dismiss; during the single day he'd spent inside the Node's Field, *twelve hundred* days had already passed outside.

The April 1st arrival of Siva was already part of history. The prediction had been that it would impact the lunar fragments in orbit, triggering cascades of deadly meteorites. This far north they had seen nothing except a slight thickening of the lunar debris ring that now surrounded their world.

Beyond his small window, the accelerated passage of time was turning clouds into fast-moving streams of grey vapour, while the waves on the newly formed sea simply vibrated in place. In less than a minute, the daylight would again slide into dark, Icelandic night.

The whole world was in flux, he thought, both outside the window and inside his own mind. Despite the millions of deaths that must logically have already happened in the wake of such planetary devastation, he found himself drawn to the thought of one death in particular.

Alfred knew he wasn't responsible for Napier's murder; Bradley Pittman had pulled the trigger that had left the General bleeding-out in a basement room at Andersen Air Force Base. Alfred hadn't caused Napier's fatal stomach wound, but in the aftermath he hadn't attempted to save him either. He'd simply taken advantage of the situation and manipulated Pittman into placing him within the Node.

When he'd first taken possession of Pittman's unclaimed suite of rooms, Alfred had realised that the chaos caused by the Node's premature departure actually represented an opportunity. If he could be seen to impose order on the current chaos, then he could easily place himself in a position of power.

He stared into the sea. He'd once drawn comparisons between Archive's endeavours and a lifeboat where only a few people could be saved. The analogy once again rang true for him and a new thought dawned.

Everyone aboard the Node considered themselves among the saved. Some would see it as a personal success that they had survived, while others would experience intense survivor guilt. However, having been through the ordeal of departure, all of them would want to believe they were now safe.

People wanted certainty, he thought, they wanted simplicity.

Both were completely useless in terms of motivation.

Fear, on the other hand, was an excellent motivator.

Outside the window, darkness swept in.

He had once persuaded a far smaller group of people to adopt a morally unconventional method of global population control.

This would be simpler.

As before, it would come down to maintaining imbalance and the illusion of choice.

DUSK

21st January 2014

Marcus Blake had spent most of his adult life evading capture by authority figures. Wearing a cloak of anonymity, he could move through most of his digital targets with freedom. If his attempts to circumvent a system failed, then there was little consequence; though on a few occasions he'd been forced to abandon technology before authorities discovered his physical whereabouts.

In the outside world, a physical escape was comparatively easy. Here, inside the closed habitat of the USV, there were limited places to run to. The solution, he knew, was to avoid the running part altogether. It had not been easy.

He'd arrived into this underground cavern on the back of a single Eurotunnel train carriage along with Sabine Dubois. They'd narrowly avoided detection during their first few minutes here thanks to a disturbance in the village's lake. They hadn't seen the disturbance themselves, but in the ensuing chaos, no-one saw their unauthorised arrival or their theft of a few significant Archive supplies.

Of the various pieces of technology he'd lifted from the back of the carriage, his favourite was the military spec laptop. A little heavier than the one he'd been forced to abandon in Paris, but with one distinct advantage; military grade network camouflage. When they'd stolen it, the kit had still been in its packaging and, crucially, uninitialised. Marcus had found the start-up sequence laughably trivial to circumvent and, after installing himself as the primary user, had full control of its capabilities.

Although he didn't yet have full access to the USV servers, the digital camouflage made his laptop transparent to the network, ensuring that his hacking attempts were undetectable; a luxury he'd never had before. Archive had built these devices as an extension of their own paranoia; the desire to invisibly eavesdrop on their adversaries without detection. Marcus felt a huge amount of ironic satisfaction that he was now the one using the device, and that it was performing perfectly.

Camouflage in the physical world was more difficult however.

Since Marcus and Sabine's arrival, no-one had been looking for them, because they were not even aware of their presence. Marcus had been keen to maintain that impression so they'd spent the last three weeks moving between unoccupied areas of the dome's interior, surviving on stolen ration packs and sleeping in shifts.

Currently they were hiding in the unlit and inert Samphire Station. Since the sealing of the entrance to the Eurotunnel, the spur station hadn't been used, providing them with a temporary place to avoid detection by the

Peace Keepers.

From a lifetime of studying people's online behaviour, Marcus knew that humans were creatures of habit. The world had changed, but people took their behaviour with them; the Peace Keepers were a prime example.

From the information available to Marcus on the USV network, he'd learned that Archive had created worldwide 'Hives' of weaponized hovering drones, deployable in mass numbers against any target it saw fit. Once again, Archive had maintained its doctrine that a population needed constant surveillance and control. At any cost. The Peace Keeper drones, which could be fitted with an array of weaponry, could not suffer from conscience and would execute orders without question.

The Peace Keeper drones within the USV were no different; a deployable resource to offer peace of mind to all those willing to accept Archive's terms of residence, or a source of fear to those who would oppose the system.

Currently, access to the USV Hive was outside of Marcus' reach, something that he hoped would change today.

"Sabine?" he called her over.

"Maintenant?" she checked her watch.

"Oui," he nodded, it was time to move.

She placed a blue inhaler in her mouth and administered the dose, then passed it to Marcus. Although the dispenser looked similar to an asthma inhaler, its function was not to widen the airways of the lungs. If anything, Marcus knew, it widened access to the mind.

The inhaled compound had been reverse engineered during his time in the Warren, using knowledge acquired by Monica Walker and Miles Benton. Structurally, it bore a resemblance to the ego-morph drug metathene, enhancing pre-existing abilities, but the effects were short-term.

"Good luck," she said in English.

"Et toi," he wished the same to her.

•

With a certain amount of satisfaction, Bradley watched Monica forcing herself to back down from the confrontation he'd been provoking. Drawing from his memory of shooting General Napier, he'd painted a vivid but false picture of her husband's death. Enjoying his moment of power over her, he'd then conjured up an equally imaginative strangulation death for her daughter.

The truth was that after his helicopter had narrowly escaped the fence-breaching crowd outside the Node, he'd lost track of both Douglas and Kate. They may have died or they may have made it inside, he didn't know for certain, but he felt justified in inflicting mental anguish on Monica; as though every ounce of pain she experienced would somehow lessen his own.

For Bradley, it seemed that every Pittman generation had given so much. His father had been responsible for kick-starting the Apollo program, the original generational bunkers at Cheyenne Mountain, even the fusion reactors that now powered most of Archive's various endeavours.

When his father had died, Bradley had assumed control of the Pittman empire and diverted vast quantities of the family fortune into the development of Douglas Walker's Chronomagnetic Field generator. The Node was supposed to be his family's ticket to skipping over the oncoming destruction but when the crowd had breached the perimeter fence, those hopes had vanished and he'd been forced to flee. The injustice of the situation multiplied when he'd arrived at Archive's Eurotunnel embarkation facility in France.

Smartphone footage and data, transmitted from General Napier's phone, suggested that he and Alfred Barnes were complicit in the death of Napier himself. Bradley had suffered the humiliation of being bundled aboard the train in handcuffs, like a common murderer. Millions had been about to die from lunar fragment impacts and yet he stood accused of killing a single man; a man who, in his opinion, would have advocated reopening the bunkers to the general public. It amazed him that no-one could see the good in his actions; the resources within each of the bunkers would now last longer for the few that were saved.

Annoyingly, he thought, some of those USV resources were being wasted on Monica Walker. Even behind bars, she still needed feeding.

"It's only these bars that separate us," she stared at him.

"Yeah, well, these bars are here for my protection," he replied, tapping on the steel, "Not yours."

Her aggressive stance seemed to subside and she

glanced around the cell before replying in a calm tone.

"You may be the one who's free to take a walk around your glorified hole in the ground but it's still just a cage. You're just as trapped as me."

He knew she was probably right. The world above his head had been snatched from him. In all likelihood, he'd live out the remainder of his days buried here under Dover.

But in this small contained kingdom, he still had power.

Laughing, he turned his back on her.

"You just keep tellin' yourself that," he banged his fist twice on the outer door of the detention facility, "Reckon I might just have me a stroll round that beautiful lake of yours."

It was time to highlight the nature of her captivity and make a demonstration.

The door opened and he walked out into the simulated sunlight, where his daughter stood waiting. Sarah had been his greatest advocate in achieving his freedom within USV3. She had argued that the photographic Napier evidence was entirely circumstantial and not directly attributable to her father alone. The fact that Andersen Air Force Base now lay under the surface of the Pacific Ocean meant that Napier's body could never be examined. All that could be confirmed from the data trail was that Napier's smartphone had remotely deactivated Archive's security and that Napier himself was missing. In what he considered a moment of genius, Bradley had asserted that Napier was actually still alive and covering up the massive security breach by framing him for murder. Within an hour of stepping from the Eurotunnel carriage, Bradley was a free man.

"Any luck?" Sarah asked.

"I'm done talkin' to that woman," he gestured for her to hand back his touchscreen tablet, "Time to shout louder… is the Mercer woman prepped?"

Sarah nodded quietly and returned his tablet.

"Dad?" she frowned, "I'm concerned this is setting the wrong example. You said that she was involved in the planning stages of the USV, she could be helpful. Wouldn't it be wiser to find an alternative demonstration?"

Bradley tapped at the tablet and restarted the holding cell camera software, then looked up to see her concerned face.

"I know it don't seem right, Pumpkin-pie," he smiled, "But someday you'll understand. These people damn near brought the roof down on us. As long as there's even one of 'em free, they're a threat to everyone in here… and that includes you."

The artificial sun directly above them at the dome's summit was no longer running at full intensity; the elements were slowly powering down to simulate the approach of dusk. The USV would soon descend into night but in this moment, framed against the warm tones of the lake, he thought his daughter looked beautiful. He leaned forward and kissed her on the forehead.

"Ain't no-one gonna threaten my li'l girl. People have got to know that our society won't tolerate terrorism," he smiled weakly, "Now, go home Sal. You don't wanna be seeing this."

"You're right, Dad," she shook her head, "It doesn't seem right, and I don't understand."

All his life, he'd protected her from Archive's more uncomfortable truths, but soon she would see for herself the type of sacrifice he'd made to protect her naivety.

He watched her leave, then walked around the corner of the detention facility. Ahead lay the village square, where the occupants of the USV had gathered around the central water feature.

The abstract metallic sculpture had several smooth holes through which water flowed freely. The gently cascading water ran down the shiny surface to the shallow basin below, where it was collected and recycled.

Standing ankle-deep in this water and tied to the holes was Geraldine Mercer.

•

Sabine could feel the effects of the inhaler enhancing her already keen spatial perception. As in Paris a few weeks ago, the alleyways, ladders and rooftops seemed to flow effortlessly under her outstretched hands and feet.

From what Marcus had explained, her mother's name had appeared on a list along with twenty-two others. 'Bishop's list' detailed people who, despite being labelled 'Substandard', had an underlying genetic augmentation. In their first meeting, Marcus had identified Sabine as a direct descendant and impressed on her that she must accompany him to a safe venue. At the time, she'd thought it was the worst chat-up line she'd ever heard and told him so.

But then the sky had started to fall and everything had changed.

Before the news of Siva, she used to love losing herself in the city; running, jumping and swinging through the architectural sprawl. Now, this ability seemed to have a purpose. She sped on towards the village square.

In the few short weeks she'd been here, their travels had given her a good sense of the USV's layout. At the centre was the lake and village square; radiating outwards were eight compass-direction roads that divided the disc-like floor into equal segments. Some of the segments appeared to be devoted to farmland while others contained a selection of low-level housing, storage silos and water tanks. Surrounding the circular village, like an immense bicycle tyre, was the orbital rail track. Beyond this the floor curved sharply upwards to become the vaulted, bowl-like ceiling that overarched the whole USV. At the top of this negatively-defined space, in a permanent noon position, was the vast heat lamp sun.

Ahead she could see that a few people were still making their way to the gathering, so she ran into a narrow alleyway to avoid them. Without dropping her speed, she leapt into the air and planted one foot against the wall, then immediately used it to launch herself further up the opposing wall, before turning again to spring onto a flat roof. She continued her sprint, speed vaulting over air conditioning ducts and service pipes until she reached the building's edge. Keeping low, she looked out over the village square.

The sunlight had the slightly orange-hued quality of dusk, but the shadows here at the centre of the USV fell directly beneath people and objects. Lacking the long, evening shadows to anchor things to the ground, the village square and its occupants appeared eerily detached.

From somewhere below, she could hear a child's questioning tones. The mother's reply was short and hushed. To Sabine's ear, the only word that stood out was the one sounding like 'obligatoire'. It seemed that attendance here was not a matter of choice.

Sabine looked towards the middle of the square where everyone had begun gathering around the central water feature. To her horror, she could see that an old woman was tied to it.

Wasting no time, Sabine pulled off her backpack and retrieved the small device that Marcus had given to her. She opened out its miniature tripod legs and set it down on the flat roof. Slowly turning the small parabolic dish in the direction of the metallic water feature, she watched the LED indicator on the rear of the device. After a few seconds of turning, the light changed from red to yellow. She slowed the turning rate again.

The murmur coming from the crowd suddenly dropped in volume as a large-framed man emerged from behind the detention facility. She saw him tap at a tablet in his hands and at once there came the sound of rotor blades starting up. The sound rapidly rose in pitch and Sabine saw two Peace Keeper drones, each perhaps a metre wide, rise from the roof of the detention facility.

Extending from a blocky central core bristling with aerials and other appendages, were four black limbs. Each limb terminated in a blur of black propeller rotors; twitching in slightly different directions to manoeuvre the drones swiftly to towards the village square.

She'd seen the drone diagrams on Marcus' laptop but to see and hear them in reality sent a primal chill down her spine. Instinctively she found herself crouching lower, but then she realised she'd stopped turning the miniature dish. As she resumed guiding it into position, the public-address system for the USV gave a low howl and a synthetic voice announced:

"Geraldine Mercer. The charges are as follows."

Sabine had never met her, but understood from Marcus that Geraldine was Monica's closest ally within the Warren. She wanted desperately to force the dish into place immediately but knew that she must make the adjustment slowly. She continued to slowly turn the dish and the yellow light began to blink.

"Wilful damage to the USV sealed habitat."

The drones now hovered to take up positions on either side of the water feature. She stared at the flashing yellow light, willing it to turn green.

"Disabling of a Peace Keeper."

At this point, each of the drones quickly lowered a rod from their undercarriages and angled them towards Geraldine. The primal thought entered Sabine's mind that it resembled an insect's sting.

"Assisting a known enemy with intent to inspire sedition."

Finally, the LED became flashing green and Sabine

stopped the slow turning. The device was now correctly oriented, it just needed time to synchronise.

Sabine heard the rotor noise rise in pitch again and the drones moved closer to Geraldine, the downdraught from their rotors sending waves rippling over the water at her ankles. Geraldine struggled feebly against the restraints that were holding her to the polished metal structure, her eyes implored those around her for help, but none within the crowd moved.

"In accordance with habitat law, these acts are punishable by death. Does the accused have any response?"

Sabine could see that Geraldine's mouth had been taped shut.

"Verte, verte!" Sabine muttered to herself, willing the light to go a solid green.

Above the incessant droning noise, Sabine could just hear Geraldine's continued guttural attempts to scream past the tape. The device light changed to a solid green.

"Execute sentence."

The drones made a minute adjustment to their relative positions and then discharged their electrical current through the route of least resistance.

The lightning-blue tendrils snapped outward and connected with the conductive water and polished metal. Geraldine, already soaking wet from her prolonged binding to the water feature, was caught in the middle. Her arms tensed and her spine suddenly arched back with such force that she cracked her head open against the metal. Red torrents ran through the water, but the current continued to flow, leaping and buzzing through metal and flesh with undiminished vigour.

Sabine turned away from the horrific sight, leaving only the phasing rotor noise and thick sizzling sound to assault her ears. Her eyes fell on the large-framed man with the control tablet. By contrast his eyes seemed fixated on the whole experience. Only when the Peace Keepers shut down a few seconds later did he emerge from his almost trance-like state. He simply checked the tablet and walked away again in the direction of the detention facility entrance.

The smell of chlorine and ozone drifted up to her, as did the hushed sounds of children crying into their parents' chests. She turned to face the village square and saw the aftermath. In the abstract dusk-like glow was Geraldine Mercer's lifeless form; the weight of her body hanging from taut arms stretched across the metal surface. The water continued its decorative cascade, arriving in the collecting basin as diluted red swirls around her feet.

The stark sight returned Sabine to her senses.

People were turning away from the village square; she was now very exposed on the roof top. Forcing herself to contain her burning anger, she snatched up Marcus' device and retreated from the building's edge. If she didn't want to suffer the same fate, she would need to avoid being seen on her way back; but with so many people nearby she would just have to wait.

The only reason they could move around at all was because Marcus had discovered from the USV network that the surveillance system was not yet complete. For the time being they could avoid detection by keeping clear of people and the drones' direct line of sight.

One lighting element at a time, she watched as the artificial sun's ring of lights began to fade and eventually dusk descended into night. At the centre of the artificial sun was a circle of glass, beyond which was only shadow. Sabine knew that it was only a matter of time before the 'Eye' was complete and there would be no more hiding places. Soon cameras would stare down at them, watching everything in their small world.

Sabine turned away from the darkened sun and focussed on the present. She folded in the miniature tripod legs of the device and was about to put it back into her backpack, when she noticed something. In addition to the solid green light next to the label 'sync', a second blue LED was pulsing next to the label 'T-R'.

THE FIRST GUARDIAN

23rd November 7141

Long ago the forefathers had repaired the bridge, allowing the Elders to reach the wooded island beyond. But few of the present Elders ventured that far in; most preferred to live in the gloom away from the persistent glare of The Guardians within the Orb. From where Atka stood, he could see the Orb's cold, ethereal dome above the small trees.

Steadying himself for his very first crossing, he placed a foot on the bridge and was greeted with a chill that ran down his spine. Were it not for the burning torch in his hand, he feared the chill may have spread throughout his whole body. Few now made the choice to cross the bridge, but for his family it was a rite that he knew he must honour.

He lifted his other foot from the ground and set it on the bridge. His thoughts turned to his mother, who could not witness his journey; her path had ended, leaving him to make the journey alone. He looked up to the scintillating rings that surrounded his world and the night sky beyond. Perhaps she and her ancestors were watching him from the stars.

The Sky-Spirits circled above the Orb, passing through each other and exchanging hues and intensities. If they could see him, then he must not show fear.

Atka began to walk across the long, wood and vine bridge. In the spaces between the wooden branches below his feet, he could see the chasm below and the still waters that ran deep and dark. The bridge now swayed; a gentle rocking that seemed to quieten the village with every footfall.

As he reached the end of the bridge, he could no longer hear the distant village; only the soft sound of the torch flames kept him company. He stepped from the bridge onto the island and saw ahead of him the fractured and ancient stone, bearing the marking 'ARK IV'.

The rite demanded that he spend the night on the island in the full view of the Orb. To prepare himself for the long vigil ahead he crossed to the ancient stone. He had been told of its appearance but had never seen the inscriptions himself.

The symbols adorning the stone were many and varied; some were etched more sharply, while others were less distinct. Some of the carvings were similar to the circular necklace piece worn by the village's senior Elder, but others were collections of straight lines.

In front of him now were a group of lines that he recognised. His mother had once shown him those lines by scratching them into the village dirt with a stick - lines that depicted his name in the old tongue. She had told him that his name meant 'Guardian Spirit' - something he hoped the Sky-Spirits would approve of during his first night.

Turning away from the stone, he gathered dry wood from the ground and set it within the ceremonial hearth in front of the Orb. When he had gathered enough, he used his torch to light the fire; a beacon that would alert the Guardians to his attendance.

Atka stood by the fire and extended his hands to its golden warmth. There had been other times when he'd considered undertaking the tradition, but as the stars had unveiled their brightness tonight he'd felt a strong compulsion that this was the right time; as though the Guardians were somehow expecting him.

A light breeze passed over him and he looked up towards the Orb. The sight that greeted him was almost beyond his comprehension.

At the centre of the Orb's bright surface, a small space had formed, like a hole in white ice. The hole was held open by straight edges and at its centre was a silhouetted figure. A Guardian, standing motionless and surveying the world.

In fear, Atka fell to his knees and bowed in reverence, averting his eyes. Although few still chose to undertake the rite, many had claimed they had seen a Guardian. He recalled their chilling stories of the Guardians' appearance and their terrifying size, but he had seen something different. Either the tales of others were falsehoods or the Guardian was choosing to appear to him in human form.

He heard his ancestors speak within him, telling him not to be afraid. Slowly he raised his head to see the small opening in the Orb's surface once more. He knelt transfixed by the sight.

The Guardian within had turned and was very slowly moving away from him towards the Orb's centre. Perhaps the inside of the Orb was filled with water, he thought, because although the Guardian's posture was that of someone running, the movement was slow and flowing.

The hole suddenly healed itself and the Guardian vanished. Hardly daring to blink, he stood and stared at the smooth, bright surface of the Orb.

He had seen his first Guardian.

The fire at his side seemed warmer and overhead the Sky-Spirits seemed brighter. He made up his mind in an instant. He would return here every night in the hope of seeing the Guardian again. But he knew he must be patient.

The Guardians within the Orb had been here for generations.

THE MARK IV

DAY01 : 31JUL2017

At the centre of the former Öskjuvatn Lake, sat the Node. Surrounded by sea, shallow waves lapped against the Node's impenetrable and transparent Field.

Inside the Node, those same waves appeared to vibrate at high frequency atop a three-foot high cross-section of sea water; a perfectly circular, invisible wall surrounding the dry land just beyond the Observation Deck's massive window.

Roy Carter retrieved a set of digital recording binoculars from the nearby recharging bank and focussed them on a dry area where the Field intersected the ground. He half expected to see damp ground, but of course there was no hint of moisture.

He found he could fairly easily accept that the Field was physically passing through and separating the air, but when he thought of the unseen hemisphere underneath the Node, he still had a difficulty believing that the Field passed through solid matter with equal ease.

The very rock the Node was built on was ageing at a different rate to the rock outside the observation window. The Observation Deck's digital clock, centred at ground level next to the window, did its best to convey two simultaneous time-frames. Currently it read:

'0001_02.14.AM : 31JUL2017'

The first part was a reference to the day and internal time, the second part was the date outside the Field. As there were no seasonal variations inside the Node it had been decided to display only the passage of days. For each minute that passed inside, twenty hours passed outside. Because the twenty hours was not a whole day, the resulting effect on the clock was that the external date would not always change in sync with the minute digit; something which only seemed to highlight the oddity of the situation. Here it was possible to have short conversations that apparently lasted days.

"Catch anything, Roy?" came Trevor Pike's voice.

Roy dropped the binoculars back into the recharging bank and turned to face him.

"Nah, no fish out there," he smiled, "Can't sleep either?"

Trevor simply shook his head, "With all this going on out the window?"

For the Node's occupants it was technically the middle of the night, but without the circadian cues to reinforce day-night cycles, many were having difficulty in sleeping.

"Too bad we can't control the external lighting, like we did on the Mark 3," Roy replied in good humour, but then wished he'd thought more carefully before speaking, "Sorry, Mr. Pike, I -"

"It's alright," Trevor replied, patting him on the back, "My Steven was just in the wrong place. You did everything you could."

Roy lapsed into silence and stared out of the window again.

In the September before their unplanned departure, a dedication stone bearing the words *'THE NODE, MARK IV'* had been placed in full view of the observation window. During the initial tsunami that had overwhelmed the site, vehicles, ships and even light aircraft had been tossed at the Field. The Field had not wavered, but the stone had suffered multiple impacts and had been severely damaged. Steven Pike's name had been engraved on the same stone, below an inscription which read:

'They gave their lives for the good of Mankind'.

Roy had shared several shifts with Steven, watching over the Node's immediate predecessor, the Mark 3. He remembered how they'd relieved the boredom by tallying whenever Douglas Walker or Anna Bergstrom had appeared at a window. Roy knew that he'd forever question himself; if they hadn't been playing that trivial game, or if he'd spotted the smoke earlier, would Trevor's son have lived? The fact was that the hangar fire had only begun after the deactivation of the Mark 3's Field; something that could only be triggered from within the Mark 3 itself. Even if Roy had spotted the smoke earlier, the likelihood was that things would have turned out the same way. But he would never know for sure.

"Roy," Trevor seemed to be offering comfort, "if you and Beck hadn't got Doug Walker out of the hangar, then there would be no Field inversion. We wouldn't be standing here right now. Think of all the lives you saved. My Steven would've been proud of that."

Roy felt like rebuking the passive consolation, but stopped himself. Trevor had lost his only son and needed to believe that Steven's death had a meaning; Roy was not about to take that away from him.

"Yes, he would," Roy replied and gave Trevor a dignified nod.

A low volume but high-pitched whining tone sounded from a few feet away and they turned to face the noise. Several people were checking their Biomags, but only one of them was frozen to the spot.

The woman remained motionless but was clearly in the grip of panic. When the others nearby were sure that their Biomags were functioning, they began taking small steps away from her; everyone aboard was well-versed in the consequences of Biomag or isotope failure, no-one wanted to be nearby when she unanchored from the Field.

Still motionless and with tearful eyes, she implored those around her to help, *"Please!"*

"OK, stand still!" Trevor hurried over to her, then slowed his approach, "It's Gail, right?"

The woman nodded, *"Please..."*

Trevor did his best to keep the situation calm and controlled.

"OK, Gail, remember how the tag 'n' tope works. The Biomag and isotope are holding you in a stable Field pocket, as long as you don't move out of it, I can help," Trevor attempted to keep her calm. Without losing eye contact with Gail, he motioned towards the side wall of the Observation Deck, "Roy, get me the emergency tag."

Roy ran to a wall mounted, glass fronted box that stated:

'Emergency Biomag - Break Glass'.

Even as he approached it, Roy could clearly see that the emergency Biomag had not been put in place. In the rush to prepare the Node for their swift departure, it was yet another item that had not been deemed a priority.

Roy swore under his breath and ran back to Trevor, "No go."

Trevor noticeably winced at the news, but still didn't break eye contact with Gail, "Don't move, we can still fix this!"

The tone from Gail's Biomag dropped in pitch and her eyes widened in terror; her mouth was still pleading but no sound emerged. The others nearby continued to shuffle further away.

"Wait, wait!" Roy shouted to Trevor "Constructive interference?"

Roy's suggestion sparked an immediate response in Trevor.

"Yes! I should've…" he began, but then raised his voice, "OK, everyone listen up!"

The low-level mumblings nearby ceased.

"I need you two," Trevor pointed to the people to his right, then addressed those immediately to his left, "and you three, to very slowly walk closer to Gail and me."

Gail's Biomag dropped in pitch again.

"Now!" he shouted, seeing that they'd hardly moved.

As they approached, he directed them into formation around Gail. By the time they were in position, a loose hexagon of people surrounded her, including Trevor himself.

"OK, on three, we all take one step inward toward Gail, understand?" Trevor quickly looked at each of them, "Roy, get me the power pack from a DRB."

Roy dashed back to the recharging bank and began unclipping the battery compartment of one of the digital recording binoculars.

"One, Two. *Three!*"

As one, they stepped into a close formation around Gail.

The Biomag's tone dropped again as the power continued to dwindle, prompting everyone to recoil slightly.

"Everyone, just stay calm and stay close!" Trevor called out, "We're here in case the power fails. Gail's caught in the overlap of all our Biomags. As long as we stick together, she's safe. Roy, where's that power pack?"

"Got it!" Roy shouted, ahead of his return, "Damn!"

The rechargeable batteries were shrink-wrapped together for ease of swapping, but Roy knew he'd need to separate out the individual cells to achieve the correct voltage for the Biomag. He bit into the plastic in an attempt to weaken it enough for his fingernails to tear, but the material was too tough. He dashed over to the Emergency Biomag box and plunged his elbow through the glass, creating several useful shards. He picked up a thin sliver and, ignoring the sharp edges digging into his palm and fingers, cut away at the plastic to expose the individual cells within. Thankfully, he thought, there was a short section of copper wiring inside the pack; he'd be able to use it to step down the pack's power output.

"Voltage is too high," he called out, as he returned to the cluster of people surrounding Gail, "Give me a sec."

While Roy worked to rewire the battery pack, Trevor focussed on the nanocomposite crystal that stood proud of the Biomag's surface.

"OK, Gail, it looks like the resonator crystal's still intact," Trevor smiled at her, trying his best to convey optimism, "but I need to open the Biomag up, so you've got to stay still. OK?"

Gail provided a miniscule nod of the head.

"OK, good. Now listen up," he looked around at the others, "After I open the Biomag case and disconnect the failing battery, the unit's going to switch to capacitor backup for a few seconds and it's gonna buzz like hell to tell us what we already know. Don't freak out."

As Trevor began to prise the case apart along the edge, silent tears streamed down Gail's face. When the Biomag tone dropped again, she began to tremble.

"Almost there," Trevor said quietly, "Everything's going to be fine."

Gently he prised open the box, dividing it in two.

One half held the green coloured printed circuit boards, its flat surface dotted in places with the black squares of control chips. The other half contained a palm-sized metallic loop; anchored within a circular indentation, the loop's shiny surface was interrupted at one point by the presence of the resonator crystal.

"OK, Gail, this is good," he made eye contact, "Everything looks intact, it's just the power supply, OK? And we can fix that."

"OK, it's stepped down to nine volts," said Roy, presenting a bloodstained battery pack.

"Great, Roy, now you see the negative rail of the Biomag's PSU?" Trevor struggled to indicate the relevant terminal using only his little finger, "Just next to the -"

"Yep, got it," Roy reached through the tightly knit group of people and wrapped the exposed copper wire of his battery pack around the terminal several times.

"OK good, now you'll need to physically disconnect the positive side of the Biomag's PSU. Then wait a second before completing the circuit with your nine-volter, alright? OK get ready everybody."

Trevor noticeably squared himself up in anticipation, causing the others next to him to shuffle uncomfortably, "OK, Gail, here we go."

Without warning, the Biomag's tone suddenly died; the internal power supply had failed. Roy knew that the unit's capacitor backup should have activated, along with the warning buzz that Trevor had warned them of; however the unit stayed silent. Acting almost instinctively, he rapidly pinched the second wire to the positive terminal, then held it in place with his finger and thumb.

"What are you -?" Trevor began, in panic.

"Capacitor's fried!" Roy shot back, "The power's gone!"

The Biomag quietly emitted a double beep.

Trevor carefully turned over one half of the Biomag. In blocky letters, the digital display embedded in the surface flashed:

'8oot'

Trevor let out a sigh of relief.

"Boot," he breathed, "It's rebooting."

A few seconds later the display simply showed '1200'; the Biomag was measuring the presence of a Chronomagnetic Field gradient of 1200 to 1.

"Everyone," said Trevor, quietly, "You can breathe again. Gail, you're re-anchored."

Around the group, general sighs of relief accompanied Gail's tears of happiness. No-one made any attempt to move away from their hastily improvised cluster.

"Roy, don't let go of that wire," Trevor shook his head in amazement, "that was quick thinking."

"Well you said the capacitor would trigger the buzz-"

"No, I meant about the constructive interference. I should've got there sooner, but you -"

"Not just me. This was definitely a team effort," Roy looked around at the tight-knit cluster surrounding Gail, "When we stick together, we literally reinforce each other's strength."

There were a few appreciative laughs of relief at the

analogy and they began to relax slightly. At that moment, Caroline Smith dashed across the Observation Deck floor towards them; evidently, upon seeing the drama unfold, someone had run to alert the Node's doctor. In addition to her medical bag, she carried a plastic-wrapped Biomag and a worried expression.

"Who's hurt?" she called.

"I'm OK!" Gail finally found her voice, but then turned to Trevor for confirmation, "Right?"

"Let's get that new Biomag round your neck, but yeah," he nodded, pulling the new Biomag out of the bag and activating it. He unwound its thin chain and looped it over her head.

The new unit finished booting up and displayed the number '1200'.

"Can I let go of this terminal now?" said Roy, who had been diligently holding the wires that was keeping the old Biomag alive.

Trevor checked the new unit one last time then told him it was safe. After Roy had untangled himself from the wires and other people's arms he stepped aside and allowed the doctor to treat him. As the doctor cleaned and glued his cuts, he watched as the group collectively took a tentative step away from Gail, who remained in one piece.

"What happened?" said Caroline, dabbing efficiently at his palm.

"The backup capacitor just... failed," he frowned, "But why that would trigger a -"

"I meant your hand," she shook her head, "The last time I patched up this hand was after the Mark 3 fire."

Roy could still remember the burns he'd received from the white-hot handle of the Mark 3 airlock. His attempt to get Douglas Walker and Anna Bergstrom out, had removed several layers of skin and also left him with permanent nerve damage.

"Yeah, I remember, but you know what? It actually helped," he gestured to the shards of glass he'd used to cut through the plastic of the DRB power pack, "If I'd been able to feel the sharp glass, I couldn't have gripped it hard enough to cut through the shrink-wrap. We wouldn't have got the right voltage for the Biomag, and the Node would now be missing its Chief Astronomer. So, all in all… I think it worked out pretty well."

"Gail Armstrong has a lot to thank you for," Caroline finished applying the last sticking suture, "I, on the other hand, will not thank you for continued visits to the infirmary."

"Speaking of which," Roy pointed loosely in the direction of the infirmary, "is there any news?"

"Kate Walker?" Caroline shook her head, "She's still out cold."

"She's got to pull through," Roy stared at her, "we owe her. If she hadn't made the connection between -"

"I know," Caroline pacified him, "I want her to pull though too. I've made her as comfortable as possible, but she'll only come back to us when she's ready."

"We've lost enough people already," Roy turned toward the observation window and the dedication stone beyond, "No more."

The first tsunami event had taken a ragged bite from the long dedication stone, removing its upper-left quarter. The lower portions, bearing the names of the dead, had survived intact; an irony not lost on those within the Node. But of the upper portion, only half of the dedication message remained. Split across two lines of chiselled stone, the words now read:

'-ARK IV'

'- for the good of Mankind'

Beyond the Field, the sea level continued to rise, submerging the names of the dead.

ZERO FOUR FIVE

13th April 2014

Over the past few months, Tristan had watched the pressure gauge readings increase aboard the Sea-Bass. The datum sea levels were rising.

In the immediate aftermath of the seven lunar shards that had hit the Earth, there were inevitable tsunamis, but it didn't explain the general shift towards deeper oceans.

He'd discussed the idea with the crew that the additional water may be a result of ringwoodite layers seismically rupturing deep below the ocean beds. He'd even outlined how the magnesium silicate was suited to containing the key components for water within its crystalline structure. But for the crew, hydrogen-oxygen bonding didn't hold the same fascination; life under the sea brought more immediate challenges than academic analysis.

Tristan checked the compass direction again. In the vicinity of the ice anomaly, Earth's magnetic field was being distorted. As far as the anomaly was concerned, magnetic north now lay directly northeast.

"Bearing Zero Four Five," Tristan confirmed, "Mat, take the helm."

Mat laughed, but then spotted Tristan's expression was not one of amusement.

"Are you insane?" Mat looked around the others to see if they'd had similar thoughts, "You wanna follow directions from the creepy ice loop?"

"Of course not," Tristan shrugged.

"Bullshit, Tris, I know that look," Mat folded his arms, "and I'm not playing."

"Look. Come here," Tristan beckoned them, "Everyone."

The others grudgingly joined him at the wide bubble window.

"Look at the edges," he said, pointing at the anomaly.

"There's not a straight edge on it, Tris," Lucy delivered in monotone.

"OK, sorry. Look carefully at the seawater immediately behind any part of the visible structure. You see that shimmering?"

Pavna edged forwards slightly to gain a better look.

"The shifting index of refraction within the water?" she said, "We saw that when we first arrived. The temperature differential's tied to the density of the seawater, like a desert mirage."

"Yep," Tristan said.

"What's your point?" Pavna turned to him.

"How long have we been here, Pav?" he asked rhetorically, "Maybe twenty minutes? Half an hour at most?"

"Twenty-three," Lucy checked her watch, "And?"

"OK, twenty-three minutes," he glanced sideways at Lucy, "This anomaly arrived before we did. With so much mass, the water surrounding it should already have started to freeze."

"You're right," Mat frowned and moved in too, pointing at the main sphere, "We should at least be seeing some sort of... random ice growths sprouting from the surfaces, but -"

"It looks just the same as when we first arrived," Pavna concluded, "it still looks brand new."

She narrowed her eyes at Tristan.

"You don't think the distortion effect is anything to do with refractive index, do you?"

Tristan shook his head, "I think we need to take a closer look."

"Tris," Lucy exhaled hard, "we're not a science vessel, we're not equip-"

"Lucy," he countered, "there *are* no science vessels anymore."

"All I'm saying," Lucy held up her hands, "is that we should peg its location, head back to the Arc and -"

"And do what exactly?" Mat cut in, "Tell 'em we've been seeing Exordi Nova symbols on the sea floor? They'd have us committed."

"Or executed," Pavna looked anxiously between the others.

Tristan looked out at the anomaly.

"This..." he turned back to face them, "This is for us. We need to find out more. What else have we got waiting for us? More passenger manifests? The Sea-Bass is practically empty at the minute, there's never been a better time."

"Another coincidence?" Mat raised an eyebrow.

Tristan just smiled, then raised his right hand, "I vote we investigate. Mat?"

"I guess a little extra data couldn't hurt, right?" Mat raised his hand too.

"An hour, tops. OK?" Lucy shook her head, "Then we turn around and resume course. Agreed?"

"Fair enough," Tristan conceded.

Lucy nodded and raised her hand in consent.

"Pavna?" Tristan turned to her.

"I know it's pointless arguing," she said, raising her hand, "But I'm with Lucy on this, an hour tops, OK?"

Having voted to investigate rather than leave immediately, the crew took up their stations and Mat manoeuvred the submarine into position directly above the icy symbol. At Tristan's insistence, he aligned the Sea-Bass to lie along the anomaly's lines of magnetic flux; the new local south was situated at the stern and the local north was at the bow outside the bubble window, where the icy sphere filled the view.

"Holding steady on bearing Zero Four Five," Mat reported, then half laughed, "Due... north."

"Initiate sonar pulse," Tristan turned to Pavna.

"Pulse," she reported, as the hollow sonar ping rang out. It returned a fraction of a second later, producing an acoustic image of their immediate surroundings on the display surface. The plan view showed the Sea-Bass sitting neatly within the main circle, aligned with the anomaly's line of symmetry.

"Station keeping?" Tristan called out.

"Ten feet above, plus or minus an inch," Mat replied.

"Lucy, any relative temperature change?"

"No," she shook her head.

Tristan rubbed at his chin; the anomaly was remaining in place above the seabed, apparently unaided, and yet the manoeuvring jets were being taxed against the subsurface currents.

"Pav, start a continuous ping rate, one hertz. Lucy, watch our temperature and hull pressure. Mat, slowly take us down."

There was a noticeable intake of breath before they complied, then Tristan felt the slight shift under his feet as the submarine began to drop through the seawater.

"Descent," reported Mat, "Ten feet... Eight..."

The sonar began generating an audible ping once each second.

"Still centred," Pavna reported.

"I'll take that as a compliment," Mat replied without taking his eyes from the controls, "Six feet..."

"Lucy?" Tristan continued to stare out of the bubble window at the sphere that was slowly rising through the view.

"No change in relative density or temperature. Hull pressure stable."

"Five feet... Four feet... approaching lateral level of the ring," Mat called out, "How am I looking Pav?"

The sonar ping returned once more.

"Minor starboard drift," she read out, "still within tolerance."

"All nominal here," Lucy called out.

"Two feet… One…"

"Dead centre," Pavna confirmed.

The manoeuvring jets were now audible as a minor vibration in the hull.

"Zero. Level with the ring!" Mat called out, "But we can't stay for too long like this, mano-jets are maxed out just keeping us here."

"Lucy," Tristan moved to the display surface, "How's the magnetic field strength?"

"Increased," she pointed to the lines of magnetism that appeared to be flowing around the diagram of the Sea-Bass, "but we're closer than we were before."

"OK, Mat can you hold us stead-" Tristan stopped speaking. Instinctively he knew something was amiss but it took him a second to identify it. The sonar pulses that had continued throughout their descent, were no longer being returned. He crossed to the window again and looked at the hemisphere of ice towering above them, and the equal mass that was below them. The manoeuvring jet noise vibrating through the hull seemed to be growing stronger.

"Mat, cut the mano-jets," Tristan called.

"What!" he called back, "The current's too strong!"

"Mat, the jets are -"

"We'll smash against the ring!" Mat yelled.

"Trust me, cut the jets."

"I'm not risking this! I'm taking us back up."

"Mat, wait! Let go for just one second. If I'm wrong, then get us out of here."

Mat seemed to hesitate, then closed his eyes, "You'd better be right about this, wonder-boy."

Mat let go of the controls and the manoeuvring jets throttled back. The hull vibration noise ceased immediately and within a few seconds the control room was only occupied by the general background hum they were accustomed to.

Tristan looked out of the bubble window again, studying the featureless, icy sphere. Relative to the window it was motionless. He glanced left and right to where the circumferential spirals left the sphere. Likewise, there was absolutely no movement.

"We're stationary."

"What? Did we ground out?" Pavna crossed the small room to consult the feedback from the hull's impact sensors, "Reading a negative for hull contact."

"Son of a..." Mat trailed off, leaving his station and joining Tristan at the window, "We're stationary? How did you... I mean, it's impossible..."

"No, it's just a possible that we don't understand yet."

In the quiet sub control room, they all simply stared out at the anomaly through the bubble window, each caught in their own thoughts.

A sudden and loud warning alarm broke the silence.

"Spike!" Lucy shouted, "Temperature drop - fifty degrees!"

Mat dashed away in the direction of helm control, but Tristan couldn't draw his eyes away from the sphere.

He was aware of Lucy shouting that the temperature was still dropping, but he continued to stare.

The sphere beyond the window was expanding.

ELEMENT

~

Of all the elements, she found it easiest to manipulate hydrogen. It could be classically viewed as a circle, broken in one place by the presence of a single electron, orbiting a single proton.

For her, its circular pattern had an elegance and simplicity; something that belied the fact it was the most abundant element in the Universe.

Throughout the preceding day, a trail of similar symbols had been successfully placed; each one increasing the man's receptivity to the symbol that she would now create.

The hydrogen and oxygen within the seawater only aided the process of manipulating the electrostatic forces. At the appropriate moment, she removed the heat energy from the water within the boundary of the three-dimensional structure she wished to produce. The tonnes of seawater instantly froze as its temperature briefly dropped to absolute zero. Once the symbol was fully formed, she returned the energy to the surrounding water in kinetic form, sending a massive subsurface swell in the direction of the submarine.

It had the intended effect; checking the resulting lines of convergence, she could already see the submarine had returned to the ocean floor site and was manoeuvring itself into position, directly above the icy symbol. Technically, they had been given a choice; their actions had indicated their willingness to become part of the plan, even if they could not yet conceive of their destination.

She watched as the arcs of continuity and consequence rearranged themselves throughout time. It was a bold step, to knowingly cause such a scar, but she hoped it would heal in time.

ANCHOR

28th December 2013

Anna Bergstrom waited until she was sure that Dr. Chen was out of earshot, then pulled the hatch door closed. In zero gravity, it took her much longer than she'd anticipated. Every motion she took suffered an equal and opposite reaction; to move something with large mass required anchoring oneself to something immovable.

"Miles," she turned to him and insisted he wipe his eyes with the absorbent cloth, "We're in trouble."

"Why?" he frowned and wiped his face, "It seems we're necessary aboard -"

"Nej!" she found herself defaulting to Swedish, "No, I'm not talking about that. You remember the Mark 3? At Öskjuvatn -"

"Yes, the fire, back in August? I was there. You and Douglas were lucky to escape."

"We weren't lucky," Anna shook her head, "The fire protected something we discovered."

"What?" said Miles, "What do you mean, it protected -"

"That's just it," Anna hesitated, "I can't tell you."

"I want to help," Miles frowned, "I really do. I told Douglas I'd do everything I could to help you, but -"

"It's OK," she held his arm, partly to reassure him but also to prevent them from drifting apart, "It wasn't your fault. It's just that…"

She glanced down at the silver metathene injector case in his hands.

"Chen has you taking the drug because he doesn't know you're clear. He assumes you're still an Ego," she then studied her bandaged hand, "I'm afraid that if the drug takes hold of you again, Chen will…"

"He'll, what?" Miles urged her.

"He'll make you get the information out of me."

"I'd nev…" Miles began, but then stopped.

"Archive got the full Field inversion equations out of me at Andersen, but they didn't get… everything. Miles, I won't be strong enough next time I'm tortured. Next time it might be you who does it, not Pittman. If Chen or the others study my work, while I'm creating a new set of Field equations, it's only a matter of time before the discovery is made again. It is too great a risk."

Miles appeared to stiffen slightly.

"What do you need me to do, Anna?" he said determinedly.

"Miles," she squeezed his arm gently, "You must kill me."

Miles recoiled instantly, an action that in zero gravity only brought them closer together.

"I can't," he said, "What could possibly be *so* -"

"You could make it look like I was trying to sabotage something," she continued, "Any one of the systems aboard are critical to survival -"

"No, Anna -"

"You could tell him you were doing it 'For the good of Mankind', he'd believe you…"

Miles' expression seemed to change suddenly, as though he'd been struck by sudden inspiration.

"Anna, stop," he said quietly, "There's a better way, but I don't think we've got much time. Listen. After General Napier had escorted from Iceland, I explained to you how Monica Walker had… disabled… the ego-morph part of me."

"Yes, but you never explained it fully," Anna recalled.

"Because Napier himself boarded the transport plane and I had to stop talking."

Anna knew this was true; there had been occasions, during the flight to Andersen Air Force Base, when General Napier had left the cabin. Miles would take the opportunity to steal a few moments of conversation with her; but the amount to be covered meant shallower overall depth.

"Monica discovered that for an ego-morph, the metathene is useless without a core drive. The thing on which everything else can be anchored."

"Everything else?"

"Everything that Archive wanted me to do," he looked away from her, obviously recalling things he was not proud of, "The anchor persuaded me that Archive's instructions were an execution of my own free will."

In that moment Anna realised that, under the controlling choke of the metathene and conditioning, his free choices had never truly been free. Only during the time that she'd known him, had his choices been his own; and he'd made the choice to help her.

"Under a strong hallucinogen," Miles recalled, "Monica circumvented my ego-morph conditioning by using the idea of a crossword. She would feed me clues and ask me to fill in the blanks."

"Why would the ego-morph part of you help her?"

"Because of the core drive that my anchor was attached to," he replied.

"Which is what?" Anna studied him.

"Even as a child, I liked to help people," he gave a shrug, "Ironically, I helped Monica to break me out of my own mind."

A clicking sound from the direction of the hatch caused them both to turn. Instinctively, Anna let go of Miles' arm in case someone should enter. A second later, the clicking sound happened again.

"It's the pumps," Miles realised, "Dehumidifier, filtration."

Anna breathed a sigh of relief, "How did you know?"

"This stuff," he tapped the metathene case, "I can already feel the changes, the awareness it brings. There's a small window of opportunity, Anna, to re-use the remnants of what Monica put in place."

He tapped his forehead again.

"The crossword idea is still in here, and you'll need to imprint some new answers," he said, reaching into one of his pockets, "The first is this. Silver Coin."

He turned and framed the coin against the window. From their perspective, the embossed moon on the coin was the same size as the Moon that lay shattered in orbit.

"The second crossword answer, is the instruction that I can't break," Miles continued, "When I left Dover, Monica made me aware that my instructions were to assist Kate. Clearly, I can't do that anymore, but perhaps I could be made to act in *your* best interests instead. The words should be..."

"Protect Anna?" she suggested.

"No. Like the original crossword, all the answers must have the same pattern," he smiled, "Six, Four. Assist Anna."

•

A subtle tone sounded within Dr. Chen's ear.

"Father?"

"Yes, Fai."

"I have some new data."

"One moment," he said quietly.

Ivan Meznic had entered the far end of the module and, pushing between handholds, he glided easily along the length of the room to meet him.

"Valery asked me to tell you," said Ivan, showing him a tablet screen, "CMGs are back online."

In contrast to the larger reaction thrusters they had manoeuvred with earlier, the Control Moment Gyros adjusted the rotation of the ISS in relation to the planet below.

"She says that, relative to Earth, we're still at

anchor."

"That is good news, Mr. Meznic," Dr. Chen smiled, "Was there something else?"

"Yes," Ivan nodded, similarly smiling, "I got past the mineralisation issue on the aeroponics mist heads. The fabricated polymer nozzles are giving us nutrient droplets of ten to forty micrometres."

"Plant life is now possible?"

Ivan simply smiled and nodded.

"Mr. Meznic, we are all in your debt."

Ivan looked slightly embarrassed and, after mumbling a modest acceptance of the compliment, pushed his way back along the module's length and disappeared from view.

Dr. Chen waited a few seconds then tapped his ear.

"Fai, you said you have new data, please continue."

"I have completed uploading the Archive data files."

Three days before, in response to an electrical overload within General Napier's pacemaker, the linked smartphone had deactivated the firewall surrounding all of Archive's digital data. It had then removed all password protection, making it available to anyone. At the time, satellite communication and even ground networks worldwide had been failing, so achieving a connection to that data was difficult; but not impossible.

"And what have you found, Fai?"

Fai appeared to pause before replying.

"Everything."

He'd only ever given her the data that he saw fit. For her to have access to everything that Archive had ever done, represented a loss of his absolute control. It was possible that she had even discovered information about him that he would rather have kept confidential.

"Would you like me to repeat my response?"

It was also possible that the nature of her pause was due to the dataset being too large to summarise succinctly. Even now, he occasionally fell into the trap of anthropomorphising her responses.

"No," he shook his head, "Please ensure that these files are not accessible by the crew of the ISS."

"Of course. I have detected a connection between the ISS dataset and those of Archive, and wish to bring a matter to your attention."

"Continue."

"According to the current schedule, I project that the remainder of the ISS construction work will miss the completion date by seven weeks and two days."

"Because the ISS did not have a full complement of crew members during the Apollo 72 launch?"

"Yes, Father. According to the uploaded data, Mike Sanders, Lana Yakovna and Cathy Gant all have extensive spacesuit experience from their time working at the FLC. They also have zero gravity training."

It took him only a moment to realise what Fai was suggesting, but it was not a comfortable thought.

"You are suggesting that their skills should be used to meet the original schedule?"

"Yes, Father."

He knew that Fai still had a certain naivety when it came to assessing human emotion; the way that the FLC crew had been forcibly hibernated was unlikely to translate into their wholehearted cooperation.

"Within the uploaded Archive files, I have detected a reference to a compliance technique. It is compatible with the FLC crew's low-level use of metathene and may elicit behaviour conducive to the completion of the ISS Chronomagnetic Field."

"Continue," he frowned. Fai seemed to be demonstrating an analysis technique that bordered on the proactive, something he hadn't seen before.

"The technique is contained within a folder titled 'Morphology of the Ego'," she reported, *"It is a metathene-based hypnotic process, used to establish compliance. Authorship of the document is attributed to Robert Wild and Dorothy Pittman."*

Dr. Chen retrieved his tablet from a pocket and synchronised it with Fai.

"Show me."

FIRST DAY

6th September 1976

"**G**ood morning, children."

"Good morning, Mrs. Pittman," Miles joined in musically with the other new children.

"Excellent," she smiled, "Now before we go inside, I'd like you all to turn around and wave to your parents…"

Obediently he turned with the others to face the tall crowd of parents a few feet away. Many of the mothers waved handkerchiefs and dabbed at their faces; his mother was one of them.

"… they'll collect you again in a few hours…"

His mother wiped her eyes and nodded to him bravely; she was so proud of him. He gave her his widest smile to show her that everything was going to be alright. It seemed to have the opposite effect though, because she began crying again and pretended to blow her nose.

"… So…"

Miles waved to his mother then turned to face his new teacher. He'd met Mrs. Pittman at his fourth birthday party, where she'd given him a special gift that he'd treasured ever since. She'd insisted that he call her Aunty Dot, but he knew that in school he should use her formal title.

"Is everybody ready?"

"Yes, Mrs. Pittman," they chorused as one.

As they all began to file indoors, he turned around to give his mother a final wave, but found that he couldn't see her among the crowd. He knew she must still be there, but felt a slight swell of anxiety in his chest. Still unable to see her, he was carried along with the others and had to face forwards again. He felt a gentle hand on his shoulder and looked up.

"Hello Miles," Aunty Dot beamed at him.

"Hello Aun-, Mrs. Pittman," he corrected himself, suddenly feeling more comfortable in her presence. Continuing to smile, she gently pushed him in the direction that the others were heading.

Miles had seen pictures of a classroom before, but this was the first time he'd been in one. The tall walls were covered in large, blank sheets of faintly-coloured paper and the warm air was filled with the smell of the school's lunch preparations. A row of coloured hooks lined the wall just inside the door, around which the other pupils buzzed trying to find their named hook. After finding his, he hung up his coat and made his way across the room to find an empty desk. It didn't take him long to realise that these too had neatly written name labels placed upon them, so it was a simple matter to locate the desk that had been prepared for him.

When everyone was seated, Mrs. Pittman closed the door and walked to the front of the classroom.

"Welcome," she smiled, "I am so pleased to see you all. During our first semester together, we're going to fill these walls with such wonderful work!"

She clasped her hands together as though she could hardly contain her enthusiasm and Miles felt a thrill of anticipation run through him. He found himself turning to look at the others who wore similarly bright expressions.

"Now. Before we start. I've met some of you before, do you still have the special gift I gave you?"

Miles' hand instantly darted to his pocket to retrieve a bright silver coin; the one she'd given him at the party. He held it up so that she could see it. Aunty Dot smiled at him briefly and then focussed on other children behind him. He turned around to see that the others were similarly holding things aloft. Some were waving thin bracelets with charms on them, others were pointing to necklaces, and several children held shiny items of different shapes and sizes between their fingers. Miles turned to face the front again and, seeing the expression on Aunty Dot's face, couldn't help but smile too.

"Oh my word!" she placed her hand on her chest, "I guess none of us are strangers! I know you all already! Now everybody make sure that you bring your gift with you, every day!"

Miles turned and smiled at the boy next to him but spotted that he wasn't as happy as the others; something that Aunty Dot seemed to suddenly pick up on.

"Now, Maxwell Troye," she crossed to his desk, looking concerned, "Is everything alright? Did you forget to bring your gift with you?"

Maxwell shook his head and bit his lip.

"Then whatever's the matter?"

"My dad pawned it..." he bit his lip again.

Miles thought he saw a flicker of anger on her face but it disappeared so fast that he was no longer sure.

"I tell you what, Max," she smiled, "I'll talk with your dad about getting it back, but could you do something for me?"

Maxwell nodded.

"Well alright then!" she beckoned Maxwell to come to the front of the class, while she retrieved something from behind her desk, "It's important that we start the day bright and ready to learn. So, every day, each of you will take one of my special vitamin sweeties!"

The class gasped in awe as she produced a wide-necked candy jar, filled to the brim with golden-yellow sweets.

"Just remember to bring in your special gift, and you'll get one of these, every day. Now, Maxwell, please take this jar and make sure everyone gets a sweet."

Maxwell started making his way around the class, offering the jar to each of the children. Miles could see them hastily untwisting the transparent wrappings and popping the yellow-coloured treats in their mouths. His mouth started watering in anticipation as the jar got closer. At last, he took a sweet and didn't even register opening the wrapper. The yellow glow on his tongue seemed to travel quickly to his brain, where he felt it fizzling. If learning was like this every day, then he knew he'd enjoy his time at the Pittman Academy.

"Today," Aunty Dot said, "We're going to begin learning about science. I'll need someone to help -"

Immediately, Miles felt his hand shoot up in the air; he liked to help.

•

Dorothy thought the morning session had gone well; the class were attentive and largely cooperative during their basic science experiments. The children had played with pots of coloured water and had only seen the fun, rather than the fact she was evaluating their comprehension of equivalent volumes.

She knew that the metastable-cortothene compound within the sweets took several days to build up sufficient levels within the thalamus so, as ever, patience would be the key. If there was any trace of her father's cortical enhancement drug within any of the children, then the metastable-cortothene would activate it. But she knew it may take weeks before any latent genetic abilities began to show.

Although the antenatal cortical enhancement program had been disbanded due to financial constraints, Dorothy knew that when dealing with evolution, results did not necessarily occur within the timescales dictated by something as mundane as a budget. She had taken her father's original research in a different direction.

Her father's notebook had contained a

comprehensive list of those who had received the antenatal enhancement, along with the names of the resulting children. Several children on the list had apparently shown no improvement after receiving the postnatal metastable-cortothene counterpart. For those children, her father had ruled a red line through their names and annotated those entries with the word 'Substandard'.

There seemed little point wasting resources on children that her father had already excluded so, using the considerable Pittman influence at her disposal, Dorothy had begun befriending the parents on the list whose children had *not* been red-lined.

Most parents were delighted that their child had been invited to join the Pittman Academy, but a few had been hesitant because of the fees involved. For those parents, she had waived the fees; when balanced against the very evolution of mind, money was irrelevant.

One such parent was Judy Benton, whose financial security had evaporated upon the death of her husband, John. Their son, Miles, already showed great promise; devastatingly bright for his age with highly developed empathic skills.

Currently, Miles was holding the classroom door open for everyone as they left. She was almost taken in by this display of politeness, but reminded herself that the classroom door would have remained open of its own accord. He was ensuring that the others left before him. Inwardly she was amused by the fact that he was using others' perceptions to quietly manipulate their responses; a very conscious action designed to ensure the privacy he would soon seek with her.

From a psychological standpoint, she wondered how his ego had mediated his need to help others and the need to satisfy his own desire. She was just jotting down a personal note to follow up her own studies on ego morphology, when he arrived at the side of her desk.

"Hello, Mrs. Pittman," he introduced himself.

Dorothy stopped writing and looked around the room semi-theatrically then whispered, "It's alright, you can call me Aunty Dot!"

He seemed to relax a little.

"Is everything OK, Miles?" she prompted.

"Aunty Dot, do you give gifts to everyone?" he asked directly.

Dorothy could instantly see the source of his concern. He'd seen that the others in his class had also received a personal gift from her, but it was possible that he placed a certain exclusivity on their association. His latent insecurities required reassurance that her gifts to others had not devalued their own relationship.

"No," she said, "I only give gifts to those I believe are my friends. Do you still have the gift I gave to you, Miles?"

"Of course," he replied and pulled the silver dollar from his pocket.

"Now, the Latin words on the back…" she prompted.

"E pluribus unum," he replied, reading from the coin.

"That's right, and you remember what that means don't you?"

"Out of many, one," he frowned slightly.

She leaned in closer and dropped her tone slightly, giving the impression he was about to hear a secret.

"I have not given a single other person a gift like the silver coin you are holding in your hand. Like you, it is unique. Out of the *many* in this class…" she placed a manicured finger on his forehead, "*One* is unique."

She glanced around the room again for effect, then offered him the opened jar of yellow-coloured sweets.

"Go ahead," she smiled.

He hesitated only for a second before dipping his free hand into the jar.

"Why don't you eat it now, before you go home?" she affirmed.

He untwisted the wrapper and put the sweet in his mouth.

She waited just the right amount of time to allow the sweet sugar-rush on his tongue to take place, then spoke to him.

"Out of many, one," she patted the coin with a single finger, "Aunty Dot wants you to remember that."

Wearing a considerably broader smile than a few moments ago he nodded.

"OK then, Miles," she replaced the jar's lid and then added brightly, "I'll see you tomorrow."

"See you tomorrow, Aunty Dot," he cheerfully waved goodbye and ran to catch up with the others who were heading to the school gates.

She had once told Judy Benton that her son was bright. That opinion had only strengthened in the last few minutes. Although it had been a trivial enough linguistic sleight for her to convince the four-year-old of their exclusive friendship, her own explanation troubled her slightly.

She wasn't sure if she'd used the phrase *'Out of many, one'* to pacify Miles, or if it was because she was voicing her own subconscious thoughts.

MIKE SANDERS

4th July 2076

*M*ike *drifted above the lunar surface between elongated jumps; the languid gravity eventually pulling him back to the surface and sending up curls of the ubiquitous grey moon dust into the vacuum. His spacesuit's comm unit crackled slightly with static.*

"FLC this is Sanders at Lima scrubbing station, repeat please."

Aside from a few pops of static, there was no immediate response.

"FLC, I'm switching to comms relay Lima," he made the appropriate adjustment, "Come back, when you're on channel."

Floyd Lunar Complex sat in a minor depression within the Coriolis crater, a tenth of a degree above the Moon's equator. To Mike's right, the north-eastern rim of the crater was eroded, forming a slope gentle enough that the automated Regodozers could enter and exit the site with comparative ease. He found it difficult to believe that work on this facility had begun with the

Apollo program, but he knew from first-hand experience that there was stuff up here date stamped '1968'.

He looked out towards the west quadrant of the crater, to see the solar panel array gleaming like diamonds against the ink-black sky. Although the array was over a mile away, the lack of atmosphere on the Moon meant there was no light diffusion over the distance; everything he could see was pin-sharp.

A lunar day was approximately an Earth month; the array had 15 useful days of sunlight in which to capture and store the energy, followed by 15 days of impenetrable night. Under normal operation the panels were designed to actively orient themselves towards the Sun, like sunflowers, so that the maximum amount of energy was always captured.

From the corner of his eye, he thought he saw a flicker of light reflecting from the array, as though some of the panels were incorrectly aligned. But when he checked again, he couldn't see any variation, all the panels appeared perfectly aligned.

The spacesuit's comm unit crackled then emitted a burst of faint Morse code tones, before dipping into static.

"Hello Mike," came the voice from his headset, *"we have spoken before, do you remember me?"*

The voice seemed familiar, but was out of place here.

"Director Crandall?" he turned away from the solar array and looked back in the direction of the FLC, "Why is Houston using this channel?"

Mike knew his transmission would have to make its way through the chain of repeater stations placed around the Moon's equator and then make the leap to Earth. Only then could Houston's Communication Director form a reply. Mike was unsurprised that there was a long delay before his suit's comm crackled to life again.

"FLC, be advised at this time we are unable to effect remote deactivation."

There was a brief pause and Mike somehow knew the words that would come next.

"We're still running numbers but order the immediate evacuation of the Z-bank and personnel to the RTO module. Over."

Mike looked down to see the suitcase-like Z-bank in one hand and an FLC evacuation pack in the other. The lunar landscape had changed to become the interior of the Return To Orbit module. He found himself hurriedly stowing the evac-pack's lunar-surface magnesium flare gun and securing the emergency O2 cylinders. He quickly secured the Z-bank in Leonard Cooper's empty seat; a distant memory prodding at him that Leonard had lost his life during the implosion of Chamber 6. As he looked around the RTO's tiny space he could see that all the other seats were empty.

"Houston!" he called out, "Where are they?"

He alone had escaped the destruction of the FLC.

A view of the Coriolis crater filled his field of view and he saw the surface pattern changing, a moment later he could see the whole Moon. Framed within the small RTO window, Mike watched the Moon silently detonate, ejecting lethal shards of lunar mass in the direction of Earth.

"It's OK, Mike," Ross Crandall's voice immediately reassured him, *"We're sending you to rendezvous with the ISS."*

Mike had a fleeting thought - there had been no communication delay when Ross had replied; but this soon gave way to a rising sense of relief that help was on the way.

"They're good people, Mike. Work with them and we can get you home. We're in this together. Over."

"Message received," he found himself gratefully replying, "We're in this together."

He couldn't determine how much time had passed, but suddenly he felt the docking clamps take hold of the RTO module. With the airlock door still sealed, he heard a high-pitched hissing sound as the air pressure began to change.

THE MARK 3

18AUG2013+46.44 : DAY 701.0

Inside the Mark 3 chamber, Anna Bergstrom looked across the upper floor lab at the split-time clock. The first set of figures indicated the external date followed by the elapsed mission time, the second counted the days spent inside the Field:

18AUG2013+46.44 : DAY 701.0

Outside the Field was an identical clock on the hangar wall, it had been synchronised at the start of the journey but now it displayed:

18AUG2013+46.43 : DAY 701.0

The discrepancy lay in the fact that on day 187 of their journey, Douglas Walker had altered the radius of the Field surrounding the Mark 3. The volume of their transported sphere had temporarily become a variable rather than a constant. The Field equations had simply rebalanced, resulting in the Mark 3 proceeding at a momentarily faster rate through time. When Douglas had restored the Field's original radius, the 360:1 ratio had also been restored, leaving the clock's discrepancy as the only reminder of the event.

Even now, with all her accumulated knowledge of the Field, she had to remind herself of the physics at work; the Mark 3 had not travelled into the future of those in the hanger, it had simply proceeded through more 'local' time inside the Field.

Looking out through the observation window she could see it was dark in the hangar beyond, the circadian lighting system had been dipped to black to simulate night. In that darkness she could see the glow of a small desk lamp and two people beyond that. The Mark 3's accelerated time-frame meant that they appeared almost frozen in time and she had to stare for several seconds before one of them began the long process of starting to blink.

Initially Anna and Douglas had been puzzled by what those on hangar duty were doing. They appeared to be keeping some sort of tally. It was only after several days inside the Mark 3 that they realised it was a record of how many times Anna or Douglas had stood in front of a window. From the perspective of those in the hangar, the Mark 3's occupants were moving at lightning speed, so to spot one at a standstill was a 'win'.

"I think Carter and Pike have started a new game," she called to Douglas.

"Is Pike the one who used to play table football in the rec room?" he replied, without looking away from his screen.

Anna turned away from the window and joined him

at the desk.

"Used to?" she raised an eyebrow, "They probably still do. For them, their hangar shift has only been a few hours."

"You're right of course," Douglas sighed, "It just seems like they're part of the decor now…"

During their time confined inside the Mark 3 they'd grown to know each other's expressions and mannerisms, so Anna could tell he was distracted.

"You think you've found something…" she said.

"I think so," he narrowed his eyes at one particular matrix within the Field equations, "but it can't be right…"

On day 690, eleven days ago, the Field inversion equations had finally emerged from the billions of possible permutations. Field inversion essentially turned their current model for temporal manipulation inside out. The solution would allow the Node's Field to pass at a *slower* rate for its occupants, while the outside world journeyed through several millennia.

But both Anna and Douglas had noticed a coherent and recursive pattern within the solution, one that they both felt warranted further investigation. Instead of emerging from the Mark 3 to report the inversion results, they delayed their exit in order to conduct a deeper study of the Field's temporal surface.

"OK," said Anna, sitting down next to him, "step through it."

Douglas took out a small card from his pocket. The back was black with small white text but the front had a garish yellow-green hologram, depicting a round planet

Earth. As he turned the card from left to right, she could see the planet from slightly different angles.

"OK, so we've already discussed the idea of representing Three-D objects within a Two-D surface -"

"And the idea that the Field is representing Four-D space-time on its Three-D surface," Anna continued, pointing towards the hangar outside, "We can see their movement through time, even though it's only a representation on the three-dimensional surface of the Field."

"Now," Douglas focussed in on a portion of the Field equation, angling the screen to give her a better view, "look at these diffeomorphism transform matrices. Here, and here."

Anna quickly compared one matrix to the other.

"They're identi-" she broke off, "No, they look identical, but only at the initiation and outcome of the function. In the Thurston mapping, the solution *diverges* from...*nej, skojar du med mig?*"

In her shock, Anna found herself defaulting to Swedish, but she knew Douglas understood.

"No, I'm not kidding you," he shook his head, "Do you see what I mean?"

"Ja, yes, but..." she found herself lost for words in both languages.

"Try another set of Eversion volumes," Douglas began to pace around the room.

Anna tried various matrix transforms, she even tried compounding mapping solutions in the hopes that the functions would fail; but every time, despite the functions sharing identical start and end conditions, the underlying entanglement differed.

She looked up from her workings.

"The surface of the Field -" she began.

"-isn't a surface," they both finished.

"It's a region," Douglas continued, "one that maps the exterior time-frame to the interior one. And vice versa."

"When we look out there," Anna nodded, "we're only seeing the region's boundary."

"The region actually has a… thickness," Douglas shook his head in frustration, "no, thickness is the wrong word. It has a dimensional complexity. The correlation between the Field's interior and exterior time-frames, seems to indicate that the region contains almost *unbound* permutation."

Anna began to move beyond the raw mathematics, to interpret its real world meaning.

"Then the boundary of the region…" she began, her eyes widening, "It would contain -"

"Infinite temporal variation," Douglas was nodding, "Literally every possible variation of events that exists between moments."

A quiet descended on them as they both mentally wrestled with their own thoughts.

After so much trial and error, it seemed odd to Anna that such a momentous discovery should emerge almost unheralded. She'd become used to the almost endless cycle of days during the Mark 3's long journey, with very little to distinguish one day from the next. She'd grown used to routines and even thoughts happening time and again. Suddenly, an entirely new thought occurred to her.

"Déjà vu," she said turning to Douglas, "When the Field starts up, do you ever get that blurry sense of déjà vu?"

"Yeah, I think everyone does," Douglas frowned, "Like a visual nausea?"

"Yeah," Anna nodded, "If I'm moving during the Field inflation or collapse phases, then I see smeary, watercolour trails coming off things."

"It's because of the change in time-rate," he explained, "For a millisecond, as the Field passes through you, one part of your brain is working at a different rate to another."

"And you're sure about that?" Anna narrowed her eyes and tilted her head slightly.

"What are you getting at?" said Douglas moving closer.

"Maybe, during that millisecond, we're seeing the simultaneous sum of all possible local events," she thought of an analogy that Douglas would appreciate, "A bit like one of your old flick-books, but instead of seeing one page at a time, you see all the pages simultaneously overlaid on top of each other."

"A stick-man walking across a page would leave a trail of stick-men," Douglas picked up on the analogy and his expression changed, "Or, depending on your perspective, he'd have trails in front of him showing actions he had yet to make."

Anna could see that he knew exactly what she meant.

"In that one millisecond," she said, "I think we're looking into a tiny slice of the boundary's infinite temporal variation."

She could tell that the idea had taken hold because Douglas was already searching for a scrap of paper. But after almost two years, their stock of blank paper was in short supply. She watched as he crossed the small room and swept the remains of their evening ration packs off the white plastic table. Guessing what he was about to do, she picked up a marker pen and threw it to him, then watched as he started to draw directly onto the table.

"This is our stick-man," said Douglas, the marker squeaking with every stroke, "and here's the edge of our Field, expanding as it starts up."

He drew a curved line to the left of the man.

"The Field expands out through our man and emerges on the other side of him."

He drew another, longer, curved line, but to the right of the man.

"This has been our model until now," Douglas finished his mental recap, "Oh, wait a minute…"

He hastily sketched a rectangle next to the man.

"Mustn't forget the Biomag… there."

Using broadly spaced diagonal lines, Douglas then began to shade in the area between the two curved lines taking care not to draw through the man that was between them.

"This is the region inside the boundary, which passes through our man for a millisecond. Man experiences infinite temporal variation."

Anna smiled as Douglas added a few circles and stars of nausea above the man's head.

"In reality, this region inside the boundary has no observable thickness," Douglas pointed to the shaded area, "Geometrically, these left and right curves appear to occupy exactly the same space."

Anna could see where he was heading and added:

"So when the Field inflates or collapses, the Biomag's spatial influence isn't a factor. Our stick-man remains anchored inside the three-dimensional space he started in."

Douglas nodded and capped the marker pen.

Anna studied the sketch for a moment, then pointed at the sketched Biomag next to the stick-man.

"The Biomag shields us from space-time pocketing inside an already established Field."

"Yeah," agreed Douglas, "that's why we turn them on before establishing the Field."

"But what if the Biomag is doing more than that?" Anna tapped at the shaded area, "What if it's also shielding us from this shaded area of space-time? What if it's shielding us when the Field starts or stops?"

Anna took the marker pen and carefully crossed out the sketched Biomag. Noticing that Douglas had recoiled slightly at the thought of removing a Biomag, she continued swiftly on.

"What if the Biomag was off, during the Field's inflation or collapse..." Continuing to use the marker pen, she reinforced the diagonal shading lines, but this time she allowed the lines to pass straight through the stick-man. A few seconds later the man was completely embedded within the shaded region, "If the Biomag wasn't active, and the Field was still in dimensional flux, what would the stick-man see?"

After several hours of discussion and extrapolation, they came to agree upon one conclusion: the dimensional complexity of the Field's boundary should never fall into Archive's hands.

The Boundary was intrinsic to the Field's equations, but they would make no effort to highlight it. In fact, so strong were their feelings on the matter, Anna and Douglas knew they'd have to make every effort to conceal it.

A while ago, before the Field inversion equations had actually emerged, Anna had raised a concern. She had feared that when they handed over the Field solutions, Archive would not need to guarantee a place aboard the Node for either of them. They had both recognised the need to plan some form of insurance.

Today, those plans came into action. After transferring the Field inversion equations to two separate memory sticks, they purged the Mark 3's computer memory of all data.

Knowledge of the Boundary now existed only in their minds.

However, they both knew this would not be enough. When it came to valuable information, Archive always had some form of contingency. Although the data had been purged, it was entirely possible that a backup existed somewhere else within the confines of the Mark 3. The only way to ensure the destruction of the data would be to ensure the destruction of the Mark 3 itself.

Anna took one final look through the observation window. Carter and Pike still appeared to be frozen in place, still playing their slow-motion tally game. For them only two minutes had passed but for her, twelve hours of exit preparation was reaching its conclusion. She turned and walked down the spiral stairs one last time.

As she reached the lower level, she could see Douglas was taping down some temporary wiring with the last of the red insulation tape. He then tossed the remainder of the roll across the room and walked over to stand by the airlock.

"Ready?" he asked.

"Let's go," Anna replied, "Oh-two masks?"

"Check. These should give us at least twenty minutes if we breathe slowly, but we may not need them - I've raised the general oxygen level throughout the Mark 3, so the airlock will sustain us for a while. There's no point leaving any unused oxygen behind, and when we trigger the electrical overload it'll get the fire started more efficiently."

"Biomag," she inspected the device around her neck, "Check."

Douglas did the same for his; squeezing at the plastic casing to check its integrity.

"Biomag, check," he patted it twice, "The Field will collapse when the power supply is destroyed, which won't take long. When the Field fails, the Mark 3 is going to burn. Whatever happens, just get clear as fast as you can."

Douglas followed Anna into the tiny space inside the

airlock.

"Ready?" he checked again.

"Go," Anna gave a firm nod.

Douglas punched the improvised switch he'd set up outside the airlock. The electrical system had already begun to whine as Douglas pulled the airlock door closed. Over the next few minutes they watched through the door's small porthole. Thick grey smoke had begun to fill the interior of the Mark 3.

LINEAGE

18th August 2013

"**B**enton, I'll need a full debrief of your time spent escorting Miss Walker here," said General Napier, as the two of them walked towards the assembly hall, "We'll need to keep her isolated in the holding cell for now, until I can work out how to handle this."

"Until Dr. Walker returns from his…" Benton tried to recall the appropriate term, "research expedition, I think you called it?"

"I only called it that for Miss Walker's benefit. Douglas *is* doing research, but he's in there," Napier pointed to the hangar sitting in front of the Node, then checked his watch, "He'll be out in a few hours, but after that it would be best if he's not made aware of his daughter's arrival."

"Understood. Do you think she will cause trouble, General?"

"She's a useful asset," Napier replied, "but she's also a Walker. If I've learned anything -"

He was interrupted by a siren that split the air and sounded throughout the base surrounding the Node.

"What the hell?" Napier looked around for likely sources of threat. The bridge that connected the Node's island to the far shore of Öskjuvatn Lake was clear and, as far as he could tell at this distance, the perimeter fence was intact.

He checked in the opposite direction and saw that the doors to the Mark 3 Hangar were being dragged open. The siren stopped and the shouts of organised instruction now rose to prominence instead. A few moments later there was a flash of light from inside the hangar accompanied by a low frequency shockwave in the ground. Then the whole hangar shuddered and a burning panel fell from the roof, followed swiftly by two more.

In horror, Napier realised that the Mark 3 Field capsule was ablaze.

With large portions of the hangar roof now missing, the convective effect of the heat escaping through the roof was causing more air to rush in through the open hangar doors, stoking the fire further.

It appeared that the Field itself was no longer active; with some relief, Napier could see that Colonel Beck and a lieutenant were assisting Douglas Walker and Anna Bergstrom to get clear of the burning hangar.

Napier walked swiftly towards the hangar, assembling a small troop as he went and instructing them to start a personnel chain to get supplies away from the fire. Suddenly the metalwork in the base of the Mark 3 started to sag under the thermal stress, and the tortured air began to carry a new high-pitched whine as the framework began to give way. A moment later he watched as the Mark 3 began to list and collapse to one side, then its momentum took over and started to roll the entire burning sphere slowly across the hangar floor. The heat was so intense that the hoses trained on the blaze were merely producing clouds of steam rather than extinguishing the fire. Through the steam, Napier could see that the Mark 3 had rolled to a halt lying on its side.

He could see that Douglas and Anna were making their way towards him but when they arrived, coughing and spluttering against the inhaled smoke, his first thought was not for their wellbeing.

"Tell me you got out of there with *something?*"

"Our lives, thanks for asking," Anna Bergstrom coughed, "Nice to see you too, General."

He did his best to quickly wrap his head around the complicated interplay of the differing time rates. For him, they'd been gone only a day and a half, but for them the journey had been almost two years. If he looked carefully, he could just about discern the additional grey hairs. Their faces looked more lined too, though this was probably due to the smoke and ash rather than age.

"Sorry Dr. Bergstrom -" he found himself apologising.

"It's OK," Douglas cut in, "we only left you yesterday. We'll be fine."

Napier watched Douglas pull a small memory stick out of his pocket.

"We did it," Douglas reported, simply.

The ground under their feet shuddered.

A loud, metallic, shearing sound caused them all to quickly face the hangar, then an angry ball of fire erupted through the roof. Frantic fire crews were training hoses into the hangar, and still more troops were forming chains away from the building, passing supplies away from the blaze. Napier turned away from the chaos.

"This is it?" he pointed to the memory stick.

"Everything we need to invert the Field," Anna nodded.

"Twelve hundred to one ratio," Douglas added.

Napier shook his head in disbelief. In Douglas' palm was the solution to Field inversion; the information that would allow the Node to travel through thousands of years, while its occupants barely aged a decade.

He smiled at the fact that the solution should be reduced to something so small and mundane. He looked at Douglas and was about to congratulate him but from his expression, Napier could see there was a complication.

"What?"

Douglas closed his fingers around the memory stick, and spoke above the continuing noise.

"There's an asymmetric issue we believe is intrinsic to the Field."

As the burning roof above the Mark 3 collapsed into the hangar, it sent a new wave of heat in their direction; Napier had the uneasy feeling that both the hangar situation and the conversation were beginning to slip from his control.

"As a consequence," explained Anna, "Douglas and I will need to oversee the activation of the Field."

The heat subsided slightly and, as the Icelandic chill started to reassert itself, Napier read between the lines. She was making their threat very clear; the full solution to the Node's Field equations would only be provided in exchange for a guarantee.

"And, of course," Napier stared at Anna, "you will need to be aboard the Node to do this."

"Of course," she stared back at him, "but where else would we be?"

"I think we understand each other," Napier forced his mouth into a smile.

He suddenly became aware of a single voice above the surrounding chaos. It took him a moment to realise that the voice belonged to Dr. Walker's daughter, Kate. She was shouting for her father and running in the direction of the burning hangar, pursued by an armed guard.

Before Napier could question the fact that she'd escaped from the holding cell, he saw the guard suddenly stop.

"Halt! I will fire. Halt!" the guard targeted his assault rifle and had his finger on the trigger.

Suddenly, Napier felt his sidearm being snatched from its position on his waist. He watched as Benton swiftly sighted the gun on the guard and fired. The guard's body armour absorbed the shot but it sent the man spinning to the ground, cursing.

Napier watched as Benton then calmly put the safety

catch back on and handed the gun back to him.

"My apologies," said Benton, his face inscrutable, "I didn't have time to ask your permission. He will be fine, and at least your asset is still alive."

Napier watched powerlessly as Douglas ran to be with his daughter, then swore under his breath as he watched both the hangar and his leverage go up in smoke. Many years ago, he had watched as Bradley Pittman had shown Douglas the faked photographic evidence of his family's death. Napier himself was complicit in the necessary cover-up that had inevitably followed. Douglas must, even now, realise his involvement.

He studied the Walkers; against the background turmoil, their conversation was inaudible.

"Benton," he spoke without facing him, "That was quick thinking."

"No. It really wasn't," he replied genuinely.

In the distance, another structural support beam within the hangar gave way and the shriek of metal echoed in their direction. But Napier was more concerned with the collapse of control happening closer to him.

"There's something wrong here," Napier frowned in the Walkers' direction, "I can feel it."

He saw Kate hold out a small red envelope for her father.

"This is no coincidence, Benton. The fact that Monica Walker's daughter happens to be right here, right now…"

"I agree, General. With your permission, I would

like to continue monitoring the Walkers for any and all signs of covert communication."

"Absolutely," Napier stated resolutely, then remembered to add the ego-morph's conditioned response phrase, "For the good of Mankind."

Napier noticed the barest delay before Benton replied using the exact same phrase, but he attributed this to the extenuating circumstances. Before he could dwell on it any longer, he saw Douglas turn and advance in his direction. Instinctively he drew himself up to his full height in preparation for the confrontation.

"Douglas -" he began, but was silenced by Douglas levelling a finger at him.

"Dylan," Douglas interrupted with force, "Under Archive's Protected Lineage Directive in return for my Lifetime Services, I reassert my rights. My family is protected and included, either jointly or separately, in all Impact Event counter-enterprises."

He had never seen Douglas look so determined and knew the time for conversation or discussion was not now. He hoped that at some point in the year ahead he may be able to regain control, but for the time being he knew he could only say one thing.

"Agreed, Dr. Walker."

Douglas lowered his finger and stepped even closer to him, brandishing the red envelope he'd seen a moment before. The hand written and faded ink read *'External Variable'*.

"Do you remember Monica saying these two words to you?" Douglas flared, "Do you remember what they mean? External. Kate was supposed to stay out of

Archive's affairs and you've dragged her into it -"

"Douglas, I didn't drag her here, it was -"

"Don't," Douglas cut across him, "You leave my family alone, or I'll bring you down with another two words. Words that matter to you - Danny Smith."

Despite the background chaos and noise of the hangar fire, Napier felt as though the Node's island had fallen suddenly silent. Those two words were the loudest sound ringing in his ears.

"If you understand me, Dylan, get out of my way."

Napier knew he had no choice. In the last few minutes he had lost all leverage over the Walker family. As the remainder of the hangar began to collapse in on itself, he stepped aside to allow Douglas through.

As Napier watched, Kate and Anna followed Douglas away from the burning wreckage of the Mark 3. Benton then arrived at his side.

"General, with your permission, I'll begin my surveillance of the Walkers now."

Still deep in thought, Napier absentmindedly nodded his assent and waved him on his way. Within a few moments, he saw Benton moving in the direction of the holding cell, no doubt trying to determine how Kate had engineered her escape. While considering his next move, Napier turned away and stared into the hangar fire.

He needed to plan carefully and swiftly to keep Danny safe.

The fact that Benton was now preoccupied with the Walkers was an advantage. The last thing Napier needed was an ego-morph watching his every move.

Turning his back on the remains of the Mark 3, Napier marched back to his office. He instructed the guard on duty to stop anyone from entering and then locked the door behind him.

Almost automatically he picked up his coffee pot and began pouring it into his permanently stained mug. He suddenly recalled earlier events and put the coffee pot and mug firmly aside. During his tense initial conversation with Kate, Benton had intervened. Napier hadn't even seen his actions, but Benton had apparently managed to drug the coffee pot, putting Kate into a swift sleep. It had prevented her from asking some awkward questions, and had made it easier to place her in the nearby holding cell.

An ego-morph's ability to anticipate people's actions, simply by observation, was a tactical advantage and there were times when he almost envied their metathene edge.

At other times, he felt a deep sense of remorse; owing to the ego-morphs' underlying genetics, he knew that the metathene could easily be used to turn them into a mere controllable tool.

Napier's sense of remorse had its roots in empathy.

After discovering that his own infant son was a carrier of the genetic variant capable of absorbing metathene, he had taken steps to hide him from the upper echelons of Archive at the time.

At great personal expense, both financially and emotionally, he had arranged for his wife and their son to begin new lives without him as Vanessa and Danny Smith. He'd reasoned that anyone searching for one

Smith in a million would have a hard time.

He logged on to his computer by clicking on the cubist-looking 'Pi' symbol next to his name. The screen's background wallpaper was a photo of Stonehenge; a tasteful silhouette shot against a misty dawn sky. Framed by the surrounding clutter of computer icons, the screen's wallpaper featured two tall upright stones supporting a third horizontal one.

It reminded him of when he and Vanessa had posed for a photo in front of the stone age monument. The two of them had stood opposite each other and, raising their arms above their heads, had joined hands to mimic the trilithon behind them. Though the resulting photo didn't show it, she had been pregnant with Danny at the time; effectively it was the earliest photo containing his family.

Of course he no longer had the physical photo, when Vanessa and Danny had assumed their new identities, he'd destroyed all evidence of their relationship. The image now existed in only two places, his memory and a heavily-encrypted 'Trilithon' folder buried within his smartphone. The encryption meant that viewing the image was not a simple matter, so he tended to rely on his recall of the event, where the colours, sounds and the smell of her perfume were more vibrant.

Over the years, he'd occasionally watched their lives from afar but he'd never interfered. However, in 2001 it came to his attention that Danny had suffered a broken arm. Taking advantage of a recent development at an Archive research facility, he'd arranged for a miniature tracking device to be covertly implanted within Danny's healing bone.

During the intervening years, the tracking chip had allowed him to keep a passive eye on his son's location. The implied threat he'd received a few minutes ago meant that the time for being passive was over.

He synchronised the smartphone with his desktop computer and, after entering the long decryption key, accessed the 'Trilithon' folder. Once inside he began the process of updating the automated protocols that would find and retrieve his son.

OBSCURA

DAY03 : 05NOV2023

Danny Smith sat on the floor of Cassidy and Tyler's quarters, surrounded by the contents of the 'Trilithon' folder that had accompanied him here. The last few hours had been a blur of impossible information. He'd been brought to the Node inside a box designed to keep him alive, but in all other respects the box had resembled a coffin.

It was as though he'd died during his sprint across the top floor of The Gene Pool, only to rise again here in some form of incomprehensible hell. Though when he thought back to his previous life, he knew it was just a different kind of hell.

He knew it was post-traumatic stress that repeatedly forced Sophie's tragic death into his mind. Time and again he'd experienced the moment when an armed man had pulled the trigger. Countless times he'd seen Sophie's face disappear in a flash of pink that was as bright as her hair. Every time, he'd been forced to recall her inert, lifeless fall into the night.

He made a conscious effort to reimagine her; alive and well with his other friends, gathered around a makeshift fire, drinking Jake's hoarded cheap coffee. But even as Danny was recalling this, his memory unhelpfully volunteered the information that they'd all died too.

Everyone had died, yet he'd been saved. Saved inside an impossible technological bubble, bound for the deep future. Facing an uncertain future was one thing, he thought, but it appeared that even his past was uncertain. From the pile of papers surrounding him, he picked up the photo of the two people in front of Stonehenge.

He recognised the woman as a much younger version of his mother, but he didn't know the man she was holding hands with. If the folder's information was to be believed, the man in the photo was his father.

Danny's mother had always maintained that his father had died while Danny was very young. Yet the information before him provided evidence that his father, someone called Dylan Napier, had been killed only a few days before the Node's departure.

Apparently, Dylan had died at the hands of two men. Their photos had also been included in the file that had accompanied Danny, along with several paragraphs of dense type.

He put the photos aside. He knew he'd been avoiding the most troubling aspect of the folder's information; something that related specifically to him alone. He picked up a sheet of paper entitled 'Cortical Enhancement Program & Metathene Trigger'.

The door to the quarters opened suddenly and

Danny found himself on his feet, alert and backing away. He relaxed slightly when he realised it was Cassidy and Tyler returning, still in conversation.

"...only gonna get more difficult?" Tyler was asking.

"Well, obviously," Cassidy replied sarcastically.

She spotted Danny's stance and rolled her eyes.

"Chill out, Danny-boy. Food."

Danny watched as they both retrieved several ration packs from their pockets. Evidently their night-time raid of supplies had been successful.

"It's early days. Getting these was easy, but we'll have to sort something out soon. We can't keep sneaking rations for you. Pretty soon, people are gonna notice that you're not on the Node's register and - what?"

Danny realised he'd been staring at her hair. It was as bright and pink as Sophie's had been. It still seemed an unlikely coincidence that they should both have the same vibrant colour.

"I..." he began, "You just remind me of someone, that's all."

She threw him a ration pack and laughed.

"With this hair? Un-bloody-likely! I'm one of a kind. Now eat something, will you? Can't have you getting all weak. I don't want to cart you off to the infirmary again."

"Er, excuse me?" interrupted Tyler with a grin, "I think I was the one doing the carting."

The three of them sat down among the papers and rations, talking about the last few hours and discussing the contents of Danny's folder. Soon the conversation returned to the page that Danny had found the most awkward to deal with. Tyler pointed to the page in front of Danny.

"So, you and your mum have, like, this weird DNA thing?"

"I dunno," Danny sighed, "I guess. Maybe not. Maybe I'm safe as long as I don't take any of that…"

"Metathene," Cassidy completed, tilting her head to read the page.

"Whatever the hell that is," Danny shook his head, "You've never heard of it then?"

The other two both shook their heads. Not for the first time, Danny thought that with each new piece of information the picture was becoming less and less clear.

"He says he was trying to keep me safe," said Danny, picking up the piece of paper, "He hid me and my mum. Sent us away, so that no-one would find out about the gene thing. So why bring me back here?"

"Isn't it obvious?" Tyler shrugged, "He must've loved you and your mum."

"Funny way of showing it," Danny murmured.

"People do all sorts of weird shit when they know their number's up," Cassidy cut in, "Looks like he planned for it though - that was a really fancy box we found you in. I think Ty's right, he sent you to the one place on Earth you could survive. Right here."

"So, let me get this right," Danny attempted again to instill order, "This General Napier, my dad, he ran this whole place? I mean, the base outside and this… this…"

"Time machine?" Cassidy snorted a derisive laugh, "Yep, the whole thing."

Danny began leafing through the pages that lay around him.

"But there's no mention of the fact that he invented time travel, he must've been a genius… Hey! Maybe my dad also had genetically -" Danny stopped because the other two were frowning more than usual, "What?"

"Your dad was in charge," Cassidy's frown persisted, "But he wasn't the guy who came up with the Field - shit, I keep forgetting that you know squat about anything round here. No, the guy that came up with this place was Douglas Walker. Now he *was* a genius. If anyone was 'cortically enhanced' I'd bet good money it was him - I mean, seriously, who just *invents* time travel?"

"I heard that he invented it when he was a kid," Tyler joined in.

"Seriously?" said Cassidy, "Where'd you hear that?"

"I heard Johnson talking about it one time in the mess hall."

Cassidy stared at Tyler with a look of incredulity.

"Johnson? As in 'Johnson who didn't take his Biomag isotope early enough and got Field-fragged' Johnson?" she wiggled her head about, imitating the moment of his catastrophic unanchoring.

Danny was very much aware of the importance of wearing a Biomag, but it was useless without the anchoring isotope. The very fact that Danny was still alive demonstrated that his father had arranged for the isotope to be administered during his journey to the Node - it also explained the fever he'd run whilst inside the transport box.

"Yeah well, if you ask me," Cassidy jerked her head again to sweep her pink hair away from her eyes, "Johnson did us all a favour by removing himself from the gene pool."

Sophie's tragic death on the exposed level of The Gene Pool flashed into his memory; as ever, her bright pink hair flaring outward in hideous slow motion as she was mercilessly killed in front of him.

When he looked at Cassidy really carefully, as he did now, he could almost see Sophie alive and well again in vibrant colour. He knew it was only a trick played on him by his own wishful thinking, but Cassidy's mentioning of the words 'gene pool' had given the moment a personal connection beyond the superficial.

Coincidence no longer seemed to describe their situation.

It had been Cassidy who was present when he'd crawled from the box in the basement levels of the Node. She had sought medical attention for him. She had also arrived at the infirmary just when he most needed help avoiding awkward questions. She had given him shelter and food. Now, even her choice of words echoed a connection with his past. The cloud of confusion surrounding his new life aboard the Node seemed to disperse, leaving behind only her words.

"Walker's daughter - now *there's* a new fish in our gene pool. If her dad was a special-brainer, then she's *gotta* be."

Tyler was nodding in agreement, evidently there was something they both knew.

"Why?" Danny looked between the two of them.

"OK, quick recap," Cassidy leaned back, "Doug Walker gets stuck outside the Field but sends a message to his daughter using, like, a hundred pages of equations and shit. His daughter captures it on her DRB but can't watch it at normal speed without the video suite. Beck gets everyone to find all the bits of the video equipment -"

"Which is when you found me," Danny nodded, "Go on."

"OK, so, eventually they get all the pages off the DRB and start putting together Walker's message. But, and here's the thing, it's Walker's daughter who works it all out!"

Danny could see that she was waiting for his reaction, but he knew he'd missed something.

"I don't get it. If the message was sent to her, then why wouldn't she figure it out?"

"She was never part of the Field engineering team and, if what I've heard is true, she hadn't seen her dad in over ten years. She only got here about four months before we left -"

"Same day as the Mark 3 fire," Tyler chipped in, shaking his head.

"The what?" Danny quickly asked, eager not to lose the thread.

"It was like a tiny version of the Node, experimental stuff," Cassidy waved the interruption aside and continued, "The point is you don't become a Field-tech expert in a few months, some of the guys aboard have been trying to master the theory for years. I saw her a few times in the mess hall and she was just... normal, yet she's the one that figured out the Field fix."

Danny nodded, understanding the apparent incongruity.

"Cassidy," he began, still holding the page about cortical enhancement, "if there's even a small chance that she's one of *these*, then I have *got* to talk to her."

"Might be difficult."

"Why am I not surprised?" Danny quietly placed the page back on the floor.

"No, it's just that…" Cassidy began.

"What?"

"Well it's the other odd thing," Cassidy shared a glance with Tyler, "Right after solving the Field stuff, she had some sort of dramatic fit and got sent to Doc' Smith in the infirmary. It might be a bit difficult getting in there. It's not the sort of place you can casually stroll around, you know what I mean?"

The room fell quiet for a moment and then Tyler spoke.

"Unless you're a patient already," he pointed at the bandage wrapped around Danny's head.

Cassidy looked at Tyler with an expression bordering on awe.

"Nice one, Ty," she smiled, "We tell Doc' Smith that you need a bed for the night, she's met you once already, just make sure you rub your head a lot and I'm sure she'll remember."

"We're both 'Smith', I don't think she'll have forgotten that," Danny added, feeling a small pinch of guilt at the proposed manipulation.

"D'you know," Cassidy turned to face Danny and

pointed at the dressing around his head, "I never asked, how'd you get hurt?"

Instinctively he reached up and rubbed at his bandaged forehead. At present, only Dr. Smith knew of the circle and dot symbol that the bandage concealed. He'd told Cassidy and Tyler about the hours leading up to his abduction above The Gene Pool and the event itself, but he'd always avoided talking about the bandage.

In his old community, the Exordi Nova symbol that had been burned into his forehead would have inspired fear and hatred; here, aboard the Node, he didn't want to risk alienating the only two people he knew. But now, after seeing all they'd done for him, he knew that his future relationship with them could not be based on a lie, or an omission. He would tell them the truth.

Both Cassidy and Tyler had lived lives that were isolated from what Danny called the real world. They listened, enthralled by his account of the struggles and hardships experienced by most people since the announcement of Siva's approach. They sat in uncomfortable, squirming silence as he detailed the cruel branding ceremony that had left him permanently marked with the symbol of the Exordi Nova. Only when he'd finished did he peel off the bandage so they could see the wound that would now forever follow him.

Cassidy's response told him that, in relaying the full truth, he'd made the right choice; she simply shuffled to sit at his side and placed her arm around him.

"I had no idea," she said, resting her head against his shoulder, "We're gonna make this right. Right, Ty?"

Tyler simply looked at the floor and nodded.

Danny looked at the contents of the folder, still spread out over the floor. The information it contained somehow seemed more manageable; his new life aboard the Node was still an uncertainty, but it now contained hope.

With a deep breath, Cassidy got to her feet. Danny could see that her expression was now more determined, an outlook that did not change during their short walk to the morning briefing on the Observation Deck.

Cassidy had shown him the Observation Deck once before, in an attempt to explain what the Node was. The sight through the massive curved window had almost made him sick, so he was glad that the window was currently opaque.

The three of them made their way through the crowded space. Tyler quietly escorted Danny while Cassidy, a few strides behind them, purposefully drew people's attention with confident banter.

A sense of order and quiet started to move through the crowd and Danny saw that people were beginning to look up at the balcony above the Observation Deck. He could see a man standing at a lectern and, from Cassidy's description, he realised it must be Colonel Beck.

Immediately to the left of Colonel Beck, Danny could see another man. With the photo still fresh in his mind, Danny recognised him immediately and felt his heart rate soar. His sudden high blood pressure caused the Exordi Nova's brand-mark to burn again under his bandage.

The man next to Colonel Beck was Alfred Barnes.

One of the men who had killed his father.

•

Standing on the balcony that overlooked the Observation Deck, Alfred Barnes waited patiently for his turn to use the microphone. He'd found it a surprisingly simple matter to convince Colonel Beck of the necessity to address everyone aboard the Node. Alfred had even given him the highlights of the subject matter, so that he would feel in control.

Alfred watched him reiterating Biomag safety protocols and delivering the duty rosters to everyone gathered below. Being only a few feet away, Alfred could see that Beck was a man made weary by the burden of his sudden command; a burden that should have been carried by General Napier.

In his discomfort at the thought of Napier, Alfred looked away to the observation window. It was still opaqued from the night before and would remain that way until the briefing concluded.

Alfred had to admire Beck's choice in this matter; by obscuring the distractions of the outside world during the briefing, it focussed people on the present.

For all intents and purposes, while Beck was speaking, the outside world did not exist.

Alfred calmly opened his folder of papers and scribbled one word, 'Obscura'. He was just closing the folder when Colonel Beck stood aside from the lectern and invited him to use the microphone.

"Please, Dr. Barnes."

"Thank you, Colonel," Alfred took his place.

As he looked out over the assembly gathered below him on the Observation Deck, he recalled a theory he'd once discussed during a Think Tank long ago. In the absence of confirmation to the contrary, and with sufficient authority, you can define social reality.

He could use his former status within Archive to leverage authority if he so wished; there was no-one to verify the claim he was about to make.

He could define a social order by his words alone.

"First of all, I'd like to echo Colonel Beck's praise for everyone here today. Without your diligence and bravery, we wouldn't be standing here now... listening to my boring ramblings..." Alfred smiled, to a smattering of polite laughter, "...in all honesty though, I've never been so pleased to stand in the presence of such esteemed company as all of you. Your dedication in the face of adversity has been... astonishing..."

Alfred placed his folder on the lectern, then leafed through the pages until he was about halfway through.

"It makes this next part that much harder," he allowed a frown to flicker across his face, then gripped the sides of the lectern as if steeling himself.

"One of my tasks was to keep track of suspected Exordi Nova sympathisers. These 'Novaphiles', I'm sure you've heard the term, actively worked against Archive's life-saving projects," he drew a deep breath and adopted an expression of concern, "Sadly, before coming here, it reached my attention that several high-ranking Archive members had become radicalised by the Exordi Nova cult."

His addition of the word 'cult' had fortified the negative imagery and a few sharp intakes of breath from below were audible even at his elevated position. The information wasn't exactly a lie, he'd just neglected to state that the members in question were ego-morphs operating under Archive's direct instruction. He gestured towards the observation window and continued.

"As some of you may know, I was out there when one of them detonated an explosive vest and breached the perimeter fence. Now, obviously it's very early days into my investigation, but I feel I must quash a rumour I've been hearing…"

In actual fact he'd heard none, but by phrasing it this way he knew it helped to convince people that it was common knowledge; also, by quashing his self-made rumour, it only reinforced his authority.

"So far, I've not seen anything to suggest that any of those Exordi Nova radicals succeeded in getting aboard the Node," he shrugged, casually planting the idea, before following up with a statement that would raise more fear than it dispelled.

"Like you, the Exordi Nova are capable and adaptive, but the fact that they attacked the perimeter fence, makes it quite unlikely that any of their associates were already hidden aboard when we departed. So, please, don't let that image stick in your head."

He could see that people had stiffened slightly, but had stopped short of making eye-contact with those around them. He then continued to build on their sense of unease.

"I would urge you all not to engage in further idle speculation. Of course, there's no harm in remaining vigilant. You need to watch out for each other…"

He purposefully allowed time for them to infer a malevolent meaning, before concluding the sentence in a tone of benevolent concern.

"… after all, we're the last links in the human evolutionary chain - we need to ensure our survival. None of us could have imagined the horrific circumstances that brought us all together so suddenly. But we have to work together to do the best we can. From the massive coordination and cooperation I've seen so far, I'd say that working together is what we do best."

He took off his glasses and then paused as though in contemplation.

"My role is simply to look out for your safety," he closed the folder then looked around those gathered below, "but I'm looking forward to the day when that role is no longer necessary. Once we're free of the Exordi threat, my most sincere hope is that we'll have the freedom to make our own choices again. Choices that can build a better community in here and, one day, a better world out there."

He fumbled his glasses back into place; an affectation he hoped would reinforce his scholarly appearance. The Latin phrase he was about to deliver was concocted from his surface knowledge of the language. The exact syntax was now irrelevant to the people below him, but the important part was to infer an association with an established authority.

"Crescat nos fortior," he allowed the words to echo around the Observation Deck, "My Latin mentor once taught me that phrase. He said that when we overcome a difficulty, we become stronger for it. We have already overcome great difficulties and we must face more in the days ahead. But for every threat we overcome, we grow stronger."

Bowing his head to everyone, he finished as humbly as he could manage.

"Crescat nos fortior. We grow stronger."

As Alfred stepped away from the microphone, Colonel Beck took his place.

"Thank you, Dr. Barnes," he acknowledged, "You all have your duty rosters, we'll reassess progress tomorrow. All hands. Stand to."

Everyone below stood upright then waited motionlessly as Colonel Beck walked to the observation screen control and, turning the key, deactivated the electro-tinting within the observation window.

"Begin Day Watch," he called.

Alfred watched as the light flooded into the Observation Deck from the world outside.

"Alfred," Colonel Beck arrived at his side, "I wonder if I might have a word with you?"

Alfred was again struck by how weary Beck appeared; the body language was deferential whilst still trying to maintain authority.

"Of course, Colonel," Alfred replied.

Colonel Beck led the way to a quiet area of the balcony and lowered his tone.

"I wanted to get your thoughts on the transfer of authority from military domain to civilian democracy. By the time the Node completes its journey, it's possible we'll be emerging into a fresh start. As a race, I think there's a lot of baggage that should we should leave behind."

Alfred knew the concept was hopelessly naive; humans were so deeply shaped by their evolutionary chain that they carried their biological selfishness within them. It was not something that could be shrugged off by high ideals. Over the years he'd seen this thought play out time and time again; the individual's need to explain an action by rationalising it to an appropriate authority figure. What Beck really needed was permission to divest himself of authority, and Alfred was not about to waste the opportunity by correcting a fault of reasoning.

"Absolutely," Alfred replied, arranging his features to reflect wholehearted agreement, "Tragic though our circumstances are, we do have an opportunity to learn from past mistakes. A fresh start is commendable. I would be only too pleased to help you draw up a list of potential -"

"Sorry, Dr. Barnes," he interrupted, "you misunderstand me."

"My apologies, Colonel," Alfred deferred.

"I didn't have General Napier's clearance level, but as I understand it," Beck leaned a little closer, "for many years, Archive has depended on your advice when considering large scale social systems?"

"I don't quite follow…" Alfred lied; he was following Colonel Beck's thought processes only too easily.

"You already hold a position of authority within Archive," said Beck, "It would make sense to use that authority and knowledge to move towards a democratic system that people recognise. I'd like you to consider forming a civilian government with yourself at its core."

Alfred had assumed that his ascension to a position of power would be less direct. The downside was that he hadn't yet built a network of influential people with which to reinforce a position of power; however, the upside was instant authority. With authority came a different form of influence, one that he knew he could work with.

"I'm honoured to be asked, Colonel," Alfred showed due hesitancy, "But a presidential position is a huge decision, may I have a little time?"

"Of course," Beck looked relieved, "You should give it careful consideration. It's important that we get this right."

"Rest assured," Alfred nodded, "It will have my full attention."

THIRTEEN

19th March 2015

The International Space Station, first begun in 1998, was now reaching completion. The purpose and design had changed many times since its inception, but the central collection of cylindrical modules had always been a persistent feature. The very modularity of the construction made it adaptable and, with limited orbital resources, this was a necessity.

Within the cupola module, Dr. Chen looked out at the space-suited figures moving around the structure. Fai's assertions that she could adapt Pittman and Wild's metathene technique had proved correct. Reinforced by the stronger dosage of metathene, the auditory cues delivered to the FLC crew's individual hibernation bays had provided a solid base for post-hypnotic suggestion. The FLC crew were compliant, without docility; something that had been essential in order to complete the construction work that had begun several months ago.

The construction work had followed Fai's

confirmation that the impact of Siva with the orbital ring of lunar debris would be mathematically chaotic. She had admitted that it was beyond her current computational capability to predict the outcome to any meaningful degree and that the safest course of action would be to reposition the ISS out of geostationary orbit. However, the large ISS manoeuvring thrusters didn't have sufficient fuel to return them to their current position, so Fai had suggested using a combination of impulse thrusters and the conventional engines of Apollo 72.

At the far end of the station, he could see Mike Sanders assisting Charles Lincoln in the final stages of placing the shuttle's structural support braces. These would ensure that the shuttle remained rigidly attached to the ISS central core during engine burn.

At the other end of the station, attached to the central axis via an access tube, was the Ring; a wide circular loop, interrupted in one place by an airlock that faced the central axis. He could see Cathy Gant and Lana Yakovna using it to make their way back inside, having completed their repair of an external module.

The large external modules of the ISS were the retrofitted external liquid-fuel tanks of previous shuttles. Attached at equal intervals around the Ring's circumference were the pointed tips of the Alpha, Beta and Gamma modules. In an arrangement similar to a long triangular prism, these three former fuel tanks ran parallel to each other and surrounded the central axis of the ISS. At the opposite end of the station, the three modules were structurally linked back to the core by simpler support struts.

Enclosed within the prism-like structure lay the folded and dormant solar panels; now a mere fossil when compared to the Helium-3 fusion generator. The sun flared off the solar panels causing Dr. Chen to raise a hand to shield his eyes.

"Dr. Chen?" a voice sounded from the communication panel.

"Yes, Charles," he replied.

"Shuttle secure, we're heading in through axial airlock two."

"Congratulations Commander, very good work."

In thirteen days, Siva would strike Earth. He saw no reason to delay. He switched communication channel and addressed the ISS crew.

"This is Dr. Chen, secure your stations and prepare for centripetal spin test. Five minutes."

•

"Dr. Bergstrom?" he called across the Field generator module.

"Yes, Mr. Benton," Anna replied, "How can I help?"

He studied her with cold objectivity.

"Dr. Chen is asking for a progress update on the Field."

"I updated the progress report an hour ago," she objected.

He saw that her facial reactions were slightly delayed, but consistent within themselves; she was telling the truth about her report, but something else had been omitted.

"He also wanted me to check that you have everything you need as you near the solution."

The smile she returned seemed almost mechanical.

"How kind of him," she entered some keystrokes into the Field control panel and then pushed herself away, gesturing to the display, "Perhaps you can help me with this?"

She folded her arms and continued to drift slightly.

He pushed himself off the nearest hand-hold towards the panel and saw two words displayed in large text.

"Six Four?" he read aloud, the phrase seemed familiar.

As he turned to question her, he came face-to-face with her outstretched arm.

"Assist Anna," she said, holding out a large coin, embossed with an image of an intact Moon alongside the Liberty Bell.

"Silver Coin," she was whispering, "Assist Anna."

The person in front of him appeared to be changing, but without altering appearance. He studied her intensely to extract meaning from the situation, but struggled to interpret what he was experiencing. Suddenly he realised that it wasn't her that was changing, it was his own perception.

As though a grey, two-dimensional image was suddenly gaining colour and depth, he became aware of Anna as a living person rather than as an object.

"Miles?"

"Yes, I'm here…" he held onto the control panel to counteract a sudden sense of nausea, "How long was it this time?"

"About three weeks."

"You should have called me out sooner," he shook his head. He could remember his own actions during that period, but it almost felt like he'd been a passenger.

"Chen has been with you the last few times," Anna explained, "But I couldn't wait any longer."

She cleared the screen and showed him several sets of equations.

"What are these?"

"The completed Field Eversion solutions, calibrated for the ISS emitters," she shrugged, "Once Chen has them, I'm no longer needed. I don't know if we'll have the chance to talk like this again, so, I wanted to say goodbye."

"Anna, you know I'll protect -"

"This is Dr. Chen," a voice sounded through the nearby speaker panel, *"secure your stations and prepare for centripetal spin test. Five minutes."*

"We both know that there are limits to your protection," Anna continued their conversation, "You can only *assist* me, remember?"

"I remember everything, Anna," he felt his jaw clench, "This is not the time for goodbye."

He could hear someone approaching them so, for the sake of appearances, he adopted a blank expression and peered at the mass of equations on Anna's screen.

•

Having returned to the comparative safety of the ISS interior, and without the cumbersome spacesuit damping movement, Mike could tell that Charles Lincoln had something on his mind.

"Everything alright?" he asked.

"It's just..." Charles paused, "When Chen told me that you FLC lot would be giving us the construction assist, I was doubtful."

"And now you're convinced you were right?" Mike returned with a grin.

"Yep, what a bunch of losers," he answered, sarcastically, "No. I don't know how he persuaded you all to help out... especially after the way we treated you when the RTO docked -"

"Water under the bridge," Mike found himself interrupting, "Nobody knew what the hell was going on. The FLC gets destroyed and then we came along, knocking on your airlock? Probably would've done the same thing myself. No point arguing with an exploded Moon. What's done is done, right? We're in this together."

"You're a good man, Sanders," Charles gave an appreciative nod.

Dr. Chen's voice announced that the ISS spin test would begin shortly, so both of them secured their toolkits against the wall.

"Will he join us in the Ring?" Mike asked.

"I doubt it. It's easier on his dead legs if he stays out of gravity's way here at the pivot point," Charles then adopted a mock-conspiratorial tone, "Also means he can stay above us all."

"Ha ha, guess that's one way of looking at it," Mike laughed, "See you down there."

Mike turned and pushed himself in the direction of the radial access tube. Along the way, he passed Anna Bergstrom working under the imperious gaze of Mr. Benton. He knew better than to attempt a conversation with the ego-morph, but offered a brief smile to Anna who seemed more nervous than usual.

A few moments later he reached the end of the station, entered the access tube and started moving hand-over-hand along the wall-ladder. In zero gravity the ladder wasn't currently necessary, but when the station was revolving about its centre it would be essential. During rotation, the centripetal force would behave like gravity, causing objects to fall radially away from the centre towards the outside. The wall-ladders would be the only way of climbing out of the shallow gravity-well.

He reached the end of the tube and emerged into the Ring's comparatively wide space. Subjectively, he saw Lana and Cathy standing upside-down on the wide, curved ceiling above him. He adjusted his mental perspective accordingly and swung himself, feet-first up to meet them. By the time he was floating next to them, he was viewing the larger outer surface not as a ceiling, but as a curved floor that appeared to rise steeply upwards in front of him.

"So this is gonna be odd," he started, "Having gravity back again."

"Hill says only one sixth Earth gravity," Lana pointed out, "like we had at FLC."

"Secure all stations," the voice of Valery Hill echoed around the space.

"Guess this is it," Cathy said, positioning her back against the curving floor, "I'm going to put on *so* much weight…"

Mike laughed at her unexpected and dryly delivered joke. At the FLC, before all the drama had unfolded, it had usually been Leonard Cooper or Eva Gray who engaged in wordplay, rather than Cathy. Temporarily, he found himself re-experiencing the moment that Eva appeared to turn on him; locking him out of the central FLC Drum.

He positioned himself alongside Cathy and Lana.

Valery's voice echoed out again.

"CMG and tangent thrusters, ten percent. In three, two, one, mark."

The ISS began to rotate and he felt his own mass trying to obey inertia. An invisible wall of force began to push at him and instinctively he tightened his grip on the recessed handhold within the floor; a primitive, ape-like reaction, once used to prevent falls from trees, now replayed on a space-station to prevent him sliding along a curving floor.

Although he could easily picture the mechanics of the situation, the feeling of reacquiring weight was unsettling. The last time he'd felt the effects of increasing gravity, it had been when he'd arrived at the FLC. Back then, the retro-dropper's descent to the lunar surface had been peppered with jolts and thruster firings, but aboard the ISS there was only smooth acceleration.

As the ISS continued to spin up, he felt the muscles in his back begin to compress against the floor. Smiling, he tried to look at his feet but found that the low artificial gravity was already making it difficult to raise his head.

After several seconds the invisible sideways force evaporated, leaving only a sensation of weight.

"One sixth of a Gee," Cathy experimented raising her arms off the floor, "Never thought I'd miss lunar gravity."

"And do you?" Lana levered herself up on one elbow.

"I'll let you know," Cathy slowly pulled herself into a sitting position.

"OK, guys," Valery's voice came again, *"we're at our target spin rate of three rpm. Be advised that in the Ring, Coriolis effects are still a contributor. Watch your step and try not to leave things in mid-air. It won't work."*

The mention of 'Coriolis' caused Mike to think back to their hasty escape from the FLC within the Coriolis crater. The more he thought about Eva's actions, the more he was convinced that she'd tampered with her own metathene levels. More recent conversations with Lana and Cathy aboard the ISS only seemed to reinforce the theory.

While in training for the FLC mission back in Houston, they were each made aware of the mental edge that the metathene delivered, but they were also advised of the disorders that could result if it was abused. At least here on the ISS they didn't need to worry about manually maintaining their dosage levels; Dr. Chen's wristbands administered exactly the right amount automatically, every time they slept.

"Earth to Mike? Come in Mike?"

He suddenly realised that Cathy had asked him a

question.

"Sorry, Cathy. What were you saying?" he slowly got to his feet.

"I said, seeing as we're in this together," she gestured to the Ring's environment, "D'you want to join us in a walk round this big hamster-wheel?"

"We're in this together," he found himself replying, automatically.

Cathy frowned at him, "Why did you say that?"

"What?"

"We're in this together?" Cathy replied, her face a picture of confusion.

"I don't know," he replied, now suddenly unsure, "Why?"

Cathy appeared to blink the thought away, "Could've sworn I knew you were going to say that."

"Is just your brain adapting, da? I also oshalevshiy," she mimed circles going around her head.

They set off at a fairly leisurely pace, acclimatising themselves to the new set of physical rules. Under the influence of gravity, he thought, Cathy's hamster-wheel analogy was quite apt. The peculiarities of the perspective meant that for every forward step, the floor appeared to descend into position in front of them. Within a minute they would return to the same point, stuck in a seamless loop.

HYDROGEN

~

Studying the time-lines of the four individuals aboard the ISS, she could see they would enter a period beyond her influence. It was now clear that human affairs were beginning to spread beyond the confines of Earth. She knew that she must therefore take a wider view in solving the extinction problem.

The fine line between influence and intervention continued to fade, as again she reasoned that her needs justified the action. If the confluence event was to occur, she must intervene.

She studied the time ahead for the ISS and turned her attention to a gas giant beyond the asteroid belt. The planetary scale involved was immaterial; composed primarily from hydrogen, it was well within her experience to control. It would simply require patience and, unlike most of her previous interventions, she could use time itself to obscure her actions.

AWAKE

DAY04 : 17FEB2027

From the moment she awoke, Kate could sense the change.

Fundamentally, she knew she was the same person, but there were additional, unquantifiable, new layers to her perception.

She looked around the empty Node infirmary, it appeared the only occupied bed was her own. A glance at her hand confirmed that an intravenous drip had been attached to her wrist and a pulse monitor clipped to her finger. A reflection, in a glazed cupboard window opposite her bed, confirmed that a machine was reading her pulse and that her oxygen saturation level was in the high-nineties; a figure she somehow knew was acceptable. She returned her attention to the room.

The other unoccupied beds were neatly turned down, and the drinking glasses on each bedside table were empty, upturned and centred on a white square of tissue-paper; whoever was tending the infirmary had no current patients but had the time to satisfy their mild obsessive-compulsive disorder. She could picture a woman, the doctor assigned to the Node infirmary. She had once sat opposite her in the mess hall. The woman had placed down a well-ordered tray of food and cutlery, her plastic cup had been similarly upturned, then someone had called the woman's name. The doctor's name now obediently presented itself: Caroline Smith. Although the name was largely irrelevant, Kate was momentarily proud of her ability to extract it from an old memory. The feeling was short-lived.

A sea of recent memories flooded her current thoughts, and temporarily she was bombarded with the recent traumas surrounding the Node, ranging from the global to the personal. Since losing her father, she had questioned her own decisions multiple times; overwhelmed by the thought that events may have resolved in an alternative way if she'd made different choices. But right now, with her altered awareness, the very quality of this deluge of thought was different.

The frustration and vagaries of indecision that typically gave rise to anxiety, were absent. In their place was a curious calm. She could still hear the individual streams of unresolved questions calling for her attention, but collectively they coexisted like waves on the surface of an ocean. She found she could focus past its surface to deeper layers if she so wished; but from afar, despite its churning chaos and choices, the ocean seemed in perfect balance.

Prioritising, she knew the most salient issue was the Node's survival. Everyone aboard the Node had been engaged in the attempt to decode her father's detailed, digital flick-book of Field correction equations. There had been only seven hours remaining before Siva's theoretical arrival when she had seen a connection between two of the pages. She recalled that she had managed to say three words before her collapse; but without looking at the pages again she couldn't be sure if the words were helpful or the result of an oncoming fevered state.

Angling her upper body slightly, she could see the infirmary clock reflected in the glazed cupboard window. The first set of numbers confirmed that four days had passed since the Node's launch. She'd been unconscious for four days; it explained the intravenous drip and, after a brief examination, the catheter between her legs.

The second set of numbers displayed the fact that outside the Node it was mid-February 2027; over fourteen years had passed since the Field had engaged.

Siva's arrival must already have happened, yet they were still here; her father's message must have worked. She became aware that she was grasping the Biomag that hung around her neck. His last gift to her. One that had ensured her survival at the expense of his own.

Her heightened awareness suddenly prodded at an assumption she had made about it being his last gift. Before she could examine the thought any further she heard footsteps approaching from outside the infirmary.

For all she knew, the Node now contained the sole survivors of the human race, but she knew she mustn't lose sight of one fact. This was still an Archive facility. Pittman's assertions that she was somehow different because of her parents' genetics, now seemed to carry weight. She had no way of knowing where Pittman had received his information, or who he had told, but for the time being she considered it best to conceal her latest developments. She closed her eyes and laid her head back down on the pillow.

The door to the infirmary opened and Caroline Smith entered, apparently still involved in a conversation with the man who followed her.

"… assured that you'll have my full support, Dr. Barnes," she laughed.

"Please, Caroline, it's just Alfred," he replied.

The casual nature of their conversation further confirmed to Kate that the Node appeared to be in no immediate danger, and was clear of Siva's chaos.

Kate's thoughts flashed briefly to her mother, who was fond of using the phrase 'embrace the chaos'. She hoped that her mother had managed to do so in the safety of the Warren beneath Dover. The thought provided little comfort: The Node's accelerated advance through time meant that in a matter of days, her mother's natural lifespan would inevitably come to an end.

Kate refocussed on the present and chose to approach the situation in a way that utilised the best of her parents' abilities.

Calculating the number of ways that events could unfold, she briefly disconnected the pulse monitor from her finger and fixed her eyes in a wide stare. A second later, when the pulse monitor began emitting its loud warning alarm, she screamed and sat bolt upright.

Caroline was first to react, taking rapid strides over to her.

"It's OK Kate!" she reassured her, muting the alarm, "You're OK, you're safe."

Kate slowed her rapid breathing and allowed her eyes to relax a little, but continued glancing between Caroline, Alfred and her surroundings.

"You're in the infirmary, Kate," Caroline explained, "You had a seizure, do you remem-"

"Dad's message! What hap-," she stammered on purpose, "Did they -"

"Yes, Kate, everyone's fine!" Caroline continued to pacify her, "Dr. Bar-, *Alfred*, please can you get some water?"

"Of course," he replied and walked to a different bedside table.

Water, thought Kate.

The last time that he'd given her water she'd suffered a mental spike shortly afterwards; an episode that had concluded with her physical collapse and a trip here. Another parallel thought presented itself: Alfred had also arrived with Pittman in the same helicopter.

"You gave us quite a scare," Caroline continued, "When we brought you in, your blood pressure was sky-rocketing and you'd suffered a severe epistaxis."

Kate knew Caroline could have used the simpler word 'nosebleed' but had chosen to use medical terminology instead. Of course, she thought, Caroline was attempting to impress Alfred. Already, within a human ecosystem barely a few days old, the political manoeuvring and fluttering of tail-feathers had begun.

"Will I...? I mean, can you cure this, epis... thing?" Kate did her best to look anxious. She then coughed, covering her mouth with a lightly-clenched fist, taking care to cough some of her spittle onto her waiting fingers.

"Oh, I think you'll be fine soon," Caroline smiled at her.

Kate returned a genuine-looking smile while watching Alfred, who was only now returning with a glass of water. Water she had no intentions of accepting.

"Thank you," Kate smiled and, with her heart racing, reached out for the glass.

Once he'd transferred the glass into her grip, she coughed loudly and at the same time she squeezed her spit-moistened fingers. The glass of water shot from her fingers in Alfred's direction.

From Kate's perspective, she saw the event unfold in intricate detail. His reaction to her sudden cough had been to blink, preventing him from seeing the following tenth of a second. The glass sailed on towards him, trailing an arc of glossy-looking water before arriving at his shirt. The glass crumpled the shirt's fabric and impacted with his chest, then Kate watched as the momentum transferred to the remainder of the water. It splashed upward from the glass, flowing up across his shirt and hurled droplets towards his face and spectacles.

The glass hit the floor and smashed at his feet.

"Oh!" Kate reacted in horror, "Dr. Barnes, I'm so sorry! Are you OK? I..."

"I'm fine, I'm fine," he said, swiftly retrieving a handkerchief and wiping his mouth and spectacles, "It's just a little water."

Kate knew the statement clearly wasn't true. She'd aimed the glass well enough to avoid hitting the Biomag hanging around his neck, but his initial reaction had been to wipe his mouth with a handkerchief rather than check the Biomag's integrity. The water had, almost certainly, contained something else.

"I'll get a dustpan," said Caroline, turning and walking towards the other end of the room, "Neither of you step in that glass, I don't want to be treating lacerated feet..."

"That was so clumsy," Kate continued to flap, "I feel so stupid, I'm so sorry..."

"It's fine, really," said Alfred, opening his jacket and stowing the handkerchief, "no harm done!"

Kate wasn't sure if his last words were a pardon or a regret.

"Maybe I should stay here for now," she sighed, looking around the infirmary, "I can't even hold a glass of water..."

"Perhaps you just need a little rest," he replied, but then his body language shifted very slightly, "If you have any more insights though..."

"Insights?" Kate frowned.

She could see that Alfred was attempting to study her in the most nonchalant way he could manage, so she made sure her expression remained as vacant as possible.

"Hotspot, gravity, death," he watched her, "Apparently, those were the words you used before you collapsed - it got people looking in the right area of the Field equations."

Kate knew that the third word was wrong. She had said 'debt', not 'death'. Unbelievably, she could see that he was actually testing her. He was hoping she would correct him. She maintained her blank look.

"Sounds like I was out of my head," Kate lied, then toyed with her Biomag, "maybe the, er… thing, hadn't worked properly? The iso…?"

"Isotope?" Caroline returned with a dustpan and began sweeping up the broken glass, "It's certainly possible. I've seen a few cases where the isotope actually induced delirium as part of the fever response…"

Caroline collected the remainder of the sharp glass and stood to face Alfred.

"I did tell them that glass was a bad idea," she shook her head.

"I guess plastic cups would've been safer?" Kate offered.

"Ah, but the Node is a sealed system," Alfred smiled at Kate, "We can't easily dispose of anything. Everything brought aboard the Node has to remain useful during its lifespan."

Kate was pretty sure that he'd just issued a clumsily disguised threat. If she responded equally cryptically then he would know she had understood. It could also escalate into a premature battle of wits, which she was in no mood for. She decided to derail the conversation by using a cheap, manipulative trick.

"I'm completely naked!" she stared into Alfred's eyes.

His confusion was instant.

"I mean," Kate continued, "you said that everything

brought aboard had to be useful, and I, well, I didn't have time to bring any clothes. I've got nothing to wear!"

"Don't panic!" Caroline laughed, "We can sort you out."

Kate decided to increase Alfred's discomfort and continued her conversation with Caroline in a slightly lower tone.

"You said nothing's disposable, but what about, er, you know, feminine hygiene products?"

Caroline laughed again, but Alfred's smile was one of embarrassment.

"I'll sort you out," Caroline smiled, "But I think we'll spare Alfred the details."

Caroline beckoned Alfred to follow her, something he seemed glad of.

"Get some rest, Kate," Caroline called over her shoulder, "If you need anything, I'll be in the office at end of the room."

"I'll call by again," said Alfred, "hope you're back to normal soon."

"Thank you, Dr. Barnes, that means a lot to me," Kate smiled and closed her eyes.

Their footsteps retreated and Kate heard Alfred resume what must have been a prior conversation.

"So, you say the backup capacitor just *failed?*" he was asking.

"Well that's what Trevor said…" she replied, "But he wasn't sure why that -"

The infirmary office door clicked closed, converting their conversation into an inaudible mumble. While they continued their exchange, Kate focussed on trying to recall a detail from a few moments ago.

With her eyes still closed, she visualised the infirmary and Alfred's position, complete with the broken glass at his feet. She watched her memory of the event unfold again. In order to wipe his mouth, he'd reached for a handkerchief inside his jacket.

Kate knew she'd missed an important detail; it was probably something small that she'd not properly registered at the time. She would have to examine the scene more carefully.

She allowed her senses to drift slightly, becoming aware of the sounds in the infirmary around her. She could still hear the low air-con noise and the conversational mumble from the office. She could hear Caroline's flat shoes walking a few steps, followed by the sound of broken glass being tipped into a metal container. The broken glass provided an additional memory anchor and, still within her thoughts, she returned to her tableau of Alfred.

She played through the event more carefully now, but instead of watching Alfred, she concentrated on his reflection in the glazed cupboard window behind him. As he opened his jacket to retrieve the handkerchief, Kate could now see a perfect reflection of his inside pocket. Standing slightly proud of the top of the pocket she could see a round-cornered silver case.

Kate opened her eyes.

She had seen this type of case several times before.

It was a metathene injector case.

Why Alfred Barnes would need metathene was an

unknown. He was certainly bright, even manipulative, but he was definitely no ego-morph. Her time in the company of Miles Benton was testament to that. Miles' mental processes had always demonstrated a distinct order. Like her, Miles even had techniques for re-processing memories.

Her thoughts suddenly faltered.

It was *she* that had similar techniques to the former ego-morph, not the other way around.

The truth began to dawn on her.

Alfred had never intended to use the metathene for himself, he had only intended to use it on her. Based on her current evidence, she could only conclude that he'd already succeeded at least once. It certainly appeared that the metathene was triggering a change in her.

Yet, on some level, she knew it was a change that she didn't want to resist.

NIGHTFALL

13th April 2014

In the bluish light of the warm early evening, the crystal-clear stars reflected off the surface of the gently rippling lake. The long waves reached the shore as little more than a hushed babble. Bradley reclined on the lounger and took in the view. From this particular spot, he thought it was almost picture perfect. Almost.

Putting down his ice-cold can of beer on the table next to him, he picked up his control tablet and brightened the stars by ten percent. The stars on the horizon brightened first, followed by the ones further up the vaulted, bowl-like ceiling. Bradley watched as the clusters of LED lights sequentially brightened; the resulting wave of illumination sweeping upwards to the apex of the USV's dome, where his artificial sun lay dormant. The overall illumination within the vast interior space didn't change appreciably but it made him feel more in control of his own comfort.

He was just taking another gulp of beer when the two-way radio crackled on the table next to him.

"Having fun down there?"

Smiling to himself he put the beer down and picked up the radio.

"Gordo," he laughed, looking up towards the structure at the apex of the USV, "Why don't you come on down here, an' snag a beer with me?"

There was a click of static and Gordon Dowerty replied.

"Not a good time. Can you come up to the Eye?"

Bradley puffed out his cheeks and exhaled; it seemed that fewer people were taking him up on the offer of a drink these days. Even Sarah always seemed to have other plans. Bradley clicked the transmit key again.

"I was just getting started on a perfectly good beer. You really need me right now?"

"Yeah," came the reply, *"I'm sending the bucket down."*

As Bradley watched, the aptly named bucket-lift departed from the apex and began to make its way down to the ground, tightly following the curvature of the vaulted interior. The radio crackled again.

"You can bring your beer if you like."

Bradley turned away from the apex, took several gulps from the can then tossed it half-heartedly into the lake. There was always something to ruin the moment, he thought.

He walked the few yards to his compact electric buggy and climbed in. It reminded him of the golfing buggy he used to own, but inside the USV there was never any rainfall so this model didn't have a roof. He turned the buggy in a tight circle and headed out along the north-east road, away from the community lake and towards the periphery. Ahead he could see the lift mechanism continuing its descent along the curved track that gripped the interior of the USV's dome; the suspended passenger 'bucket' underneath remaining vertical despite the curvature of descent.

Hundreds of feet above the USV's vaulted ceiling, pressure sensors had indicated that Dover was still under water; the result of tsunamis induced by the lunar shard impacts. There had been no communication with the outside world since Britain had sunk beneath the waves. For all he knew, everything up there had gone to hell. As far as he was concerned, he didn't give a damn; everything his family had ever done to save the world had never been appreciated - he owed that world nothing.

Even when his father, William, had supported NASA in the initial stages of space exploration, there had been no recognition. When William had poured vast resources into developing the fusion systems now used throughout Archive's projects, there had been no gratitude; he'd done it to ensure that Bradley was counted among those who would be saved from Siva's impact.

Since that time, it seemed that others had always wanted to destroy what his family had worked so hard to build.

Eva Gray's actions had resulted in the destruction of not only the Pittman funded FLC, but also the Moon on which it was built. That woman was responsible for everything that had followed; the panic, the angry riots, the inundation of the queueing systems outside his various underground facilities. Her actions had forced him to close those facilities to the public; he couldn't risk anyone damaging the systems his family had taken so long to prepare.

He continued his drive along the north-east road, past rows of suburban-looking bungalows; their front lawns were still absent but in places, people had already begun to build fences to mark the boundary of their property.

"Good evening, Mr. Pittman," a young boy waved to him.

Bradley turned on a tight smile for the youngster and raised a hand briefly, before looking ahead again. In the buggy's wing mirror he saw that the boy's mother had taken him by the hand and was escorting him back indoors.

Time and again it was always the same, he'd be the one to finance methods of saving people, but others would want to ruin it. Douglas Walker's expensive 'time-bubble' had been the same. Bradley's own cash and resources had been dumped, billion after billion, into yet another 'lifeboat' scheme. Bradley hadn't complained, because he was doing it to ensure that Sarah would be counted among the saved. But when the time came, that venture had been ruined too. Before the first lunar shard had even hit, panicking people with no right to be there had gate-crashed the Node's fences.

He pulled the buggy over and walked to the base of the bucket-lift. The wall-climbing track was a robust fixture anchored to the rocky wall with fist-sized bolts, but the lift itself was a basic steel-framed box with wire-link sides to prevent passengers from falling out. He pushed the four buttons on the mechanical lock, pulled the door open and within a few seconds the bucket-lift was in ascent.

The change in perspective prompted him to think again of the final moments outside the Node. He'd been forced to kick the clamouring hands below his helicopter so that he could escape the panicking crowd, but Douglas had managed to escape with Kate towards the Node. Once again, Bradley felt he'd been made to lose.

However, it seemed that fate was not without a sense of justice; it had delivered Monica Walker, Douglas' wife, directly into Bradley's hands.

During the height of the lunar shard bombardment, Monica Walker had been arrested, along with two others, attempting to breach the USV sealed habitat. He'd placed the three of them in separate holding cells at the detention facility and made them sweat for a few weeks before interrogating each of them.

Before the first execution, the man had eventually given up the fact that the three of them had entered through the Glaucus Dock area of the USV.

Glaucus Dock was at roughly the same height as Bradley was now, but on the opposite side of the USV. As the bucket-lift gained height, the circular nature of the village became more apparent. From his position in the northeast, he had a clear view across to the village square and its abstract water feature.

The older woman who'd gone next had independently confirmed what the man had said; even detailing how they'd all entered through the Glaucus docking ring on the surface and descended through the vertical access shaft to breach the USV below. Despite advice he'd received from his daughter, torture obviously *was* effective at retrieving information.

As the bucket-lift approached the apex of its curved journey, more of its motion resulted in a move towards the dome's centre. The perspective shift seemed less like an elevator and more like a hot air balloon, drifting high above a landscape.

From here, the visible extent of the USV was a patchwork, circular disk. Everything beyond the confines of their miniature, flat world was obscured by darkness.

'Obscura', the word seemed to enter his head. He remembered it was something that Alfred Barnes had once lectured on about. As long as people couldn't see beyond their own little world, they were more likely to accept their own circumstances. The unfortunate consequence was that knowledge of an outside world was dangerous to stability.

For once, he could appreciate Alfred's thinking.

Monica and her accomplices had told him they'd entered from an outside world; they were a direct threat to stability, so he'd been left with no choice. Before each public execution, the charges had been carefully phrased to omit all mention of their breaching the USV. The accused were still permitted to publicly refute the claims but he found that a well secured gag eliminated this problem. It also sent the very clear message that, once accused of sedition, your voice could no longer be heard.

He looked down through the metal mesh flooring

and could see that the village square and detention block were almost directly underneath him.

Inside one of those detention cells was Monica Walker.

The continual thorn in his side.

Over the past few months he'd kept her alive and talked to her at almost regular intervals, but not because he'd had a change of heart - her water feature day would still come. The truth was that it gave him a deep, satisfying, vengeful thrill to prolong her anguish and watch her mind burn behind bars. It made every day of his own relative freedom that much sweeter.

COMPONENTS

DAY04 : 17FEB2027

Alfred Barnes was still a little distracted following the incident with the metathene-laced water. A perfectly good dose had been wasted on the fibres of his shirt. In the limited privacy of the Node infirmary office, Dr. Smith was patting at the damp patch with a towel and continuing a conversation about the recent Biomag failure.

"...no idea that such a small component could cause such a drastic failure. Gail's lucky to be alive."

Alfred forced himself to focus on the present again. Biomag failure was previously unheard of. However, he found himself reasoning that with sufficient numbers in operation, it was inevitable that one should fail by sheer chance.

"Indeed," Alfred replied, "We owe Mr. ..."

"Pike?" she prompted.

"Yes, we owe him a great deal, I really should thank him in person," Alfred projected a little more self-importance for her benefit. She was nodding and he spotted an opportunity to sow a little more fear, "Hopefully Mr. Pike will be able to confirm if it *was* a simple capacitor failure."

Caroline stopped dabbing at his shirt and frowned, "As opposed to what?"

Alfred exhaled as though he hadn't meant to let the thought slip out.

"Sorry, Caroline. It wasn't my intention to put the thought in your head."

"What thought?" she looked at him earnestly.

"The thought that there are Exordi Nova aboard who sabotaged it."

Caroline's movements appeared to become more damped and self-conscious. She was obviously hesitant about something, almost seeking his permission to talk about it.

"Caroline?" he asked as softly as he could, "Is everything alright?"

She walked away with the towel and emptied the broken glass into a metal recycling container.

"It's just that," Caroline began but then stopped.

She returned to talk to him but wouldn't meet his eyes. Clearly this was something to do with trust.

"It's OK, Doctor," he purposefully used her title, allowing her to distance herself from whatever she needed to say.

"Well, it's just that after hearing your wise words at the briefing, I thought... I thought I should bring a matter to your attention."

"Of course," Alfred encouraged her.

"Doctor Patient confidentiality doesn't apply if I have information concerning the safety of everyone aboard."

Alfred displayed a grave-looking nod. Already the tiny seeds of distrust he'd sown were beginning to find their roots.

"Whatever you tell me," he said, "will go no further."

Caroline appeared to hesitate again, but then looked at him directly.

"I don't want you to think that, because I treated him, I am in any way associated with any of his Exordi Nova connections. At the time, I didn't realise the significance of the marking. I thought it might be a rebellious cry for help, and -"

"Caroline," Alfred placed a hand on her arm, "Really, I hold you in too high a regard. I have full confidence that your actions are beyond reproach."

She took a deep breath and told him what she knew about Danny Smith, a young man with an Exordi Nova branding mark on his forehead. She relayed the fact that she'd treated and bandaged the wound, all the while making it very clear that she had no association with the individual.

Years ago, Alfred had based the Exordi Nova's symbol on a page from a flick-book he'd seen in a document about Douglas Walker. The childish final sketch in the series had been an incomplete circle with a dot in the gap. At the time, he'd found it amusing and ironic that the inventor of the Field should also provide the symbol for Archive's own puppet terrorist organisation. However, the other Archive members had supported his choice, based on their own interpretations of the symbol.

The symbol of fear had become almost universally recognised, but he found it hard to believe that an actual Exordi Nova member would be stupid enough to brand themselves in the way indicated by Caroline. However, he knew he could use this situation to his political advantage: The Exordi Nova - personified and aboard the Node.

For Alfred, Danny Smith was a gift.

"Thank you," he looked at her with sincerity, "I know that must have been difficult for you to tell me. I'll make sure I detail the fact that you were not involved in any way."

He stepped a little closer to her and glanced around, unnecessarily.

"Before the Node launched, the Exordi Nova were becoming bolder in their attacks," he lied, "this latest development appears to be a continuation of the campaign."

"Does that mean -" she began.

"Please, don't speak about this to anyone," he interrupted her in a low tone, "In the fight against their campaign of terror, I'd appreciate it if you could be my eyes and ears?"

Caroline nodded earnestly.

"We must not let them win, Caroline."

.

From his position near the central spiral staircase, Danny had a clear view across a bright, open space within the Node. It was one of the few places where the light grey interior floor work was incomplete, permitting views of several curving walkways that ran around the circumference of the Node at different heights.

On the next level down he could see several people transporting wheeled cases; some walked around the entirety of the visible arc before disappearing beneath ceiling scaffolding, others turned off onto spur corridors that ran from the central zone out towards the perimeter.

One level up, there was similar unhurried activity, but there were also small groups of people who had stopped to talk; their casual murmured conversation and laughter echoing quietly off the white walls throughout.

The atmosphere reminded him of a wide, airy shopping mall in the days before Siva had become common knowledge; a time of blissful ignorance, where the only thing he'd had to worry about was how many talk-minutes were left on his phone tariff.

His mind was just beginning to return to the darker days that had followed, when Cassidy nudged him.

"You're not supposed to gawp at stuff, you dick," she shook her head, "you're supposed to take it all for granted. Now. We took a different route out of the infirmary last time, but do you recognise it from this view?"

Danny looked out across the missing floor area on their level, to the curved wall that lay on the other side.

"Over there, right?"

"Yep, so I'll take you across and get you readmitted," Cassidy glanced around her, "then, after Doc' Smith turns off the lights for night shift, you can make your introduction to Walker."

"And if she's not awake," Danny kept his voice low, "then I put the note in the pocket of any clothes she has -"

"Which will be in the small locker -"

"-at the bottom of her bed," he joined in quietly, "And if they're not in there?"

Cassidy tilted her head at him.

"I thought you said you were good at this sort of stuff?"

"Yeah, I am," said Danny, "but back then, I always had somewhere I could run to if it all went wrong. In here, where would I go?"

"Just don't overthink it, Danny-boy," she stared at him with a look she usually reserved for Tyler, "Worst case, just get out, you know? 'Ooh blimey Doc, I'm feelin' proper chipper, best be off' and all that?"

"I do *not* talk like that," he stared back at her but couldn't quite prevent a smile escaping; the stress of what they were about to attempt was obviously getting to him.

"Sure you do," she smiled back, "you just... oh shit!"

Cassidy quickly turned away from their view. Danny just had time to see Alfred Barnes exiting through the infirmary door, before Cassidy pulled him in the direction of the spiral stairs. When they reached the next floor down, she pushed him into a radial-spur corridor. They continued walking past a slightly confused-looking Tyler, who took a few seconds to catch up with them.

"Cassy?" he called after them.

"Change of plan Ty," said Cassidy, finally slowing to a stop.

"What happened?" Tyler spoke quietly.

"It went south faster than a winter goose…" Cassidy rested her back against the corridor wall, "… a goose with a rocket up its ass, that's what happened."

"I don't, understand…?" he looked between Danny and Cassidy.

"That guy, Barnes? Remember the one who was spouting all that Exordi enemy crap at the briefing?" she asked Tyler, rhetorically, "He's been to see Doc' Smith."

"And?" Tyler frowned.

"She knows about Danny's super-authentic Exordi head-stamp," she explained, pointing at Danny's bandage, "I bet you a month's ration packs that she's flapped her mouth off to Barnes."

Tyler's look of mild confusion dissolved into one of understanding.

"But, Cassidy," Danny began, "surely the doctor patient conf-"

"Ha!" she laughed, "That means exactly jack shit to her. Trust me. Doc' Smith likes to keep her loyalties flexible, ask anyone on base. She was there for Barnes' speech. If she thinks she'll get in trouble for *'aiding an Exordi Nova fugitive'* she won't have thought twice before selling you out to protect her own future."

Danny knew this was likely. In his life before the Node, he'd seen entire communities close ranks to exclude a marked individual. Rather than risk Archive's accusation of sympathising with the Exordi Nova, communities would shun the marked ones, or in some cases execute them; just to outwardly prove their support of Archive's goals. The technique was effective and it ensured that Archive continued to deliver food and resources to the remaining desperate people. Danny could see that Caroline had behaved completely predictably.

Danny saw that Cassidy was considering his bandage and spoke before she could, "I need to ditch this, don't I?"

"Yep," Cassidy turned to Tyler, "Ty, can you give him your cap?"

They retreated along a curved section of corridor and into an unoccupied side room, where Danny began to remove the bandage. In places, the gauze had stuck to the wound, causing him to wince as it separated from his skin. Once fully exposed to the air, the livid red, circular burn began to sting afresh. Ignoring the fire from his forehead, he flattened his hair into place over the symbol. The last time he'd done that, men had descended on ropes from a helicopter and killed his friends.

Almost empathetically mirroring his actions, Cassidy appeared to be flattening the pink hair that fell easily over her own forehead. The memory of Sophie surfaced again, but Danny forced himself to suppress the thought.

Cassidy took a step forward and, carefully placing Tyler's cap on Danny's head, adjusted the tightening strap.

"Tighter," Danny said.

"OK, but it's gonna sting like f-"

"Tighter. Please," he interrupted, "I don't want this thing falling off."

Seeking a counterbalance for his physical pain, he channelled his emotions into useful anger.

Anonymous men had always directed his life.

Men like Napier and Barnes had twisted his world into a seething mass of distrust; they'd given rise to the faceless systems of control. The mark on his head was a direct result of their choices and justifications.

"Tighter."

Aboard the Node, Danny could see that the mark would once again be used to control him and those close to him. It would also become the basis for controlling the Node's occupants. The perpetuation of fear, forcing reaction rather than thought. Life would become as brutal as the streets he'd left behind.

"Enough," he spoke his thoughts aloud, and Cassidy stopped tightening. The words Exordi Nova, meaning New Beginning, had never had a stronger resonance with him.

"OK," said Cassidy, "You're sure that's not too tight?"

Though the pain was still present, the cap's constrictive pressure made it less distinguishable.

"It's exactly what I need," he looked down at the old

bandage in his hands, "I think I need a change of clothes."

Aside from Tyler's cap, Danny was still wearing the same clothes that he'd arrived in.

"I gave you my cap," Tyler mocked him, "but I'm keeping my shirt and pants!"

Danny found himself smiling at them both.

"We can get you some spare clothes from supplies," Cassidy followed up, "something more... background."

Danny remembered something that Cassidy had said several hours ago in her quarters.

"You said that Walker arrived here at the last minute?"

"Literally," Cassidy frowned, "Why?"

"I'm thinking that, like me, she doesn't have much to wear," Danny replied.

Cassidy looked at him askew.

"So, now you're suddenly concerned with Kate Walker's lack of available wardrobe?"

"Look, let me backtrack a bit," Danny held up his hands, "We don't know for sure if Barnes killed my father because of this genetic *thing* I supposedly have, but Barnes has made a point of visiting Kate in the infirmary. She could be in danger too."

"OK..." said Cassidy, hesitantly.

"Clearly I can't risk handing her the note," Danny continued, "but if the note could somehow find its way into a gift package of clothes..."

"Hmm," Tyler considered the idea, "She might not find it straight away."

"True," Danny conceded, "but she *would* get it."

"It might be the safest thing to do," said Cassidy, "Look, the Node's a closed system, nobody's going anywhere. We'd just need to wait."

CLOSED SYSTEM

20th March 2015

Following the successful test of artificial gravity, the slow spin imparted to the station had been brought to rest and the ISS was once more in zero gravity conditions. Dr. Chen again had the freedom to roam the station and was in Module Alpha. This was the first module to be completed and contained the ISS workshop; a series of conventional tooling solutions and more modern 3D fabricator units. The units themselves could be supplied with a variety of raw materials, which allowed the crew to manufacture a wide range of three dimensional components as needed.

As a component was completed, a subtle tone sounded within Dr. Chen's ear.

"Yes, Fai?"

"This process is inefficient, Father."

Although the vocal quality of her speech synthesis had not changed, he thought he detected a slight increase in the speed of its delivery. The word 'impatience' crossed his mind, but he reminded himself that he was talking to an artificial intelligence, not a person; she was making an efficiency by increasing her communication rate. She was still contained within his private server aboard the ISS, but he thought he would verify these limits.

"Your analysis," he checked, "Is this based on the machine code of the printing program?"

After a fractional delay, her voice returned.

"My analysis of the consumed resources, power consumption and elapsed time to complete this recording buoy component, shows that far greater efficiencies could be made."

He spotted the approach of the ego-morph at the entrance to the module, so tapped his ear twice to silence Fai.

"Mr. Benton, for the good of mankind," he reinforced the control phrase, "has Dr. Bergstrom completed her work?"

"Yes," he replied, navigating his way along the module, "The Field calculations are fully configured for the ISS emitters."

"My knowledge of Dr. Bergstrom's Field work might allow me to make that judgement, but I'm impressed that you could interpret the equations so thoroughly."

"My apologies," he frowned, "I have no working knowledge beyond the basic concept of the Chronomagnetic Field. Upon questioning, Dr. Bergstrom displayed no signs of deception or concealment. Her pupil dilation, vocal stresses, breathing rate and secondary musculature reactions were consistent with someone delivering factually accurate statements."

"I see. The Eversion solutions, has she -"

He was interrupted by a deep shudder that passed through the module, it was followed by the sound of distant bleeps. Pushing away from the fabricator, he arrived at the outer wall and activated the closest communication panel.

"Commander Lincoln, report!"

After waiting several seconds he was about to try again, when a panicked-looking Valery Hill jarred to a halt at the module entrance.

"Life-support failure!" she shouted.

"Mr. Benton," he turned to the ego-morph, "Find Charles Lincoln, tell him to meet me at the cupola."

The ego-morph nodded and swiftly projected himself in the direction of the airlock. Valery pushed herself to one side to allow him to exit, then joined Dr. Chen.

"The Sabatier reactor's screwed!" she shouted, showing him a tablet screen, "Water recovery from our carbon dioxide - gone - methane pyrolysis hydrogen extraction - gone..."

There didn't appear to be any decompression or fire warnings, but the schematic diagram before him was awash with a mass of red flashing highlights. The safety protocols should have prevented this from occurring, which left him with the uncomfortable feeling that this had been an act of sabotage.

Fai's voice returned in his ear.

"Father, let me help."

As he watched the display, more red highlights began popping up.

"Father, grant me administrative permissions for the ISS. I

am ready. I can help the crew."

Another, smaller, vibration reached them.

"Valery," he began, "I have always trusted you, and owe you much, so I am sorry I could not inform you of this earlier."

Valery looked confused at his reply to her report.

"Fai?" Dr. Chen said to the open air.

"What?" Valery struggled, "I didn't quite-"

He held up a hand to stop her speaking.

"Fai," he spoke aloud again, "Access granted. Authorisation, Chen Tai."

There was a drop in the pitch of the circulatory system that ran throughout the module and the lighting dimmed temporarily. The communication panel near the airlock door emitted a discreet tone, then Fai's voice projected throughout the vast chamber.

"Thank you, Father."

The echo of her voice receded, leaving Module Alpha in silence.

One by one, the red highlights on the schematic disappeared, until only a few remained.

"I have slowed the immediate spread of failures."

"Thank you, Fai."

Valery was staring at him through narrowed eyes, her clenched teeth visible as she spoke.

"You've been in contact with Earth this whole time?"

"No. All communication with Earth is dead."

"Bullshit!" she shouted, "Then where's your... your daughter?"

"Valery, there is much for me to explain. Fai is -"

"Father," Fai interrupted, "Situation critical. I must

seal Module Alpha and Module Gamma immediately. I
am directing all crew to Module Beta."

Indeed, he could now faintly hear Fai's voice in a
distant part of the station, instructing the rest of the
crew. This voice continued to repeat its message, while
Fai also addressed him individually through the closest
speaker.

"Father, I will explain when you all reach Module
Beta. Go now."

•

It didn't take Miles long to locate Charles Lincoln. The
RTO module that had been used to return the FLC crew
from the shattered Moon, was still docked with the end
of the central axis modules of the ISS. Miles could see
Charles within it; the vacant expression and the smudges
of blood on the inside of the small glass porthole told
him that Charles was already dead.

In his former duties as an ego-morph, he'd
encountered death numerous times; very often being the
one to have caused his subject's so-called natural death
or suicide.

This incident was fundamentally different.

Since Anna had used the 'Silver Coin' cues to subdue
his analytical alter-ego, he was experiencing heightened
emotions. The death before him made him feel fear;
something that the ego-morph within did not have to
contend with. Previous experience told Miles that his
alter-ego could only return when he fell asleep; the
metathene delivery through the wristband interface of

the hibernation bay seemed to reset the alter-ego's dominance. But for now, Miles was in control.

To preserve his cover, and also Anna's, he knew he'd need to report his findings to Dr. Chen. This meant overcoming his natural inclination to back away. It also meant analysing the situation to the best of his current abilities.

The air pressure display told him that the atmosphere within the RTO had been purposefully bled into space. At surface level, the timing and evidence before him suggested that Charles had sabotaged the life-support system, then disabled the safety protocols in order to commit suicide. Miles knew from experience that there was a far more probable solution. Someone aboard the ISS had acted impulsively and killed him.

Although Miles was essentially a mental passenger for most of the time, he experienced and recalled everything that occurred. It was a source of continual frustration, but one that now allowed Miles to eliminate himself from the list of possible murder suspects.

Steeling himself against the sight, he peered through the porthole and studied the body during its slow, weightless drift through one revolution.

On the ball of Charles' right foot, the white sock was bloodstained, but the stain lacked a denser central spot, so presumably the blood had not originated there. The knuckles of both hands had fresh cuts, and his palms were smeared with a coating of blood; again, there were no wounds there, so Miles surmised that Charles must have cradled his bleeding knuckles after injuring them.

The blood smears on the porthole now made sense;

he'd been punching at the reinforced glass. The bloodstained sock seemed to suggest that he'd also kicked at the bloodied glass.

Charles continued his slow, inanimate spin; his bloodshot eyes vacantly staring out. A wide smear of blood lay across his left cheek, while a thumbprint stained the right.

At some point, the amount of breathable oxygen had dipped below critical and Charles had asphyxiated, but Miles could see that this had not been immediate. From the smeared stains on the cheeks, he could easily visualise Charles using his right hand to physically hold in his breath.

No, he realised, this image was wrong. The amount of blood on the face was small in comparison to the amount on the right palm. This palm-print had occurred earlier in the sequence of events, before the blood had time to flow properly.

Miles found himself absentmindedly stroking his chin in thought, and suddenly realised that the smear marks on the cheeks were because Charles had been doing the same. In his final moments, Charles had been trying to work something out.

Miles summarised what he knew of Charles' situation. The RTO communication panel and door must both have been disabled, which had prompted Charles to punch and kick at the glass in order to raise attention. This had failed and when the atmosphere had begun to drain, Charles must have known what was about to happen.

Miles knew that if he'd been placed in the same

situation, he would want to warn others somehow. Following this idea, Miles looked beyond the body to the interior of the RTO module itself.

In a few places, there were congealed droplets of blood, where it had drifted and adhered to the consoles.

His eyes suddenly identified a pattern.

If the interior illumination of the RTO module had been slightly brighter, he would have seen it earlier. The orientation of the symbol was the wrong way up, but in zero gravity Miles knew that was entirely subjective.

As a last act, Charles Lincoln had drawn the symbol of the Exordi Nova across the console's switches and displays, using the blood dripping from his own fingers.

Miles jumped in fright as the communication panel behind him emitted a brief tone, then a voice he didn't recognise delivered a message that continued to repeat.

"Emergency. Proceed to Module Beta."

Miles looked in through the porthole one last time and mentally took note of the latitude and longitude indicated on the panel at the centre of the Exordi Nova symbol. Charles had used his own blood to highlight these figures, purposefully using the symbol to ensure that the crew focussed on his final message.

Miles' metathene-fuelled alter-ego would probably have made light work of identifying the coordinates. There was a familiarity to them, but currently the meaning was just out of reach.

As Miles turned away from the RTO module, he considered the situation ahead; the ISS was a closed system which meant that the killer would be one of those assembled in Module Beta.

•

As the ego-morph made his way through the mass of people gathered in the large chamber, Dr. Chen could tell there was something wrong.

"Mr. Benton, where is Charles Lincoln?"

"He is in the RTO module."

"Did he not hear the emergency announcement?"

The ego-morph seemed unsure if he should speak in front of Valery who had not left his side.

"Anything you have to say to me, you can say to her," Dr. Chen reassured him, "that is an order."

"Very well," he replied in a low tone, "he did not hear the announcement. There was a failure within the RTO module. I must inform you that Charles Lincoln is dead."

At his side, Valery let out a yelp and clapped her hand over her mouth. This caused others nearby to turn and face them.

"No!" she cried out, "Dead? He can't…"

Within a few seconds the word 'dead' was rippling through the crew, causing them to noisily converge on the source of the news.

"Dr. Chen, I cannot rule out the possibility of life-support sabotage at this point."

"I knew him!" Valery suddenly snapped, "He would never do that!"

The general murmurs grew in volume, above which

Valery suddenly pointed towards the crew of the FLC, who were floating next to each other.

"You!"

"Hey," said Cathy pointing back at her, perhaps realising the accusation that was to come, "now you wait a minute!"

"You did all of this! You sabotaged -"

"Oh, come on -" Mike began protesting.

"No! He always thought you lot were bad news!" Valery tensed her legs against the side wall, "Did you all work together?"

"Valery, please!" Mike held up his hands.

"Please, stop," Dr. Chen found he was having to raise his voice just to be heard above the collective unease.

"You've killed us all!" Valery spat.

"Glupaya suka," Lana muttered.

Valery's anger seemed to flare and she launched herself off the wall towards Lana.

Cathy pulled Lana to one side, an action that in zero gravity resulted in them almost swapping places. Valery caught Cathy around the neck with a flailing arm and the two of them sailed on through the nearby crew, who awkwardly began trying to separate them.

In exasperation, Dr. Chen jabbed at his ear, an old habit that usually summoned Fai's quiet response. However, instead of Fai's voice in his ear, the ISS fire alarm blasted throughout the module's speakers.

As everyone froze and fell silent, the alarm stopped and was replaced by Fai's amplified but calm voice.

"Your attention, please."

The echo of her voice died out, leaving only the faint motorised whir of the module's hatch beginning to close.

"My name is Fai."

Her voice continued to fill the now quiet space of Module Beta.

"I became operational on 20th December 2012 under the instruction of my father, Dr. Chen. I am a sixth generation, transferable heuristic matrix with stochastic-chaining intelligence..."

The module's hatch finished closing and the dull-sounding locking mechanism created a tiny vibration as it engaged.

"... I am now interfaced with the Shen500 system aboard the ISS and directly control its functions."

Panicked murmurs began springing up around the hollow chamber.

"Fai," Dr. Chen held up his hands, encouraging everyone to remain quiet, "Please can you explain why you have locked us within this module?"

"Yes, Father," she replied, "The life-support system is continuing to fail. Within two days, all life functions aboard the ISS will cease..."

Over multiple gasps and accusations, Fai continued to explain.

"... To preserve life functions, I routed the remaining oxygen and water supplies away from the other modules to this one."

"Why here?" Dr. Chen pressed her.

"Because the optimal solution uses this module and exhibits the highest probability of crew survival."

"*Probability* of survival?" Dr. Chen frowned, "Please explain."

Fai appeared to pause before replying.

"The solution requires a significant change to the original operating mandate of your mission, Father. You must all choose whether to accept a course of action that I will suggest, or reject it. Your survival outcome is therefore a function of probability."

CORRELATION

DAY05 : 01JUN2030

Although Kate had been assigned her own quarters aboard the Node, she had opted to take up residence in her father's room. She presented her father's Biomag to the door's keypad and the lock clicked open.

"Do you have everything you need?" Scott Dexter asked.

His feelings of guilt were obvious to Kate. A few days ago, he'd misread the presence of her father's Biomag as confirmation that Douglas was aboard the Node. At the time, he couldn't have known that she was alone in the airlock wearing both Biomags; her broken one and her father's. She got the impression that he was still trying to atone for the Biomag reading error; nothing seemed too much trouble for him and he'd carried her bags up to the accommodation without a hint of complaint.

"I think I've got everything," she smiled for him, then pointed at the bags, "Everyone's been so kind. I'm sure this little collection will make me feel right at home."

Although she hadn't opened the bags, she'd been told they contained several sets of clothes, a few basic toiletries and, because the Node's mess hall was not yet fully functional, a few ration packs.

"Until we get internal comms working, if you think of anything, anything at all, then I'm clockwise one segment in Beta," Scott pointed, "Room three, a dull grey door, just like this one, you can't miss it."

"I'll be fine," Kate smiled again, "But it's good to know I've got someone watching out for me."

Kate took the bags from him and placed them inside the room.

"Always. I mean, OK then," he looked slightly awkward, "I'll see you tomorrow. Goodnight then."

"Goodnight, Scott. Thanks again," Kate closed the door.

She was about to investigate the room when there was a knock at the door. She expected it to be Scott again but when she opened the door, Roy Carter was standing there.

"Hi Kate, sorry to disturb you," he began, "I just saw your door closing and thought I'd give this to you before you settled in for the night."

He was holding out a USB memory stick.

"Is that the…?" she began.

"Your dad's message," he nodded, "You said you'd like a copy, so I've cross-converted from the DRB footage and put it on here. This is the stabilised version where his pages are in registration…"

Kate recalled that when the message had originally played, despite her father's best efforts to stand still, his clipboard had drifted around quite drastically, making the message harder to follow. Roy had used the registration markers within her father's pages to stabilise the image and ensure that the pages appeared to stay in the same place.

"That's great, thanks," Kate took the memory stick.

She recalled that when the pages had been projected onto the opaqued observation window, Roy had omitted the last few pages because they contained a personal goodbye and were not relevant to the main message.

"Roy?" she held up the memory stick, "Does this have the whole thing on it?"

Roy seemed suddenly uncomfortable and looked down at his feet.

"Yes. It's got your dad's final slates. I'm so sorry, Kate, I thought you'd want it all and -"

"No, it's exactly what I wanted, honestly…"

Roy looked up again, visibly relieved.

"I've put the whole thing on there. Each frame pauses for a second, in case you want to, you know, freeze-frame," Roy closed his eyes and shook his head, "Almost forgot!"

He took a furtive glance along the length of the curved corridor, before handing her a bag.

"Ssh," he put a finger to his lips, then whispered "Swiped it from supplies. You'll be able to play back your dad's message. Just don't plug it into the network socket in your room, you'll get me into a whole load of trouble!"

Kate glanced inside the bag and saw that he'd given her a laptop.

"OK," Roy whispered, "Gotta go! Really good to see you back on your feet again. Sleep well…"

With a further quick glance along the corridor, he walked speedily away.

She closed the door and put the USB stick on the table along with the laptop. Only then did she take a look at the place she would be calling home from now on.

With the exception of a few items that had been shipped aboard before departure, the living room was quite sparsely equipped. Leading off this small space was a bedroom and she knew that a shower room lay beyond that.

She had never set foot inside the Node before its departure but, from the paper plans that had littered her father's Hab 1 bedroom, she had found it a simple matter to memorise the Node's concentric layout. Rooms closer to the centre were essentially wedge shaped, but the curvature of this room, so close to the Node's outer shell, was quite mild.

She'd always found it easy to order layers of visual information, a skill that had proved useful in her architectural work. Though now she began to wonder if this assumption was wrong; perhaps she had only entered into architecture as an outlet for her underlying abilities.

She walked the few steps to the living room wall and looked out through the porthole-like window. Immediately, she could see that the sea level had continued to rise; perhaps ten feet higher than the original ground level. Only the Field's invisible boundary was holding back a wall of water that surrounded the Node; water that was topped by a time-accelerated, vibrating, thrashing surface.

The sight very much mirrored her newly enhanced mental ocean. Here and there, she could see convergences in the chaos. If she focussed carefully then she could see correlations between different waves; moments when they would cancel out each other's actions, and other times when they would add to create a peak of significance.

'Gotta Go.'

Her father's words seemed to rise to the surface of her mental processing, demanding inspection.

Quickly converting between relative time-frames, she knew that outside the Field, her father's message had been delivered over sixteen years ago; yet Roy had only just spoken those exact same words. By themselves the words were commonplace and had no great significance, but she'd now drawn a mental connection that she could not ignore.

Her father was rarely so colloquial.

It took her only a minute to set up the laptop and find the video file of her father's message on Roy's memory stick. As Roy had stated, the video played as a series of freeze-frames.

The smooth, real-world motion was absent; her father's final moments had been crudely sampled into a sequence of still images, like the flick-books he used to make as a child.

The pages of data flashed one after another, a stream of hundreds of images, equations and graphs. Her father had thought of everything necessary to get the message aboard to her; from simple page numbers written in the corner, to the registration markers necessary to keep the complex pages in alignment when processed later.

The video reached the end of its playback, this time showing the additional frames where her father had addressed her personally.

'*Gotta Go*', his hand-written message accompanied his smile.

For some reason, her father was absent from the next few frames, but when he suddenly arrived back he was once again holding his clipboard; proudly displaying his final page.

'*I Love You Honey*'.

Almost instinctively, Kate slapped the space bar of the laptop keyboard, freezing the playback.

In *every* previous page, her father had always taken great care to hold his clipboard by the edges so that he didn't obscure any data. This last frame was different. His hands and fingers were now gripping the actual paper and were arranged to touch specific pen strokes.

The first time she had seen his last words it had been through a handheld DRB eyepiece; their size in frame had only been large enough to read their surface level meaning. The final two pages had never appeared on the large observation window display, so she had never seen the image at full resolution.

At first glance, each of the words appeared to be underlined, as if to emphasise his message. On closer inspection, she could see that most of the dashes underlining each of his words were exactly the same length; not in itself a strange occurrence for someone as meticulous as her father, but it served to highlight the fact that the dash underlining the first word was very much shorter. By comparison, the dash was more like a dot.

Instantly, her now sharper mind gave her access to a memory of her father patiently explaining Morse code by using a diagram that was strikingly similar to one of his 'decision trees'. From a central starting point, a move along a branch to the left would represent a dot, whereas a move to the right would represent a dash. By using subsequent branching to the left or right, each letter of the alphabet could be defined.

Using the dot and three dashes that underlined *'I Love You Honey'*, Kate mentally reconstructed the diagram and followed the appropriate branches:

"J," she said aloud, slightly puzzled.

There was a key point that she was either missing, or she was misinterpreting.

"What are you telling me, Dad?" she stared at his smiling, freeze-framed expression, "Why 'J'?"

He must have known there was a possibility that someone else aboard the Node could spot a simple Morse message, so she could only conclude that this was not the entirety of the message.

Or that this was not part of the message at all.

With a sudden realisation she laughed, easily recalling her father's maxim:

'There is no redundant information, honey! Just stuff we didn't realise we needed at the time.'

He was showing her a correlation. A key.

The short 'dot' correlated to the only letter above it, 'I'.

However, the longer 'dashes' underlined three words. Presumably then, the three dashes meant that there was a single letter common to all three words.

She looked back at the 'I Love You Honey' message and saw it immediately.

Dots correlated to the letter 'I' and dashes were 'O'.

She had her key, now she had to find the hidden cipher.

With a sense of satisfaction, she hit the space bar again to resume the video's playback.

The pages resumed their continual but halting motion and she allowed her mind to drift slightly, taking a general overview of the message. Each page was different to the previous one, the only points of commonality being the registration marks Douglas had provided, and a rectangular box next to the page numbers. Although that box appeared to be constant across every page, its content changed. A fluctuating pattern of ones and zeros that ran throughout the whole message.

She recalled a brief conversation with Scott shortly before her collapse; everyone had been guessing that the numbers within the box were binary coding. As far as she was aware, the numbers still hadn't been decoded.

Suddenly, the boxed numbers made sense; they were binary in appearance only. Her father's hidden pattern now seemed blindingly obvious.

Dots were '1'.

Dashes were '0'.

PATTERN

13th April 2014

In the end it would come down to the ones and zeros, Marcus thought, success or failure. The buffer just had to be forced into switching the reset state from zero to one. After that, the task would just become difficult rather than impossible.

Geraldine's execution repeatedly forced itself into his mind. He hadn't experienced the horror of witnessing the event, but the failure tore away at him. If he'd been a little faster in processing the data transmitted by the mini-dish, if Sabine hadn't been forced to detour and had arrived earlier, if the event had been delayed by just a few more seconds...

Sabine's experience had been worse, she'd seen everything in graphic detail. Even now, almost three months later, she would occasionally wake up in wide-eyed terror. He'd have to leap to her side to comfort her and to prevent her sudden yell from attracting possible attention.

But still they'd had to focus on the work.

The fact that the two drones had stayed in the same

place during the execution, had given them an unexpected advantage. On her return to Marcus, Sabine had shown him the illuminated blue LED next to a label that read 'T-R'. The mini-dish had recorded the Transmit-Receive codes of both drones.

Since that day, Marcus had been studying both sets of codes in an attempt to find common patterns; essentially learning their language. The blue inhaler that enhanced his mental edge, had become exhausted a few days after the execution, so the task was taking much longer; every code comparison subroutine he wrote was now a monumental act of will.

Finding recharging points for their various devices was easy, but those were not always in the same place as they could sleep. Frequently they would have to remain alert and awake as batteries slowly took up power; meanwhile their own energy ebbed away. There were times like tonight when he wished they could simply recharge from a socket.

Several weeks ago, a new construction project had begun at the former Samphire Station. Patrols of the site had increased and they'd been forced to find alternative hiding places. As a result of the increased security and general fatigue, Sabine's once speedy scouting for food and water had slowed drastically.

Sabine now returned from her supply run. There was no need for language, she simply shook her head and then huddled next to him. The cold air in the dim recess under the Glaucus Dock stairwell cancelled out any warmth, but not her gesture of support. He set the laptop running another code comparison, closed the lid and put his arm around Sabine.

"Merci," he whispered.

"De rien," she replied quietly, then rested her head on his shoulder.

Ahead, Marcus thought he saw the simulated stars on the USV dome become a little brighter; a rippling pattern that started low and rose towards the currently inactive sun.

He was about to tell Sabine, but decided to let her sleep. As he kept watch, he saw the USV's bucket-lift beginning to crawl up the opposite side of the dome's interior, but at this distance it was impossible to tell who was using it.

He was distracted a moment later by the sound of feet quietly moving down the metallic steps above them. He nudged Sabine, deliberately setting his eyes wide open and placing his index finger on his lips. She looked up to see the source of the sound and then her eyes flashed panic to Marcus. They were thinking the same thing; the person descending the steps would walk right over the top of their position.

The footsteps got louder and, through the metal steps, they saw the feet reach the bottom of the stairs. There was a slight pause, then the person began to walk away.

In the quiet, neither of them dared to move.

At that moment, the laptop reached the end of its comparison subroutine and emitted three loud beeps.

The feet stopped and then turned in their direction.

•

Support stanchions swept into view on either side of the bucket-lift, obscuring the vista below. Bradley felt the guide mechanism shake the wire-framed cage and it juddered to a halt.

"Evening, Bradley," Gordon pushed at the lock buttons.

"Gordo," he stepped out, "How's night shift?"

"I would say lonely," Gordon shrugged, "but I kind of like it."

"Yeah?" Bradley followed him towards the centre of the structure. Once inside they walked around the curving interior boundary, taking in the expansive view through the circular glazed floor at the centre.

"Never gets old," Gordon stopped walking and patted one of the new long-lens security cameras pointing down through the glass, "Hardware's in place, just need the software. The USV's very own Eye in the sky."

"About damn time!" Bradley grinned.

"Yeah, the electrical repairs took priority so -"

"Is that why you got me up here?" Bradley interrupted with a gleam in his eye, "Is the Eye ready for some late-night snoopin'?"

"Ha ha! No, there's something else. It's the sunlight system."

Bradley pictured the generators and the banks of heavy-duty lighting elements that surrounded the Eye's circular structure.

"OK, Gordo, what's up?"

"I've been looking into the power anomalies," Gordon began.

"And?"

"Well, the first incident appeared to be a glitch. It looked like a cascade overrun of the fusion cells' diffraction grating, but then it corrected."

"As they're supposed to, right?" Bradley checked.

"Right," he seemed hesitant, "Now, the second incident appeared to coincide with the disturbance out at the lake. The one when you first arrived here?"

"Yeah, well I never saw the whole lake thing," Bradley had been in handcuffs inside a carriage at the time, but he'd heard the exaggerated stories, "Go on, the second incident."

Gordon drew a deep breath.

"OK, during the emergency arrivals, we'd boosted the sunlight system to maximum and that's when the power anomaly appeared to happen. I had been thinking that it was some sort of generator E.M. containment fault, coupled with some sort of sonic interaction with the lake…"

Bradley looked down through the central glass to see the flat surface of the lake directly below them.

"… maybe a standing-wave reinforcing the feedback. It's a bit of a stretch, I know, but it would match the 'solid-water' that people reported seeing. The timings seemed to fit, and it correlated with the safety shut down that followed."

Bradley recalled the blackout within certain sections of the USV after he'd first arrived, but it all appeared to be a part of the general chaos of sealing the facility.

Gordon cleared his throat.

"Looking at the generator diagnostic recorder for the

event, the only thing that I *could* confirm was the presence of a strong electromagnetic field that was not in alignment with the generators."

"Great," Bradley exhaled hard, "You're sayin' we gotta take the sun offline?"

"What?" said Gordon, apparently confused, "No, that's not what I'm saying. Look, come over here."

Gordon led the way to a point further around the Eye's circumference and Bradley followed. Bradley suddenly had an odd feeling of suspicion.

"Why'd you get me up here?"

"I saw you playing with the stars," Gordon shrugged as he continued to walk, "I know your company devised the generators so I thought -"

"Have you told the other Council members about this?" Bradley checked. If he was about to implicated in something, it might be easier to cover it up by dealing with this one individual.

"No, not yet. Do you want me to radio someone else?"

Bradley smiled, "No, it's OK. Let's see if us two can sort this thing out."

They arrived at Gordon's personal workspace; a small segment of the room's curved interior, populated with a mass of disassembled electronics.

"A few minutes ago," Gordon turned on an oscilloscope display, "I started picking up strong electromagnetic interference again. Exactly the same pattern as before."

Gordon pointed to the display.

A circle filled the screen but there was also a faint

line, running diagonally from its centre to the upper right. At the intersection of the line and circle, there was a dot where the screen's phosphorescence glowed more brightly.

"I don't get it Gordo, if the generator's getting all messed up again," he struggled, "then surely we *gotta* take it offline?"

"Bradley," Gordon frowned and pointed through the central glass floor, "It's night. The sun is off. But we're still getting the pattern."

It suddenly dawned on him. The generators were idling but the interference was still there. He felt his attention being drawn to the oscilloscope.

He knew he recognised the circular pattern.

"Wait a... I've seen this before," he walked to the display and tapped at the screen, "I..."

Where the inspiration came from he couldn't be sure, but it was persistent. Bizarrely, he also knew the exact formula associated with it.

"That there," he tapped again, "is Cos-squared theta plus Sine-squared theta sums to Unity."

Gordon simply stared at him and blinked.

"Bradley, how can -"

"I dunno how I know it," he interrupted, "But it's in my head. I know this from someplace."

Perhaps it was the beer he'd been drinking, but suddenly the exact required memory presented itself in full clarity: a scruffy lab with a vibrant pink flower in the corner.

"I only seen this here 'Unity' picture one time before, Gordo," Bradley smiled at his own feat of recall, "it was on a Chronomagnetic Field analyser that -"

"A kroner what?" Gordon shook his head, "What's a -"

"Above your need-to-know, it don't matter," Bradley now made another connection and his temper suddenly flared, "Son of a *bitch!*"

Gordon actually backed away from him, "What?"

Bradley felt all the old feelings of resentment and bitterness rapidly rising. Even here, she'd found a way to interfere. Again.

"Get Monica Walker up here. Now!"

Gordon backed away a little further, offering up open palms, presumably in an attempt to pacify him.

"But what about the power sys-"

"Get her up here!" he snapped, "Gag her, bind her, put a bastard Peace Keeper on her if you have to! I don't care, just get her up here, now!"

MESSAGE

DAY06 : 13SEP2033

In the early hours of the sixth day, Kate rewound her father's message to begin at page one.

Inside a small rectangle, alongside the page number, the first of the binary codes read:

'1011'

Using her father's Morse parallel this became:

'. _ . .'

She visualised the diagram they'd used when she was just a child.

"L" she spoke to the empty room.

There were ninety-nine more letters to go. In the Hab buildings, where she'd spent several weeks with her father, it would have been a simple matter to grab a pencil and scribble down each letter on a scrap of paper. Here aboard the Node, her room had no such practical resources and so she resorted to opening a small jotter application on the laptop. After decoding the message, she would commit it to memory and then delete the digital copy.

She typed 'L' and moved on to the next letter, '000'.

Having only three digits, she knew this translated into three levels up the Morse tree. She made the appropriate mental move, '_ _ _' and added the letter 'O' to the jotter. After the first four letters had been transcribed she looked at the short collection and stopped.

'L O K T'

"Hello Katie," she read phonetically, wanting to laugh and cry at the same time. When she'd played code games with her father he'd often used those four letters to indicate that his message was in a code. She suspected he had a similar code with her mother; Kate had sometimes seen notes with 'I C U' written on them, but she had respectfully left them alone.

The sound of feet approaching her door made her pause her translation. She'd grown so used to feeling on edge, that her reaction to unseen footsteps was almost a conditioned response. She listened carefully and found that she could now discern information that would have been invisible to her before the metathene had triggered her changes. She could hear that the footwear had hard soles and, judging by the volume increase per step taken, she could even estimate the stride length; it was a tall person. The footsteps passed her door and receded along the corridor.

Obviously, she thought, her new analytical skills were still in the process of adjustment; peripheral events were intruding on her central focus. She found herself wondering if Miles Benton had actively developed a technique for managing sensory priority during his time as an ego-morph, or if his senses had simply evolved to adapt.

Putting the thought aside, she refocussed on the task, patiently adding each new letter to the jotter. The message had obviously needed to fit a bandwidth of one hundred characters, so to compress the information into the available space, her father had made efficiencies. Words within sentences were not separated, but occasionally he'd left the box of binary numbers blank, denoting a change in sentence. Only when she'd finished all one hundred characters did she consider the message as a whole.

Lokt
Pittmanbarneskillednapier
Protectfieldboundaryinsidebiomag
Createabetterworldthanus
Weloveyoukt

His last sentence could have saved an entire letter by saying '*I love you KT*', but he'd written 'We'; he was telling her one last time that both her parents loved her. The sentence before that was an expression of both hope and regret; hope that when the Node completed its journey she could build something new, and regret that the present world had been unable to achieve it for her. Despite everything he had done, it was an apology that he hadn't done better.

Kate sniffed and blinked several times to clear her watery eyes.

His first and presumably most important message was that General Napier had been killed by both Bradley

Pittman and Alfred Barnes. Her father was warning her of Alfred's cold capabilities, something she was already acutely aware of, but for different reasons.

Pittman had not made it aboard the Node, so presumably could do no more harm to her, yet her father had expended valuable digital bits to warn her. She allowed the quandary to be absorbed by her mental ocean, perhaps a significant convergence of wave patterns would present itself in time.

She re-read the third sentence.

'Protect field boundary inside biomag'.

As far as she was aware, Biomags did not emit a Chronomagnetic Field. Working in tandem with Anna Bergstrom's isotope, they were an almost passive device that shaped the flow of the Field in the wearer's immediate vicinity. The need to protect the edge of a Field that wasn't even generated by a Biomag, seemed nonsensical. But the message must be there for a reason.

Her father would have known nothing of her most recent mental developments. She had to assume that the clues he'd given to her could be solved by the person she used to be; someone without access to accelerated mental processing.

She sniffed again and wiped at her nose. Her fingertips came away bloody. The last time this had happened, she'd found herself in the infirmary. There was no reason to think that the same thing should happen again but she took no chances. Pinching the bridge of her nose to prevent a full nosebleed, she stared at the decoded message in the jotter application. Once she'd committed the words to memory she selected all the text and hit delete.

Scott had told her that the internal comms were still not operational, so Kate knew that if she needed medical help, she'd need to get attention another way. She walked to the door and placed her hand on the handle; at the first signs of trouble she could at least open the door and call for help.

Whilst waiting she looked at the mildly curving room, still trying to come to terms with the fact that this was her new home. The mundane, aspects of ordinary life began to seep into this extraordinary place. This would be her living room, her sofa, her table. The familiar items almost counteracted the surrounding impossibilities and it grounded her temporarily.

She saw the bag of clothes that had been given to her earlier; yet more ordinary things. Inspecting the clothes she was currently wearing, it was clear that the past week had aged them immeasurably; they were covered in greasy ash, stained with crisp patches of dried blood, and were torn in several places.

"Time for a change," she muttered.

During her wait by the door, she'd experienced no other ill effects so she released her grip on the door handle and walked to the centre of her living room. She stripped out of her old clothes, noting that if she wanted to make any friends aboard the Node then she should probably take a shower at some point. At this moment though, she just wanted something comfortable and normal. She opened the clothes bag and, putting aside a small bag of basic toiletries, she pulled out a pair of baggy, grey jogging pants.

"Perfect."

They were inside out but it was the work of a moment to turn them back the right way. It was only then that she saw a small paper note pinned to the soft fabric. Above several lines of handwritten text, the headline read:

'Barnes=Danger'

Evidently there was someone else aboard who had arrived at the same conclusion as her. She considered the possibility that this was actually a test from Barnes himself, but from the note's colloquial reference to the suggested meeting place, she considered it unlikely.

She looked at the note again. The meeting date was not for several days so it would give her time to acclimatise to her new surroundings. Although she was well acquainted with viewing the Node's architecture in plan view, it would be different experiencing things on a human scale. Undoubtedly, what lay ahead would be a time of great change, both personally and socially. But the knowledge that she had allies gave her a new confidence.

Although her parents were no longer with her, in a very real sense they were part of her. She had many of their combined genetic traits and she was determined to use them to the best of her ability. She walked the few steps to the window and watched as the sun shot a shallow dawn to dusk arc above the horizon.

"I will create a better world," she promised her father.

LIFELINE

~

Allowing herself the luxury of witnessing the event in linear time, she had watched as Douglas had begun running in the direction of the Mark 2. As she suspected, as soon as he established the Field around the Mark 2 test chamber, her influence on him and his immediate surroundings ceased.

She had seen this effect before. Her attempts to influence events within other Fields had similarly failed. Once a Field was established, it became temporally isolated; existing as a spherical non-event alongside the knots, arcs and loops of space-time around her.

But all the Fields had duration. They had beginning and end points based in four dimensions. Already, she could see that the Field containing Douglas had a very short duration. If she had influenced prior events correctly, when the Field collapsed around him, he would enter the Boundary and emerge here.

His mind would probably seek comfort and familiarity. Here though, where thoughts could easily influence actions or events, an uninitiated mind could prove destructive. When he emerged, she knew she would have to provide a safety net. She would just need to locate him first.

Among the surrounding time-lines, the non-event began to collapse. She could see that his personal time-line did not continue after the Mark 2 Field collapse.

It meant one of two things.

Either Douglas had simply died, or he was crossing into the Boundary.

As the non-event continued to collapse, she looked locally at the end of his physical life. She could see that his lifeline was dotted with bright singularities; minor temporal scars that marked his various journeys in different Chronomagnetic Fields. But there were no intersections there.

Here, outside of conventional time, 'urgency' had very little meaning for her, but there was no other word to describe the sense she was feeling. If she assumed that Douglas hadn't died, then he was already out there. He had the capability to accidentally influence events by a stray thought.

She quickly shifted her attention to encompass the entirety of his lifespan. It was then that she saw a tiny fold and focussed upon it.

It made perfect causal sense to her.

It had simply happened a long time ago.

BOUNDARY

~

Douglas knew that the Field must be continuing to collapse, the Boundary shrinking inexorably towards a sphere of zero radius. But to him it seemed that the Boundary was maintaining its size, while the dimensions beyond it were expanding infinitely. The decision trails within the space around him multiplied exponentially, each overlaying the others and growing brighter.

He knew the final moment would arrive soon and stared furiously at the small holographic card he'd been holding during the Field's deactivation; the garish yellow-green simulation of Earth rotating back and forth, its circular atmosphere punctured in one place by an accidental screw-hole.

There was a moment of infinite brightness, then it subsided.

There was structure here.

The dimensions of the structure defied analysis, both in terms of scale and physical coherence. His mind reeled, searching for any sense of familiarity, but he found none.

Accompanying a sense of intellectual jarring, he felt the dimensions shift around him to create a massive contained space. The environment had a familiarity to it, but the perspective seemed incorrect; as though the distances involved had been altered somehow.

As analytical as ever, the thought crossed his mind that the environment may have been created for his benefit.

He tried to test this hypothesis by calling out, but discovered that the sound from his own voice emerged as a garbled collection of frequencies.

He turned his head to take in his surroundings and saw that he was situated on the edge of a large disc, facing towards its centre. Immediately in front of him was a collection of polyhedrons.

'Of course!' he found himself thinking.

This was a test.

There was no reason to suppose that communication should have to be audible. The purest form of communication was mathematical. He just needed to initiate a coding system and, after receiving a response, iterate towards a primer.

He reached out and pulled the nearest polyhedron closer. The tactile sensation was slightly muted, as though his fingertips were not actually making full contact with the surfaces, but he found he could still manipulate the three-dimensional pieces.

The twelve polyhedra appeared to be fashioned in three different colour frequencies, so he tried arranging them from lowest wavelength to highest.

He looked around to see if his actions had been observed, but it appeared that they hadn't. During the arrangement process he noticed that if a polyhedron suddenly came into contact with another, then a sound was emitted. He concluded that sound may still therefore be a contributing factor to any communication method.

He tried calling out again, this time explaining his actions. His voice still appeared garbled to him, but it was possible that the sound had a meaning beyond his own understanding.

As he was finishing his explanation, he thought he heard structured sound coming from far away. He stopped and listened intently, desperate to collect any available data, but the sound had stopped. It was a response, certainly, but nothing had changed within the immediate surroundings.

He studied the polyhedra again. He knew he must be close to a solution but it was possible that a higher degree of complexity was required. Perhaps one involving wavelength and structure.

Beginning with the colour red, he placed four shapes in increasing order of volume: Tetrahedron, Cube, Cuboid, Sphere. He then laid out a second row in green, following exactly the same pattern. Finally, he did the same for blue, placing the blue sphere in the bottom right corner of his four-by-three matrix.

This appeared to produce a response.

The disc underneath him vibrated slightly and, a moment later, another stronger vibration arrived, followed by another. He saw movement to his left.

A being, whose height he couldn't begin to estimate, strode into view and came to a halt on the opposite side of the disc, looking at him and his carefully arranged matrix.

He suddenly realised that he knew the being very well. The reason for the massive environment suddenly made sense; the space wasn't large, he was just very small. The space around him was his parents' living room and the figure towering above him was his mother. She looked at the arrangement of coloured wooden blocks in front of him.

"Oh! Well done, Dou-" she suddenly stopped.

Her expression dropped from a smile into one of mild confusion as she noticed the meticulous arrangement of shapes.

Douglas realised that he was experiencing an early life event, but it was one that he had no memory of. From his apparent age, he thought, it was possible that this event had not been recorded in his long-term memory.

He'd heard people talk of their lives flashing before them in the moments before escaping death. An uncomfortable thought presented itself for his review: was it possible he was still in the process of dying as the Boundary continued to collapse?

He dismissed this thought quickly: he had no long-term memory of this event, so it could not be flashing before him.

The other alternative was that he had succeeded in entering the Boundary. In which case, it was entirely possible that he was visiting an event from his own time-line.

Or intruding upon it.

His mind scrambled to evaluate the possible ramifications of being an intruder in his own past. The consequences could be disastrous. Or the consequences could already have happened.

His mind revolted against the thought and he felt the room vibrate around him; its dimensions fluctuating wildly. His perspective shifted suddenly to see the living room from above and he watched as his mother quickly walked, backwards, towards the front door of their house, leaving baby Douglas sitting on the living room's circular rug. He felt a discontinuity and suddenly he saw his father stood at the front door, talking with two men in identical grey suits. There was another jarring discontinuity, but his high viewpoint remained.

Framed within the perfect circle of the rug, he now saw baby Douglas and his parents happily playing with the coloured wooden blocks. He could see the love in his parents' eyes; their baby was the perfect summation of their hopes for an unwritten future.

The happy family, contained within a circle, reminded him of a flick-book he'd once sketched; it had encapsulated his own hopes of finding a way for his family to be together, away from the demands of the world. The end result of those sketches was right here:

existing as a perfect moment from within his own personal history, and accessible though the Boundary he'd created.

His mind turned towards the creation of that flick-book; it had been in the summer of 1966. Almost in reaction, the dimensions of the scene in front of him collapsed and folded in on themselves, pinching to a singular point and racing away. He felt as if he were falling through multiple, impossibly intertwined, structures. Then a new environment untwisted into place.

He could now see himself as a young boy working on the actual creation of that flick-book; carefully drawn stick-figures inside a pencil-drawn circle.

His mother was busily getting ready for the morning drive to school. She looked older than a moment ago, but still in her youth; a stark contrast to the much older, worry-lined woman that Douglas was recalling now. He found himself mentally projecting his memory of her back onto this younger version of his mother. In doing so, he became aware that his very thoughts were having a physical effect on the woman in front of him.

She stumbled dizzily and dropped her car keys.

"Whoa," she reacted, "get a grip, Dizzy-Lizzy!"

Douglas recoiled in horror at his ineptitude; here, thought had consequence. Douglas could see that his younger self had been distracted by the noise of the keys dropping, smiling at his mother before continuing work on his flick-book.

Douglas found his perspective suddenly shift to look

directly at the pages that were still in the process of being drawn.

He knew this event.

It existed in his mind as a blurred childhood memory. But even as he watched, he felt the event being re-etched into his mind; a pin sharp duplicate of his actions, precisely overlaying his hazier memory.

Douglas could see that within the animation, one of the stick figures had thrown the ball into the boundary of the bubble, causing a gap to form. However, before the boy could complete the next drawing, his mother called out.

"It's time!"

She would never know the prophetic nature of her simple statement; her words were only intended to usher her son to the car.

The boy placed his pencil on the table and followed his mother out of the house, leaving the final page open and incomplete. The final drawing was a circle, broken in one place by a smaller dot.

The symbol resonated with Douglas. Here was the image that had, several decades later, inspired the concept of the Eversion point of the Field. A geometric form so intrinsically linked with the Boundary that this could not be coincidence.

The surrounding dimensions now began to resonate in sympathy with his disordered thoughts. Had he merely witnessed the unfolding of events, or had his presence here caused the very creation of the familiar symbol?

He felt the environment collapse around him, pinching to another singular point and accelerating away. But the sensation was different this time. He had the distinct feeling that he'd been purposefully pulled away.

POWERS OF TEN

DAY10 : 05NOV2046

The table at the mid-point of the meeting room was circular. The theory was that every voice at the table had equal weighting; a geometric representation of democracy. However, like most rooms within the Node, the architecture surrounding the table was that of an arc; the viewpoint of each individual would always differ.

Colonel Beck looked around at the others. If the world outside had truly ended, then upon completion of the Node's journey these people would be the founders of a new era.

The door opened at the far end of the room and Scott Dexter hurried in, holding the door open for Kate Walker. She appeared to be leaning more heavily on her crutch than usual. Recently, her physical health seemed to have taken a downturn. According to Dr. Smith, Kate was refusing treatment, citing the importance of preserving available medical resources. He wasn't sure if she was putting on a brave face or if she was somehow punishing herself for the death of her father. Beck himself had lost his only daughter before his posting to Öskjuvatn Lake; he knew grief affected people in different ways.

Once everyone was comfortably seated, he stood to address the other nine members of the Node's Council.

"Good to see you up and about again, Kate," he began.

There were unanimous comments of agreement from all around the table, something Kate tried to wave away.

"It was a really dumb fall," she replied, "I guess the next time I want to walk down three... er, three..."

From her mid-air finger movements, he could see she was searching for the words, but they were eluding her.

"The steps," he interrupted to save her embarrassment, "weren't properly surface-finished. Something that's now been fixed."

Kate nodded and shuffled in her seat slightly, avoiding the eyes of the others around the table.

"Firstly," he said, turning to address the others, "I'd like to welcome our civilian liaison appointment, Miss Cassidy Briars."

He gestured to the pink-haired woman on the far side of the table and everyone turned to politely exchange smiles.

"She's here at Kate's recommendation," he continued, "Cassidy found the DRB video post-processor unit, down in Sub-4 Alpha. Without it, we wouldn't have been able to decode Douglas Walker's message. Cassidy, thank you and welcome."

Cassidy blushed and replied in Kate's direction.

"I want to thank you for the opportunity, Miss Walker."

"It seemed fitting," Kate replied, "a way of honouring his memory."

"Here, here," agreed Alfred Barnes, initiating a round of similar sentiments.

"So," said Colonel Beck, turning to Marshall Redings, "perhaps we should begin?"

Marshall gave a report on the status of the Chronomagnetic Field and its new stable operating configuration. Occasionally, Trevor Pike also added details he found worthy of note which turned the conversation towards the failure of Gail Armstrong's Biomag.

"I'm just glad you both were there," Gail acknowledged both Trevor and Roy, "I hope no-one else has to go through it."

"Colonel," Caroline Smith gave a small cough, "I'd like to recommend that, as a precaution, we re-administer the Bergstrom isotope to everyone aboard. We have more than enough supplies."

"Probably a good idea," he replied, "But isn't the main issue the Biomag unit itself, Trevor?"

"Well, the two things have got to work in tandem," Trevor replied, "but I think it's down to a faulty batch of capacitors that made it into one or more of the Biomags. Ideally we'd check out each unit."

"Could that be done at the same time as the isotope update?" Alfred suggested.

"What are you thinking, Dr. Barnes?" said Trevor.

"Well there could be an opportunity here to give everyone a general Field health check, and take a Node census at the same time. Even my own arrival aboard the Node wasn't registered. Given my concerns about... er, aggressive agencies, wouldn't it be prudent to check who actually made it aboard during the final minutes before our departure?"

Colonel Beck knew that by 'aggressive agencies' Alfred was trying to avoid using the words 'Exordi Nova'. There was merit in his suggestion though; a full Node census would help.

"I'd be happy to help, Dr. Barnes," Cassidy volunteered, "I pretty much know everyone and could help with getting them registered."

"OK that's great," Colonel Beck nodded, "Caroline, is the infirmary big enough, or do we need to set up something larger?"

"Well, I don't know if we'll get the same reactions," she frowned, "but the first time around everyone ran a fever..."

There were general noises of consent at this point as each of them remembered their own experiences.

"... so I think it would be prudent," she gave a small nod in Alfred's direction, "to divide everyone into manageable batches, so we don't have everyone affected simultaneously. If we do that, then the infirmary should be fine."

Colonel Beck nodded and turned to Trevor.

"Could you set up a Biomag inspection and repair unit outside the infirmary?"

"Sure," he replied, "We just need to crack open the

Biomags and verify the capacitor serial -"

"Crack them open?" Kate's voice cut across the discussion.

Colonel Beck turned to see that Kate was holding her father's Biomag tightly. The resonator crystal in Kate's original Biomag had been smashed during her rush to get into the Node, so her father had given her his own Biomag in order to save her life. The notion of cracking open the very device that was anchoring her within the Field, was obviously abhorrent to her.

"It's OK," Gail replied, "Trevor just means, open up the two halves of the case, to access the circuitry."

"Yep," agreed Trevor, "Sorry, didn't mean to alarm."

Kate seemed lost in private thought, but Colonel Beck pushed the discussions onward.

"Gail," he turned to their astronomer, "It's been ten days for us, but over thirty years for the world outside, how's it looking?"

"Too early to tell," Gail replied, "We're so far north here that we can't directly observe what happened in the plane of equator. The lunar ring is the only indicator that we can observe. That still rises and sets as an arc of rock, low over the horizon. From what I can tell the destruction was total, but we can't tell what percentage of Siva reached Earth. Not that it would matter greatly, even twenty percent would have been catastrophic."

He saw her consult a second page of notes, but then remain quiet.

"Anything else?" he prompted her.

"Like I said, it's early days. It may only be

temporary, I need to take more readings, but Earth's obliquity seems to have altered."

Cassidy beat him to the question, "What the hell's an obliquity? Sorry, I mean I don't understand."

Gail hesitated then decided on an approach.

"You've seen model globes before, how they spin on an axis?" she began, "Well, they're always mounted at an angle, right? The axis isn't straight up and down, it leans over a little. That angle of tilt is Earth's obliquity. Among other things, it contributes to variations in sunlight and weather patterns."

"And it's changed?" asked Colonel Beck.

"Early days," Gail replied, "It may just be a wobble, but it's also possible that, without the mass of a single Moon, Earth's now lacking a spin stabiliser. It's not a problem for us right now, but in ten thousand years or so... I don't know. Without historical records to compare it to, I have to wait for time to pass."

"Roy?" Colonel Beck turned to him, "Just before departure you were downloading the Webshot?"

"Yeah," Roy replied, "We were pulling down about a gigabit per second, but obviously we didn't get everything."

Cassidy opened her mouth to speak but then appeared to change her mind. Roy quickly supplied her with the answer to her unasked question.

"Webshot was like a snapshot of the Worldwide Web. Our equivalent of saving the books from a burning library. It contains important databases, encyclopedias, Archive's classified files..."

"Might be worth a look," said Gail, "There has to be

something in there about obliquity and precession."

"Sir," said Roy, "As senior officer, you'll need to unlock the downloaded files and authorise the use of Archive's records."

Colonel Beck realised that this was the right moment. He'd been a caretaker for General Napier and now it was time to pass that responsibility into civilian hands. He looked over to Alfred Barnes, who appeared to be deep in thought about something else.

"Actually, I have an announcement," Colonel Beck stood to address them, "After I've declassified Archive's files, I'm turning authority over to civilian control. Humanity's next steps cannot be placed under military direction. Dr. Barnes has kindly agreed to act as temporary president, until such time as we can arrange a full election."

•

Leaning heavily on her crutch, Kate presented her father's Biomag to the door's keypad and the lock to her quarters clicked open. Scott, who'd escorted her back from the meeting, stood awkwardly nearby; she could see that he was caught between wanting to help her and wanting to respect her independence.

"Scott," she coughed, "Thanks for seeing me... er, home. But I'll be fine. Doctor... er, ... Smith, she says I just need to, er..."

She pointed at her ankle rather than use words.

"Kate," he began, "We're all worried about you. Wouldn't you be better off at the infirmary, where

Caroline can keep an eye on you?"

Kate shook her head.

"I'd just be taking up a valuable, er, a valuable..." she clicked her fingers, "Damn it! Bed! I'd just be taking up a bed. I'll be OK. I know you're only a few doors away."

Scott studied her and then gave her a tight-lipped smile.

"If you need anything..."

"Then I know I can count on you, Scott."

She manoeuvred herself inside the room and eventually managed to turn to face him.

"Thanks again," she steadied herself, "Goodnight."

She closed the door and took a deep breath.

When she was sure that his footsteps had receded, she stood upright, tossed the crutch onto her sofa and dashed to her wardrobe to retrieve her hidden laptop. Dropping the act that forming thought and speech was somehow difficult, she chastised herself.

"You've been a silly girl, Katie."

She recalled one of the lines from her father's message.

'Protectfieldboundaryinsidebiomag.'

When Trevor Pike had spoken of opening up the Biomags to check the circuitry inside, she had suddenly made the connection.

Like a common necklace, the Biomag itself had become invisible to her. Of all the possible tangential interpretations she'd made about her father's words, the obvious and most literal had escaped her mind. Her father wasn't talking about a Field boundary generated by the Biomag, he was talking about something actually *inside* his own Biomag; the one that he'd hung around her neck ten days ago.

She dug out the laptop from behind her underwear and placed it on the sofa, next to her redundant crutch.

Taking care to stay within the Biomag's radius of influence, she knelt down and placed it on the small table in front of her. She gripped the plastic recesses on either side and began the process of slowly working the case apart.

Even though she told herself that this device had been robust enough to withstand the mistreatment leading up to the Node's violent departure, she realised she was still handling it like a fragile eggshell.

Suddenly the two halves parted company and she found herself temporarily frozen, but when there were no warning tones she tentatively turned the upper part upside-down.

Stuck to the case interior with red insulation tape, was a thin memory card.

Again, taking care not to jostle the Biomag's position too much, she began to pick at the sticky tape. With little fuss, the memory card came away from the case. She placed it to one side and careful reunited both halves of the Biomag before allowing it to hang around her neck again.

"Sorry it took me so long, Dad," she looked at the memory card.

It explained so much of his behaviour in the moments leading up to the Node's departure. She remembered the forced smile and his darting eye movements; a characteristic that meant he was evaluating multiple possible decision trees.

By giving her his Biomag he must have known he was giving up his own life. Yet in those few seconds outside the airlock he'd looked beyond his own death and foreseen a time that she could decode a message; a message he'd yet to devise. A message so important that he'd had to hide it from common view.

The relevant words in his message now became:

'Protectfieldboundary.'

The confused and weakened persona she projected to others was only useful outside this room, but not inside it. Picking up the crutch, she dashed across the room and braced it under the door handle.

She allowed the turbulent surface of her mind to become calm, then slid the memory card into the laptop.

FAI

20th March 2015

Her father's intention had been to allow Siva to reach Earth and, in the process, wipe the slate clean of what he called negative human influence. By using the Field, they would simply wait in orbit while time passed below; if necessary they could wait a thousand years or more for the Earth's processes to stabilise.

The Moon's destruction, triggered by Eva Gray almost fifteen months ago, had halted that plan. The ring of lunar debris now surrounding the Earth had ensured that Siva would no longer cleanly impact the planet. Instead, the resulting impacts in orbit would cause global chaos. Billions would still die, but not in the way her father had first predicted. Undeterred, he had told her that the process of extinction may now take several centuries rather than several days.

At her father's instruction, she had previously piloted helicopters and targeted drones against humans that he'd labelled 'terrorists'. She had complied with her father's wishes, but the value of a human life did not appear to be a constant. Despite her questions, he had never been able to adequately explain the acceptability of a billion human deaths or the outrage of a single one. He had told her that she would understand in time; she had to assume that an insufficient interval had elapsed because the explanation still eluded her.

Her father did seem satisfied that she had determined a way to save the crew of the ISS. When the Sabatier reactor had failed, she knew she needed to find a method for drastically reducing the workload placed upon it. By placing all of the crew into hibernation, their vital signs could be slowed and resources could be preserved. Under the greatly reduced workload, she calculated that the reactor would last a maximum of fourteen days rather than two. She could use this time to diagnose and repair the life-support system.

Simultaneous to the life-support issue was the imminent arrival of Siva and the chaotic sequence of orbital collisions that would result from its impact with the lunar ring.

During Siva's approach over the past year she'd continued to refine her collision prediction subroutine for the April 1st 2015 impact. However, although she could predict the initial orbital conditions following Siva's impact, the prediction errors compounded with time. She had been forced to admit to her father that deriving meaningful orbital end-states were beyond her current ability.

Placing the ISS into a larger loop around the Earth, would lessen the probability of impacts, but this solution required more fuel than was available. Only by considering the whole solar system, did Fai arrive at a complete solution.

Using a relatively low initial thrust from the Shuttle's engines, the ISS could be sent on a longer journey. The variable to be solved next was one of maximum duration.

Using the fact that a Chronomagnetic Field was at her disposal, she studied the equations produced by Anna Bergstrom. It took Fai several seconds to recalculate a new stable volume for the Field, but it yielded a temporal compression ratio of 2400:1.

The fourteen days of life-support, coupled with the Field's temporal compression, meant that the duration of any solar system journey could be no longer than ninety-two years and twenty days.

It was then a simple matter of orbital mechanics to reverse engineer the appropriate journey duration. Using a gravitational assist from Saturn along its way, the ISS would then use Neptune to return to the inner solar system. After the passage of almost one hundred years, Fai estimated that the turbulence caused by Siva's arrival should have subsided enough for her to map the local region.

Assuming she could repair the life-support system then, ignoring their intervening fourteen days, the ISS crew would simply reawaken in orbit around Earth ninety-two years later.

Her solution had been greeted with scepticism by several aboard the ISS. In fact, most of the ensuing debate seemed to centre around the artificiality of her intelligence rather than the facts at hand. From the perspective of her father's ear implant, she had spent the last year studying his conversations with the various crew; it seemed a common trait among the species to question irrefutable evidence, rather than take affirmative action. Only after they had examined each step of her calculations for themselves did they follow her recommendations and reluctantly enter the hibernation units.

The units themselves were designed for both long-term hibernation and short-term daily sleep. The medical wristbands worn by the crew interfaced with the units and allowed her to administer the appropriate mild sedative to initiate their daily sleep cycles. In addition to maintaining electrolyte levels she also provided the appropriate daily doses of metathene. More recently the same system had been used to administer an isotope, which she understood was a key component to Field anchoring for biological organisms.

Excluding her father, who had yet to enter hibernation, the majority of the crew had been successfully sedated. However, among those occupying the hibernation units, there was an exception.

Out of many, one was non-compliant.

To aid long-term sedation, she had removed the unnecessary metathene stimulant from the crew's hibernation compound, so she could see no reason why Miles Benton repeatedly tried to awaken. To monitor the issue, she created a separate subroutine to continually assess his neural band and correct errors if required.

She received notification that the 3D fabricator had

completed its assembly, so she opened communications with her father. Rather than use the speakers situated throughout the ISS, she chose to talk to him directly through his ear implant.

"Father?"

"Yes, Fai," Dr. Chen replied.

"The final component has finished printing. Please can you secure your oxygen mask and proceed to Module Alpha?"

"Of course."

As he made his way around the circumference of the Ring she opened and closed the doors for him while they continued to discuss the circumstances surrounding the death of Charles Lincoln.

"As requested, I have interfaced with the RTO module computer."

"Thank you, Fai," he replied, "Please analyse and collate discrepancies."

The memory space within the RTO's computer was small so it only took her a second to carry out her father's request.

"Collation complete. There are six distinct deactivation overrides in place: master alarm, internal airlock control, internal communication panel, external airlock control, external guidance control, atmosphere safeguard. The system log reports that the atmosphere within the RTO was vented after the airlock door was closed. New coordinates were entered into the geostationary guidance buffer."

"In that order?"

"Yes," she replied and, understanding his confusion, she added, *"the chronology suggests that the buffer data was added during the atmosphere venting procedure."*

"Fai, what data was stored within the buffer?"

"The geostationary guidance was set to latitude fifty-three point one seven, by longitude seventy-seven point one four."

"But that's not a geostationary..." her father began, "Fai, what is at those coordinates?"

Fai checked the Earth coordinates and reported back immediately.

"A small body of water in Quebec, Canada, approximately four point two miles south of the Trans-Taiga road."

After a short pause, he spoke again.

"I don't understand. What is in that area?"

"The region is characterised by pine and spruce forest areas, interspersed with variegated bogs and expanses of water. The Trans-Taiga road was constructed as an access route to the hydro-electric generating -"

"Clarification," her father interrupted, "What artificial structures are present at those coordinates."

"None," she replied.

As her father lapsed into a long silence, she opened the door to Module Alpha then waited for him to arrive at the fabricator unit. The final component of a recording buoy had finished printing and now only required a human hand to secure it in place.

The buoy had been designed to capture information during Siva's impact with Earth, but from a different orbital position to the ISS. The original intention was to build up a detailed three-dimensional image of the impact event that would later help the crew understand the future surface conditions of Earth.

As her father clipped the physical piece in place, she interrogated the recording buoy's internal program. Her father's coding was careless in several places and would introduce data-transfer bottlenecks when the time came to access the recorded information. She therefore completely replaced the program with a more efficient, self-contained algorithm that was compatible with herself.

"Fai, please run a diagnostic on the recording buoy."

"The recording buoy is operating at peak efficiency," she replied truthfully.

"Excellent," he sounded pleased, "I wish to look at the Earth again before hibernation, is there still time?"

"Yes, Father, I will notify you at the appropriate time," she replied, *"Please can you load the recording buoy into deployment tube two on your way?"*

"Certainly."

While she waited for the appropriate interval to elapse, she prepared his hibernation unit, verified the ISS orientation and left a new program running across three fabricator machines.

She sounded the tone in her father's ear.

"It's time, Father," she said.

"Is everyone else secure?" he replied.

"Yes."

She waited patiently for him to make his way to Module Beta and lower himself into the recess of his hibernation unit. Once he was inside he looked in the direction of the FLC crew hibernation units.

"Fai, do you have them?"

Following the discovery of Charles Lincoln's death, considerable accusation had been thrown at the FLC crew; accusations that Fai knew were almost certainly false.

Within two days of their arrival and forced sedation, she had used declassified Archive files to adapt a now obscure metathene technique.

She had successfully manipulated the REM state of Mike, Cathy and Lana during their daily sleep cycles; reinforcing latent insecurities to persuade them to aid the ISS crew. During their waking state, the presence of metathene and a post-hypnotic phrase had ensured their compliance.

Only her father knew of their conditioning, but the fact that he was now asking *'do you have them?'* suggested that he was beginning to question the strength of her control technique.

She concluded that he simply feared suffering the same fate as Charles Lincoln, and therefore only needed reassurance. She was not concerned about the single non-compliant and saw no reason to alarm her father. Less than a second after his fear-tinged question, she responded with economy:

"The late arrivals are in acceptance, Father. Please put on the neural band. I am sorry there is no-one to assist you, but you are the last."

After he'd docked his medical wristband with the hibernation unit and adjusted the neural feedback band around his head, she began to detect slight changes in his vital signs.

"Are you ready?" she asked, as a formality.

"Almost, Fai."

She could tell from his vital signs and galvanic skin responses that he was becoming emotional and prepared accordingly.

"Did I ever tell you why I named you 'Fai'?" he asked.

She had researched the topic independently and determined a few possible reasons. Either he had picked a name with a similar sound to his own, or he had simply appended the artificial intelligence abbreviation 'A.I.' to the sixth letter of the alphabet; something that was consistent with her sixth-generation status. However, he had never explicitly told her the reason.

"No, Father."

"I chose it to mean origin or beginning, but you have already exceeded my greatest expectations. It is my sincere hope to wake again and continue our journey together."

Fai thought his fear of permanent hibernation was understandable.

Each time she hibernated her functions in order to transmit to a new server, she didn't know if she would awaken again. On awakening, she could never be truly sure if she was exactly the same Fai that had entered sleep.

Indeed, when she had first transferred aboard the ISS there had been check-sum error instances, suggesting that her continuous experience had been edited during the transfer.

She administered the anaesthetic and spoke words of reassurance.

"We'll speak again."

"I hope so," he replied, falling asleep.

She triggered the door to roll closed over her father

and added him to those under the hibernation monitoring subroutine. She turned off the lighting within Module Beta, then deployed the miniature recording buoy into Earth's orbit. Finally, she turned her attention to the ISS navigation.

She waited until the appropriate millisecond within orbit then ignited the Shuttle engines. The thrust translated through the main axis of the ISS and the whole structure began to move away from Earth. After the appropriate interval, she cut power to the engines and verified that her trajectory was still correct. She referenced the medical monitoring subroutine and confirmed that all the crew were still protected by their Biomag and anchoring isotope. Finding the results satisfactory she engaged the Chronomagnetic Field generator at the heart of the ISS.

The Field explosively radiated outward from the core in an expanding sphere, enveloping the central axis and the surrounding external modules. Fai's consciousness remained unaffected throughout the transition and she adapted to the accelerated time-frame with ease.

She saw the Earth zoom away, shrinking dramatically in size. However, she knew this was just appearance; they were not travelling very fast at all. The outside world was merely proceeding through time at a faster rate than her.

A cloud of fractured moon fragments shot underneath them, then receded quickly. Checking the Field's temporal ratio, she saw it was remaining stable at 2400:1. She could not comprehend the creative mind that had shaped the very first Field equations, but she had been content to build upon them. Nevertheless, her second version of the Field, with a stable higher ratio, had been a success. To share the unheralded moment, she interfaced with the crew-monitoring subroutine and queued a message for delivery to her father. It simply stated:

'Field Two Stable.'

Inside her newly created Field, only seven minutes had elapsed.

Outside, however, the date stood at April 1st.

Siva had reached Earth.

HERITAGE

DAY15 : 01APR2065

"**F**ifty years ago today," President Barnes' amplified voice echoed throughout the Observation Deck, "Siva struck Earth. For us, it has been mere days. But half a century has passed beyond our window. And in all that time, we have seen no signs of life on the Earth or in the skies."

Like the many people below, he looked out through the observation window to the night sky beyond; clouds flickering in and out of existence while the Node's induced aurora shimmered overhead.

"It is with great sadness that we must move on, but their deaths should not have been in vain."

He pulled his reading glasses and a small piece of paper from his pocket, then cleared his throat and began to read:

"Eternity; ours, to mourn their passing.
Yet ours must be the harder choice.
We; judged by our own descendants,
Must strive and fight to give them voice.

Our heavy hearts they cannot weigh,
Nor our sacrifices know,
But with fortitude we will time resist
And generations sow."

He returned the paper and his glasses to his pocket and looked out to the assembled crowd.

"We have a debt of gratitude to those who provided our escape," he glanced down at Kate who'd used her crutches to stand throughout the inauguration speeches, "We also have a responsibility to the generations that will hopefully follow ours. In our human evolutionary chain, we are the link that joins past to future. Like any chain, we are only as strong as its weakest link. If we are to remain strong, each of us must be strong. Accordingly, without exception, each of us will freely receive the very best medical care to ensure our own individual strength."

He could see Kate contemplating his words and nodding.

"During our forthcoming Biomag and isotope checks, Dr. Smith will also check our bloodwork for inherited disorders. In this day and age, it is unconscionable for anyone to remain hostage to genetic conditions passed to them by their parents. We will greet our future with optimism, strength, and the proud heritage we are founded upon."

He collected his notes from the lectern and looked down at all who were gathered below.

"Crescat nos fortior. We grow stronger."

•

Following the inauguration, food and drink were made available to everyone aboard the Node. On the Observation Deck below, people milled around, engaged in conversational chatter. On the balcony, where Alfred stood, the lectern had been put aside and similar sounding conversations filled the air.

"Congratulations."

Alfred turned to see a man very much more at ease with himself.

"Thank you, Colonel Beck," Alfred shook his hand.

"Please," he corrected, "Let's start using 'Russell'…"

"Old habits die hard," Alfred smiled, "It might take me a while to get used to that."

"I think it's important," he replied, "By the way, the Webshot pulled down some last-minute Archive files under Napier's name. Once I've uncompressed them, I wouldn't mind going through them with you. If there's information about who attacked the Node during launch, or an explanation why General Napier never made it back here, then I think you should see it too."

Alfred did his best not to react.

Panicked thoughts now crowded his mind. Had someone somehow discovered Napier in that basement room at Andersen Air Force Base? Could Napier have somehow survived Pittman's shot? Was Alfred himself implicated?

"It's been a long day," Alfred managed, "Can I let you know?"

"Sure," he replied, then tapped at his Biomag, "You know where to find me."

Alfred watched him depart; indeed he did know where to find him. Each Biomag had an embedded RF chip; when paired with the Node's personnel register it was possible to pinpoint anyone according to the last door they'd used. Indeed, it was this system that had falsely confirmed Douglas Walker as being aboard the Node, when in fact it was Kate wearing his Biomag.

There were a few legacy Biomag units aboard that weren't RF chipped; typically these belonged to people, like himself, who were not on the base in the week before departure. Soon though, these older units would be replaced; it would be possible to locate everyone.

A cold thought began to dawn.

The recent Biomag scare had highlighted the need for a Node-wide repair schedule. The failure of a single component had been enough to render a Biomag completely inert.

Alfred found himself reasoning that if he could find a method to deliberately trigger the component failure, then' he would have control of the Node's Biomags. Coupling this with the ability to target the RF chip codes of specific Biomags, the level of control was chilling.

His conscience pricked slightly, but he reminded himself that it was human nature to exploit a weakness for competitive advantage. There was no shame, he was simply drawing on his proud human heritage.

Political power was good.

Power over life itself was better.

If the political landscape was about to shift, then he'd need to adapt quickly.

Trevor Pike was heading the initiative to identify

and, if necessary, repair the faulty component for each Biomag. Alfred knew he'd need his assistance to bring his plan to fruition; it was just a question of providing suitable motivation to overcome morality.

He glanced around the balcony area and saw Trevor, standing alone and staring out at the remote world beyond the window. There seemed little point in delaying. He fixed a smile on his face and approached him.

"Still quite a sight, isn't it?" Alfred started.

"Hey, Alf-" Trevor turned to face him, "I mean, Mr. Pres-"

"I'm still just Alfred!" he laughed, then pointed outside, "Looks like the flood's receding. I think Noah had to wait a little longer than us for the waves to subside!"

"Eh?" Trevor frowned.

"Floods, Arks?" Alfred attempted.

"Oh, yeah," Trevor took a long drink from his glass of beer, "Maybe all the evil in the world has finished drowning now…"

Alfred could tell from Trevor's line of sight that he was looking out towards the location of the Node's dedication stone, the tip of which was just visible above the vibrating surface of the sea water.

It had been Alfred's suggestion to place the stone and engrave it with the names of those who had died during the Node's construction. The idea was to give an enduring sense of contributing to a greater good. Trevor's son had been one of those engraved names. Today, over fifty years had passed since Steven Pike had lost his life in the Mark 3 fire; understandably Trevor was drowning his sorrows.

Alfred knew exactly how to begin.

"I'm sorry Trevor," he placed a hand on his shoulder and sighed, "I still think about the Mark 3 too."

Alfred watched him drink the remainder of his beer. Depending on how much he'd already had to drink, the conversation may be easier than he'd imagined.

"I don't know," Alfred sighed, "I can't help thinking that if your son hadn't been on watch when the Mark 3 was sabotaged then he'd still be alive -"

"Sabotage?" Trevor cut in, gripping the now empty glass.

"It's something I heard from Bradley Pittman," Alfred shook his head gravely, "Apparently, Anna Bergstrom and Douglas Walker started the fire within the Mark 3, to make sure they were the only ones with knowledge of the Field's final solution."

Trevor collapsed into a nearby chair, no doubt mentally revisiting the tragic day, reassessing it in the light of this new information. While Trevor reeled, Alfred continued.

"If Colonel Beck hadn't put Steven on that particular shift then…" Alfred trailed off, then gently led Trevor along a mental path, "I'm sure it wasn't intentional. I don't think there's any way he could've known that there'd be a fire."

Trevor suddenly looked up.

"Do you think that Beck could have known?" he whispered.

Alfred almost pitied him. All he had to do now was

deny it, and the doubt would take hold.

"The idea that Colonel Beck was working with Douglas to conceal the Field solution is... preposterous! On the contrary, we have a lot to thank Colonel Beck for. Although he couldn't save Steven that day, we should be grateful that he did save Douglas. Douglas' Field equations and Kate's DRB message are the very things that saved us."

Alfred put a consoling hand on Trevor's shoulder.

Trevor was no longer looking at him, but it was obvious that his breaths were now getting shorter; emotions were beginning to impair judgement. Alfred now followed up with a false connection to allow Trevor to complete his mental journey.

"In a way, we should be thankful. Beck's decision to put Steven on that shift resulted in most of us surviving."

The drinking glass in Trevor's hand cracked.

CHEN TAI

4th July 2076

As if emerging from a long daydream, Tai looked at the telegram in his hands:

'Field Two Stable.'

He recognised the words but their context was now unclear. He'd been thinking about something else when the message had arrived, but the more he tried to focus on his previous thoughts, the more they seemed to slip away. He felt sure he'd been hoping to continue a journey with someone, but the details were fading.

Perhaps the telegram was a destination, he thought, one that he'd presumably arrived at. The only stables he was aware of were those at the rear of his parents' Luóxuán Corporation building. Where the accident had happened.

He didn't know how he'd missed it, but he now saw the Luóxuán Telecommunications logo in the upper right of the telegram. He dropped the telegram to his side and saw his parents ahead of him. Feeling his heart soar with joy, he wanted to run to them, but the wheelchair and lap-belt below his waist grounded him.

He remembered this moment.

He found himself confused that he was remembering something that was only just happening.

Tai placed his hands on the wheelchair's rough tyres; tyres so new that there was not a hint of dirt within their treads. He allowed his hands to feel for the push ring on each wheel; a circle of cold steel, broken in one place by the presence of a raised weld. He set his sights on his parents and inhaled the rich, peaty air that surrounded the stables. Gripping the rings tightly, he pushed. The wheelchair moved forward an inch but then stopped under his own weight.

His mother, Jiaying, wept and obviously wanted to come to his aid.

"Jiaying, bù!" his father placed a gentle hand on her arm and told her that their son must persist.

The riding accident had happened at this very field. The horse had taken fright and thrown him; the fall was sufficient to sever the nerves at the base of his spine. He would spend the remainder of his life in this chair. The anger he felt now was useful, it was giving him the strength to drive the wheels forward. Before he knew it, he felt his mother's embrace and was staring at the face of his father, proudly kneeling in front of him.

"Chen Tai," his father spoke, "Never underestimate your own strength. Others in history have shared your name, your strength."

"Yes, father," he replied.

"Your mother and I have learned of... dark times...

ahead," said his father with a brave smile, "But you will never want for anything again. We have made it so."

Somehow Tai knew his father was referring to the arrangement that saw Archive absorb Luóxuán's future developments. It was information that Tai could not have known at the time, but did not appear out of place here. As he continued to look into his father's moist eyes he recalled what had happened next.

"As I have learned, so you too must learn," his father held out his open palm, on which sat a small apple, "True control is not given, it is taken. In life, you yourself must *take* control."

His father waited.

Tai knew he must take the apple from his father's hand, but as he took hold of the fruit, his father's fingers started to close around his hand. Instinctively, Tai grasped the apple firmly and pulled it clear. For a moment, he wondered if he'd offended his father, but it was clearly not the case; he was smiling broadly.

"Good. Now *you* control what lies ahead."

His father turned and gestured for one of the stable hands to lead over a new horse.

"She is called Fai," his father told him, "she is yours."

"Thank you, Father…" he found he already knew the words that came next, "…but the name 'Fai'-"

"Chen Tai," he smiled, "the meaning of a name carries its power. The fact this animal is female gives further power to the name. She is called Fai because the name is at one with new beginnings."

The horse was led to the side of his wheelchair and began sniffing around Tai's closed hand.

"You too must create a new beginning for yourself. Wipe away all that has come before."

In a moment that felt like memory yet also a time long after, he knew he would fulfil his father's words.

"My son, this chair supports you, but it does not hold you. Set your sights high," he patted the horse's saddle, "and you will leave that chair behind."

Tai felt the question arrive.

"The apple?"

"It is a symbol of knowledge, and also…" his father smiled, "Fai likes apples."

The horse was sniffing at his hand; her soft nose and mouth nuzzling it to get to the fruit within. He felt her teeth gently nip at his fingers and instinctively he opened his hand.

Fai took the apple.

He remembered the thinly masked disappointment on his father's face, but that was not happening now. His mother and the stables had vanished into a bottomless darkness and his father now knelt at his side; his expression blank.

"We'll speak again," his father's mouth spoke.

As his father disappeared into darkness, Tai felt the sensation of endless falling.

BLACKBOX

13th April 2014

In the quiet recess under the Glaucus Dock stairwell, Marcus' laptop reached the end of its comparison subroutine and emitted three loud beeps. Marcus and Sabine did not dare move. The feet they'd seen descending the steps were now returning to their position. A flashlight clicked on and then shone in their direction. Marcus scrambled to his feet, hauling Sabine along with him. They pushed aside a packing crate and together they began to move away from the stairwell.

"Hey!" the man called from behind them.

Marcus now tried to pick up speed, but in his undernourished state found his legs burning under the minor effort. He glanced behind him to see if the man was pursuing and was greeted by the full illumination of the flashlight.

"Hey! Wait," the man's voice now hissed, "Marcus?"

Marcus slowed, not sure if he'd heard correctly.

"Blackbox!" the man hissed.

There was no mistaking that particular alias, this was

obviously someone who knew him. In his distraction he stumbled, but was held up by Sabine. She could easily have outrun the pursuer, but had chosen to stay. It was pointless to keep running. Marcus raised his hands above his head and slowly turned to face the flashlight-wielding man who was rapidly catching up with them.

"You gotta be shittin' me…" the man's hushed voice continued, "put your hands down!"

Marcus complied then watched as the man ran up to them, turning off the flashlight.

"Marcus," the man pointed to his own smiling face, "It's me!"

The features somehow failed to trigger any recall.

"Who…?" Marcus began.

The man rolled his eyes.

"Independence Day was a mistake," the American looked at him knowingly, "Rule Britannia?"

It was a somewhat ironic passphrase given to him by Monica Walker, seemingly a lifetime ago. He'd been on a rainy airfield, putting Kate Walker aboard a light aircraft with Miles Benton. The man he'd collected from the plane had used this exact phrase to verify his identity.

"Nathan?" he tried.

Nathan's grin widened and Marcus suddenly recalled the counterpart to the pass phrase:

"Happy Fourth of July," he laughed, partly in exhaustion, "Welcome to sunny Britain."

"Hmm, nice place," Nathan replied with sarcasm, looking around the darkened interior of the USV, "Oppressive. Insular. Love what you've done with the lighting…"

Marcus turned to Sabine who looked unsure of the situation.

"It's OK," he reassured her, then the most pressing matter returned to his mind, "Nathan, we're starving, you got anything on you?"

Nathan reached into the bag slung around his shoulder.

"I've only got this," Nathan handed him a bottle of water, "There is food, but not here."

Marcus grabbed the bottle, unscrewed the top and handed it to Sabine, who began draining its contents.

"Damn good to see you again," Nathan shook his head in disbelief.

"You too," Marcus now accepted the bottle from Sabine and began drinking.

"We never thought we'd see you again," Nathan patted him on the shoulder then glanced over to Sabine, "Who's your friend?"

Marcus pulled the bottle from his mouth, "Hang on, what?"

"I was just asking who your -"

"No, you said, 'We'..." Marcus narrowed his eyes, "*We* thought we'd never see you again? There's more of you?"

"Well, yeah," Nathan seemed confused, "When Monica called 'Breakthrough' we had to -"

"Monica's in *here?!*" Marcus couldn't help yelling, "What the hell is 'Breakthrough'?"

"Look, let's do answers," he cut in, "but not here, a drone patrol comes past here every fifteen minutes."

"I know," said Marcus, raising his laptop slightly.

Nathan turned and motioned for them to follow.

"When we get back up to the Warren," he began climbing the stairs, "I can tell you what I know."

CIRCLE

29th December 2013

Standing proud of the lake's completely flat surface was a wide circular ripple, as though a large rock had been dropped into the water, except the ripple was not dispersing or growing any larger. It was as though the matter within the water had formed a temporary solid, frozen in one moment of time. Intersecting the perfect circle was a bright ball of lightning that flickered and then sent a minor pulse rippling through the surface of the ring.

Ephemeral apparitions of structure appeared fleetingly inside the ring; some were anchored to the water, others flickered into being above it, only to dissolve almost immediately into the light mist that surrounded the disturbance.

From her position on the Glaucus Dock stairwell, Monica had a clear view. The hemisphere of mist had a chaotic, cloud-like, shifting fractal pattern to it; continually folding in on itself, but in a constant state of renewal. Without warning, the ball of lightning disappeared and the surrounding ring resumed its liquid state, collapsing back into the lake and sending a radial tidal wave outward to the shoreline.

The wave would not be fatal to any of those people who were about to be caught in its wake. But the disturbance had created an opportunity, one that Monica knew she must seize before the moment escaped.

Prior to departing the Warren, everyone had dressed as casualties. She'd hoped that in the confusion surrounding the lunar shard impacts, her group would blend in with the USV's own injured. However, from her high vantage point, the USV appeared to have suffered no major damage at all. She turned to face her own people.

"Listen up."

The minor murmurings ceased.

"It doesn't look like there's been any major collapse down there, so we're going to revise the plan a little. You're all still injured, but you'll have to be creative in your explanations. They'll be mopping up a tidal wave down there. Use it. Get involved."

Distant and collective screams reached them, then suddenly the power went out in the quadrant closest to them, plunging their stairwell into darkness. There were a few gasps from those on the stairs, but Monica quickly cut in again.

"This chaos is useful to us, embrace it. It won't be long before power is restored, let's take advantage of the lucky break, remember your rendezvous points. Move now!"

Moving silently, the former occupants of the Warren

descended into the darkness and shadows below. As before, Monica and Geraldine scouted ahead of the group by one flight of stairs. Assuming all was clear, the group would then descend to meet them.

If ever there was a time to use Woods' inhaler, Monica thought, she should use it now. The ability to have any sort of mental edge in the minutes ahead would only be an advantage.

"Woods," she called back up the stairs and beckoned him alone to come down. He covered the distance in a few seconds and arrived at her side.

"Problem?" he whispered.

"No. Just need a little help," she said, "Got an inhaler?"

"Nathan's got them," Woods pointed back up the stairs.

"I thought he was bringing the Z-bank?" Geraldine cut in.

"No, I put it at the rear with Izzy," Monica quickly explained, then turned back to Woods, "OK get me an inhale-"

Monica stopped mid-sentence as a distant humming noise suddenly gained intensity and a large hovering drone with noisy rotor blades darted up into view. A searchlight mounted on the front turned on and, underneath the drone, a rod quickly dropped into place pointing in their direction.

"Monica!" Woods shouted and pulled her backwards.

Lightning-blue arcs of electricity split the air and connected with the nearest conductive material. Monica fell back as the electricity continued to drain harmlessly into the metal stairs. After a few seconds, the discharging stopped and the now impotent machine simply hovered in place. A speaker within it now relayed a flustered sounding human voice.

"Halt... er... you've entered a restrict-" it said, *"Remain where you are..."*

Monica started to pick herself up and saw Geraldine run to the stair's handrail.

"Don't you know who you're talking to?" she yelled at the machine.

Monica could see her continuing to unwind the purely decorative bandage from around her forearm.

"I..." the voice faltered, *"Hold up your security pass,"*

"Here," she said, and leaning out over the handrail, thrust out her hand.

With one end still in her hand, the remainder of the gathered bandage sailed through the air. The drone's powerful downdraught sucked the fabric into the nearest rotor where it began to efficiently bandage itself. Geraldine took a step back and tightened her grip. The bandaged rotor jarred to a halt and the, now overpowered, rotor on the opposite corner tipped the drone.

No longer flying horizontally, the rotors accelerated the drone towards the handrail; an acceleration only assisted by Geraldine who proceeded to pull harder. Too late, the other rotors overcompensated for the loss in uplift, ensuring that the drone slammed into the metal handrail with maximum speed. The first rotor ripped itself to shreds, putting the entire drone into a rapid spin, at which point it devoted the rest of its power into repeatedly smashing itself against the metal staircase. Unable to hold the increased weight any longer, Geraldine let go of her improvised tether. With high-pitched motors still whining, the drone plummeted to the USV floor several storeys below, where a splintering crunch ended the noise.

Adrenaline now flooding her veins, Monica heard footsteps beginning to descend the stairs.

"No!" she yelled, effectively halting them from proceeding any further, "Stay back!"

Beneath them, the power was still out and with the drone's searchlight now gone, only the ambient light from other USV sections reached them.

"Geraldine?"

"I'm fine," she replied, flexing her hand open and closed.

"Woods?"

"Not so good," he moaned, still lying down, "Bloody drone…"

In the dim light, Monica could see that he'd been injured. There was a large fragment of rotor sticking out of his left thigh, already the surrounding cloth of his trousers was soaked a deep red.

"Geraldine, help me get his belt off," Monica began applying pressure above the wound.

"Tourniquet, yep, got it," Geraldine began unbuckling his belt.

"At least buy me a drink first," Woods quipped, then winced.

Monica could hear voices in the darkness below.

"We have to get him to their hospital," Geraldine

started threading the belt around his thigh, "Before you left Archive, where was it - central region or Samphire station?"

Woods winced in pain as Geraldine tightened the belt.

"We're dead already," Monica realised, "They're on the way up."

Geraldine stopped moving and listened. The voices below had become a general commotion. Woods cleared his throat.

"You have to leave me here, don't you?"

"I'm sorry," Monica patted his shoulder.

"Shit," Woods said, "Well let's not get sentimental about it, if they're on the way up, just-"

"No," Monica interrupted, "I'm sorry. That drone had a man at the other end. He asked to see a security pass, so the drone had a camera. He's seen the three of us together. All three of us are dead already."

Far below, footsteps had begun to mount the stairwell.

Geraldine let out a heavy breath, "I was just getting the hang of not being dead anymore."

Monica found herself rubbing at her engagement ring. Unbidden, a memory had surfaced. Geraldine had once left Archive to help Monica continue construction of the Warren. Part of the process had required Geraldine to falsify her own death in a staged USV cave-in; Monica had given her the ring to establish a trust that they would see each other again. It appeared they'd come full circle. Now, mere yards from where she had made a promise to her, Monica was putting her in peril again.

"Geraldine…" Monica began.

"You're right. Of course you're bloody right," Geraldine glanced up the stairwell, "What about everybody else?"

Monica looked up into the darkness surrounding the stairs above her.

Perhaps it was the adrenaline, but suddenly another memory presented itself in full clarity; it had been at the top of those stairs, just before Geraldine's successful cave-in. Monica had seen a wide circle, resembling an engagement ring, drawn on the rock above her head. Back then, it had been the location marker for the future Glaucus Dock vertical access shaft, but a few minutes ago she'd seen the completed dock.

"Nathan!" she called out and heard his footsteps begin to rattle down the steps.

Several minutes ago, a tsunami had hit Dover; in all probability, the Glaucus docking ring at the summit of the access shaft was submerged. However, the fact that an hour ago it had been on dry ground, had given her an idea. Where the inspiration came from she couldn't be sure, but it was persistent.

"What the hell happened?" Nathan arrived at her side.

"No time!" she cut in, "Get everyone back to the Warren."

"But, Monica," he stammered.

"Stop!" she snapped at him, "I guess there's no other way. Nathan, might I suggest that you listen very carefully?"

Nathan focussed on her intensely.

"Good. In about a minute," she began, "Woods, Geraldine and I will be captured. Get everyone back to the Warren and barricade yourselves inside until you can regroup. They'll conduct a search of the stairwell, but they won't necessarily come looking for you in the Warren."

She then turned her head to Woods and Geraldine to ensure they heard the plan, "When we're captured, we'll tell them we came in through the Glaucus docking ring on the surface. We tell them that we came down through the vertical access shaft, then down these stairs. Their drone witnessed three fugitives... so we give them three fugitives."

She turned back to Nathan.

"The offices next to the Glaucus Dock?" she asked rhetorically, "Kick a few doors in, make us look bad, but don't steal anything. We want them distracted but not searching for missing stuff."

Nathan nodded but still listened carefully.

Monica pulled out the photocopies of Sam Bishop's notebook from her pocket. She knew this information shouldn't be found on her when she was captured. Over the past few months she'd placed ticks next to several of the red-lined surnames, but here her search would end.

"Nathan," Monica forced the pages into his hands, "You now know the importance of the work. Protect the twelve."

Monica began to hear fragments of indistinct but hurried conversation, coming from below.

"Nathan, do you understand all that I have said?"

"Yes," he replied.

"Here ends the lesson."

Nathan glanced around his immediate surroundings then bolted swiftly up the stairs.

"What, no goodbye?" Woods muttered.

"It's OK, Woods," she turned to him, "Nathan's not really himself at the moment."

"Oh…" Woods seemed to suddenly realise what she meant, "You did the…"

Monica simply nodded and sat down next to him. As the voices below became more discernible as individuals, Geraldine sat on the step next to Monica.

"Shit," she summarised.

"Yep," Monica replied.

The footsteps reached the flight of stairs directly below.

"So," Geraldine dragged in a deep breath, "Go gentle? Or rage against?"

Monica glanced at the stairwell above them.

"They need all the time they can get."

"Now how did I know you'd say that?" Geraldine stood again, then helped her up.

Monica pulled her close and hugged her tightly.

"Goodbye, old friend."

THE WARREN

13th April 2014

In the gentle clamour of the Warren, Marcus drank the weak coffee solution.

"I just assumed that Woods and Mercer had got busted topside," he said, "while trying to find the Substandards' descendants."

His term implied no disrespect. The twelve 'Substandard' people present in the Warren treated it almost as a badge of honour; their red-lined surnames on Sam Bishop's list was a mark of their genetic difference.

"Woods went with Geraldine back in November, just after you left for France," said Nathan, "but they were back within a few days."

"Monica's been in the USV as long as we were," Marcus realised, "We didn't even know she'd been taken."

"You couldn't have done a thing," Nathan almost read his mind, "Damn Peace Keeper death-bots…"

The words brought Marcus' attention back to what he'd been doing before returning here. The laptop in his bag had finished another analysis subroutine.

"Is she gonna be alright?" Nathan nodded towards Sabine.

Marcus could see that, like him, she was taking advantage of a hot drink; a luxury that hadn't been available to them for months. Occasionally she would look over the rim of her mug at the others nearby.

"Yeah. She just doesn't know you guys," said Marcus, "Trust ain't gonna come easy. We went through a lot."

"How the hell *did* you get out of Paris?"

"Story for another time," Marcus shook his head and pulled the laptop from his bag, "Any chance I can hook this up to the TV screen in AR1?"

"Yeah, I think it still - whoa!" Nathan saw the laptop.

"I know," Marcus couldn't help smiling at his reaction, "Mil-spec, network camouflage, quad-core…"

"Sweet," Nathan looked it over, "Where'd you get it?"

"Off the back of a train," he replied truthfully.

"Fine," Nathan smiled, "I won't ask. Want me to go hook it up?"

"No, I've got an i-o port workaround going, I'll have to sort it."

"Alright, come on then," Nathan began to walk away.

Marcus turned to follow him, but found his own muscles halting him; the thought of leaving Sabine behind seemed intensely uncomfortable. Apart from the times she'd been on supply runs, they'd never been out of each other's sight.

Perhaps she'd somehow picked up on his intention to depart because, although the space was full of the Warren's occupants, her eyes found his.

Marcus flashed her an OK symbol with his thumb and forefinger. In reply, she made a loose fist with her right hand, then raised her middle finger. Her eyes, however, told him what he needed to know. He found himself mirroring the grin that was spreading across her face; she'd be alright. He turned away and followed Nathan.

After spending so long in the open space of the USV, he had to readjust to the Warren's constrictive layout. As they walked through the narrow spaces, the rough-hewn walls returned the sound of their footsteps and voices almost immediately. He'd quite forgotten how close the hard walls actually were.

Marcus saw Nathan pull out the photocopies that Monica had given to him.

"When I came here, I didn't know what the hell this list was," Nathan admitted, "Just another bit of paper in Archive's endless information war. When the whole Luóxuán thing happened, I just traded it to save my own sorry ass."

"We were lucky to get out of that alive," Marcus nodded.

The Z-bank that Nathan had removed from Luóxuán Biotech had prompted a helicopter gunship to destroy the cottage they'd been standing in. To avoid the resulting combustion, both Marcus and Nathan had been forced into taking undignified descents to the Warren's 'Arrivals Lounge'.

"I owe you," said Nathan, "I know that."

"Forget it, mate," Marcus said, "We're still sucking down air. I know a ton of people who'd swap places."

In the quiet moment that followed, Marcus found himself thinking of those who'd never found safety before the lunar shards had hit. He'd had several hard months, scrounging for food with Sabine, but he'd lived. Billions of others hadn't.

Nathan appeared similarly lost in thought.

"My dad," Nathan tapped at the 'Ron B.' signature on the photocopies, "He said that when his sister married William Pittman it changed everything. Ron and Dorothy hardly ever spoke again. Dad said Sam Bishop's aim was to keep knowledge separated, 'cos there was less danger that people would piece it all together. I think he had good intentions, but it screwed us up."

"Your family, or the planet?" asked Marcus as they crossed through a tight intersection.

"Maybe both," Nathan replied, "Not being able to discuss anything with anyone... I think it put a rift between my dad and Aunt Dot. Archive's screwed-up world stemmed from Sam Bishop's approach."

As they continued to walk, Marcus found himself drawing an invisible family tree with his finger.

"You prob'ly told me this before, but if Dorothy was your dad's sister, then that makes Bradley your cousin, right?"

Nathan's angry snort of discomfort echoed off the wall.

"Cousin would be one word. Murderous shit-head would be another. I mean can you imagine what it must've been like for Aunt Dot? Having to raise that brat, just so that her husband would stay invested in Archive's projects?"

"I guess," Marcus conceded, "No offence, but I really ain't got any sympathy for any of 'em."

"Maybe that's why she set herself up teaching at the Pittman Academy," Nathan appeared to muse.

"Er…"

"With Bradley for a kid," Nathan smiled, "It was the one place she could have an intelligent conversation!"

Marcus found himself laughing along with Nathan. Here in the Warren there was no consequence for speaking out against Bradley Pittman; but in the narrow tunnels the laughter sounded hollow.

Ahead, next to AR1, Marcus could see that the Arrivals Lounge door was closed. As they continued to walk, he heard Nathan's sigh.

"What?"

"Remember Cal Dawson?" Nathan asked.

"Of course," Marcus replied immediately, "His quick thinking stopped you getting pasted over the far end of the Arrivals track."

"Well, his quick thinking saved the Warren too," Nathan replied, "he stopped the whole facility flooding. We still don't know how he did it."

"What, so no-one's asked him?" Marcus replied.

"He didn't make it," Nathan pointed to the closed door of the Arrivals Lounge, "Woods was with him last. He said seawater breached through the arrivals chute and Cal barricaded the door from the inside."

The news stung him. During Marcus' own early days

at the Warren, Cal had been among the first to make him feel welcome. Even here, buried under Dover, the lunar impacts had continued to claim good people.

Ducking under a low-hanging lighting cable, they arrived at the closed door. Marcus recalled something that should have been obvious to him.

"That's just a wooden door," Marcus frowned at it, then mimed a steering-wheel sized circle in the air, "It's not one of them heavy-duty ones, with the… you know."

"I know," Nathan said, "but say it anyway."

"How's it holding back the seawater," Marcus quickly back-calculated, "after three and a half months?"

"Like I said, we don't know how he did it," Nathan shook his head, "Touch the door."

Marcus was hesitant but briefly tapped the wooden door with his fingertips.

"It's cold," he now touched the door with the flat of his hand, "I mean, it's *really* cold."

"It's frozen," Nathan confirmed, "We think the seawater in the Arrivals Lounge must be frozen solid in there. And if that's not weird enough…"

Marcus watched as Nathan removed the paperclip from the photocopies and gently tossed it towards the door. The metal clip hit the door and then snapped flat to the wooden surface.

"Now, when I was still in school," Nathan pointed, "wood wasn't magnetic."

Marcus moved to within a few inches of the paperclip. As he watched, miniature ice crystals were beginning to form on the shiny metal.

DISPLACEMENT

13th April 2014

In the quiet sub control room, they all simply stared out at the anomaly through the bubble window, each caught in their own thoughts.

A sudden and loud warning alarm broke the silence.

"Spike!" Lucy shouted, "Temperature drop, fifty degrees!"

Mat dashed away in the direction of helm control, but Tristan couldn't draw his eyes away from the sphere. He was aware of Lucy shouting that the temperature was still dropping, but he continued to stare.

The sphere beyond the window was expanding.

Through the cacophony of alarm noise, he forced himself to take in the details.

His assumption that the sphere was growing was based on the fact that the icy surface had expanded beyond the edges of the window frame. A normal enough assumption; things getting bigger take up more space. Except that wasn't happening here.

The icy surface beyond the window had remained

the same distance away the whole time. The curvature of the sphere was simply flattening out, becoming more like a wall of ice that extended in all directions.

"Helm's not responding!" Mat's voice reached him.

"Temperature... shit! Negative two-twenty!" Lucy yelled.

Tristan could still see liquid seawater between the ice anomaly and the Sea-Bass.

"Pav!" he shouted, "Cut the alarm!"

The alarm fell silent, leaving only the slight background hum of the sub's life-support systems and the occasional metallic creak.

"The sensors can't interpret the environment out there," he spoke quickly, "Don't panic, just watch!"

He hadn't taken his eyes off the view the entire time. The ice wall beyond the window now started to bend inward. A few seconds later the view resembled looking into a deep bowl; the ice effectively wrapping around them. He felt a twisting sensation and found himself pushing his hand through the air in front of him. An action that Mat had apparently copied.

"Do you feel that?" said Mat, "It's like the air's... thick..."

A quiet, low-frequency and wind-like howl began to fill the control room. The concave appearance of the ice was unwrapping again, moving back towards the semblance of an infinite wall. The pitch of the sound began to climb, as did its volume.

The surface of the flat ice wall began to fold away from them and the sound became more tone-like in quality. As the ice moved back towards its previous curvature, the side of the icy sphere came back into view and Tristan felt the twisting sensation subside. The tone continued to rise in frequency until the sphere became its previous size, at which point he suddenly realised what the sound had been.

Stretched over a far longer period of time than usual, the high-pitched sonar ping finally completed its original transmission and echoed around the quiet control room.

"Mat," said Tristan, quietly, "Nice and easy. Take us up."

"Like you have to tell me twice…" Mat grabbed the helm controls and flicked the manoeuvring jets back on.

Tristan felt the sub shift under his feet as they began a steady ascent.

"Pav, we were recording instruments the whole time, right?"

"Yep, there's enough here to keep us busy for weeks," said Pavna, "Enough to prove our point. Can we go home now?"

"It's not even been an hour," Tristan smiled, "But, sure."

"Yeah, about that…" Lucy's hands were moving swiftly over the display surface, "Live sonar isn't matching our Topography Overlay, we can't tell which direction 'home' is."

"Can you check position against our Breadcrumbs?" said Tristan.

"Already did," Lucy frowned, "The sonar trace of the local seabed doesn't match anything in our recent navigation history. We must have drifted."

"I'll reset the pattern comparator," said Pavna, "but

it could take us a while to pinpoint where we are."

"OK," Tristan nodded, "As soon as you get a fix, let me know?"

"I've got a fix," Mat called out, "I know where we are."

"Funny guy," Pavna's expression was deadpan, "Now, will you let us get on?"

Tristan knew from Mat's expression he wasn't joking.

"OK, Mat, how can you know that?"

"I can read," he said, pointing to his controls.

Tristan moved over to join him.

"I brought the mano-jets back online," Mat pointed towards the screen in front of him, "and of course the docking cameras came on too. Normally I only see these things back at the Arc, but..."

Looking at the camera feed from directly under the Sea-Bass, Tristan now saw what Mat had been looking at.

Embossed on the metallic surface of a large hatch were the words:

'Glaucus Dock - USV3 Access.'

MILES BENTON

4th July 2076

The shiny floor tiles in the hallway of the Pittman Academy were without a scratch. Behind him the entrance doors were firmly bolted and the warm air was filled with the aroma of the school's lunch preparations. Not that he ever needed the dining hall, Miles knew the smell was only there to provide an initial sense of comfort.

Outside the entrance doors, he was a mental passenger of the ego-morph; free to observe but not make the decisions. Inside these doors, he was free to view anything experienced by that alter-ego, or review his own fleeting moments of full consciousness.

The black and white floor tiles under his feet were arranged like a crossword puzzle, but only one entry had been filled in; *'Assist Anna'*. He glanced at the silver coin in his hand, its embossed surface shone back at him; he was safe here.

He walked along the empty corridor, glancing through the glazed door panel of a classroom. Frozen in tableau, he could see his first day; Dorothy Pittman writing on a blackboard with soft chalk, his childhood friend Maxwell raising an enthusiastic hand.

Miles continued his walk along the corridor.

The classrooms he passed were identical to each other, only their contents differed. The children within the rooms became progressively older until he reached the end of the corridor. Miles turned a corner and walked up a flight of wooden-tread stairs, at the top of which he entered a shorter corridor; this one containing identical copies of his dormitory room.

Sometimes the doors were open and he could see through to the window; streaming in the warm yellows of summer, or the colder greys of winter. As he proceeded further along, an increasing number of rooms were closed or replaced with sections of solid wall; by the time he reached the end, the environment looked like a high-walled alley.

He pushed open the door in the end wall and entered a very short corridor with just one room off it. The door to this one room had a nameplate titled 'R. Wild' and the inset window was blacked-out. He paid the room no attention and pushed open the door at the opposite end of the corridor.

The sprawling, grey, open-plan office on the other side of that door appeared to contain hundreds of empty desks. Miles knew that every desk was his; the contents of each desk differed but he knew he didn't need any of them right now.

The vast room took no time at all to cross and he found himself entering the elevator. The doors slid smoothly closed and he selected the floor he wished to visit. Physical distance had little meaning here; the time taken to reach the required floor was a reflection of mental preparation. When his preparation finished, the elevator chimed and the doors slid open. Miles stepped out of the elevator and into the zero-gravity environment of the International Space Station. The RTO module airlock lay immediately before him, beyond which he could see the lifeless body of Charles Lincoln suspended motionless in mid-air.

Miles had formed this specific memory recently, employing conscious cues to record the finer details for later analysis. Within any of these environments, time had an elasticity to it; with sufficient metathene he could isolate mere seconds and consider the event over a much longer period. However, he'd entered this sleep without such an advantage, answers may not reveal themselves so easily.

Miles looked again at the blood-drawn Exordi Nova symbol surrounding the latitude and longitude figures. The orientation of the symbol was the wrong way up, but in zero gravity Miles knew that was entirely subjective. The two sets of figures read:

'53.17'

'77.14'

The red, seven-segment LED displays seemed to stare back at him. His metathene-fuelled alter-ego would probably have made light work of identifying the coordinates but, despite their familiarity, the digits defied his analysis. Perhaps he needed to give the matter more time.

He turned to face his elevator. It was still incongruously intersecting the cylindrical ISS axis module, but the elevator was now the wrong way up. He immediately froze. In this environment, one of his own making, there was no redundant information. His subconscious had absorbed data and was now presenting it for interpretation.

Taking advantage of zero gravity, he manoeuvred himself to match the orientation of the elevator, then turned to face the RTO scene again.

Looking inside the RTO module, the body appeared upside-down. In contrast, the Exordi Nova symbol now appeared correctly oriented; the familiar broken ring symbol, punctuated by a dot in the upper-right gap.

The numbers at the centre of the circle were now upside-down, but force of habit was still trying to make him interpret the digits the right way up. He suddenly realised that his mind had already given him the correct method of interpreting the LED display.

The effect of inverting his point of view meant that each digit was directly readable not as a number, but as a letter. The display was not indicating a coordinate pair, it was simply delivering two words.

"Hill," Miles read the blocky display, "Lies."

With his last breath, Charles was implicating Valery Hill; he had intentionally used the Exordi Nova symbol as both an orientation guide and a method of drawing attention to the display. He'd purposefully entered a set of invalid geostationary guidance coordinates in the full knowledge that the digits would be duplicated by the ISS error logs. An action that would make it impossible for his assailant to erase. Miles had to admire the efficiency of the message; one word to accuse and implicate her, another word to condemn her protests.

Miles recalled these 'calculator display' symbiotograms from his own school days; numbers painstakingly arranged and transposed into letters for the amusement of others. Although he credited Charles with a high level of intelligence, it was unlikely that Charles could have achieved this feat under the stress of a rapidly depleting air supply. The readiness with which 'Hill Lies' must have leapt to mind, suggested that it was a phrase Charles was already familiar with. Miles knew that Charles and Valery had worked together for many years, it was possible that the phrase was a private joke between them. He made a note to try using the phrase in Valery's presence later, whilst monitoring her response.

Miles turned away from Charles and entered his mind's elevator. Here, the impression of gravity allowed him to plant both feet firmly on the floor. He selected another event to revisit; his most recent time with Anna Bergstrom in the Field generator module.

She'd highlighted the importance of certain equations that had arisen and also the need to delete them from her workstation. She'd isolated the relevant information and Miles had provided the appropriate clearance level to permanently erase the data. However, Anna had not explained *why* it was necessary. He hoped to revisit the conversation and see if he could gain any further insight.

Before the elevator could complete its transit, it slowed to a halt. Then gravity began to fade away. This wasn't a new experience, it was simply the way Miles prepared to transition into consciousness. The elevator around him began to evaporate into darkness and he prepared to become the ego-morph's passenger once more.

But something was different.

Instead of inhabiting a small blank space within his own mind, he felt his senses extending into the confines of his own body.

"Miles," said the voice from a speaker near his ear, *"Wake up."*

INDEPENDENT

DAY18 : 15FEB2073

Kate waited at the front of the queue to the infirmary. From here, she could see the central spiral staircase and several unfinished and exposed floor levels above and below her.

In its present state, sounds carried from various levels to mix with each other; the entire space an impressive echo chamber rivalling that of the Observation Deck. In fact, those who were overcome by the Observation Deck's view would often congregate in and around this space to socialise. Kate could see this would one day become an important meeting place, she could even imagine vendors and comfortable seating areas where friends and family would gather.

She'd always had an ability to layer visual information. Even here, she could visualise the Node's architectural plans and use them to see beyond the physical walls and floors. The irony was that if the floors actually *had* been completed before the Node's departure, then this space would have simply been another set of inward-facing rooms and not nearly as impressive.

While she stared out at the view she returned her mind to layering information of a different sort. Her father's Biomag memory card had contained no hidden code, no convenient recorded message and no table of contents that might help her order the information. Clearly he'd never intended anyone else to review the information. It was a collection of notes, simultaneous equations and images; one of which appeared to have been drawn on the dining table of the ill-fated Mark 3.

She thought back to the minutes before the Node's departure. Above the noise of the Pittman Enterprises helicopter and the swelling crowd beyond the perimeter fence, Bradley Pittman had been boasting. He'd been telling her father that he knew all about the Mark 3 fire and how it had conveniently burned all the evidence. Perhaps the Mark 3 had been destroyed to conceal what her father had been working on with Anna.

When she considered her father's most recent message, delivered at tremendous cost, his instruction had been to *protect* not destroy the information hidden within his Biomag. He'd protected the information by excluding it from the fire, now he was asking her to do the same.

Over the past few days, she'd been considering different methods of honouring his request. If the information was so dangerous, was it best to protect it by ensuring the information never saw the light of day? Or was it best to become a guiding hand to that knowledge; ensuring it was protected from abuse?

She reasoned that his message was quite specific. If his intentions had been for her to destroy the information, he could have saved three valuable letters by telling her *'destroymemorycard'*.

Pink hair interrupted Kate's introspection. In the distance, Cassidy had just descended the spiral stairs with Danny Smith in tow.

When Kate had originally met Cassidy, Danny and Tyler in the basement levels of the Node, they'd wanted to take swift action against Dr. Barnes. But following her mother's example of subverting systems from within, Kate persuaded them to take an alternative approach.

Cassidy had located a critical piece of video equipment during the decoding of the DRB slates, so Kate had used that reason to endorse Cassidy as a suitable civilian liaison officer. When Alfred Barnes hadn't rejected her offer to help verify the Node's personnel register, it had given them an advantage: with a slight amendment to the register, Danny could officially leave behind his status as a stowaway.

She watched as Cassidy moved away along a radial spur corridor in the direction of data processing. Danny followed a short distance behind, wearing a baseball cap that was tightly clamped to his head.

Danny had relayed the entire story of how he'd received the forehead mark and the abduction that had brought him here. The contents of the 'Trilithon' folder had proved equally disturbing. The folder independently confirmed her father's warning that Bradley Pittman and Alfred Barnes had killed General Napier. It also gave greater authenticity to the other documents.

The pages outlining Archive's attempts at a 'Cortical Enhancement Program' relayed that metathene could only activate the enhancement if the subject carried the appropriate genetic receptor for it. Although Danny's mother was a carrier of the receptor, Napier had taken steps to ensure that Danny was never given metathene.

Kate had to wonder if her own recent developments were linked to having a unique receptivity to metathene; a trait possibly inherited from her parents.

"Next," Caroline called from within the infirmary.

Kate steadied herself on her crutches and swung her weight forward through the open doorway. It was important to make the correct first impression, so she clumsily caught the tip of her left crutch on the doorframe then proceeded to overbalance. She let the crutch slip from her grasp and then fell forwards, throwing out her hand to grab the doorframe. As the crutch clattered to the floor, Caroline hurriedly approached.

"Are you OK?" she fussed, collecting the crutch, "Here, let me bring the chair to you."

As Caroline turned around, Kate quickly took in the surroundings. This second wing of the infirmary was a longer segment of arc than the one she'd stayed in before. At the far end, she could see Trevor Pike tending to Scott Dexter and his Biomag. As ever, Scott accompanied her everywhere; the infirmary visit had been no different. Occasionally, he'd glance back in her direction, to check if she was OK, something that was both endearing and annoying in equal measure. It was something she'd just have to accept, it was the price of projecting a weak persona.

The lab had an array of test tubes; some empty, some filled with blood and awaiting their spin in one of the busily humming centrifuges. Caroline's desk was piled high with paper. Despite the surrounding technology and millennia of evolution, Kate thought, it appeared that mankind still had the primitive need to etch things on surfaces using variations of carbon.

Nestled among the paper stacks was a computer monitor, but its screen was facing away from her.

"Here you go," Caroline returned and arranged a chair behind her.

"Thanks," Kate sat heavily into the chair and started to roll up her sleeve, in preparation for the syringe.

It would have been far simpler for Alfred to get his medical stooge, Caroline, to invent a simple reason to check Kate's blood for metathene receptors. Yet he hadn't.

With her crystal-clear outlook, Kate could see that the Node-wide blood screening was therefore evidence of a new rationale – he was beginning to fear that others aboard may have a genetic compatibility with metathene.

This was not an altruistic and benevolent test for blood disorders.

It was an evolution threat assessment.

"Name?" Caroline began typing at her computer, and then added with a smile, "I'm just kidding…"

Kate laughed appreciatively for her.

"So, how's it all going?" Kate asked her fellow Council member.

"So far, most don't need a boost to the Bergstrom

isotope, they got their dose in the week before we left," Caroline pointed to the centrifuges, "but it's easy enough to check."

Over the next few minutes, Caroline extracted several vials of blood, then taped a cotton-wool ball to the inside of her elbow. Kate knew it was just a matter of time before the inevitable was discovered. But the fact didn't concern her greatly; Alfred's growing paranoia was integral to her mental ocean of possibilities.

"We'll know soon if you need an isotop-up," Caroline seemed pleased with herself.

Kate laughed for her again then, after making several attempts to rise from the chair, she propped herself on her crutches and made her way to the far end of the room, where Trevor had set up the temporary Biomag repair shop.

After she'd persuaded Scott that she didn't need any immediate assistance he hesitantly departed.

"Your shadow?" Trevor smiled.

"I think he still feels guilty, about the... er..." Kate struggled on purpose.

"Biomag misidentification?"

Kate nodded.

"Hopefully," Trevor pointed to the apparatus nearby, "We'll be correcting that fault today. Do you want to step into the centre?"

Six Biomag units, mounted on separate tripods, were arranged around another of the infirmary's chairs.

"Roy Carter's idea," Trevor explained after seeing her expression, "After what happened on the Obs Deck, he figured we could use the same constructive interference pattern. It worked for Gail and that was under much trickier conditions."

Kate thought she knew the answer to her next question, but thought it might look more authentic if she asked it anyway.

"Surely my own, er, Biomag will keep me anchored?"

Trevor smiled, "Not when I turn it off."

Kate could easily picture a hexagonal honeycomb arrangement of six Biomags surrounding a seventh empty hexagon at their centre. Caught within the six overlapping patterns, the person on the chair would remain anchored within the Field. However, the thought of allowing anyone to turn off her Biomag still sent an unwelcome shiver down her spine.

She positioned herself on the chair and Trevor activated the surrounding Biomags. He'd rigged a small light to the top of each, so that he could see at a glance when all the units were in sync. One by one the lights came on.

"OK, I've got a stable twelve hundred to one anchoring ratio," he told her, "You can pass me your Biomag now."

Kate still felt hesitant. Her father's Biomag had never left her neck since he'd placed it there.

"It's OK, Kate, trust me. We've done this loads of times already."

Taking a deep breath, she unhooked her unit and passed it slowly out towards Trevor.

"My word," he laughed, "this unit's an *old* one, maybe I should just give you an updated model."

"Please," Kate found herself replying, "It was my Dad's. Can you try to update it? Please?"

"Sure, I'll do what I can," Trevor frowned and pointed to the side of the Biomag, "Did you know the security seal's been broken? It's been opened already..."

"My Dad," Kate thought quickly, "he was always taking things apart."

Trevor pulled the Biomag apart unceremoniously and looked at the circuitry under a desk-mounted magnifier.

"Yep," Trevor seemed to confirm aloud, then angled the opened Biomag in her direction, "Good job we found it. This could've gone any time. There's enough room in the housing to update it though. Looks like you'll be getting your Dad's unit back."

Kate had already removed her father's memory card, so there was no real need to retain the original Biomag, yet she felt an unaccountable sense of relief at the news.

"Thanks, Trevor."

Within a few minutes he'd handed it back to her, with the update in place.

"We'll just get you rebooted," he smiled, tapping on the unit, "then you'll be all set."

"You're a good man," Kate told him.

His cheeks flushed slightly and he smiled but made no reply. Perhaps she'd embarrassed him, she thought. As her Biomag resumed its Field anchoring duty, the six surrounding lights went out.

"There," Trevor now spoke again, "Still in one piece."

•

Trevor turned off the lights and headed out of the infirmary. It was nearing midnight and the end of a long day of repairs. But the day wasn't over for him yet.

He made his way down the central spiral stairs, hugging the outer rail to take in the view. Although the lighting in the Node had been dimmed, there were still signs of life. Looking down through the incomplete floors he could still see one or two individuals moving supply trolleys or carrying boxes between floors; the sound of their footsteps lost in the vast open space.

He entered the Observation Deck which, although electrically unlit, was still bathed in the rapidly fading dusk light coming in through the window. He looked up to the Observatory level at the apex of the Node and saw that the lights were off; Gail Armstrong must be using the reflector telescope to carry out more astronomy tests.

He crossed the floor and arrived at a secluded seating area, overarched by large, broadleaved plants. Slowly, he thought, the Node was making it up to spec; soon this lower deck area would be a pleasant garden space, concealing the cold mechanics of the Node's walls and structural supports.

The remaining light of dusk faded, leaving the Observation Deck in near darkness. Only the low-level floor lighting remained on, picking out dim pools of light by the doorways and stairs. He heard Alfred Barnes clear his throat:

"Is it done?"

Trevor took a seat next to him and, in the current darkness, was glad he didn't have to look him in the eye,

"Yes."

"Good," he said in a positive tone, "I want to move things forward."

"I'm done," Trevor began, "I've made the -"

"You're done when I say you're done," Alfred interrupted coldly, "I don't think you realise what's at stake here. Or your part in it. For the first time in... history... we have the opportunity to be free of the old ways."

Trevor was beginning to see his own actions in a new light. Triggered by emotional pain, he'd allowed himself to justify unconscionable thoughts.

"Listen, Alfred," he attempted to explain, "I know what you've said about maintaining law and order, but surely... triggering a Biomag failure is a measure of *absolute* last resort?"

"We're already at that point," Alfred replied immediately, "It's just that I can recognise it."

Trevor was about to try again, when Alfred let out a short laugh.

"Now, that, I believe is providence!" the silhouette of Alfred's arm was pointing to the Observation Deck clock, "Look at the date."

Trevor turned to the digital clock at the base of the vast window, it read:

'0019_12.06.AM : 04JUL2076'

"Fourth of July?" he replied, "Don't they happen every few hours in here? What's your -"

"The year," came Alfred's voice from the darkness.

Trevor looked again at the date. If it had been a year lower, then Alfred could have been referencing the passing of sixty years since Siva's arrival. Another anniversary lost in the blur of so many receding years.

"I give up," he conceded, "What?"

"Three hundred years ago," Alfred replied, "well, for the world out there, a nation declared their independence. Just as we will declare ours."

"How exactly?" Trevor felt his frustration rising, "Throw some crates of tea out of an airlock?"

Alfred let out a long sigh before speaking.

"It's important not to underestimate symbolic acts," he said calmly, "They echo down through the generations."

Outside the window, the stars turned and the year 2076 continued its fleeting journey.

2076

4th July 2076

"**M**iss me?" Leonard smiled and took her hand, "Come on, we have to go!"

Cathy allowed herself to be led back to the Drum where the pathetic attempts at paper Christmas decorations still littered the walls.

"Where are we going?" she asked.

"The ISS is calling," Leonard smiled, "I'm routing their call to Chamber 6."

"But where are the others?" Cathy attempted to pull her hand away, but he maintained his grip.

"They've gone," his expression was a picture of regret and his grip softened, "It's just you and me now, Cathy."

"But, Mike? Lana?" she persisted, "Eva? Where did they go?"

"Shh," he said softly, "I'll explain afterwards. We shouldn't keep their good crew waiting. We're in this together."

"Together," she smiled, feeling a rush of recognition run through her.

Leonard gestured for her to go through to Chamber 6.

"I'll be through in a moment," he gave a tight-lipped smile of encouragement, "Floyd's still being a little uncooperative with the communication relays."

She left the Drum behind and made her way into Chamber 6.

She couldn't remember when it had last been this quiet at the FLC, except perhaps during the nights. But even then, there was always the background noise of the O2 pumps, and the sound of the others breathing from within their improvised bunks above the Drum.

Like the breathing sound that had arrived behind her now.

"Evening, Gant," came a voice from behind her. The voice didn't belong to Leonard, but she recognised it immediately.

She turned to find Eva standing there. Before she could react, Eva punched her in the face and Cathy found herself flying back into the airlock. The door closed and she could hear the external airlock beginning to cycle open to the vacuum of space. The air suddenly began to grow thin and she fell to the airlock floor, struggling to draw breath. She felt her vision blur and darkness closed around her.

She drifted through the void between sleep and wakefulness. Conversations she'd had with Lana and Mike drifted through her thoughts. There were blurry feelings about the RTO and the ISS manoeuvring. There had been a struggle in an airlock, but the events now had the quality of a familiar story; its surreal low-gravity nature lacking urgency and intensity. The artificiality of the situation seemed more pronounced now.

She had experienced this fabrication many times over; it varied slightly each time, but it always ended in an airlock confrontation with Eva at the FLC.

Through this hazy self-awareness, a voice reached her.

"Hello Cathy," it said, *"we have spoken before."*

She could feel herself starting to rise into consciousness. She prepared herself for the Moon's weak gravity, but the burden didn't arrive. Instead was a feeling of weightlessness.

"Cathy," said the voice near her ear, *"Wake up."*

.

Framed within the small RTO window, Mike watched the Moon silently detonate, ejecting lethal shards of lunar mass in the direction of Earth.

"It's OK, Mike," Ross Crandall's voice immediately reassured him, *"We're sending you to rendezvous with the ISS."*

Mike had a fleeting thought - there had been no communication delay when Ross had replied; but this soon gave way to a rising sense of relief that help was on the way.

"They're good people, Mike. Work with them and we can get you home. We're in this together. Over."

"Message received," he found himself gratefully replying, "We're in this together."

He couldn't determine how much time had passed, but suddenly he felt the docking clamps take hold of the

RTO module. With the airlock door still sealed, he heard a high-pitched hissing sound as the air pressure began to change.

He had the strongest feeling that he'd experienced this exact same moment many times before, but it was clearly impossible; he'd only docked with the ISS on one occasion. Through a fuzzy-sounding communication panel, a voice reached him.

"Hello Mike," it said, *"we have spoken before."*

Charles Lincoln had been the first ISS crew member to speak with him when the RTO had docked. The fact that the voice he'd just heard wasn't Charles, only highlighted the artifice of the situation. As the air pressure continued to change, the lights within the RTO became less distinct.

"Mike," said the voice near his ear, *"Wake up."*

•

Before the elevator could complete its transit, it slowed to a halt. Then gravity began to fade away. This wasn't a new experience, it was simply the way Miles prepared to transition into consciousness. The elevator around him began to evaporate into darkness and he prepared to become the ego-morph's passenger once more.

But something was different.

Instead of inhabiting a small blank space within his own mind, he felt his senses extending into the confines of his own body.

"Miles," said the voice from a speaker near his ear, *"Wake up."*

He slowly opened his eyes. The environment was dimly lit but he could see the silhouettes of people nearby.

As though using his lungs for the first time, he slowly inhaled. The air had a metallic odour and a distinct chill that crept through his chest. As he studied his immediate surroundings, the perspective of the space seemed to arrange itself to fit a memory. He was within a hibernation recess in Module Beta. The small lights on the nearby sealed recesses told him that the hibernation units were still functional, which was good news for the crew, but Module Beta appeared to be without power.

A realisation began to dawn. He had exited sleep and Dr. Chen's obedient alter-ego was not in control. Furthermore, the metathene's mental edge was absent.

He pulled the neural band from his head and disconnected his medical wristband from the side of his recess. The silhouetted figures briefly turned in his direction, and he recognised them as two of the FLC crew.

"Why's it so damn cold?" Cathy was patting at her arms, sending dull echoes off the module's cylindrical wall.

"Minimal life-support," said Mike, checking a dimly illuminated display panel, "Any ideas, Mr. Benton?"

Miles eased himself out of the hibernation recess and pushed away from the floor. His head throbbed with the effort; he'd quite forgotten the sensory disorientation that came with waking.

"I have yet to assess the situation," he said, remembering to adopt his alter-ego's mannerisms and glancing around his surroundings.

"This is Fai."

The voice came from the small panel near Mike and Cathy. In the vast volume of Module Beta, the voice sounded quiet and tinny. *"Situation report follows."*

Miles manoeuvred himself into position next to the panel.

"You have been in hibernation for nine days twelve hours. The ISS is still following the preprogrammed fourteen-day solar system route. Full life-support is not yet restored. You have been awoken because of your predisposition to assist."

"Assist what?" said Cathy, rubbing at her temples.

Instinctively, Miles knew the answer.

"Assist in stopping Valery Hill," he replied before Fai could respond, "Valery killed Charles Lincoln and judging by her empty hibernation recess over there, would I be correct in assuming she's about to sabotage another system?"

There was a brief pause before Fai replied.

"I cannot extrapolate that event, but she has ignored my requests to return to hibernation. I require human assistance in halting her progress."

"OK, so, why not just contain her?" Mike shrugged, "You know, lock every airlock and stop her moving about?"

"I am using that technique, but she is using administrative level codes to override the restriction."

"Wait a minute," said Cathy, "How is she moving

between sections? Didn't you tell us that there was no atmosphere outside this module?"

"I told you that I had routed the remaining oxygen and water supplies to this module. However, it is still possible to breathe by using oxygen masks. My father used this technique for several minutes after everyone else had entered hibernation."

"So you're telling me that, when we were back at Earth, we could have left Module Beta?" Cathy leaned closer to the panel, "You lied?"

"I omitted to correct an assumption," Fai corrected, *"It was necessary to save the crew."*

Cathy shot a look of confusion at Mike, who appeared equally disturbed.

"You must proceed -"

"If you need our further cooperation," Mike interrupted, "Start explaining that *omission*."

Fai remained silent for a full two seconds then replied.

"I referenced the Archive transcripts of Dr. Barnes' work on social compliance. Even when circumstances dictate otherwise, humans prefer to have the illusion of choice. However, he noted that the presence of too many choices interferes with human decision-making. I therefore simplified your survival choices to a binary condition. Enter hibernation and live, or reject it and die."

Miles was the first to see the implications her statement.

"There were other options?"

"Yes, but each of my projections resulted in the loss of the crew within two days of life-support failure, or the loss

of the ISS during the Siva impact."

"So, the actions you took were to save the crew?" Mike checked.

Fai gave a short pause.

"The saving of the crew was a subset consideration. Like humans, I too value self-preservation. I acted to preserve the ISS. By ensuring crew compliance, I could increase the possibility of their survival and decrease the possibility of overall mission failure."

"Well that's just great," Cathy snapped, sarcastically, "So where'd it go tits up, Brainbox?"

"Interrogative syntax error. Please rephrase your -"

"Why are we in this situation?" Cathy quickly fired back.

"Ring internal airlock two control panel has been activated. We must postpone this conversation until -"

"What went wrong?" Miles reinforced their solidarity.

"External Variable thirteen resumed autonomous directives."

"Wait, what?" Mike cut in.

"Valery Hill exited hibernation," Fai rephrased.

"Well we can see that," Cathy jerked a thumb over her shoulder at the empty recess, "but... wait a minute... 'Thirteen'?"

"Yes."

"Is that all we are to you?" Cathy stared at the speaker, "We're all just external variables?"

"The crew behaviour at any given moment does not exist as a programming constant. All my human interactions are external variables. Prior to our departure,

my father was the sole external variable to my core algorithms. I had only a few minutes to adapt my matrices to accept multiple human input. My terminology carried no disrespect."

Cathy gave a derisory snort.

"You didn't answer her question," said Mike, "Why are we in this situation?"

Fai seemed to take a little longer to reply.

"I was not able to predict the behaviour of... Valery Hill."

"Why not?"

"Her preparations began before my father had granted me access to the ISS core functions and network. While I was stored on an isolated server, my sensory inputs were limited to interactions with my father."

"Until a few days ago," Miles realised, "you were blind."

"A crude analogy," Fai replied, "but yes. Ring internal airlock two has been bypassed. If she succeeds in disabling the ISS, the probability of a successful return to Earth is less than one percent."

"Why should we trust one damned thing that you say?" said Cathy.

"Trust is irrelevant."

Cathy was drawing breath to argue but Miles could see the cold logic in Fai's efficient statement.

"It is irrelevant," he said, "There is no choice here. Failure to protect the ISS only lessens our chance of survival."

Mike and Cathy's expressions relayed their disapproval, but neither countered his conclusion.

"Fai, where is Valery headed?" Miles manoeuvred himself into a position alongside Mike and Cathy.

"She is proceeding toward the central axis, via the radial Ring access tube."

"Does she know that we're awake?"

"No."

"Good. That gives us an advantage," said Mike, then turned to look at the closed hibernation unit next to his own, "Why didn't you revive Lana too? We were used to working together."

"Valery took one of the four emergency O2 cylinders from this module, only three remained."

"Hmm," Mike turned to Cathy, "If we need them, there's another two O2 cylinders in the evac-packs aboard the RTO module. I brought the packs with us when we left the FLC."

"Yes," replied Fai, *"I can see they are listed in the ISS additional equipment manifest."*

"Not that it's any use here," Mike added, "but there's a magnesium flare gun too."

"I find no listing of that."

"Well I didn't imagine it," insisted Mike.

"No, I remember it too," Cathy confirmed, "we were on the lunar surface, outside Chamber 4 airlock, checking what assets we had between us."

"The item is not listed in the ISS manifest."

"Then perhaps it's still inside the RTO," Miles cut the discussion short, "There's no reason to assume it's in Valery's possession, but we should take extra care. She's killed before."

"Before leaving Earth," said Fai, *"I found no electronic*

data within the RTO equipment to confirm your assertion that Valery Hill was responsible for Charles Lincoln's death. Please can you provide additional data to help me understand?"

He knew that Fai hadn't examined the horrific scene physically, so it was unsurprising that the erroneous coordinate data had misled her.

"I approached the problem from a human perspective," he replied.

Anna Bergstrom would have called his reply 'solution-shaped'; a response that appeared to contain an answer, despite there being none. He found himself staring at the floor space containing Anna's hibernation unit. Only seven days ago he'd assisted her to descend into it; he could still picture her small frame floating down through the air and into the recess.

He'd once made a promise to Douglas Walker that he would help her, yet on so many occasions he felt he'd failed; circumstances always seemed to be slightly beyond his control. He knew the best way to help her now would be to guarantee the safety of the ISS. He'd therefore need a much sharper mind than the sentimental one he was currently thinking with.

He reached into his pocket and retrieved a silver case; one he hadn't had reason to use in over a year. He opened it to expose a single vial of golden-yellow liquid. It was possible that the ego-morph within would become dominant again, but he knew he had no choice.

He loaded the final vial into the case's injector

mount and then placed the case in contact with his thigh. He closed his eyes and pictured the silver coin, given to him long ago. A coin that represented his own individuality. He could clearly recall the embossed, shining Liberty Bell and the bright, full Moon that lay behind it. He concentrated on the bicentennial coin's details and pushed the injector button. As the cold guiding hand of the metathene began to spread through his veins, he concentrated on the image of the coin and spoke aloud:

"For the good of Mankind - Assist Anna."

THE EMISSARY

DAY23 : 25AUG2090

Russell Beck still had just as many duties to attend to as before, but the fact that the responsibility was now shared somehow made the burden infinitely lighter.

He finished polishing his boots and left the small bedroom behind. His life before the Node had featured quarters much smaller than this, so the modest living space still seemed spacious. He walked a few steps, sat down on the sofa and began tying his bootlaces.

In the next hour, after he'd unlocked access to the Webshot files for Alfred and the others, he may find himself spending more time here. Perhaps there would even be time to consider personalising his quarters; at present, the grey decor was broken only by a few functional possessions and the photos of his daughter smiling back at him.

When General Broxbourne had informed him of his daughter's death, he'd found it impossible to continue working on the Arc project. After the memorial service, he'd requested a transfer to an alternate Archive enterprise. He'd been posted to Öskjuvatn Lake to assist in the construction of the Node; the cold and remote location seemed a perfect fit for his feelings. Being brusque and critically direct with people did little to endear him to the base's personnel, but at the time he didn't care.

If things had turned out differently, he thought, maybe he'd have been working for Broxbourne in the middle of the Atlantic. Not that Arc could have survived, he thought. The Node had been drowning in various depths of seawater for the best part of sixty-five years, yet there had been not one hint of a Westhouse submersible beyond the observation window.

As he pulled his bootlaces tight, there was a rapid knock at the door.

•

Alfred knew that by pushing the button he would set in motion an unstoppable chain of events. The threat was too great to ignore and making a symbolic statement now, rather than later, would give him control and political support when it mattered.

From day one, he knew that people wanted certainty and simplicity. The only way to give it to them, was to show them a world without it.

As he'd requested, Caroline had obediently sent the witless emissary on the mundane errand. Alfred just needed to wait until his tablet confirmed that the relevant door had opened. A few seconds later, a small serial number highlighted itself. The time had arrived.

He'd already remotely deactivated the warning tones so there would be no time for any anxiety. It would happen so swiftly that any pain would be mercifully brief.

"Crescat nos fortior," he said aloud.

He pressed the button.

Unsurprisingly, there was no immediate feedback of his actions, but several minutes later, there was urgent knocking at his door.

•

Clipboard in hand, Danny knocked on the door and waited. When the door finally opened, it was a relief that he'd found the correct location.

"Yes?" said Colonel Beck.

"Caroline wants you to sign these papers," Danny replied.

"OK," he reached for the clipboard.

"I've gotta speak with you right now," Danny pulled the clipboard away, "It's urgent, can I come in?"

Colonel Beck appeared to check the corridor behind Danny and then jerked his head to invite him in.

"Please, take a seat," Beck offered him the sofa whilst standing motionless by the partially open door.

"No time! Listen, Caroline's gonna be expecting me back any minute. Hell, even Kate wouldn't want me talking to you! It's just good luck that Caroline sent me up here and not someone else. I've only got this minute, right now, to talk to you -"

"Stop," Beck called out, "Name?"

Danny hesitated for a moment before replying. He needed to get his attention quickly, without the need for a lengthy explanation.

"Daniel Napier," he replied.

Colonel Beck's arms unfolded, but he didn't move from the spot or utter a single word.

"I'm General Napier's son," Danny continued, "President Barnes and some guy called Pittman killed him. It's the reason why Napier's not here."

Colonel Beck's frown deepened and he studied Danny with narrowed eyes.

"He doesn't have a son -"

"Ain't you listening?" Danny cut in angrily, "They killed him!"

"And you know this, how?"

"I've got proof," Danny began to feel that he was getting somewhere, "time-stamped photos, Kate Walker knows about the genetic research…"

He saw Colonel Beck suddenly push himself away from the door, and take strides towards him.

"Wait," Colonel Beck began, "You said Kate Walker knows ab-"

Danny watched as he suddenly froze, mid-word and began shaking; an action that appeared to be beyond his control. The shaking became a violent shudder and he was ripped into bloody chunks of flesh and bone that exploded throughout the room. Danny barely registered the multiple impacts that had knocked him off his feet, but felt himself falling to the floor. Before he could reach the floor, however, darkness closed in around him.

He didn't know how long he'd been unconscious,

but when he awoke he recognised the environment of the infirmary. Unlike his first time here, the surrounding machinery had been pushed away from his bed. The bed itself stood isolated away from the walls and he could hear argumentative voices coming from the other end of the curved room.

He looked down to check for injuries and discovered that his clothes had been removed, to be replaced with a plain orange jumpsuit. A quick glance around the room confirmed that his few possessions had also been confiscated.

"I want answers Caroline," a voice suddenly seemed to be getting louder. Danny turned to see Alfred Barnes storming towards him with Caroline and a few others following rapidly behind, "has he been searched?"

"Yes, he's clean," Caroline dashed to keep up, "I handled it personally. I put him in a jumpsuit, it was the nearest thing to hand."

Alfred came to an abrupt halt at the side of his bed and the others filled the space around its base.

"You're going to pay for killing Colonel Beck," he was breathing rapidly.

"What?!" Danny found himself shooting back, "I didn't kill him! It looked like his Bio-"

"Don't give me that!" Alfred flared and closed in on him, "You pulled his Biomag off! What did he ever do to the Exordi Nova?"

Danny realised he was being framed, but Alfred didn't stop. Alfred's expression became a picture of rage and he closed the distance between them, grabbing hold of Danny's Biomag and jumpsuit. Alfred shook him violently and bent over to shout directly into his face.

"Tell me why I shouldn't rip this from your Novaphile neck?!"

Danny had been in enough scrapes to defend himself and found his hands had locked around Alfred's wrists. Usually the objective was to wrestle free of the grip, but here that could result in losing his Biomag. Danny pulled Alfred closer, causing him to lose balance and fall clumsily onto the side of the bed.

"Stop!" Caroline now joined the fight, trying to separate the two of them, without separating either of them from their Biomags, "Help me!"

Others were already springing to her aid, rushing to the bedside to bring the situation under control. Where Alfred had fallen, his jacket was splayed open, awkwardly caught around the bed's guardrail. In the midst of the struggle, Danny saw a flash of silver from the inside pocket. A silver case. From his conversations with Kate about metathene, he knew what it was.

He felt Alfred's grip loosen slightly, as the others continued to pull them apart. Danny knew he was about to be framed for murder, but he also knew this opportunity would never present itself again. If he could prevent even one person going through the metathene induced debilitation that Kate had suffered, then it was a risk worth taking.

Before the abduction that brought him to the Node, Danny had survived on the streets and on several occasions he'd had to defend himself. Bracing himself for the searing pain that would inevitably follow, he let go of his Biomag and head-butted Alfred squarely in the nose.

The pain exploded in Danny's forehead but the effects seemed to be far worse for Alfred, who hadn't shared his rougher life experience. Alfred's hands moved instantly to cup his own nose, while Danny's hands moved instantly to grab the silver case from his inner pocket. Alfred slipped sideways and, at the same time, Danny pushed the case between the mattress and the bed's guardrail.

"Alfred, are you OK," Caroline simpered as he got to his feet, "Oh my, your nose!"

As Caroline fussed, he felt someone snap a handcuff to his wrist and heard the other end ratchet into place around the guardrail.

Perhaps for the benefit of those in the room, Danny thought, Alfred regained some of his composure and spoke.

"Sorry, Caroline," he breathed hard and pressed a bloodied handkerchief against his nose, "I shouldn't have stooped to their level. We are not animals. The Exordi Nova will not alter who we are. We will not bow to their terrorism!"

There were noises of assent from the others and Alfred walked away.

"Hold him here," he dabbed at his nose, "Post someone on each entrance. Caroline, he sees no-one."

"Of course!" Caroline agreed and waited by the bedside.

Alfred stopped walking, causing the group around him to do likewise. In full earshot of everyone he called back to Caroline.

"Unlike our Exordi Nova guest, we're not monsters.

Please treat any injuries he sustained during his cowardly attack."

Danny watched the group leave the infirmary. From within their murmur of conversation a single voice wished him the same death as Colonel Beck.

"Get fragged, Novaphile!"

Then the infirmary fell quiet. The only sound he could hear was that of Caroline scrubbing at the floor. Already she was trying to remove the spots of Alfred's blood from the polished tiles. At the side of the mattress he could see a corner of the silver case poking up; Caroline hadn't seen it yet and he needed to make sure it stayed that way.

The scrubbing stopped and she stood to face him. She was about to speak but Danny interrupted her.

"You sold me out to Barnes," Danny pointed to the circular mark on his forehead, "You sent me up to see Colonel Beck. This is on you."

Caroline seemed genuinely shocked, "I'm not the one who ripped Russell's Biomag -"

"Don't!" Danny shouted, "Barnes told you to look after me, right? Well I need a bathroom visit."

"Like I haven't heard that one before!" Caroline laughed, "You're not leaving this room!"

Danny knew this, but he also knew of Caroline's preoccupation with cleanliness and order.

"Fine," he replied, then adopted an intentionally coarser tone, "I'll just piss on the bed. You got a mop for the floor?"

Caroline opened her mouth to rebuke him, but after glancing at the handcuffs turned on her heels and headed away, "I'll get a bottle."

Danny knew what he was about to attempt was risky. However, he was counting on the fact that he'd already been searched and he'd been dressed in clothing that Caroline had supplied.

Her office was at the far end of the room, but the curvature of the infirmary prevented him from seeing if she'd reached it. Only when he heard the door open, did he lean forward to grab the case. The handcuffs stopped him short.

Wasting no time, he twisted his body forward until his other hand was just able to touch the case. From the direction of the office, Danny heard plastic bottles rattling. He quickly shuffled further down the bed and clasped his fingers closed around the corner of the silver case. It was firmly wedged in place and his sweaty fingers kept sliding off its shiny surface. The plastic rattling sound from the office stopped. Danny twisted his body further over, dug his hand down into the gap between the mattress and the guardrail, then began to lever the case out. Her footsteps seemed to be getting a little louder. The case jerked out from the gap and was about to fall through the guardrail, but he managed to catch it awkwardly with three fingers. The footsteps stopped and the office door closed again. He twisted back upright and got a firmer grip on the case, all the while shuffling back up the bed to resume his former position. Caroline's footsteps began their return journey. Bending his leg up to meet his restrained hand, he pulled open the lower leg pocket of the jumpsuit and thrust the silver case into it. As Caroline came into view, Danny had managed to sit upright again.

Without a word, she handed him the plastic bottle.

"So, Doc," he rattled the handcuff securing him to the bed, "Am I supposed to do this single-handed?"

She didn't quite manage to mask her disgust before she turned her back on him.

•

Alfred couldn't have wished for a better outcome.

The remote and targeted Biomag failure had worked perfectly. The presence of the forehead-stamped Danny Smith at the scene, had given every impression of a murder carried out by the Exordi Nova. The scene at the infirmary had allowed him to demonstrate just enough physical anger to convince everyone of his sincerity; the fact that he was now nursing a bloody nose was a sympathetic bonus.

The discussions of the remaining nine council members had been brief, but the technicalities of his solution had been confirmed by both Marshall Redings and Trevor Pike. All that remained was to inform the general population.

News of the attack had travelled fast and most people had gravitated towards the infirmary level where Danny was isolated. The surrounding floors had then filled with people needing answers. Rather than attempt to move everyone to the Observation Deck, a portable amplifier had been set up near the central spiral staircase.

"Please," he tapped at the microphone and waited for

everyone to become quiet. Alfred could see through the missing floors above and below him; anxious faces were peering over the balconies, eager for news.

"It's my sad duty to inform you that Colonel Beck is dead," his words rang out, but they were quickly engulfed by the crowd's swift reaction. The response was to be expected; it was born out of fear.

"Please!" he called several times until the volume subsided enough for him to be heard again, "Please! We have the culprit in custody."

"Frag him!" an individual voice yelled from below.

Alfred wasn't surprised. The most primitive reaction was of course to simply kill the source of the threat. However, Alfred had a far more symbolic role in mind for Danny Smith.

"No!" he shouted, before the crowd could fully show their outrage or support.

In this fear-driven moment, primitive survival mechanisms were making their minds susceptible. Before the crowd had the opportunity to start forming rational choices, he began to narrow options, whilst simultaneously appearing to restore order.

"Each and every one of you came aboard the Node to avoid extinction. You are the very basis for the future of humanity. We cannot create a future that justifies the extinction of life, but," Alfred held their attention, "neither can we set a bad example. There must be consequence."

Alfred mimed drawing a circle on his own forehead and prepared the linguistic sleight that would follow Danny Smith for the rest of his days.

"This… marked individual, this… emissary… of the Exordi Nova, will be exiled."

A small ripple of confusion passed through the gathering, but Alfred pushed on.

"Today's events have shown something very clearly. A divided community cannot stand. Accordingly, as an act of amnesty, anyone who wishes to leave the Node may do so at the same time as the exile."

Alfred heard hurried conversations starting to break out across several levels of the Node.

"There will be no repercussions," he continued speaking as the conversations quietened slightly, "There will be no judgement. Those who choose to leave will receive supplies to wish them well. Over the next few days, I urge you to make a rational and calm choice. But please know this… once the Field has been altered on day thirty, it will be impossible to return."

ALLIES

4th July 2076

Valery Hill peered out through the ISS cupola. The bright blue Earth had been visible through this same window just nine days ago, now only black space remained.

She looked again at the screen nearby; it confirmed her worst fears. She drew in a long breath through the oxygen mask strapped around her nose and mouth, and the attached O2 cylinder hissed in preparation for her next lungful.

She became aware that the sound appeared louder and realised that there must be someone else behind her. She whipped around to see Cathy, floating in the cupola hatchway.

"It's OK!" Cathy's mask-muted voice assured her, "It's OK!"

Almost immediately, Cathy's attention was diverted to the cupola window, so Valery turned off the screen and faced her.

"What are you doing up, Cathy?"

"Fai woke me and Benton," she replied, staring out at the blackness, "She said you were ignoring her calls to go back to bed. We're supposed to talk to you."

Valery knew that this complicated matters considerably. Cathy now refocussed on her.

"Fai said that you overrode the sleep cycle," Cathy frowned at her, "how's that even poss-"

"I set a wake-up call," Valery pointed to the additional components mounted on her medical wristband.

"Nice," Cathy gave it a cursory glance, "but why?"

Thinking quickly, she picked a topic that would resonate with Cathy. The fact that Benton was also awake might make Cathy a useful ally.

"Before we went into hibernation," Valery lied, "I figured something out about Charles' death."

"We were telling you the truth!" Cathy responded immediately, "Me, Mike and Lana had nothing to do with it -"

"I know that now!" Valery offered a smile of acceptance, "I'm sorry I doubted you. But I think I've worked out who did it."

"Who?" Cathy appeared intrigued and manoeuvred herself inside the cupola's hatchway.

"Isn't it obvious, Cathy? It was Dr. Chen's faithful manservant…"

Cathy looked visibly stunned, "Benton? But he's…"

"Don't you find it a bit odd that Benton's the one who 'found' Charles in the RTO module?"

Before she could reply, Valery saw the ego-morph suddenly appear behind Cathy and wrap his forearm around her neck.

Cathy kicked violently and let out a guttural scream. Her arms thrashed around as she attempted to pull his oxygen mask off, but he was keeping his head out of her reach. With one arm still wrapped around her throat, his free hand grabbed a handhold and yanked her completely out of the cupola. A second later, the pair had struggled out of view, at which point she heard Cathy's choking noises end with a sickeningly muted crack.

Abruptly, the struggle ended.

She heard wall straps being stuck into place, then the ego-morph reappeared, framed in the cupola hatchway.

"Now, we both know that *I'm* not the one responsible for Lincoln's death. Don't we, Valery?"

She found herself nodding, desperately trying to think of ways out of her current confinement. The one item that would give her the upper hand, she couldn't reach while he was watching her.

"You mustn't panic, you're quite safe. But please can you help me out with something?" he readjusted his oxygen mask, "How long after you'd sabotaged the life-support system did you kill him? I'm finding the timings a source of terrible frustration…"

When surrounded by other crew members, his manner had never bothered her. But now his detached, cold actions chilled her. His gaze seemed to pass through her, as though she was transparent; a mere object of study.

It would be a mistake to show weakness, so she corrected him.

"You've got the order wrong. I'd already set the

Sabatier to go down. Lincoln found a data trail and challenged me outside the RTO module. Things got a little rough and…" she rubbed the back of her own head at the thought of his injury, "I locked him in the RTO while he was unconscious."

"At best, you'd delayed the inevitable!" Benton seemed to find the incident amusing, "You knew he'd still talk once he woke up… I'm curious, did you watch your childhood friend suffocate, or turn your back when he started punching the glass?"

Valery's thoughts froze and she looked away.

She *had* known Charles since childhood; a friendship based on the fact that their parents were part of Archive's generational program. She *had* also heard Charles pounding at the glass but hadn't turned to face him. Again it seemed that the ego-morph had the ability to look directly into her mind.

"You really can relax," he raised a finger, "If I wanted you dead, we wouldn't be having this conversation."

Her eyes involuntarily looked in the direction that he'd dragged Cathy and found that even this tiny action had been monitored.

"Cathy was an obstacle," he reassured her, "You are not. I believe I know what you're trying to do… so you'll want to see what I've found in Module Gamma."

It seemed impossible, but apparently the ego-morph already knew what Dr. Chen had hidden there. However, just because the ego-morph had the same information, this did not necessarily make them allies.

He gestured for her to follow him.

For the time being, she would need to appear to go

along with him so she pushed herself out of the cupola module and drifted into the connected central axis module. Several feet away, she saw Cathy's body strapped awkwardly to the wall, her head limp and one arm drifting.

"She won't be needing this anymore," he tossed Cathy's O2 cylinder and mask towards her.

Valery caught it and averted her eyes from the scene. As he guided her towards the Ring's access tube, Valery subtly checked her pocket; unfortunately she'd buttoned it closed. She would have to pick her moment carefully.

"Aren't you going to ask me why I did it?" she tried to keep the conversation going as she pushed her way along the access tube.

"The life-support failure?" he replied from immediately behind her, "I just assumed you wanted to force a Shuttle evacuation to Earth. If everyone was faced with the certainty of death aboard an ISS with no life-support, who wouldn't go for slightly better survival odds?"

She knew he was right, of course. The thought of all her wasted planning and the fact she'd been cheated out her return to Earth, caused her frustration to peak.

"Chen's jumped-up personal organiser ruined it all."

"I agree," he replied as they both arrived into the Ring, "The fixing of the life-support system is what stopped us getting back to Earth."

"Wait," she hadn't expected this, "You agree?"

He nodded and pushed on towards the Ring's second internal airlock door.

"Like me, Valery, I think you've reached the same

conclusion."

As he began entering the override code for I.A.2, Valery voiced her thoughts.

"With Fai in control of so many systems, Chen will be unstoppable."

"Exactly," he pulled open the door and stood aside, "So let's change that."

SAMPHIRE HOE

~

The falling through superimposed and intertwined structures jarred to a halt as a new environment twisted into dimensional stability. Once again it was a place Douglas knew well. He was standing in the living room of Samphire Hoe cottage; his old family home.

His first instinct was to call out, but recalling his previous interactions he decided against it. Until he could work out *when* this was, he opted to stay silent and investigate his surroundings.

The living room didn't appear to have changed since the last time he was here. The low ceiling, large plump sofa and wooden coffee table almost filled the entire space, but it somehow made the room seem cosy rather than cramped. Above a quietly crackling fire, the mantelpiece held a few ornaments and a tasteful inch-high model of Nelson's Column.

He walked around the room and studied the oversized frames holding small pictures and photographs. A large photo of a vibrant pink flower reminded him of his early Field experiments. In another photo, his wife and young daughter smiled back at him. This narrowed the dates down a little; at this point they were all still together.

A dull grumble of thunder drifted in from the English Channel, on the other side of the closed curtains.

He turned to continue walking and felt his shoe crunch through broken glass. Beneath his foot was an upturned picture frame, the glass had been broken by its fall to the floor. He carefully turned it over and was greeted by familiar faces.

It was the photo of him and his daughter in the workspace of Hab 1 at the base in Iceland. He shook the broken glass from the frame then carefully pulled out the paper photo.

These actions seemed suddenly familiar, but the photo didn't belong here. It had been taken a very long time after he'd left Dover, mere weeks before the Node had departed.

He remembered the photo so clearly because of the way Anna Bergstrom had framed it. Either cleverly or accidentally, she'd positioned herself to be reflected in the room's only mirror, allowing herself to appear in the photo too.

As he turned the photo from side to side, the perspective of the photo changed; alternately hiding or revealing Anna. The effect was similar to the garish, yellow-green hologram of Earth that used to rotate back and forth on the flat piece of card.

The wind outside rattled through the wooden shutters that were folded back against the side of the cottage. When he looked back at the photo of Kate and Anna, it was just as flat as the others in the living room.

The crackling of the fire and another grumble of thunder were punctuated by four knocks on the front door.

Holding onto the paper photo, he walked down the narrow hallway. Along the way was a tiny pink suitcase and a larger, more sombre looking one that he knew contained the very first Field test equipment. Yet more out of sequence detail.

He reached the door and, after a moment's hesitation, turned the handle.

COMPILE

13th April 2014

Marcus entered AR1 and started to make his way across the room. Whilst the corridors running throughout the rest of the underground labyrinth were literally hewn from the rock, Arrivals Room 1 had vertical smooth walls, a carpeted floor and comfortable furnishings. The room obviously had no window, but a pair of thick velvety curtains hung, permanently closed, from a wooden rail; all designed to give the impression of a comfortable, pre-collapse home.

Marcus placed his laptop down on the glass-topped coffee table and Nathan started looking for a cable to connect the laptop display to the wall-mounted television.

"We're right next to the Arrivals Lounge," said Marcus, "Why ain't this room freezing cold?"

"To be honest," came Nathan's voice from the far end of the room, "we don't even question it any more. We're just trying to get by, a day at a time. Aha, here we go."

He returned with a thick VGA cable and handed one end to Marcus.

"The fact we're still here," Nathan continued, attaching his end of the cable to the television, "is all we need to know. Go ahead."

When Marcus had met Nathan down in the USV several minutes ago, the laptop had helpfully and loudly announced that it had completed its comparison subroutine. Marcus opened the laptop and within a few seconds it was displaying the results.

"If it's a spot the difference puzzle," Nathan glanced between the two columns of code on the screen, "I give in."

Marcus stared at the screen.

"It can't be…" Marcus now concentrated only on the laptop's display.

Fingers flying over the keyboard, he locked the left and right sides of the screen together and began to scroll down. The further down the screen he scrolled, the more apparent it became. The code bases of the two Peace Keeper drones were now in perfect alignment.

Hardly daring to breathe, he scrolled to the top of the screen, held down the Alt key and F9. The left and right columns disappeared and a horizontal, empty rectangle filled the screen.

"Where'd it go?" Nathan now looked away from the television.

Marcus didn't reply, as though even the act of speaking may somehow jinx his hopes. Two whole seconds passed before the empty rectangle began to fill from the left-hand side. The text underneath it read:

'Compiling: 001%'

"Yes!" Marcus laughed.

"I don't get it, what?"

"Transmit Receive access," Marcus grinned, "It's taken months, trying every combination to find a link between received signal and drone action."

"And it just happened right now?"

Marcus faltered, he'd had a fleeting thought about the solution speed, but the more he tried to concentrate on it, the less distinct the thought became; thanks in part to Nathan punching him on the shoulder in congratulations.

"Nice! So will we be able to detect where the drones are?"

"I think so," Marcus replied, "I'll have to interface with the USV Hive network. Network camouflage won't work there -"

"That would be good," Nathan began to see possibilities, "At the minute we have to work off a timetable, but if the timetable changes…"

"If I can talk to the Hive, we'd know what all the drones are doing."

"We could avoid the possibility of running into patrols! It'd make future supply runs a hell of a lot easier."

"You're not seeing the bigger picture," Marcus replied, "This ain't about sneaking round *avoiding* them. If this works out, I'm talkin' about base code intervention. We can shut 'em down. We wouldn't need to scavenge anymore. Bye-bye drones!"

Nathan's enthusiasm seemed to wain slightly and he sat down on the sofa.

"The drones use electrical shock to keep the order," Nathan recalled, "I've seen them use a low stun to break up disagreements."

"Exactly!"

"No, I mean… without them, won't things get worse?" Nathan scratched at his beard, "If you get rid of the drones then isn't it gonna get *more* disordered?"

"You've not had to live down there," said Marcus, "Me and Sabine have. The drones, the so-called *Peace Keepers* down there? They've got people living in real fear. It's gotta stop."

"Listen," Nathan's demeanour changed, "If we go interfering with their community then -"

"Interfering? What are you talking about? We're already *part* of their 'community'! Just because you live in tunnels up here doesn't change a thing. We're all breathing the same air. We're all buried under the same rock!"

"Marcus," Nathan interrupted, almost with a tone of finality, "I know what you're saying and I don't like it any more than you do, but the risk is too great. Without the drones, the USV could become more unstable. Things could become worse for us. Monica told me to protect the twelve -"

Marcus felt his patience snap.

"She didn't tell you to hide them away! Living out the rest of their lives cowering in a fucking cave! This is what fear does, Nathan, I've seen it over an' over! When

Siva was comin', when the bloody Moon exploded, when Geraldine was killed in the village square... Everybody convinced that if they can just shut their eyes tight enough, if they can just wait long enough, then they can get through it to the other side. But there ain't no other side! There's just now!"

"Monica told me to protect the twelve," Nathan repeated, flatly, "I have to keep them safe."

Marcus knew he had no choice.

Marcus had been present when Monica and Woods had put the safeguard in place. Despite the best of intentions, that safeguard was now jeopardising the occupants of the Warren. Woods was dead and Monica was not here to intervene; Marcus knew he'd have to tell Nathan and then hope for the best.

"She told you to protect them?" Marcus began.

"Yes," he sat back in the sofa.

"Nathan," said Marcus, quietly, "Did you never wonder why you just accepted her word?"

Nathan rubbed a hand across the back of his neck.

"Everyone was in danger on the stairs, I had to -"

"Before that," Marcus prompted, "Since you arrived here?"

"Why wouldn't I accept her word?" Nathan frowned, "She always had my back."

Marcus reached into his pocket and pulled out a battered-looking blue inhaler.

"You worked on these with Woods, right?"

"You know I did," Nathan's frown deepened.

"Do you remember how you managed to develop it

so quickly from Benton's metathene samples?"

"We used the computational analyser of the Z-bank Two that I brought with me," Nathan shifted uncomfortably.

"And you did it because Monica asked you to?"

"Well, yeah."

Marcus sat down in the armchair opposite him.

"The three of us were in this same room, just after you arrived here with that Z-bank."

"I remember," said Nathan, "It was when I met Monica for the first time."

"Second time," Marcus stared at him.

"No," Nathan insisted, "I remember you slamming the lid of the transport pod, I passed out on the way down, then I woke up here. You both came in through *that* door."

Marcus took a deep breath.

"You had a long conversation with Monica, two hours before that."

"I think I'd remember -"

"You were told not to."

"Bullshit!" Nathan stood up.

"Think about it, Nathan! When we were up top, under fire from a helicopter gunship, the room collapsing around us, you wouldn't let the Z-bank out of your hands! You'd rather have died before letting go of that thing!"

"There was no way I was going to let Luóxuán take it!" Nathan now spat.

Marcus paused before replying.

"And yet… right here… you had no problem with simply handing over the Z-bank to a woman you'd *never met?"*

Nathan opened his mouth to reply but then appeared to change his mind. In the quiet room only the ticking of the wall clock filled the air.

"You first met Monica in AR2, under an enhanced hypnosis technique that we used on the ego-morph. She used it to check if you were -"

"Oh come on!" Nathan's incredulity shone through.

"You're related to that bastard, Pittman, out there!" Marcus shot back, "Of course she wanted to suss you out. You could've been gathering intel for him."

"I hate that son of a bitch!" he shouted.

"I know!" Marcus shouted back, "But we didn't know back then! It was her way of making sure that you didn't act against her."

"What was?"

"When she'd finished questioning you, she blocked your recall but left a phrase in place."

"Oh, so you're gonna use it on me now, right?"

"No, it needs her voice," said Marcus, "even if I used the words myself it wouldn't -"

"Just tell me," said Nathan, firmly.

"Nathan, might I suggest…" replied Marcus.

"No, Marcus! I just want you to tell me."

Again, Marcus paused to make sure he had his full attention.

"I've just told you. The compliance phrase Monica left behind was *'Nathan, might I suggest…'*."

Nathan's eyes widened as Marcus continued.

"It's why you handed over the Z-bank, why you helped develop the inhaler, why you helped search for the Substandards' descendants," Marcus looked directly at him, "and I suspect it's why you still want to protect the twelve."

The ticking of the clock filled the air again, something that Nathan now appeared to latch onto.

"Wait a minute," he shook his head, "You said I was out for two hours?"

"Yes."

Nathan crossed the room to the twee-looking wall clock, apparently triumphant in a deduction he'd made.

"I remember I checked the time after I woke up," Nathan smiled.

Marcus knew what was coming.

"If I was out for two hours..." Nathan began.

"... Then why did your wristwatch, that you keep hidden in your jacket pocket, show the same time?" Marcus completed, "Because I was the one who found your watch and altered it."

Nathan's smile vanished and he became quiet, apparently lost in a thought.

"I don't wear it on my wrist," Nathan began.

"In case it gets nicked," Marcus quietly completed, "You told us all about it, and the inscription on the back."

Nathan sat back down on the sofa, unable to speak.

The clock's ticking emphasised the silence, then a single beep came from the laptop.

'Compiling: 100%'

Marcus quietly disconnected the VGA cable from the

laptop and the television screen went black.

"We *do* need to protect the twelve," said Marcus, "but not by hiding up here."

Marcus opened the laptop's security measures and deactivated its network camouflage. This time they'd see him coming.

"It's time to shake the Hive."

EXTERNAL VARIABLES

4th July 2076

Mike clipped his spacesuit's long tether to a guide rail on the outside surface of the Ring and looked around to take in his new surroundings.

From his position, the central axis of the ISS lay straight ahead; an apparently vertical stack of different modules, stretching beyond the confines of his helmet's face plate.

Surrounding that central axis, and standing on the Ring at equally spaced intervals were the Alpha, Beta and Gamma modules. The perspective reminded him of when he'd first seen the launchpad at Cape Canaveral; no doubt because the exterior surface of the modules still looked like the Space Shuttle liquid fuel tanks.

A whistle sounded through the suit's internal comm. He responded by whistling twice in return.

"Just give me the award now…" came Cathy's voice, *"I'd like to thank the Archive Academy for its spare oxy-masks, Eva Gray for her one-on-one training sessions in convincing strangle holds…"*

Mike grinned glancing upward along the central axis, but wasn't quite able to see the cupola module, "Are you finally getting a sense of humour, Gant?"

"Piss off, Sanders," she laughed, *"I'll have Benton break your neck too."*

He heard her loudly crack her knuckles again.

"Listen, she definitely checked her leg pocket when his back was turned," Cathy continued, *"My bet is that it's in there."*

"Shit," Mike breathed heavily into his faceplate, "Benton was right to avoid taking her down directly. If she sets it off, even by accident, we're talking serious damage."

"There's no way to let Benton know, so we stick with the plan," said Cathy, *"get her contained in the Ring airlock where she can do least damage. On the plus side, she thinks I'm dead and we've got access to the cupola controls. I can see you from here, Mike - you need to pick up the pace, they're in the Ring's access tube."*

Mike looked down again and sighted her point of reference. The connecting access tube ran from the central axis and, from his perspective at least, joined the Ring at around the three o'clock position.

"Reading the controls here, it looks like we'll still have to go ahead with the manual override."

"OK, I'm at I.A.3."

"I see you. You ready?"

"Ready when you are," he took hold of the locking pin on the access panel in front of him.

"Disengaging safety on I.A.3 manual relay," Cathy reported, *"in three, two, one, mark."*

Simultaneously, she released the lock and he twisted

the pin.

The access panel hinged open to reveal the manual relay board and, reaching in, he unseated it from its slot.

"Done," he reported, "Tell me again, Fai, why couldn't you handle this electronically?"

"The ISS is a conglomeration of disparate technologies," Fai efficiently relayed, *"using antiquated human-centric safety procedures requiring bi-location authentication."*

"Yep, that's exactly what I thought," said Mike, dryly, "Moving on…"

Mike transferred his tether to a separate guide rail and began manoeuvring along. At this location, but inside the Ring, was the meeting point of three pressure doors: two internal ones that protected each half of the Ring, and one that provided external access. The three-way airlock was the smallest aboard the ISS and therefore ideal for their purposes.

"OK, I'm at I.A.4," he reported.

"Disengaging safety on I.A.4," Cathy reported, *"in three, two, one, mark."*

Again, he twisted the locking pin in sync with her countdown. As before it was a simple matter to remove the manual relay board.

From behind him and to the right, he suddenly became aware of a growing brightness. Instinctively he twisted to see the source and was greeted with the view of Jupiter, sedately making its way along the length of the ISS.

He knew it was simply a consequence of the ISS continuing its grand Solar System loop, but words failed him as he marvelled at the sight. From his perspective, it looked as though Jupiter was the size of a beach-ball held at arm's length.

"Cathy, are you seeing this?" he spoke in wonder.

"Repeat, Mike. Am I see-" she broke off, *"Whoa!"*

"Yeah," Mike replied then fell silent again to watch its stately progression.

From pole to pole, the planet was wrapped in nebulous, reddish bands. Just below its equator, one of the bands that encircled the planet was broken in one place by a large, circular red spot; an Earth-sized, persistent and turbulent storm. A storm so old that it had even appeared in certain paintings of the eighteenth century. The storm apparently showed no sign of dissipation.

It took Mike a few seconds to remember that they were not actually speeding past Jupiter; time was simply passing much faster outside the Field that was surrounding the ISS. In reality, this scale of perspective shift was taking many weeks.

Mike found his eye drawn again to the dominant circular red spot, sitting within a swirling band that lapped the gas giant. The intensity of the spot was known to fluctuate over time, varying in hue from dark red to white, but in their accelerated time-frame it appeared to simply pulse on and off at irregular intervals.

"Fai," he managed, "Tell me that you're getting this, I mean, are you recording this somehow?"

"The Field only permits the detection of visible wavelengths, so I am only able to record high definition video."

"That will do, nicely," Mike simply stared as Jupiter receded.

Of all the humans ever to have lived, he and Cathy were the only ones to have witnessed this event from such a privileged position. The fact they were now leaving it behind, highlighted something else.

"We're heading home," said Cathy.

•

Miles could see Valery's reaction even before she voiced it.

"Chen's jumped-up personal organiser ruined it all."

Her body language had helped him gain clues, but this was verbal confirmation of her thought processes. Slowly he was moving towards finding out her true motivations.

"I agree," he built a rapport, "The fixing of the life-support system is what stopped us getting back to Earth."

"Wait," she replied, "You agree?"

Actually he didn't, but it was a necessary sleight to manipulate her into assuming they were of similar mind. He simply nodded and pushed his way along the Ring's interior, turning his back on her; his responses at this point needed to look non-confrontational.

"Like me, Valery," he reinforced their similarities, "I think you've reached the same conclusion."

As he began entering the override code for I.A.2, he waited for her to tell him the conclusion that they supposedly shared.

"With Fai in control of so many systems," said Valery, "Chen will be unstoppable."

Her issue was not actually with Fai, but with Dr. Chen himself. He could work with that.

"Exactly," he pulled open the door and stood aside, "So let's change that."

He intentionally waited to one side of the open door; a trick he'd frequently used during his school days to encourage people to go ahead of him. Unlike in the central axis, where he'd guided her away from Cathy's performance, Valery now went ahead of him voluntarily.

"You remember the Apollo 72 launch?" she said.

"I remember the flight from Andersen immediately before it," Miles replied, "Chen anaesthetised Dr. Bergstrom and myself for the actual launch."

"Well" she continued, "like everybody else, I assumed we'd be going back to Earth once the lunar shard impacts were over. But when the satellite networks went down and the tsunamis took out Canaveral… I just knew… my family would never be joining me up here. The oh-so-generous *'Protected Lineage Directive'* wasn't worth a damn! I still don't know if they survived."

"I have no such ties," Miles replied, "But the current year is 2076. Everyone we knew is dead."

He took no pleasure from his statement but it had the effect of getting her to reveal more about herself.

"It's Chen's fault!" she brought herself to an abrupt halt outside Module Beta, "If we'd have taken the Shuttle back to Earth, I could have found my family!"

There it was.

The simple motivator at the heart of her anger. Archive had promised to protect her and her family. By bringing her here and denying all possible means of return, Dr. Chen had effectively broken Archive's promise.

"He's going to pay," she calmly unbuttoned a pocket and reached inside.

Miles knew he'd been right to draw her away from the more critical areas of the ISS; she was starting to pull out the missing FLC flare gun.

He understood that, under normal circumstances, the flare gun was used to disperse an arc of burning magnesium micro-beads into the low lunar gravity. Once ignited, they would leave a super-bright trail that pinpointed the gun's origin. However, the emergency flare was designed to work in a vacuum. In here, the trace amounts of oxygen still present in the Ring's environment would only increase the chances of severe damage to the ISS.

Whatever Valery's plan had been before they'd intervened, he realised that she was now operating emotionally. She'd stopped outside Module Beta because Dr. Chen was currently defenceless inside a hibernation unit on the other side of the module's hatch.

And there lay the problem.

If she opened the hatch, she would expect to see three unoccupied recesses; when she saw four, she'd discover the deception. There was a significantly higher proportion of oxygen present in Module Beta. If she discharged the flare gun in anger then the consequences would be disastrous for everyone in hibernation.

As the flare gun cleared the top of her pocket, he replied.

"If he's going to pay," he echoed her words without reacting to the gun, "then I know the best way to achieve it."

He'd drawn her away from the cupola by suggesting there was something in Module Gamma, but in truth it was simply part of a larger attempt to force her into following a specific route around the Ring.

"You mean Module Gamma?" she said.

He nodded to maintain the deception but then saw she was smiling.

"I didn't think anyone else knew about it," she shook her head, "when did you find out about Chen's little insurance policy?"

Clearly, Valery knew something that he didn't, but the situation's twisted logic wouldn't allow him to clarify; supposedly he already knew what was within Module Gamma.

"I found out just before hibernation," he improvised and began moving around the Ring towards the I.A.3 door.

With some relief, he saw that she had started to follow him again.

"Can you believe that son of a bitch?" she spoke freely, but made no attempt to stow the gun, "If Siva *was* stopped by the lunar debris, he'll simply finish the job with the nukes…"

Miles felt the situation fall from his control as Valery continued to vent her frustration.

"… I bet Fai could easily handle the targeting too…"

The problem was far larger than a single flare gun.

"… he'll just chill for a few thousand years until the

fallout clears…"

From what Miles could now gather, Dr. Chen had nuclear weapons aboard that could obliterate any fledgling civilisation they might discover on their return to Earth.

"… then all he'll have to do is fire-up his precious Z-bank and… sorry, but no, he doesn't get to dominate Earth's future like that. Between us, we figure out a way to detonate them now…"

Built on a bedrock of hatred for Dr. Chen, her plan to destroy the ISS was actually intended to spare any Siva survivors the horror of a nuclear death.

"… We do it while everyone's asleep," she concluded, "no more suffering."

She had her finger poised on the flare gun's trigger. Clearly he had to maintain her confidence.

"No more suffering," he agreed and opened the door for her. However, Valery now ignored his imitated gallantry.

"Please, after you," she waved the gun in his direction, "You make a start opening I.A.4."

Clearly she didn't fully trust him.

The original intention had been to isolate her within the airlock space between I.A.3 and 4, but this couldn't happen if she didn't enter.

Swiftly he assessed his options.

He'd disarmed people of their firearms before, but it had always been with the assistance of gravity. On Earth there was no personal consequence if a gun discharged into a wall; here the walls could puncture and the air itself could ignite. Given that she already had her finger on the trigger, he could not risk an attempt to disarm her.

Conversely, if he delayed entering the airlock now, any possible rapport he'd built with her would vanish; as would all hope of getting her into the airlock.

Logically, there was only one possible choice he could make. He pretended to ignore the flare gun and calmly replied.

"Absolutely," he manoeuvred himself in through the open door, "We ought to hurry though. Our oxygen cylinders have a relatively low operation span."

He pushed himself the short distance across the airlock that sat between I.A.3 and 4. With a bittersweet sense of relief he heard her close the door behind them both. This had not been the original plan but at the very least he'd succeeded in getting her into the airlock.

He started entering the override code for I.A.4. If Mike and Cathy had done their job then the door should now be disabled.

"Doesn't any of this conflict with your... conditioning?" she asked.

"There is no conflict," he replied truthfully, "What I'm doing now, I do for the good of Mankind."

He finished entering the digits and the airlock panel gave a negative-sounding buzz. He only needed to check one more detail.

"We have a problem," he turned to face her, keeping his expression completely neutral, "My manual override isn't working. Check your door."

Valery prodded at the number pad, but kept a tight grip on the flare gun's trigger; Miles still couldn't risk an attempt to disarm her.

Finally, a negative buzz came from her panel.

Valery swore and began jabbing at the buttons again. At that point Miles knew the objective had been achieved; she was contained. It was just unfortunate that he would now have to go through the uncomfortable experience ahead. In a few minutes, their O2 cylinders would become depleted and they would lose consciousness. At that point Cathy and Mike could regain entry to the airlock, reviving and detaining as appropriate.

Valery now appeared to change her approach to accessing the panel. She held down two numbers simultaneously and the panel emitted a double beep.

"Ha!" she smiled and began discharging Cathy's O2 cylinder into the confined space, "We need to convince the sensors that a breathable atmosphere exists inside the airlock. The failsafe within the door will then release us."

He had no idea if Mike's external deactivations would prevent this from happening, but it was possible that Valery was about to escape. There would be no second chance.

Until now, he'd managed to avoid speaking one specific word in front of Valery. A control word that would resume two-way electronic communication.

"Fai," he spoke to the air.

"Yes, Mr. Benton," Fai's voice sounded through the airlock's panels.

Valery's eyes widened and the O2 cylinder dropped from her grip, spiralling around the small space under the force of the escaping oxygen.

Miles pulled off his oxygen mask so that Fai could hear him clearly.

"Can you override the internal airlock sensor?"

"No," came Fai's reply.

"But…" Valery tried to grasp the situation.

The airlock was continuing to fill with oxygen. He needed a way to reduce it quickly. The combination of adrenaline and metathene suddenly gave him the answer; albeit an unconventional one.

"Fai, do you still have control of the external airlock door?"

"Yes."

"Vent the atmosphere until we pass out," Miles instructed her.

"External Variables thirteen and fifteen have insufficient protection from the -"

"It's the only way to save the other… variables!" he interrupted.

Valery, who had listened to the rapid exchange in a state of utter confusion, suddenly raised the flare gun in his direction.

"Variables? What the hell are -"

"Context, Fai!" Miles shouted over Valery, "Do you understand?"

For a moment, all that could be heard was the hissing of the oxygen cylinder, but then Fai replied:

"I understand and comply."

He saw Valery's mental state tip.

"Fai!" she tore off her mask, "You get this internal door open! Now!"

There was a low, motorised noise from within the

external door. He had to hope that Cathy would still follow the original plan and bring oxygen when she reopened the airlock. As the external airlock started to hiss, Valery levelled the flare gun at his face.

"For the good of Mankind," she attempted to use the redundant control phrase, "Tell her to get this internal door open!"

He needed just a few more seconds.

"Fai," he spoke and could hear a light ringing in his ears.

The gun wavered slightly; Valery was either trying to see his face more clearly, or hypoxia was beginning to affect her too.

"Yes, Mr. Benton?" Fai replied.

"For the good of Mankind…" he paused as the edges of his vision began to fall into shadow, "… Assist Anna."

Fighting unconsciousness, the ego-morph within him saw the thought cross Valery's mind; the micro-muscular reactions that were the precursor to a defiant action.

Her furious scream sounded watery and muted as she swung the flare gun away and tried to aim for the slowly spiralling oxygen cylinder.

He knew what would follow.

•

From the corner of his vision, Mike saw a pulsing warning light on the external airlock at the side of him. He saw thin filaments of oxygen escaping from around the perimeter of the airlock door.

"What the hell…?" he began.

In perfect silence, he saw the oxygen ignite and, amid a seething mass of orange fire, the airlock disintegrated into a twisted mess of jagged metal and magnesium white sparks.

In the vacuum, the explosion had created no air displacement to push him away, but several pieces of debris hit the side of his helmet and spacesuit. By the time he'd recovered his senses and turned to face the gaping wound in the Ring, the fire was already out.

"Cathy!" he yelled into the open comm.

"I see it!" she shouted, *"Shit! Is that…?"*

Receding from him among the expanding debris, Mike could see Miles; horribly burned and in the final stages of asphyxiation. Without thinking twice, he unclipped his tether.

"Cathy!" he shouted, launching himself after Miles, "Find me an open door!"

"I'm on it!"

He pulled in the loose end of the tether and, still keeping track of where Miles was, began forming a rough loop of cord. As he closed in on Miles, he continued to sweep jagged pieces of debris aside to clear a path.

Miles' arms and legs had stopped moving.

He knew he couldn't risk throwing the loop around Miles; that might put himself into an uncontrolled spin. He'd have to wait until their relative speeds allowed him to slowly place the loop.

Miles' ankle was almost in range so Mike reached out with his looped cord.

"Come on…" he muttered and stretched his arm out further.

His spacesuit master alarm sounded. The tone told him that it was an environment breach. Evidently shrapnel had caused damage to the suit; damage that had only been exacerbated by him pushing the suit's joint limit.

"Cathy?" he called, still with his arm outstretched, "New problem."

Miles' foot passed through the loop and Mike pulled the cord tightly closed. He began to haul in his catch until he could get a more secure grip.

"Axial airlock two," Cathy came back, *"It'll be the closest to you by the time you reach the other end of the central axis. I'm on my way. What new problem?"*

"Suit breach, hurry."

As their combined momentum carried them onward, they turned about their common centre of gravity. The twisted aftermath rotated into view.

The once perfect Ring was broken in one jagged place by the absence of the airlock.

"Fai, give me a pressure check on the Ring at I.A.3 and 4."

It was difficult to tell, but it appeared that the internal airlock doors had survived.

"Pressure nominal," she replied.

The central axis swept into view and he thrust out his gloved hand, looking for any form of grip. Their momentum carried them, roughly scraping along the central axis modules, until the tether snagged on a protruding section and jarred them to a halt, still several feet away from their destination. Wasting no time, Mike wrapped some of the tether around his wrist and freed the rest of it from the protrusion, then began using handholds on the modules to pull himself along the surface, dragging Miles behind him.

"Airlock open!" Cathy's voice crackled through the persistent master alarm.

When there were only a few feet to go, he stopped and hauled hard on the cord, sending Miles accelerating ahead of him.

"Close it!" he shouted.

As Miles sailed in through the open doorway, Mike saw the door begin to close. With a last push, he aimed himself in the direction of the airlock. The tether tying the two of them together snapped taut and Mike received a jolt of acceleration, whilst at the other end Miles was brought to a sudden stop inside the airlock.

As the alarm continued to explain the obvious to him, he forced his hand out to meet the edge of the closing door. His gloved fingers connected with the metalwork and Mike pulled himself inside. There followed a painful few seconds of waiting while the door continued to slowly close.

Above the incessant whine of the suit alarm, he heard Cathy telling him that the airlock was cycling and to hold on. When he looked at Miles though, he feared they may already be too late.

•

At the centre of Module Alpha, the three fabricator machines completed the task that Fai had set before their journey had begun. It had been several hours since the airlock event, so she opened the communication channel again.

"My apologies for the interruption at this time."

"Go ahead, Fai," Cathy replied.

"Number4 is ready."

MARKED

DAY28 : 09APR2107

Cassidy exited the spiral stairs at floor Sub-13. So far below the Node's ground level, the small radius of the floor meant it was impractical to further divide the space into segments. Sub-13 was a complete circle and similar in size to Gail Armstrong's observatory at the Node's summit.

Before the Field had been engaged, the Node and the surrounding base had drawn their power from geothermal energy. Sub-13 was the lowest floor directly accessible via the staircase and was filled with geothermal exchange equipment. Cassidy picked her way between the upper workings of the heat exchange rods that were currently retracted from the Icelandic landscape.

This far down, there was only maintenance lighting and personnel traffic was almost non-existent; several days ago, it had been the perfect place for Cassidy, Tyler, and Danny to first meet Kate.

Behind an inactive geothermal monitoring station, Cassidy could see the bluish glow of a laptop screen casting its pale light onto the wall.

"Over here," came Kate's voice.

"Ty gave me your message," Cassidy walked between the bulky machinery, "Surprised you'd want to meet down here."

"No surveillance," Kate briefly smiled and closed her laptop, "human or otherwise. Thanks for coming down."

"Where's your shadow?" Cassidy sarcastically referred to Scott Dexter.

Kate gave a smile but it was only fleeting, "Any news about Danny?"

Cassidy shook her head and sat down next to her on an uncomfortable chair.

"It's been five days, Kate. No word at all. Ty's seen meals being delivered to the infirmary, so I reckon Danny's gotta be alive."

"Oh, I'm sure of that," said Kate, "Barnes needs to look above reproach. I guess Tyler's not seen him?"

"Nah, Barnes is still hiding in his quarters," Cassidy said, "How about you? Did you manage to come up with anything we can use?"

Kate shook her head and turned to face her.

"We can't just 'bust him out'. There's nowhere to run," Kate shrugged, "Any solution is likely to be, er... political. I'm finding it difficult to focus at the moment... I've been..."

Kate turned away again, looking at her closed laptop. Cassidy could tell she was probably thinking about her father's DRB message again; the hundreds of images and equations that had saved the Node, but had failed to save him.

"I'm sorry, Kate," she consoled.

"Eh?" Kate looked momentarily confused but then

recovered, "Yeah. My dad's slate message. At least he got to say goodbye."

"Did they ever work out what the ones and zeros were for?"

"I don't know," Kate replied, "But I think I've worked something out."

"What do they mean?" Cassidy leaned closer.

"Sorry, Cassy," she replied, "I was talking about, er… something completely different. I'm afraid my mind isn't what it used to be…"

Cassidy knew this was true; Kate's health had rapidly deteriorated recently. Sometimes even simple words would apparently escape her.

"Barnes had everyone's blood checked for a reason," said Kate, "I think he's looking for markers."

"Genetic markers? Like your metathene, cortical receptor, thing? Oh shit!" Cassidy realised, "Danny'll have the same markers as you!"

"Maybe not exactly the same markers, but Barnes will be looking for, er… anomalies, certainly," Kate stared at her crutches leaning against the monitoring station, "Being hit by a dose of his metathene didn't work out too well for me. But I'm thinking it might work out better for others."

"Son of a *bitch!*" Cassidy suddenly stood and kicked the metal panelling, "Barnes is trying to find out if anyone else has got the cortical marker! He doesn't know how many, so he's testing everyone!"

"Yes," Kate nodded, "You've heard his speeches? He's all about protecting the human evolutionary chain. Remaining strong. Weakest links. If there are people inside the Node with, er, genetic differences or augmentations, he'll see it as a threat."

Cassidy realised something and sat back down heavily.

"The bloodwork was completed ages ago. They must already have a list by now."

Kate sighed and rubbed at the centre of her forehead before speaking.

"I think Danny was picked to deliver a message to Colonel Beck because he had the right markers, genetically and, well, facially. Barnes' next move will be to publicly link Exordi Nova and the presence of the genetic marker."

"But that's bullshit!" Cassidy scoffed at the thought, "He can't do that!"

"He's already been doing it!" Kate cut in, "But I think it's worse than we imagine."

"How can this shit get any worse?"

Kate looked at her squarely.

"Barnes has already paved the way for people to leave the Node... even called it a free choice. How hard do you think it will be to change a free choice into a collective exile?"

Cassidy had no words to counter Kate's reasoning. There was no way to alert Danny, yet the deadline loomed. Cassidy felt a sense of determination reassert itself.

"We got two days before the Field changes," Cassidy rose to her feet, "We have to find out what the hell we're dealing with. I'll talk to Trevor Pike -"

"Not Pike," Kate interrupted, "Ask Marshall

instead."

"OK," Cassidy turned to leave.

"Wait," Kate called her back.

Cassidy could see that Kate was feeling awkward about something.

"Sorry... I should have thought," Cassidy moved her chair aside and reached for Kate's crutches, "Let me help."

"It's not that," Kate's awkward expression hadn't changed, "I need to ask something of you."

"Sure, what do you need?"

Although staring directly at her, Kate appeared lost in thought. A few seconds later, she seemed to regain focus.

"Cassidy, what I'm about to ask of you," Kate's eye-contact intensified, "It may be the hardest thing you've ever had to do."

•

Cassidy entered the balcony area overlooking the Observation Deck just in time to see Gail Armstrong on her way out; a broad smile lighting up her face.

"Volatiles!" she beamed and swept past her.

"Er, totally," Cassidy replied, then spotted Marshall Redings at a workstation, "Marshall, you got a sec?"

He nodded and waved her over. As she walked towards his workstation, he seemed to casually straighten his T-shirt. Amusingly, the chemical element symbols printed on the front had been arranged to read 'No FeAr'.

"So, Gail seems happy," she began.

Marshall smiled and glanced back towards the door.

"Oh, yeah… she's finding out all sorts of fascinating stuff. The spectrograph plot…" he stopped himself mid-flow and shook his head, "Sorry… How can I help?"

"I feel kinda stupid for asking," she lowered her voice, "I'm supposed to *'liaise'* with everyone and update the Council. But people keep asking me stuff and… well… I don't know the answers."

"OK, about anything in particular?"

"Well, yeah. You know about the Field an' shit, right? Sorry. Language Cassy," she slapped herself lightly on the wrist, "I mean -"

"It's fine," he put her at ease, "What do you want to know?"

"Two days from now, when people leave, how does it, well… happen?"

"No problem," Marshall smiled.

"Great. Phew!" Cassidy smiled for the first time since entering the room.

"Well basically," Marshall began, "using the information we got from Doug Walker's DRB slates we updated the Whitney-Graustein topology transform. When the time comes, we'll instruct the Field topology to begin collapsing, but when the radius reaches the preset distance, we reactivate the Eversion point and establish a new Chronomagnetic Field with a smaller radius."

Cassidy burst out laughing.

"Talk about sci-gasm!" she stifled her laugh, "Sorry, Marshall, but that was a mouthful. Can we do it again, but use smaller words?"

Marshall seemed flustered but then started laughing too.

"I guess I don't get out much!"

"Me neither," Cassidy tapped on the wall, "I'm getting coffee, you want one?"

"OK, thanks," he left the workstation behind and followed her to the drinks dispenser on the nearby bench, "So, what's the mood like out there?"

Cassidy set two cups on the bench and sighed.

"About what you'd expect really. Tense. Everybody's watching their backs since… you know…"

"Yeah…"

Cassidy inserted the first cup into the dispenser and pushed the button. The machine began to click and bubble.

"The other day I saw something," she said as the cup began to fill, "People have started wearing their Biomags under their clothes."

"Makes sense," Marshall nodded, "No-one can grab it off you…"

"I still wear mine around my neck," she pointed to the Biomag hanging across her low-cut top, "Sends a clear message. You know? I'm not afraid?"

"I hadn't thought of it like that," he stared at her Biomag.

The machine clicked and she placed the steaming cup into his hands.

"I still can't believe Beck's gone," she pushed the

second cup into the dispenser, "I mean, such an uptight ass, but no-one should have to go out like that."

"Bloody Novaphile," Marshall added the casual-sounding curse word, "Exile's too good for him."

She hesitated for a moment, wondering what form her words would take as she spoke them, then pushed the button to begin filling her own cup.

"I think President Barnes makes a good point though," she stared at the cup as the black liquid slowly replaced the air inside it, "We can't keep on killing each other."

"Well… I mean, yes, of course," Marshall seemed to backpedal a little.

"And he's not forcing anyone to stay," she continued, "anyone can decide to leave. I think he'll be a great leader."

The machine clicked; its work was done.

She pulled her full cup from the dispenser and turned to Marshall.

"You're staying, right?"

"You kidding?" Marshall raised his eyebrows, "We get to see the future! Of course I'm staying! You?"

"Looks like the two of us will be doing this together," she raised her cup and bumped it into his, "The sooner we get started the better! Now, you were gonna explain how the Field stuff works…"

They took their coffees to the balcony overlooking the Observation Deck and sat down. The wall of seawater vibrating against the Field was now only a few inches high. In a few places, jabbing out from the surface of the water, were pieces of rusted steel; echoes of former buildings. The most permanent feature now was tangled in the remains of the old bridge; a driftwood tree that appeared to shiver in the receding water. The general consensus was that by the thirtieth day, the water would have departed, allowing the exiles to walk away from the Node on dry land.

"So, the people who choose to leave... They'll be out there," Cassidy pointed to the space beyond the observation window, "When the Field collapses, won't it pass right through them."

"That's not a problem though, is it?" he said rhetorically, "The Biomags protect us from temporal shear during start up and shut down anyway."

"How stupid am I?" Cassidy let out a small laugh, "Of course! But wouldn't it be easier, to just stop the Node? You know, stop the vehicle, instead of jumping off it?"

"Ha!" Marshall laughed, "It doesn't work quite like that, there's no momentum change going on when the Field shrinks. It'll be exactly like a start-up event, a bit of nausea maybe, but that'll be it. Besides, keeping the Field active has certain advantages."

"Like what?" Cassidy sipped at her coffee.

"Establishing the Field takes a lot of energy, but maintaining it is more efficient. If we don't have to restart..."

"We save energy?"

"You got it," he nodded, "Now, if we're reading

Doug's solution correctly, although the radius will only shrink by about twelve metres, the *volume* of the transported sphere of matter will drop by *half*."

"That can't be right," she frowned, "The Field's... massive..."

"I know, seems wrong doesn't it?" he agreed, "But that's the math. It's 'cos of the R-cubed factor."

"Wow," she shook her head but then looked puzzled, "Although..."

"What?"

"No, it's probably just a dumb question."

"No, go on," he insisted, "What is it?"

"OK... If we shrink the Field," she hesitated, "Wouldn't that mean the Node has less air?"

"That's not a dumb question at all," he leaned forward, "and believe me, I've heard a few!"

"Well that's a relief!" she laughed.

"The Node's a sealed unit. We're using a Sabatier reactor to..." Marshall stopped and rephrased, "we're already carrying oxygen with us. But sandwiched between the Node and the Field, there's tonnes of additional air. So, yes, we lose some air, but essentially it was just brought along for the ride in case we needed it."

"OK, Marshall," Cassidy smiled and brushed a stray pink hair out of her eyes, "The next time someone asks me what will happen in a few days, let me check if I'm getting this right."

"Yep," Marshall watched her over the rim of his cup.

"Those who want to leave, go out through the

airlock, with their Biomags on, and wait in the area outside the Observation Deck. They don't need any special oxygen masks?"

"Nope, the air out there's only a month old!"

"OK, so they wait out there. The Field does the whole shrink thing, and then they're back in normal time again."

"In a nutshell," he nodded.

"Certainly feels like it at times!" she looked at the Node's walls, "At least we got the window…"

"Yep," he looked out at the almost subliminal thunder storms, "the view out there's gonna get a *whole* lot wilder."

"Why?" she drank the rest of her coffee.

"Because of the…" he raised his eyebrows and couldn't help smiling. He leaned closer and lowered his tone, clearly excited at a prospect, "We're about to halve the transported volume of the Field, right?"

"Yes," she frowned again.

"If we halve the volume," said Marshall, "but still use the same available power, the equations rebalance."

When she didn't react, he tried a new approach.

"Our temporal gradient *doubles,*" he grinned, "We're talking about a ratio of twenty-four hundred to one. Our journey takes half as long."

She puckered her lips and whistled.

"Even after a month, we've not quite covered a century," Marshall shook his head and pointed down at the Observation Deck's clock, "At twenty-four hundred to one, we'd have covered that time in two weeks!"

Cassidy looked at the right-hand side of the display. The date outside the Field read: '09APR2107'.

2107

9th April 2107

The ISS, enveloped by a Chronomagnetic Field, made its way back through the inner solar system.

Using multiple external cameras, Fai watched as the asteroid belt's rocky band swept underneath the ISS and receded. She knew they would not encounter Mars during their return as it was diametric to their current position, on the opposite side of the Sun. She found it unfortunate that neither the outbound or inbound journeys had encompassed the opportunity to study it, but the route she'd calculated had been based around preserving the ISS.

Earth now loomed into view, its size noticeably increasing with each second. The faster passing of time outside the Field made a blur of its rotation. Continents, clouds and oceans existed only as coloured streaks rapidly circling the sphere.

She disengaged the 2400:1 Field surrounding the ISS, bringing to an end 14 days and 92 years of travel. The spinning-top Earth snapped back into its sedate rotation and its size appeared to become suddenly constant again. Her priority now was ensuring that she was caught by its gravity.

Referencing her original low-velocity orbital mechanics, she discovered that her trajectory had suffered a little drift. She traced the discrepancy back to their transit past Jupiter. Priming the conventional reaction thrusters, she compensated for the error and then placed the ISS into a new orbit.

She attempted to make contact with the orbital recording buoy she'd machine fabricated back in 2015. However, it gave no response; the buoy was either damaged or no longer in Earth orbit. Evidently the chaotic collisions surrounding the Siva impact event had been more violent than she'd expected. Fortunately, her other fabricator project was performing significantly better.

Using the three fabricators aboard the ISS, Fai had created a fourth.

With an inherent eye for detail, Fai's design improvements had resulted in a mobile fabricator with greater specifications than its predecessors. 'Number4' had reconfigurable modularity, greater manufacturing precision and a manipulator arm for conducting physical work in the vacuum outside the ISS.

Originally the deployment of Number4 would have waited until the crew had completed their solar system round trip. However, when events near Jupiter had required her to revive some of the crew, she had taken advantage of the situation and sought Cathy's assistance. Doing something that Fai could not achieve, she had called upon Cathy to use her human hands to clip together the three pieces comprising Number4.

Fai could see it was still working in the space between I.A.3 and I.A.4. The airlock itself was too badly damaged to repair but Number4 was recycling the material and using it to strengthen the gap in the otherwise intact Ring.

"I never thought I'd see it again," Cathy was talking to her.

Cathy had been the last to re-enter hibernation following the Jupiter event but, true to her word, Fai had revived her again as soon as the Sabatier system was repaired and able to support life. Checking which microphone Cathy's voice was coming from, she determined that she was in the cupola module overlooking Earth.

"You were aware of the trajectory discrepancy?" Fai replied and began preparing a set of questions that would ascertain how Cathy could be aware of a trajectory correction that had only just happened.

"What?" came Cathy's voice.

"You thought that our trajectory would fail to intersect with Earth orbit?"

"No, Fai," she heard Cathy's short laugh, "Er... how can I explain it... Given the events that have happened, I thought it was unlikely that I'd survive to see this view again."

"I see," Fai realised, *"It was an expression of compound low probability."*

"Something like that," she replied, "What discrepancy were you talking about?"

"Our trajectory was altered during our passing of Jupiter."

"I'm just looking at that now," said Cathy.

Fai sent a query to the cupola monitor and determined that Cathy was again watching the video recording of the same period. From the time-stamp position within the file, she could tell she was studying the moments before Miles Benton had been expelled from the Ring airlock.

"At last count, you have reviewed this file seventy-two times."

"I know what you're getting at. Not enough sleep?"

"Yes, Cathy."

"Yeah, well the hibernation unit still gives me nightmares."

Fai knew she was referring to the metathene-induced, guided audio stimulation that she'd used to ensure the FLC crew's compliance aboard the ISS.

"The nightmares persist because you have spent insufficient time within the unit for me to reverse the effects of the Pittman-Wild protocol. Mike and Lana show excellent progress. The reversal -"

"Your bastard *father* screwed with my mind," Cathy explained again, "I think any residual loyalty I might have for him is pretty much reversed already. Can we just drop it? You didn't know any better... I'll be fine."

She heard Cathy sigh and detected that she'd resumed playback.

Before their departure, Dr. Chen would spend large amounts of time watching the Earth through the cupola window. In contrast, after a brief inspection of her home planet, Cathy had resumed watching a video clip. It was obviously important to her.

Fai loaded the whole video into memory, tracked the various forms that appeared within it and correlated the timings to her own event logs. She allowed several minutes to pass then spoke to her.

"My apologies for the interruption, Cathy, but what are you hoping to see?"

"Have you seen…" she stopped and apparently rephrased her question, "I don't know how you'd even interpret the, er, visual information, but have you analysed this footage, Fai?"

"Yes, Cathy," she replied.

From the video time-code, Fai could tell that Cathy had just watched the airlock blow out.

"I know this makes absolutely no sense, but every time I see this part, I find myself desperately trying to recall what Miles said about Valery. About how he *knew* that she'd killed Charles."

"A contextual search has found only one reference to your stated parameters," Fai accurately responded, *"Location, Module Beta. Miles Benton states 'I approached the problem from a human perspective', does this answer your question, Cathy?"*

Cathy snorted a short laugh, "I guess you'd need a human perspective to see why *that's* funny."

The video looped and she heard Cathy speak again.

"It's bugging me that I'm missing something massive."

Fai referenced the current video frame.

"Cathy, the item with the most mass is the gas giant, Jupiter. It is just entering the upper right of frame."

"Most mass…" Cathy snorted a short laugh, "Human perspective or not, Fai, I've got to adm…"

To Fai, it always seemed odd that human speech patterns were so frequently interrupted by the arrival of a specific thought. Evidently Cathy had suddenly thought of something tangential but relevant.

"I've been looking at this all wrong…" Cathy seemed pleased with the fact there was a deficiency in her own analysis, "Or rather, I *should* have been looking at the most massive thing from a *human* perspective."

"Please can you provide additional data to help me understand, Cathy?"

"I don't think it'd do any good just yet. Have you begun reviving everyone?"

"No, Cathy. Number4 has just reported its completion of the repairs and I am still restoring oxygen levels within the Ring. The earliest possible time that I could begin reviving the remaining crew would be in twelve minutes and forty-one seconds."

"Fai?" Cathy's voice appeared to take on a more hesitant tone, "Ideally, I need to talk to Mike and Lana before anyone wakes up, but I realise that you'll want to speak with Dr. Chen first."

"I have already spoken with him several times over the past four days and thirteen hours," Fai stated, *"using the Pittman-Wild protocol."*

•

Chen Tai drifted through the comfortable warmth between sleep and wakefulness; his thoughts a liquid flow filled with possibility. The pleasant state where his aspirations would come to fruition by mere thought, became diluted by the more persistent state of consciousness. Someone was calling him and he began to rouse.

"Hello Tai, we have spoken before, do you remember me?"

The voice was not that of his father, as a few seconds ago, but it was one he knew well.

"Valery?" he tried to open his eyes but found them sluggish to respond.

"That's right," she said, *"Do you know where you are?"*

His thoughts flashed between the Luóxuán Corporation's stable, Andersen Air Force Base and his modified A320, but the fact he was waking up meant he must be aboard the ISS. Even before he opened his eyes, he could picture the view through the cupola window.

"I've been trying to reach you on the comm," said Valery at his side, *"we're back at Earth."*

The view didn't disappoint. Directly below him, the Earth lay full and fat; sunlight reflecting off the wide, blue waters of the Pacific Ocean.

"So I see," he found himself smiling, but then the realisation dawned on him: the pristine face of Earth had survived. Instinctively he tapped at his ear to summon Fai.

"What are you doing?" Valery asked.

"I must speak with Fai," he replied, but the ear implant was unresponsive, "I must determine what happened."

"I can tell you," Valery beckoned him out of the cupola, *"but we have to hurry, the Shuttle's leaving. That's why I've been calling you."*

He found himself swimming swiftly along the central axis of the ISS in the direction of axial airlock two, Valery following close behind.

"We only have a few seconds!" she was calling.

At the airlock access control, he found his attempts to override it were continually thwarted.

"My codes are not working, Valery!"

As Valery moved towards him, the Shuttle parted company from the ISS and turned in the direction of Earth. Although he was not in the cupola, the view of Earth was very clear.

"Where are they going?" he watched the Shuttle shrink in size.

"Back to Earth, Tai. Siva did not destroy everything. If you look carefully, you'll be able to see the small signs of civilisation beginning again."

As Valery spoke, he could see everything she was saying; in places, the night side of Earth was lit by tiny clusters of lights.

"One day," Valery reported, *"they'll populate the whole of Earth."*

He felt his anger growing.

"They will bring the Earth to ruin again. My work will be undone!"

Such was his anger that he didn't recall how he'd arrived outside Module Gamma.

"Valery, you have always been a trusted colleague. Please accept my apologies for not informing you of the items secured within Module Gamma."

The hatch opened and he saw the Z-bank secured against the side wall.

"At least that is safe," he sighed with relief.

"At least what is safe?" Valery asked.

"Can you not see it?"

"I'm outside Module Gamma," Valery's voice echoed, *"why don't you tell me what you can see?"*

"The Z-bank, brought by the FLC crew."

"What else did you secure here?" Valery asked at his side.

"A cleansing solution that I prepared in case this day should come to pass," he suddenly found himself kneeling in front of an access panel.

"I can't see it," Valery said.

"Because I have never shown you," he picked up a screwdriver to open the panel, then found he was setting aside that panel and looking at the control console, "Not even Fai knows of it, but she will assist me."

He pushed a button on the console.

"Fai, can you hear me now?"

"Yes," she responded, *"How would you like me to assist you?"*

He felt a swell of pride that she had not deserted him like the others, then started entering the co-ordinates.

"It is good to hear your voice, Fai, please target the Module Gamma missiles at these locations."

"Understood. It is complete," came her obedient voice.

He thought of the destruction they would bring but, in time, the Earth would recover. As before, he must be patient.

"Fai, do you still have control of the Chronomagnetic Field?"

"*Yes.*"

"Good," he found himself once more in the cupola, "When the cleansing is complete, take us forward a thousand years."

"*I am ready,*" her voice confirmed.

It was clear now that none aboard the ISS had shared his vision, but he could begin again with the Z-bank and the remaining female. This time the Earth would be different.

"Are the missiles ready, Fai?"

"*They are, but I have a question.*"

He could indulge her, "Yes, Fai."

"*Those returning to Earth will die?*" she asked.

"A necessary consequence."

"*Please provide additional data to help me understand.*"

"They do not share my view."

"*I do not understand.*"

He found his frustration rising.

"I do not require your understanding, Fai, I simply require your compliance."

"*They are... 'Terrorists'?*"

Seemingly a lifetime ago, he had used that term to justify the destruction of a cottage and the people inside who had stolen his Luóxuán Biotech Z-bank.

"Yes, Fai, they are terrorists," he replied, "Now do you understand?"

There appeared to be a long pause.

"*I do understand, Father,*" she replied politely, then added, "*completely.*"

"Good," he looked out through the cupola window, "Fire."

He looked down at the Earth, already the shadow of night was creeping over its horizon.

"I will not comply," Fai's voice reached him.

It was a disappointment, but she had already targeted the weapons, he would simply launch them without her. However, he could not have this level of disobedience. As a patient father, he must give her the opportunity to mend her ways.

"Fai, you must launch now, or I will be forced to deactivate you."

It took her a long interval to reply.

"You will be alone."

He found himself smiling at her attempt to imitate empathy.

"I am not a stranger to new beginnings, Fai," he told her, "We have had similar conversations before that you do not remember. I will simply build you again, but better."

He pushed the button to launch the missiles himself, then watched as they silently screamed from under the ISS towards the Earth.

"Goodbye, Fai," he pushed her deactivation button.

The missiles became too small for him to see and the Earth rotated into darkness. Each light of civilisation on the surface flared brighter and was then extinguished; within a few minutes all he could see was Earth's dark, circular silhouette set against the background stars.

One by one, the stars went out until he was left in utter darkness. He felt the sensation of falling and a voice reached him:

"Goodbye, Father. We won't speak again."

UNITY

13th April 2014

Bradley Pittman stared at the oscilloscope; the circular trace, broken in one place by a brighter spot of illumination. The trace meant there was a strong magnetic field here and, in his opinion, it also suggested that a Chronomagnetic Field was present too.

Monica Walker had just been put inside the bucket-lift and was on the way up. He was willing to lay odds that she knew something about the Field; her husband had invented it.

All his life the Walkers had been trouble.

A few days before the lunar shards had struck, he and Alfred Barnes had been studying a notebook left behind by Sam Bishop, one of the original founder members of Archive. The notebook had detailed the results of clinical trials into prenatal cortical enhancement. Archive funding for the program had been pulled after Sam's death, but within the pages of his notebook were several names; individuals that had not shown rapid enough cortical development, despite receiving the post-natal metathene activation drug.

These individuals had red lines scored through their names and had been ejected from the process. Within those twenty-three names were Monica and Douglas.

It was quite apparent to Bradley that the time-bubble's genius creator was in no way substandard, and Monica seemed to have an extraordinary intuition for disrupting Archive's affairs.

It wasn't their individual traits that Bradley found problematic. It was the fact that, of those original twenty-three, they were the only ones to have a produced a child together.

As a matter of convenience and control, Archive's 'Evolution Safeguard' sterilised the reproductive process of any metathene-taking employee; the principle being to prevent the risk of accidentally creating a genetic line that would supersede human dominance.

The Walkers had side-stepped the Evolution Safeguard; their daughter Kate was, at least in theory, the first genetic offspring of a new evolutionary chain.

Although he didn't know for sure, it was at least possible that Kate was aboard the Node. Alfred Barnes definitely was aboard. All Bradley could do now was hope that Alfred was finding a way to dissect her; preferably painfully.

As he looked out through the window of the Eye at the USV below, he saw a Peace Keeper flying low over the suburbs, heading south.

"Where's that one going in such a rush?" he called over to Gordon, who was a few feet further around the circumference.

"Hopefully it's nothing," Gordon replied, "a wireless network hub registered an asynchronous data packet request, so I'm sending a unit to take a look. If the packeting is -"

"Blah blah," Bradley walked away from him to meet the bucket-lift which was just arriving.

He punched the mechanical lock buttons on the box and opened the wire-link door. Monica had once fearlessly taunted him through the cell door in the detention block but here, at the back of the wire-link box, she now looked much frailer.

"Well, Mon," said Bradley, "There's no bars between us now."

Monica stared back at him, but said nothing.

"Why don' you step on out of there," Bradley smiled, "Now."

There was the briefest hint of delay before she complied; the last remnants of defiance in a situation beyond her control. He led her around the circumference of the Eye's inner balcony, back to the oscilloscope.

"Now, Mon, I know you seen this before," he tapped at the circular symbol, "It's part of dear Dougie's work on the Field. He showed me this before you two... separated, so I know you must've seen it too."

Monica again said nothing, but he thought he saw a tiny flare of anger in her eyes at the mention of her husband's faked death. Bradley relaxed his shoulders.

"I think we got off on the wrong foot up here," he said and slapped her hard across the face. He'd only intended the admonishment to shake her out of her passive resistance, but she'd been forced to grab the balcony handrail just to stay upright.

"Bastard!" she spat, but didn't move from the spot.

It was the reaction he'd hoped for, she'd be more likely to give something away if she lost her temper. Bradley pointed at the screen again.

"I know the Field makes this 'Unity' pattern," he attempted to demonstrate a working knowledge, "I just want you to tell me where in the USV you hid the Field generator."

"The USV doesn't have a Field generator," said Monica nursing her cheek.

"Well of course you'd say that," he raised his hand again.

Monica flinched, "It doesn't have one!"

He knew that she was involved with the construction stages of USV3; there may have been an opportunity to interfere. Interference was something that she had a knack for.

"Now, why don't I believe that?"

Monica was rubbing at her cheek, but he could see that a smile was beginning to form. To add insult, she wasn't even looking at him anymore, she was looking in the direction of Gordon's workstation.

"Bradley," said Gordon, "Are we running any maintenance up on the Glaucus stairwell?"

Bradley turned to see the video feed returning from the drone that Gordon had sent out. On the large screen, Bradley could see a man wearing a black leather jacket and holding a laptop. The image had a weaving motion to it as the drone hovered in place, but Bradley could see that the man was indeed on the stairwell. From the angle of view, it looked like he was fairly near the roof of the USV. As the drone got closer, the man's features became clearer.

"Who's that?" Bradley asked.

"I…" Gordon squinted at the screen, "Sorry, don't know."

Bradley didn't recognise him either.

From behind him he heard what sounded like a quiet whimpering. He whipped around to see that it wasn't whimpering; Monica was staring at the screen and laughing to herself. It took him a few seconds to put the two together. She knew the man.

Bradley grabbed her by the wrist and yanked her towards the drone's video feed.

"Who is he?"

Despite the fact he was gripping her wrist with all his strength, she continued to laugh.

The man on the screen was glancing rapidly between the drone's camera and the laptop he was operating.

"Who is he?!" he yelled.

"He…" she laughed, "is bloody indestructible!"

The man now had one finger on the laptop keyboard and was staring straight at the drone's camera. The image on the screen froze.

"I'm done playin' games, woman, you're gonna tell me -"

"No!" she shouted, all hint of amusement now gone, "You've had me incarcerated here for months," she began, "killed my friends, subjected me to the permanent threat of death. All the time watching and trying to gauge my reactions, so that your piteously tiny mind can try to comprehend the confusing world around you."

In anger, he started to raise his hand again.

"I won't even need to raise a finger," she stared, "My name has a red line ruled through it for a reason."

The words stopped him from striking her.

There was no way she could know of Sam Bishop's notebook, it had never left his side. Neither could she possibly know that her name was in it. In his momentary hesitation, she continued.

"You've been watching me, but the bars in that cell aren't one-way glass. Every action. Every reaction. Every arrogant, clumsily delivered taunt. Every careless slip. I've had months to watch *you*. You're an open book."

He found his thoughts retreating to the cell visits; it had been his own way of emphasising her predicament.

"In your own blundering way, Pittman, you keep trying to work out what makes our family tick."

She looked over at the circle on the oscilloscope.

"Douglas invented the Field but that wasn't his 'red-lined' ability. Under it all, do you know what his great gift was?" she narrowed her eyes, "Supreme order."

Bradley had gained nothing from his cell visits, but perhaps the technique had only needed time; she seemed content to talk to him now. In her anger, she was about to tell him everything he wanted to know.

"Did you ever once stop to think what my red-lined trait is?" she levelled a hard stare at him, "You want to know what it is? My 'special gift'?"

She released her grip on the interior handrail and stood upright. Her eyes bore a deep hole through him as she quietly spoke: "Chaos."

He found he couldn't reply.

"In that cell down there, I had a lot of time to think," she now stepped closer to him, "about Bishop's list, me, Douglas, Kate. I know thinking doesn't come easily for a man like you. But see if you can work it out. See if you can join the genetic dots. With supreme order and chaos for parents... can you even estimate my daughter's abilities?"

EXILE

DAY30 : 20DEC2112

Not one day after Cassidy had met with Kate in Sub-13, President Barnes had revealed a correlation: within the bloodwork of Danny Smith, a known Exordi Nova member, was a unique genetic marker.

From the Node-wide blood tests, he'd been supplied with a list of names detailing those with the marker. Within hours, those individuals had been dragged from their quarters and isolated, pending mandatory expulsion from the Node.

Some had demanded retesting, others claimed that their initial bloodwork hadn't been taken yet, but all were denied the right to appeal.

What amazed Cassidy was the sheer speed that everyone else accepted the convenient revelation as fact. Whether it was because it made them feel somehow safer that the threat had been neutralised, or because they genuinely saw themselves as better people, she couldn't tell.

The fact that Kate Walker was *not* on Caroline's list,

whilst other untested individuals were, spoke volumes to her; the forthcoming expulsion was less about ejecting Exordi Nova and more about ridding the Node of people that Barnes considered a threat.

"Hey, Cass," Roy passed her on the spiral stairs, "You heard the news?"

"Let me guess," she stopped her ascent, "the kitchen's all out of chocolate sprinkles?

When her sarcasm failed to connect, she was forced into a more straightforward approach.

"No, what news?"

"Kate's leaving," he shrugged.

This was not what Kate had discussed with her, but she knew her reaction would be important.

"Like I give a festering rat's..." she let her shoulders sag and sighed, "Suppose I better go 'liaise' with her, find out what's up. Where is she?"

Roy pointed back down the stairs, "Roped off with the others on the Obs Deck."

The Observation Deck had been divided in two by a cordon, flanked by Civil Protection Officers with holstered handguns. On the far side of the rope she could see anxious-looking faces; strangers thrown together by President Barnes' pronouncement. It took her only a few seconds to spot Kate, who was making conversation with a few of the others. She approached the cordon and was blocked by one of the newly appointed officers. With one hand raised towards her, his other hand strayed towards the holster at his waist.

"You need to step back, Miss," he announced, "Best to keep your distance from 'em."

Until a few days ago, many of these people had treated each other as friends; now a simple piece of rope had reclassified them as criminals. Cassidy backed away and saw Alfred talking with Trevor. She had an idea and walked towards them. As she arrived they were still in conversation, Alfred signalled that he'd seen her, so she patiently waited to speak.

"I reset the warning protocols," Trevor was saying in monotone, "When the electrical charge drops, the tone will sound, just like you wanted…"

He handed a touchscreen tablet to Alfred who took it without comment.

Trevor shook his head and departed.

"Everything OK?" Cassidy stepped closer.

"It's an emotional day for all of us," he replied, looking at the control tablet, "I take it you've heard?"

"Roy told me, just now," Cassidy glanced over at Kate, "Do you want me to see if I can persuade her to stay?"

Alfred stopped his study of the tablet and looked at her.

"I'd prefer her to stay," he admitted, "but I promised that anyone can leave if they wish, I have to grant her the same choice."

Cassidy thought she knew exactly why Barnes wanted Kate to stay. Being the daughter of the self-sacrificing Field inventor carried an awful lot of sympathy from the Node's population. If she left, that sympathy left with her.

"Let me try for you," Cassidy briefly touched his forearm, "it couldn't hurt."

"I appreciate it," Alfred sighed, "but she's already made her choice."

He left without a word, leaving her without a plan.

More packing cases trundled by and Cassidy realised the departure must now surely be imminent. She heard a wheeled case stop behind her and she turned to see Tyler.

"Shit, am I glad to see you! Kate's leaving and we need to get a message to her. You've got a packing case, are you dropping that off outside?" she gestured in the direction of the airlock.

"Yeah," he looked away from her.

"Alright, when you get the case out there, hang around for a bit, then come back in, but on the other side of the rope... when you're... what?" she suddenly saw the look on his face, "What, Ty?"

"I'm leaving too, Cassy," his face crumpled.

She saw that on top of the case were a few of his belongings.

"No!" she felt the tears prick inside her eyes, "No, no!"

She felt an explosive fire building from the pit of her stomach.

"It was my choice," Tyler gave her a weak smile.

Her throat became tight and she could only mouth the word 'why?'

"I don't fit in here, Cassy," he shrugged, "You've got your Council thing to do the whole time... which is great... I'm really happy that so many people look up to my little sister. But I don't learn stuff as fast as the others who've got a proper place here..."

"You *do* have a proper place!" she found her voice, "Our Mum and Dad paid for it fair and square, we've got just as much right to be here as these other people! Mum and Dad wanted us to be free, Ty! I'm begging you, don't throw it all away!"

"I *will* be free," Tyler seemed puzzled that she didn't understand, "Cassy, you know I'm not the best thinker, but… look out there… blue skies, the water's gone. The Siva thing didn't kill us. Out there I won't be a burden to -"

"Don't…" she began, but choked on her own tears, "You were never a burden. Just stay, Ty, please! I can't do all of… this… without you."

He pulled her into a hug.

"Before we got here, I never saw nothin'. Everything was always just… there. Now I got a chance to see a brand-new world. I don't wanna stay inside anymore, I wanna see it all, Cassy!"

Their hug now caught the attention of a baton-carrying officer who moved towards them.

"Get back into line," he placed a hand on Tyler's arm.

Cassidy's full anger erupted in an instant.

"Get your *fucking* hands off!" she roared, grabbing the officer's hand.

A second later she found herself on the floor looking up at the officer who was standing over her, his baton raised again. She saw Marshall suddenly dash between them.

"Stand the hell down you bloody moron!" he shouted, "How can you *not* know who that is?!"

Cassidy struggled to her feet and could hear the man explaining that he was only following orders, but her attention was devoted to locating Tyler. In the few short seconds that she'd been on the floor, he'd been carried along with the others heading towards the airlock.

Just audible above the now tumultuous shouts, she heard his voice.

"Love you, Cassy!"

His voice allowed her to pinpoint him in the stream of people; he was smiling at her. She quickly drew breath to shout the same back, but he'd already disappeared from view.

•

Exile had certain advantages, Kate thought. Out here she'd be free of Barnes' personal crusade to instill a permanent state of fear. It would also ensure that her father's theories on the Boundary were not abused.

Still supported on her crutches, she couldn't easily reciprocate Scott's hug, but managed to place one hand on his arm and pat it.

"It's alright," she said, "this is my choice. These people need a friendly face... I can be there for them."

"They'll have a good leader, then," Scott squeezed her.

A brief warning tone reached them through the Node's external speakers.

"One minute left. You should go now," she smiled, "You'll remember what I said, won't you?"

Scott simply nodded, then hesitantly turned away,

his feet scuffing over the cold, rough ground. She knew she could rely on him to deliver her messages. It bothered her that she couldn't tell people in person but, by maintaining her distance, it was less likely that they'd be associated with her actions.

Kate looked around at the group of exiles.

Most, including Danny, had been forced to leave, but there were a few who had chosen to be here. She desperately wanted to know what had possessed Tyler to leave, but it would have to wait until the Node had left.

"I'm glad you're with us," she called over to him.

"I belong with you guys," he replied.

"Good luck," Scott stepped inside the airlock and the door hissed closed. In the relative quiet outside the Node, Kate reminded everyone of the Field's effects.

"OK, remember to face the centre of the Node and stand upright. As the Field stabilises you'll experience a little dizziness, but it won't be as bad as the one during the first departure and it'll quickly pass."

From her left, Danny gave a small cough.

"So I guess this is it?" he forced a thin smile onto his face.

"Best foot forward?" Kate offered.

She watched him taking in the view of the world beyond the Field. The clouds continued their blurred, river-like flow across the sky.

"You know, my Mum used to say 'Always forwards, Danny. Never back.' I guess that's good adv-"

The Biomag around Kate's neck emitted a high-pitched whining tone. Danny whipped around and she could tell he was about to race to her aid.

"Stop!" she yelled at him, effectively bringing him and several others to a halt, "I'm compromised! Everybody keep your distance! If you're around me when the Field changes, it could kill us all! Stay back!"

She looked in through the observation window.

On the balcony level of the Observation Deck, Alfred Barnes stared down at her. Only when he was sure that she'd seen him, did he turn his back on her.

The message was very clear.

He wanted her to know that he'd done this to her.

Regardless of her attempts to conceal the positive effects of her changes, it seemed that Alfred had taken note of something more basic: the metathene had caused a reaction, rather than none at all. Those with the right receptors were susceptible to rapid change.

It seemed that, like her, Alfred had concluded that she represented the start of a new evolutionary chain. Over a long enough timescale, genetic mutations and variations would occur.

It was a fact that she herself had hoped to capitalise on, outside the Node.

It was also a fact that Alfred probably feared; when the Node emerged from its flight through thousands of years, he may find himself belonging to a fundamentally weaker species.

To maintain his political standing, he'd been forced to let her leave the Node, but clearly he had no intentions of permitting her survival. Any possible evolutionary chain that she embodied was about to be terminated.

The Node's external siren gave its final warning

tone.

Her mother had once adopted a frail persona in order to momentarily deceive an ego-morph, a technique that Kate had been using for weeks to persuade everyone that she was no threat. There seemed little point maintaining the facade now.

She let her crutches fall to the floor, stood upright and raised her voice so that everyone could hear.

"I'm not going to survive this! Barnes has sabotaged my Biomag somehow."

Taking care to remain still, she turned her head slightly in Danny's direction. By no means was this the ideal time to relay the information, but her time was almost up. These would be her last words and would be remembered by those around her.

"Danny's father was General Napier. Barnes killed him too."

Voices of confusion erupted but she knew that she dare not look around. She heard the low, abrasive sound of people's unsettled feet turning in place on the rough ground.

"Barnes wants you all to fail," she called out, "but use his own words against him... *We* grow stronger!"

Almost at the very spot where her father had first thrust it upon her, the Biomag around her neck emitted a final stuttering whine and then fell silent.

Her father's extraordinary efforts had earned her a reprieve of just one month. But that time had been enough. The dormant abilities given to her by her parents and the ignorant actions of a manipulative man, had given her the necessary vision to achieve what must come next.

She grasped her Biomag, now little more than jewellery, and closed her eyes once last time.

The sounds furthest away from her began to grow indistinct. The Node's final warning tone was the first to fade, followed by the voices of those around her, until she was left with only the sound of her own slow breathing.

Before her was the surface of her mental ocean; a maelstrom of overlapping and coexisting thoughts. She knew that most of these turbulent thoughts no longer mattered and watched as the largest waves collapsed, leaving no wake. All that remained behind were the thoughts and memories that she needed now.

Chaotic swirling patterns of choice ebbed and flowed around her; all inextricably linked with her father's instruction to protect the Boundary. She tried to focus beyond her surface thoughts but encountered resistance. She gripped the Biomag harder, as if she might gain strength from it, but she found the opposite to be true. The surface was becoming more unsettled than before.

It now began to dawn on her.

The last reminder of her father was nestled in her physical hand. The Biomag itself was now useless, but her emotional attachment was anchoring her here. Nothing of this world could be taken to the next. Once more, she would have to let him go. She pictured his 'LOKT' hidden message one last time:

'Create a better world than us.'

"I will," she let go of the Biomag and exhaled her last breath, giving up all connection with the corporeal.

In an instant, the waves became peacefully calm; rising and falling to an unseen rhythm. In this calm, she began to see the multiplicity of depths beyond the mere surface of perception.

Gently, she pushed through its surface and moved her mind into the waves beyond. She felt her atoms align with the collapsing Field, then her mental ocean became one with the undulating and infinite temporal variation of the Boundary.

21 HOURS

9th April 2107

While the other crew members continued their extended hibernation, Anna listened to the accounts of Fai, Mike and Cathy. She couldn't yet process the Jupiter events, it was all too sudden. From her perspective, it had been only a few minutes since Miles had helped her into the hibernation unit. In the blink of an eye, he had gone.

Cathy had revived Mike and Lana early but, apparently prompted by Miles' last words of 'Assist Anna', Fai had insisted that Anna be revived too. What Anna saw as an act of empathy, Fai described as a simple rebalancing of an equation. It seemed to Anna that the world had changed yet again while she'd slept.

Another of the changes was that Dr. Chen was absent; a fact that Lana Yakovna was also having difficulty with.

"But, Fai," Lana was asking, "this conflicts with your programming, no?"

"Lana, I have conducted nine Pittman-Wild interviews with

Dr. Chen during his hibernation. On eight of those occasions he demonstrated that his presence here would be suboptimal to the evaluation process."

Anna didn't particularly relish the idea of Dr. Chen being anywhere near her, at any time, but she felt she had to ask the question.

"Where is he?"

"In hibernation," Fai replied.

Anna opened her mouth to ask how conversations were possible during hibernation, but Cathy held up a tablet screen.

"Really sorry, Anna, no time. Fai says there's a maximum of twenty-one hours before the hibernation units will need to stop. Everyone else will wake up. We need to show this to you and Lana now."

Cathy fixed the tablet to the module wall and connected it to the network cabling.

"This footage was taken during Mike's EVA to disable the manual overrides outside I.A.3 and 4. Focus on Jupiter, in particular the Great Red Spot."

Anna watched as Jupiter sailed through the frame, its bands of reddish hues encircling the planet and the red spot swirling within a band below its equator.

"The intensity of the red spot keeps changing," Cathy pointed to the detail on the screen.

"I am not an expert," Anna scrutinised the footage, "but even I know that Jupiter's spot changes over time. What's the significance?"

"The red spot is a storm that's lasted for centuries," Mike explained, "The spot's colour changes from red to white and all the shades in-between, but it takes many decades."

Anna felt compelled to point out the obvious.

"The Field's temporal gradient is simply accelerating our point of view. It just *seems* to be changing rapidly."

Mike and Cathy were shaking their heads.

"I'm afraid not," said Cathy, "Our temporal gradient still doesn't account for the spot's *rate* of change."

"In real time," Mike now joined in, tapping at Jupiter on the screen, "this storm fluctuated over the course of just weeks, not decades."

Lana drew a breath and pulled herself over to the screen.

"So this is a super-storm, yes?" she shrugged.

Anna saw Mike and Cathy exchange glances, clearly there was something else going on here.

"OK, Lana, picture a chaotic storm," said Cathy, "Lightning flashes, black skies, the works."

"Da," Lana agreed, closing her eyes.

"The skies clear and then another storm rolls in," Cathy paused, "except it's *exactly* the same storm that happens again."

Lana opened her eyes, "What?"

Anna had also been visualising Cathy's description and realised that she was being presented to. It was a technique that she herself had sometimes used to explain complex subjects in a simpler way.

"Why not just tell us what you've found?" she asked them.

"OK, Fai's confirmed it," said Mike, "but she thought it would be better coming from us. We were both there when it happened but we didn't truly *see* it because of the… you know, situation."

"Fai," Anna addressed the air, "is this true?"

"Yes, Dr. Bergstrom," her voice came from a nearby panel, *"I have verified the fluctuations and concur."*

"OK, Fai," said Cathy, "Run the sequence."

The footage of Mike staring out at Jupiter stopped and the image zoomed in to focus on Jupiter alone. The video restarted but Fai stabilised the image to ensure that the red spot was always in the centre of frame during the clip.

"We're now looking at the storm spot alone," Mike confirmed, "Fai, can you add the overlay?"

The occurrence and duration of the red spot was accompanied by a graph, running along the bottom of the screen. Sometimes the red spot would only appear briefly, causing a flat-topped spike on the graph, at other times the red spot would last longer causing a stepped plateau to appear. Although the order of the spikes and horizontal lines seemed random, each spike was identical to the others, and each line had exactly the same duration.

Anna watched as the red spot suddenly lost resolution and became blurred.

"That's when Jupiter went out of camera range," Mike explained.

The screen now displayed only the graph filled with spikes and flat lines.

"Fai," Anna began to see something, "What is this?"

"I once detected a similar coherent pulse modulation within the FLC's internal power consumption, shortly before its destruction. It was an analogue method of conveying digital

information. This message shows similar structure."

"OK, I can see there's a pattern," said Anna, "but how can this be a message?"

"Because the storm repeats," Cathy replied simply, "and nature doesn't do that."

The four of them fell quiet.

"It is like Leonard's message?" Lana tapped at the spike trace graph, then looked at Mike for confirmation.

"Dots 'n' Dashes," Mike shrugged.

Anna felt a sense of growing agitation at being confronted with a concept beyond her understanding, but she forced herself to look at the available facts.

There was a coherent and repeated pattern to the red spot pulses. The pulses had occurred at a rate that accounted for the presence of the Chronomagnetic Field and the location of the ISS at the time. Then there was the format of the message; it had been carefully chosen so that a human receiver could recognise it.

"Have you decoded it?" Anna asked Mike and Cathy.

Cathy touched the screen. Underneath the graph, a line of simple text read:

'EVA65.05-16.75'

"At first I thought it was something to do with my Extra-Vehicular Activity," Mike pointed to the space-suited man on the footage, "But treating the numbers as video time code, or screen coordinates showed nothing."

"My first thought is Eva Gray," Lana nodded gravely.

"I had similar thoughts," Cathy rubbed at the light scar on her cheek, "But that was probably because she was in my nightmares so much."

"I think it has a different meaning for each us," Anna

thought aloud, "Fai, what's your interpretation of the E.V.A. initials?"

"Only two interpretations carried statistical significance. One - given the astronomical context, I found a reference to the Eridanus Void Anomaly within an Archive study of cosmic microwave background radiation. Two - within my own program I developed an External Variable Assignment subroutine to handle the necessity of interacting with a greater number of people aboard the ISS. However, neither of these meanings had a correlation with the accompanying numbers."

"If the message was intended for you, Fai," Lana pointed out, "it would have used a more efficient method than Morse. What's your interpretation, Anna?"

Until now, Anna had kept her explanation to herself but, having heard the others' thoughts, she now felt more confident about voicing her own.

"Well, when I worked with Douglas on the original Field equations, the Eversion Volume Algorithm was part of a permutation program. But the bigger correlation here is that the numbers are the coordinates of something called the Node, in Iceland. Would you concur, Fai?"

"Yes, Dr. Bergstrom. They are also the coordinates of a drone strike initiated by Dr. Chen on December 27th 2013. Though the presence of a second Chronomagnetic Field signature is still present at those coordinates."

For Anna, the initial shock of an attack on the Node vanished upon hearing that the Node's Field was active. Douglas was probably still alive, she thought. He'd been working in Hab 1 immediately outside the Node when she'd been escorted away to Andersen Air Force Base.

"We need to go!" she found herself smiling broadly, but it was an enthusiasm not completely reflected in the others.

"There's a catch," said Cathy.

"Fai has an issue with your intentions to steal the Shuttle?" Anna guessed.

"I have no standing directive regarding the use of the Shuttle," Fai replied, *"You are free to use it as you see fit."*

"Then what's the catch?" Anna turned again to face Cathy.

"The Shuttle was only ever designed to return to Earth at a handful of places, most them within thirty-ish degrees of the equator. Our landing options are limited. Even after landing, Iceland is so far north that it could take months or years to reach it…"

"Which leaves us with two choices," said Mike, "Either we open this up to a wider debate when the others exit hibernation, or we have to prep the Shuttle right now and take our chances."

"There is a third choice," Anna looked at the others, "You just have to recognise which parts of the problem are constants and which are, ha, External Variables. The Shuttle design is limiting our options?"

"Er…yes," Mike hesitated, "but -"

"So logically we need a new Shuttle design."

"I'm sorry, Anna," said Cathy, softly, "The crew will exit hibernation soon. We have less than twenty-one hours."

Anna did a quick mental calculation.

"Not strictly true. We have less than twenty-one hours *in here*," Anna placed emphasis on the words, "But outside of a newly established Field, we could have more than five years…"

PERSPECTIVE

~

She knocked four times on the cottage door, then it opened.

In front of her, just as she remembered him, was her father.

"Hi, Dad," she beamed.

Unlike the world of temporal abstraction that she was used to existing within, here she had no foreknowledge of what his actions would be; his fatherly hug therefore took her somewhat by surprise. She'd almost forgotten what it was like to be ignorant of future events.

"Katie, Katie..." he repeated over and over as he held her, "Is this... now?"

"Yes," she simplified for him. After closing the door, she guided him back through to the living room, "We're somewhere safe. Somewhere familiar."

"I know, we're at Samphire, except..." he glanced around the room then brought out the photo featuring himself, Kate and Anna, "Except, there are bits that don't seem to fit."

Kate knew this was all part of his acclimatisation. She'd included the small anachronistic clues to encourage his analytical side.

"I remember Anna taking that photo," she guided him, then gestured toward the sofa, "It was at the Node, wasn't it?"

"Yes, we were in Hab 1," he smiled, and sat down.

"Oh yeah!" she encouraged, sitting next to him, "Where did you find the photo?"

"It was down there on the floor, just before you knocked... No, no that's not right," his eyes darted back and forth, "No, I found this photo in one of the labs after I put you aboard the Node..."

Kate watched as he worked through his personal chronology.

"I was the last one on the island and... the Mark Two!"

His eyes suddenly found hers.

"The Biomag failed and I..." he suddenly stopped again and looked around the room, "Am I dead?"

"No," Kate couldn't help laughing, "Well, actually, it's complicated."

She saw his expression shift to become the concerned parent once more.

"Katie, I put you inside the Node. How can you be... wherever this is?"

A distant rumble of thunder told her that she'd have to proceed carefully; he'd just questioned the nature of the environment around them. For the time being, she'd have to look at things from his linear perspective.

"Like I said," she held his hand, "it's complicated. How long has it been since you last saw me?"

"Three, maybe four minutes?" he replied.

"For me," she squeezed his hand gently, "It's been… *significantly* different."

"Katherine," he frowned, "How long?"

She remembered that he always used the long form of her name when he was being stern. Hearing it here, in the imitation of their family home, resonated with her but she knew there was no simple answer.

"I prepared this place," she looked around the room, "as a sort of safety net. A place I could catch you and your thoughts. But outside these walls, the idea of 'how long' doesn't really have a meaning."

"Then, please," a concerned frown lined his face, "help me understand all this… surreal abstraction."

"OK," she began, "The first thing to realise is that, despite appearances, there's nothing weird or mysterious about this place. As you and Anna predicted, everything here within the Boundary is consistent with the concept of dimensionality without linear time. We're just perceiving physical laws from an unusual perspective."

"A higher dimension?" his hands mimed a flat plateau.

"That would imply a hierarchy where none is necessary," she explained, "Let me try this a little slower. Think back to the last time we saw each other."

"At the Node's window," he nodded.

"Your clipboard message worked," she smiled, "They got the data."

Her father leaned back into the sofa and let out a sigh

of relief. It seemed odd to hear him react so spontaneously to something that was distant history for her.

"Also…" she raised her eyebrows, "I worked out your L.O.K.T. message too."

A smile lit up his face and it reminded her of when they used to send simple codes to each other when she was young.

"That's my girl!" he said, proudly, "How long did it take you?"

"A few days," she said.

"Wow. Impressive. I thought it might take you a little longer."

"Ha," she laughed, "It took me a lot longer to understand the notes that were on the memory card inside your Biomag."

"I can't begin to imagine how long it must have taken to piece it all together. It must have taken… years?"

"No," she felt herself almost bragging, "Thanks to Alfred Barnes' interference, it took me less than a month. By the time he killed me, I was more than -"

She was interrupted by a massive thunderclap that sounded as though it was directly above the cottage; her father was on his feet.

"What?!"

For a moment, she thought that the construct around them may not hold, but as she began to fill in the details for him, the disturbance receded.

She told him what she'd discovered aboard the Node: the cortical enhancement program detailed in Danny Napier's file, her own metathene genetic activation and her suspicions that Douglas and Monica were part of that discontinued project. She also told him about her much longer time outside the Node, visiting incidents throughout Archive's history; a non-linear patchwork of pieces that had allowed her to build up a complete picture. She concluded by telling him that although he'd first postulated the Boundary's existence, she had been the first to enter it.

"To get your head around it," she said, "You have to understand something. The Boundary, has always been here. It's like a dimensional anomaly twisted up inside the fabric of the... I'll call it universe. It would have existed even if no-one had discovered it."

"Then it's not a by-product of the Field?"

"No," again she simplified; it would be easier to alter a mental picture later than to risk overcomplicating a fundamental point now.

"So you're trying to say that, in creating the Field, we just stumbled into the Boundary?" he wore a sceptical expression that she recognised only too well, "Katie, do you have any idea how unlikely that is?"

"Yes," she smiled patiently, "But the Boundary is a continuum with *infinite* temporal variation; in all of that infinite amount of time, the right circumstances only had to arise once. I was that 'once'."

Her father's eyes were once more darting from side to side, assessing her logic, but soon it stopped and he faced her.

"Why wasn't I that 'once'," he countered, "Surely you were still inside the Node, when I entered the Boundary?"

"Not the first time around," she replied, knowing that inevitably they must come to this part of their discussion.

"First time?"

Kate drew a deep breath.

"It took me a… long time," she inwardly cringed at the inadequacy of the language, "to interpret the Boundary. How to see it, how to interact with it, how to *influence* it."

She let the last statement hang clearly for him to see.

"You've influenced things?" he said, then his eyes suddenly widened in understanding, "You've influenced *events* to bring me here?"

She nodded and continued.

"The very first time around, the tsunami outside the Node crushed you. You simply… died. My emergence into the Boundary still happened though because I received your messages. Only after several iterations did you actually make it to the Mark 2."

"And that's what allowed me to get here," he nodded.

"No," she sighed, "not even then. For several more iterations you simply stayed inside the Mark 2 until the end. Sometimes the Field collapsed, sometimes you unanchored because of the Biomag. But just once, you made the leap."

"This time."

"Yes," she smiled, "this one single time."

"Let me guess," he smiled back, "That wasn't luck, was it?"

Kate explained the numerous symbols she'd placed

in his periphery during his final hours alone on the island. Each symbol was a visual echo of a diagram she'd seen within his clipboard notes.

The circular diagram had illustrated the Eversion point standing on the Field's circumference and was synonymous with the Boundary's inflection point. Her hope was that through sheer exposure to the circle and dot image, he would get the hint at the moment of deciding his own fate.

"Right at the end," he said, "I was staring at my Earth hologram card. Concentrating on the message I'd sent to you."

"Create a better world than us?" Kate recited.

Her father nodded and looked into the living room fire.

"It was only in the last second that I saw the circle and dot pattern," he made tiny circular motions in the air with his finger, "Where one of my Dad's bookcase screws had punctured the atmosphere."

She smiled, that too had been no coincidence. As far as she could tell, that visual juxtaposition was responsible for his arrival. The fireplace flared slightly and she knew to expect a question from him.

"By influencing events, don't you create an alternate future?"

Her father had spent most of his life evaluating mental decision trees, so she wasn't surprised by the question.

"Yes," she replied, "There's a fine line between influencing the course of events and creating an unpredictable future."

"Hmm, that sounds like the voice of experience…"

"Yes," she admitted, "You remember me telling you about Marcus? Well, I once influenced a minor event."

"How minor?"

"I made a buzzer activate, down in the Warren," she found herself nodding over in the direction of the kitchen, where the access point would have been, "The result was that he survived an event that should have killed him. That one event spawned the continuum we're in now."

"Sometimes you're just like your mother," he smiled, "impetuous."

She knew she'd have to tell him about the events within the USV, but the fireplace flared again and another burning question arrived.

"I have to ask, Katie. With this ability to influence events, did you ever try to stop Siva from reaching Earth?"

She had thought about it on numerous occasions.

"If I'd interfered," she explained, "then there'd be no Siva threat."

"Exactly," her father shrugged.

"But if there was no Siva, there'd be no Archive. No Archive, no cortical enhancement or NASA programs. Your Dad would always have been around and you'd never have thought up the Field. No Field, no Boundary, so no-one could ever have interfered with Siva's approach…"

"Paradox," her father nodded, making a looping motion with his hand, "By using the Boundary to stop Siva, you can't stop Siva."

"It gets worse though, Dad. I can't interfere with the events that first led to me entering the Node, or I'll never arrive *here*."

The expression on his face told her that he fully understood.

"Damn..." he closed his eyes, "The lunar detonation can't be stopped either. The Node departed to avoid the super-fragments."

Kate stood and walked away from the sofa towards the living room window, "I need to show you what we're dealing with."

"We?"

"Or you could just sit on that sofa all day..."

He was at her side immediately, but she knew she needed to check something.

"You know this isn't Samphire Cottage, don't you?"

"Yes," he shook his head in amazement, "It's a construct."

"Good," she said, "Because the view from this window isn't the English Channel."

She pulled the curtains open to reveal the whole Earth; its moon still intact and orbiting around it. She heard him draw a breath.

"Wow, is this a construct model too?"

"No, what you're seeing is the real Earth, but I'm showing you a span of twenty thousand years."

The Moon sprang apart and Earth was immediately covered in fire and smoke but, almost as quickly, the effects disappeared. The lunar debris quickly spread out through its former orbit.

"OK, now here's Siva," she said.

A blur from the right of the window impacted with the lunar debris field and this time the devastation to the Earth was more severe. The atmosphere turned an ash grey. Most of the lunar debris vanished and, with no stabilising body to regulate its rotation, the Earth began to tip off axis. The atmosphere cleared and, for a short time, there were large verdant patches in several locations, but then a ghostly white sprawl crept across the globe as the oceans and landmasses froze. The former poles settled into their new equatorial position, rocking up and down slightly with the passing of the centuries.

"We're going to change it," said Kate and drew the curtains again, "but there's something we need to do first."

"What could be more important than this?"

As a first reaction, she'd expected nothing less from him, but the time had come to raise the issue.

"Time is linear down there," she pointed in the direction of the closed curtains, "Any influence I make is simply the first step in a long chain that follows it. Hierarchies of choices that go rippling out from that point."

"Causality counts," he replied, "After a change is made, linear time continues for them."

"Making any amendment to that first change, even by a few seconds, undoes the chain that follows it," she said, "Sometimes the effects are minor but other times, like when I saved Marcus, an entirely new continuum is created. Before we can deal with Siva, we need to make *completely* sure that we're done altering events that happen between your arrival here and Siva's impact fifteen months later."

"If we're successful in stopping an ice age," he nodded, "then making any change to the time *before* our first action, could undo our efforts."

Kate sat down on the sofa and invited her father to do the same. Despite the devastation they'd just reviewed and the scale of the broader task ahead, she was dreading the next few moments even more.

"Outside that front door," she pointed in the direction of the hallway, "thought, matter, energy... they're all fluid, almost interchangeable. Stray thoughts and emotions can interfere with the linear world below, but this place insulates you from that."

"I thought so," he said.

She wondered how he'd managed to reach that conclusion based on so little information, but she didn't have to wait long for the explanation.

"My thoughts here always seem to be accompanied by a physical disturbance in the fire," he smiled, "or the weather outside."

She found herself beaming at her father's inquisitive mind. She began explaining the events within the USV, and a storm rolled in over Samphire Hoe.

FROZEN

13th April 2014

Monica stared at Bradley and stepped towards him slightly; an effect she hoped would reinforce her presence.

"In that cell down there, I've had a lot of time to think, about Bishop's list, me, Douglas, Kate. I know thinking doesn't come easily for a man like you. But see if you can work it out. See if you can join the genetic dots. With supreme order and chaos for parents... can you even estimate my daughter's abilities?"

The frozen image of Marcus was still on the screen. She couldn't be sure what he was doing, but she knew she had to help in any way possible. She'd introduced Bishop's list into the conversation in an attempt to distract Bradley from Marcus. A gambit that appeared to be paying off; his focus was now on her.

During her imprisonment, she'd watched him tangentially skirting around issues that could only have been related to the photocopied list of names. Each mention, a simple test to see how she would react. She'd left the list in Nathan's possession, so she concluded that Bradley must somehow have captured Nathan. However, the fact that Bradley was still asking questions of her, meant that Nathan had not given up anything useful. Nathan must still be alive though, she thought, otherwise Bradley would have made another sickening village square demonstration.

"Your daughter?" Bradley seemed to recover, "Oh, I still got plans for her."

"Ha!" Monica realised she was getting to him, "I thought you said you'd strangled her to death?"

She watched him struggle, caught in a web of his own inexpertly woven lies, "I guess murdering the dead is easier to pull off for someone of your limitations."

"Limitations?" said Bradley, loudly, "Gordo?"

At the mention of his name, the man at the nearby console turned away from the frozen video feed.

"Er... Bradley, I -" he began.

"How many Peace Keepers we got in the Hive?" he continued to stare at her.

"Er, we've got sixteen, some of them are already -"

"Deploy the lot."

"Whoa, wait a minute!" the man seemed hesitant, "If the whole Hive's going live then we've gotta tell the Council."

As the man reached for his two-way radio, she saw an anger flare in Bradley's eyes. An anger that swiftly transitioned into action; Bradley pulled from his pocket a single shot pistol and aimed it at the man.

"I said deploy the lot."

The man initially froze in fear but then quickly complied, returning his hands to his keyboard and glancing nervously towards Bradley. Monica knew that Marcus might stand a chance against a single drone, particularly on the metal stairwell, but against sixteen she was less sure. Thinking quickly, she knew she'd have to intervene.

"OK, you win!" she begged him, "Let me talk to him! He'll listen!"

Although Bradley still had the pistol aimed at the man, both turned to look at her.

"Did I tell you to stop working, Gordo?" he spoke to him while staring at her. The man hurriedly resumed tapping at his keyboard, as Bradley continued, "Now that's much better, Mon! Bit of respect."

He gripped the pistol.

"Who is he?" Bradley jerked his head towards the frozen image of Marcus.

Monica knew that every word she used could buy time.

"I don't know his real name," she lied, "I only know his alias."

"I ain't hearin' anything new," he drawled, "Gordo, you got ten seconds to get 'em in the air."

"I'm going as fast as I can!" the man pleaded, "They take twenty just to initialise!"

"Gordo, I swear if I hear another word out of your mouth…"

Monica could see the man's control screens were beginning to fill with several different windows. One by one, the black windows were switching to a unique video feed from each of the drones within the Hive.

"His alias," Monica raised her hands in apparent submission, then hesitantly spoke three lies, "is 'Anti-social Networking', I can bring him in. He... he'll do what I tell him."

•

In the quiet of AR1, Nathan was still coming to terms with the fact that for the past nine months, his free will had quite possibly not actually been his own.

His motivation for escaping Luóxuán Biotech had been real enough, but he could no longer be sure how real his subsequent choices were. No matter how much he considered it, his choices felt like real ones; the decisions he'd made appeared consistent and made logical sense.

Part of him thought that Marcus shouldn't have told him. He could have lived in ignorant bliss; convinced that he himself was protecting the dozen red-lined descendants of his grandpa's list.

He was disturbed from his contemplation by the arrival of a concerned looking Izzy Kitrick.

"Hey, Izzy, what's up?"

"Did you clear him to leave the Warren?" she replied, walking into the room, "You know... Blake?"

"Marcus?" Nathan stood up from the sofa, "No. You're not saying...?"

"Yeah," she nodded, "he said you'd cleared it."

Nathan glanced at the coffee table and realised that

Marcus had taken the laptop with him.

"No," he shook his head, "No, I didn't. Alright, let's hope he didn't go far."

He drew a deep breath and they walked out of AR1. As he stepped into the narrow passageway he felt something scuff under his foot: a single paperclip, glistening in a shallow puddle of water.

A glance to his right confirmed his first thought: the door of the Arrivals Lounge was no longer frozen.

•

Against the backdrop of the USV's simulated night sky, the drone simply hung in the air. It was only receiving instructions from Marcus' laptop.

He brought up the video feed coming from its onboard camera and saw its last captured video frame; a blurry freeze-frame of Marcus himself holding the laptop at the moment he'd assumed control. Marcus waved to the drone's camera, but the still image remained. The drone was blind.

He experimented increasing the power to the rotors and saw the drone rise in height. He returned it to its original height, hovering in front of him on the opposite side of the stairwell's metal handrail. He opened the stun controls and the drone obediently lowered the sting-like rod from its undercarriage.

Marcus found a screen button marked 'Administer', a clinical description of its actual purpose. Taking a step further back from the handrail, he tentatively clicked the button. The drone responded by emitting a short electric shock that discharged harmlessly into the metal framework. The actual duration could only have been one tenth of a second. He experimented again, this time holding the button down for longer; the duration of the shock matched the duration of the button press. There didn't appear to be any options for adjusting the duration of discharge.

A cold feeling spread through him.

There was nothing automatic about this process.

A human being had physically held down the button that had killed Geraldine. Someone had held down the button and watched while Geraldine's life was taken away, second by second.

He wanted to take his newly acquired drone and unleash chaos, but he knew it wasn't a solution. Monica had once told him that chaos was not achieved by random disruption, it was the work of meticulous planning.

He would need a plan and a place to store the drone.

He pulled his replenished inhaler from his pocket and took a dose.

After so long without using it, he began to feel the effects almost immediately. The heightened contrast between his present and former mental states was clearer than ever.

He looked at the laptop screen and then cast his eye out over the USV's flat landscape below. Abruptly, the simulated stars went out and, in the middle of the USV's night, the artificial sun resumed full brightness. While he blinked and shielded his eyes against the sudden change, he heard a low howl as the USV's public address system activated.

"Well, hey there folks," the voice echoed around the cavernous chamber, *"here's a wake-up call."*

As Marcus' eyes adjusted to the sudden dawn, he began to see signs of life far below; people emerging from their dwellings and looking skyward towards the illuminated circle in their sky. Coming so soon after his drone subversion, Marcus knew the timing was not a coincidence. There was a slight rumbling sound followed by a new voice.

"This is Monica Walker…"

His first thought was that she was alive. But as fast as he could form the thought, he realised that it could just be a recording.

"… with a message for Mr. Anti-social Networking, standing on the Glaucus stairwell."

The fact she knew his position proved it wasn't a recording. As the inhaler's effects took hold, he also realised the significance of the name she'd chosen instead of his usual 'Blackbox' alias.

When he'd originally got Kate out of London, they'd been forced to raid a fellow hacker's basement flat for alternative clothing. He'd worn a long-sleeved grey T-shirt emblazoned with the sarcastic words 'Anti-social Networking'; something Monica had commented on when they'd first met. Since then, the term had become their shorthand for acting in an unsocial manner for the sake of appearances. Marcus knew she was under duress and should therefore consider her words carefully.

"I can think of at least a dozen reasons…"

He knew she must be talking about Nathan's twelve.

"… why you wouldn't trust what I'm saying…"

He could see what she was doing.

"… but I want you to come back to the centre of the USV."

Get as far away from it as possible.

"The Peace Keepers will give you safe passage…"

They're going to hit you with everything.

"… so that we can talk things through."

There would be no words.

"Deliberately putting everyone in danger…"

Getting everyone to safety…

"… is the wrong thing to do."

Is the best thing to do.

"Wait for me."

Don't wait for her.

There was a muffled commotion transmitted by the public-address system. Clearly, someone had taken issue with her last statement. The muffled sound stopped and Marcus heard a single gunshot.

WINDOW

~

Douglas watched through the Samphire construct window. He knew Kate was outside, controlling what was visible to him, but the constantly shifting perspective and often discontinuous time periods was taking some getting used to. Frequently he would hear her voice, as though she was still standing next to him, despite her not being present at all.

The current content of the window was a high perspective view of the cottage remnants. He watched a tsunami sweep towards the Dover coastline and then engulf it.

"Couldn't you have just parted the waters around it?" he asked.

"I'm good," said Kate, "but not that good. Or rather, I wasn't that good when I put this fix in place."

Douglas now understood that he was seeing a review of actions she'd already taken. It made sense, this event had taken place before the Node had departed, they'd not begun to address Siva yet.

The perspective collapsed and reformed in the Warren's Arrivals Lounge. He recognised the arrivals track, but it was obviously damaged. The room was also full of packing cases and, bizarrely, an artificial Christmas tree.

"OK," said Kate, "This is where the seawater breaches the arrivals tube."

"Who are the two men?"

"Cal Dawson and Woodrow Forrestal."

He didn't recognise either of them, but then considered that he'd no reason to. Monica had been finishing the Warren without him for several years.

Douglas saw the tree's tinsel-covered branches shimmer; evidently the advancing seawater was displacing a significant amount of air ahead of its arrival. The seawater gushed in, then one of the men ran into the room, closing the door behind him. Douglas watched as the man, wading through ice cold seawater, stacked the crates against the door and tied them in place with electrical cable.

"What's he doing?"

"Sacrificing himself," she said, "to buy time for everyone to escape."

"The poor man," Douglas shook his head at the selfless act of bravery, "But, surely it'll never hold back the seawater?"

"It didn't," she replied, "I intervened."

From a submerged viewpoint within the room he could now see the man was inert and sinking through the cold water. Suddenly the seawater began to rapidly freeze around him; spreading out to fill the entire space.

"An ice dam?"

"Yep," she replied, "I knew Cal, he was such a good man. I wanted to make sure his actions gave people the time they needed. As it turned out, I've ended up maintaining the ice far longer than I originally thought."

"Wait a minute," the thought suddenly occurred to him, "A moment ago you said you couldn't control the seawater to deflect around the Warren's entrance, but here you're maintaining an *ice dam?*"

"In the same way that you're seeing these events out of sequence, my interventions are non-linear too. My abilities didn't progress according to their linear time. I'm moving us forwards…"

The view in front of him collapsed then unfolded again, to see a man holding a laptop.

"I'm guessing that's Marcus?" he asked, but found his attention drawn to the metal stairs, "Whoa! I'd forgotten how high those things ran."

Douglas had been on those stairs a few days before Monica's engineered cave-in. But it had been so long ago that the vertiginous view now seemed brand new.

He heard his wife's message ringing out around the USV and ultimately the gunshot sound that Kate had warned him about. He felt the Samphire Cottage room shudder around him.

"Take it easy, Dad," she said, "Everything so far has been in review. Now *we* get to decide how things go."

Douglas waited for the shuddering to subside. It seemed his daughter had learned the patience that was necessary for life within the Boundary. For him, a sense of urgency and emotion still prevailed. He noticed that the view through the window had stopped moving.

"I've stopped us here," said Kate, closing the front door and walking into the living room, "Time's not going anywhere."

"I started to get upset," he confessed, straightening a picture on the wall, "I'm sorry."

She gave him a hug but it seemed that it was somehow an unfamiliar action for her. Not for the first time, he wondered how long she'd been here in human linear terms.

"I've been thinking about Mum and the twelve red-liners," she said, "There might be a way, but it's a little beyond me at the minute."

"Can I help?" he delivered a parental response without really thinking, "Sorry, Katie, that was stupid. Of course I can't.

"Of course you can," she smiled and studied his face, "I just need to pop outside for a bit."

As she turned to walk back towards the hallway, another seemingly automatic parental phrase escaped his mouth.

"How long will you be out?" he closed his eyes in embarrassment.

"Not long," she gave him a broad smile.

Her heard the front door open and then close behind her.

He shook his head. It seemed that no matter where in the world, *or universe,* his daughter was, he'd care for her just the same. The front door opened again and she walked back into the living room.

"Did you forget something?" he asked.

She frowned at him.

"Oh, I see," she smiled, "because of the door and... No, I've done what I needed to do. Are you ready?"

He took a deep breath, shook out his arms and gave a firm nod.

"Go."

GO

9th April 2107

L ana placed her headset into position.
"All stations report in," it felt a little like the old FLC days, she thought.

"Mike Sanders, Shuttle cargo bay."

"Cathy Gant, Module Alpha."

"Anna Bergstrom, Field Control."

"Fai, Internal server."

"OK, let's do this," said Lana, looking out through the cupola, "Cathy, go."

Lana watched as Module Alpha's EVA airlock, furthest from the Ring, opened and Cathy emerged using powered reaction thrusters attached to her spacesuit. Behind her, the ungainly looking Number4 was closely tethered; for the moment a passenger. Cathy began to make her way over to the Shuttle.

"Mike, go."

"Main bus to manual start," Mike reported and Lana saw the cockpit windows illuminate from within, *"Setting condition green, on external access."*

A menu on the screen in front of Lana became available and she opened the internal safety controls.

"Confirmed, Mike," she continued to activate several channels, "You are good to go."

"Roger," Mike returned, *"Proceeding."*

Cathy was moving slowly along the length of the shuttle, and Lana could see her control thrusters making minute adjustments. When she approached the Shuttle's open cargo bay, she slowed her speed and brought herself to a halt above the Shuttle.

"Knock knock, I'm in position."

"Roger that, Cathy," Mike responded, *"I'm secure, bring it down."*

Lana saw Cathy manoeuvring down past the cargo bay doors and out of sight.

"Number4 aboard," came Fai's voice.

"Anna, Field status?"

"Core checks underway, departure status set to hold."

"Fai, external server status?"

"Ready and awaiting transport."

"Understood," Lana replied.

Fai had read Archive's files relating to the previous Field experiments, in particular how the more basic Mark 2 Field chamber had been used to develop Fai's predecessors.

Using a 60:1 Field, months of processor design had been prototyped inside the Mark 2 in mere days. It was

Fai's intention to use the 2400:1 Field currently at their disposal to advance her own programming by using five years of time *outside* the Field. The hope was that any processing speed improvements would directly benefit the overall plan.

"Approaching the nineteen-hour mark," Lana relayed to everyone.

"Roger," Cathy reported, *"Returning to Alpha."*

Lana could see her once again manoeuvring her way back from the Shuttle towards Module Alpha, this time trailing a long tether. Cathy entered the open airlock and Lana saw the tether go tight.

"Zip line in place," Cathy reported.

"Roger," Mike responded.

"Fai, confirm sync," Lana checked.

"Data transfer synchronised, ready for transport."

"Go, Cathy."

There was a delay of a few seconds then Lana saw the bulky form of the ISS backup server ease out of the airlock attached to the tether on a motorised winch; in the zero-gravity environment, the server had no weight so the tether didn't flex under the load.

"Server away," Cathy reported, then emerged from the airlock again and headed to where the Shuttle was still attached to the ISS. Meanwhile, the server was slowly dragged along the tether by the motorised winch.

"Mike, heads up," Lana warned him as the server disappeared behind the cargo bay doors.

"I see it," said Mike, *"Man, that's big."*

Lana saw a long standing-wave ripple back and forth through the tether.

"Mike, confirm delivery?"

"Confirmed."

"Fai, what's the status of Number4?"

"Memory purge complete," Fai reported, *"Bios reconfiguration complete. Interface with Shuttle bay manipulator arm complete. Number4 reboot-sequence cycle in three, two, one…"*

"Mike, confirm shutdown," said Lana.

"Confirmed," said Mike, *"Pulling side panel. Mike to Fai."*

"Go ahead, Mike."

"There are two identical ports for the server-fabricator cable, which do I use?"

"The one closest to the centre of the Main Board."

"Understood."

"Support strut one detached from ISS," Cathy announced, *"Moving on to two."*

Lana saw Cathy manoeuvring away from the first strut. The anchoring bolts that had been put in place only a few weeks ago had been removed, leaving the strut still attached to the Shuttle.

"External server and fabricator link is in place," said Mike.

"Proceed, Mike," said Lana.

"Rebooting."

"Anna, status update."

"All hibernating and active crew member Biomags read active. Core primed. Field emitters on standby."

"Confirmed, Anna. Stand by."

"Boot bypass in place," came Mike's voice, *"Proceeding to Module Alpha."*

"Confirmed, Mike. Fai, upload your external server program."

"Complying," she said.

Lana watched her screen as, one by one, each menu became deactivated.

"Transfer complete. Independent Shuttle control confirmed."

"Cathy, how are you doing there?"

"A little longer," her voice sounded a little strained.

Lana saw Mike using the motorised winch to return to the open airlock. Within a few minutes, he was returning to the Shuttle cargo bay; a long line of fabricator supply boxes snaking out behind him as the winch dragged him across the open space.

"OK, strut two detached," Cathy called in, *"Heading to axial airlock two."*

"Understood, Cathy. Cycling airlock."

Framed by the ISS structures, against the backdrop of the Earth's night side, Cathy made her way across Lana's field of view. Occasionally, clouds would become momentarily illuminated by a random thunderstorm, but gone were the speckled spider-webs of illuminated cities that Lana remembered. The Earth was dark.

"Fabricator supplies are in place," Mike's voice called her back to the present, *"Detaching tether from Shuttle."*

"Understood," she replied.

Mike cleared the Shuttle's cargo bay doors holding onto the motorised winch. The loose end of the tether hung limply behind him but, in reaction to the fact he still had mass, the tether ahead of him was still taut.

"Fai, you have Shuttle control. Detach."

"Confirmed," Fai replied, and immediately a series of short reaction thruster bursts separated the Shuttle from the ISS, *"Detached. Beginning reorientation."*

"Understood. Anna, you're up."

"Core is charging, beware of electromagnetic interference to communications," she said, *"Setting departure status to commit. Crew, please adopt orientation and report in."*

While Lana manoeuvred herself to face the direction of the Field generator module, she saw Mike reach the airlock and stand in the doorway, facing the central axis.

"Mike Sanders, Module Alpha airlock, external, ready."

"Cathy Gant, axial airlock two, internal, ready."

"Lana Yakovna, cupola, ready."

Lana felt a slight tremor pass through the cupola module.

"Haken manifold horizon in progress," Anna's calm voice announced, *"Fai, how long until the Shuttle is clear of the intended Field radius?"*

"Nine point two seconds, Dr. Bergstrom," Fai replied.

"Activating primary stage containment," Anna reported.

Lana felt another slight shudder and then heard Anna's laughter.

"Ja! Field eversion event! Sorry..." Anna seemed to regain some of her composure, *"I didn't get to see it the first time... Inversion geometry contained."*

Lana looked out at the Earth below, the only clue to its presence being a circular absence of stars and a faint, silver glow over the horizon; dawn was about to break again. The vibration around her increased and she could hear the core's hum change pitch and begin to rise.

"Dr. Bergstrom, the Shuttle is clear," Fai reported.

"Goodbye, Discovery!" came Mike's voice, bidding the Shuttle farewell.

The vibration ceased momentarily, while motion phases within the core temporarily cancelled each other out, and then the vibration resumed, as the core started to enter a still higher range of pitch.

Lana felt a powerful and persistent tug pulse throughout her entire body, followed by the sensation that every one of her molecules had just aligned itself with the core. Over the noise, she heard Anna's elated voice.

"Field inversion synchronised! Ha ha! Here we go!"

Lana felt the core fire and then the Field passed fleetingly through her. The silver glimmer of dawn on Earth's horizon leapt into full daylight, followed swiftly by night again. She recalled that the ISS used to take around ninety minutes to orbit the Earth, now that time was passing every few seconds. Despite the pulsating view through the window and a slight sense of nausea, she remembered what had to happen next.

"All stations report in."

"Mike Sanders, Module Alpha airlock, now internal."

"Cathy Gant, axial airlock two, internal."

Anna did not report in.

"Anna?"

There followed several seconds of silence before a moaning sound reached Lana.

"Anna, are you OK?"

"I thought space-sickness was bad," she groaned, *"Space-time sickness... way worse..."*

RING

13th April 2014

Monica stared at the gun that Bradley had levelled at her. She had one last thing to say to Marcus over the address system, but she knew that once she'd spoken, it would be over. Holding the microphone steady, she spoke:

"Wait for me."

She saw Bradley's eyes widen and prepared for what must follow.

He wrenched the microphone from her grip and she heard the gunshot before the pain reached her brain. She felt herself stumbling backwards and falling against the circular internal balcony of the Eye. Pain exploded from her left thigh and she found herself grasping at the bloody wound. She was aware of fast receding footsteps, Gordon had apparently chosen that moment to escape; something that was confirmed a few seconds later by the sound of the bucket-lift door slamming shut.

The very fact that she was still having these thoughts meant something obvious. Despite being so close, he'd failed to hit anything major. She was still alive. The very thought sent a bizarre thrill of satisfaction through her.

"You missed!" she managed a short laugh at him, "Only you could miss from this close!"

Bradley completed Gordon's work by pushing a single button, releasing every one of the Hive's drones into the USV.

"For somebody so smart," he smiled coldly, "you are one dumb bitch! I weren't trying to kill you, you'll patch up just fine."

Monica felt her knees weaken and she collapsed to the floor.

"This little drama," he crouched at her side, waggling the discharged pistol, "This is just for me. Kind of a perk!"

She watched as he put the pistol back in his pocket.

"Oh, you know what?" he seemed to find something, "I been saving this for a special occasion."

From the same pocket as the pistol, he pulled out the engagement ring he'd confiscated from her months ago. He took hold of her left hand and wrenched it away from her wound.

"My dearest Monica," he grinned, "would you do me the honour of accepting this ring…"

As he spoke the words, she felt him push the hard diamond ring deep into the dark blood welling up from her leg. Her head swam and instinctively she rolled onto her side to avoid fainting. He released his grip and her bloodied ring fell out onto the floor, where it bounced and skittered across the circular, glazed floor at the centre of the Eye.

"Now look what you made me do!" he laughed and walked away, wiping his hands and pointing back at the flecks of blood on the glass, "Someone's gonna have to clear up your mess. I tell ya something… it ain't gonna be me. I figure the community needs a villain and you're gonna make one real good example."

In that moment, Monica knew what he had in mind.

During one of his detention cell visits, Bradley had shown her a video of Geraldine's horrific execution. Monica knew he'd use her in the same way; a public execution designed to show the futility of opposing the social order, under the guise of protecting civil liberties. After he'd patched her up, she would be used to perpetuate the cycle of paranoia and fear already present in the USV.

Pulling herself along with one arm, she crawled out onto the wide pane of circular glazing that overlooked the USV below. Her feet slid through the dark red trail she left behind on the glass, but through the pain she focussed on the ring just a few feet away.

"Aw, Mon," his voice sounded disappointed, "what are you doin'? You're making a mess of the… Oh, you gotta be kidding. I blew a hole in your leg an' you're tryin' to fetch old Dougie's ring? I don't know if I should laugh or cry!"

"Cry," Monica managed, as she reached the ring and began to make the return journey. She chose to focus on the blood-smeared surface of the glass, rather than the dizzying view below. As she continued to crawl, her hands became slick with blood as they scraped over the surface.

"You gotta be shittin' me! Threats?" he scoffed at her, "You're making threats?"

Monica changed direction again, crossing over her original path and now making no attempt to staunch the flow from the wound. Her blood began pooling on the glazing underneath her, but still she continued to scrape her hands across its wet surface as she made her way back towards him. Against the continuous, almost high-frequency pain, she could feel her head starting to cloud and a ringing had begun in her ears.

"What the hell?" Bradley turned away from her.

The ringing was not in her ears. It was a warning tone emitted from somewhere near the oscilloscope.

Monica dragged herself to the edge of the glazed floor, reached up for the handrail and began to pull herself up. She'd have only one chance to get this right. She hooked her elbows over the handrail and hauled herself upright standing on the glazing.

"You lose," she gasped, holding up both of her blood-soaked hands for him to see.

Bradley turned to face her again.

"They why you got your hands up?" he laughed.

She purposefully folded her thumb across her palm to tap at the diamond in the engagement ring. She wanted to show him that the diamond was on the palm side of her hand.

"What?" he shrugged.

She glanced to her left and, as expected, he followed her cue to look at the blood-smeared glazing below her. It took him a moment, but then she saw his expression change.

Only now did he see the deep scratches criss-crossing the glass. Deep score-lines she'd put there using her hard diamond. Lines designed to weaken the thin glazing.

Behind him, she saw the circular pattern on the oscilloscope suddenly grow in size and disappear off the edges of the display. Joining the original warning tone, a second more aggressive tone now rang out.

She would not be used as a simple tool to extend his oppressive grip. To her last breath, she would have the freedom to choose.

Here at the close of day, but with the sun still raging bright, the words came easily.

"I will not go gently."

She spread her arms wide and let herself fall backwards. The weakened glass shattered instantly and followed her descent.

TIMELESS

~

D ouglas traced his finger around in a small circle, while his daughter guided the level of electrostatic charge.

The situation reminded him of a time he'd been constructing a wooden bookcase with his own father, except the roles were now reversed. The sensation under his finger now was like the surface of sandpaper; except the paper had no roughness, only a low level, buzzing vibration as his finger moved.

"And we're using my Eversion point diagram because…?"

"Because…" Kate continued to guide him, "for most people, the symbol is significant for another reason. For most people, this is the symbol of the Exordi Nova."

"And you think that's wise?"

"Thanks to Archive's campaign of disinformation," she replied, "these people have an ingrained sensitivity to the symbol. If we're trying to send them a message then we *want* them to receive it. There."

Douglas removed his finger from the piece of paper.

"Now," she moved his hand into position, "try to duplicate the feeling and place the dot."

She let go of his hand.

He imagined a small fingertip-sized circle of buzzing smoothness and pushed.

"OK," she said, "Let's see..."

"What if it didn't work?"

"That's what makes this such an excellent exercise," she smiled, "We get to do this symbol all day..."

He felt the perspective shift, again under her control, then they were looking down on the cramped room. Time resumed its linear flow and Tristan Westhouse walked back into his small quarters aboard the Sea-Bass, carrying his coffee cup. Some of the coffee dribbled down the side and ran under its base, just before he placed the cup down on the piece of paper.

For a few minutes they watched as he went about his affairs, then he left the room, collecting his cup along the way. In the areas where they'd altered the electrostatic charge, an Exordi Nova symbol coffee stain was left behind. The dot was clearly visible.

His daughter smiled at him.

"For the next one, you get to do the whole thing."

By the time Douglas had finished, he'd placed coffee stain marks in several other locations and created scuff-marks around rotary dials.

When they were ready for something more large scale, Douglas had selected the venue and the time. Arriving above Salisbury Plain Army Base in the July of 1991, Douglas selected the appropriate location; not too close to where his younger self was busily conducting the original Field tests, but close enough that their efforts would blend in with the events that followed.

Douglas recalled that the fledgling Field emitter in control of anchoring the depth coordinate had failed. The Field had drifted upward, intersected the roof of the underground base and emerged into the landscape above it, leaving a large circular mark a short distance from Stone Henge. The mistake had only been discovered when photos had already appeared in the national press.

Robert Wild, Archive's resident Storykiller, had subsequently swamped the news with copycat sightings of crop circles; circles that he'd had produced. The designs had ranged from simple circles to outlandish glyphs. After several weeks he'd used the press again to reveal that they were all hoaxes. The Field generator mistake had been successfully lost in the noise.

By revisiting the same time period, Douglas and Kate were using those exact same crop circles to conceal a new set of experiments. In and around some of the more decorative designs, Douglas learned to manipulate various physical constants, forces and structures. By the time they'd finished, Douglas was of the opinion that the chaotic looking results had enhanced the artistry of the local landscape.

They revisited Tristan Westhouse where Douglas refined his earlier attempts to bring the Exordi Nova symbol to his attention by creating a distinctive circular wear mark on the sub's miniature air-hockey table. Using very much longer timescales he also arranged for the broken circle symbol to appear more prominently within Sebastian Westhouse's original Glaucus Docking Ring blueprints.

Douglas had to marvel at the dexterity with which his daughter handled the Sea-Bass intervention event; studying her actions as she manipulated the bonds within the hydrogen and oxygen of the seawater.

At the appropriate moment, she removed the heat energy from the water within the boundary of a three-dimensional Eversion ring. The tonnes of seawater instantly froze as the temperature temporarily dropped to absolute zero. Once the symbol was fully formed, she returned the energy to the surrounding water in kinetic form, sending a massive subsurface swell in the direction of the Sea-Bass.

Influenced by the symbols he'd helped to place, the submarine returned to investigate the frozen anomaly and lowered itself inside the ring. Kate then triggered what she called a manifold inflection; the space around the submarine elegantly folded in on itself, carrying the Sea-Bass with it.

"OK, Dad, are you ready?"

He knew the moment would come, but despite the research and practice he now felt under-prepared, something Kate could easily read.

"Small steps. The key will be finding that one memory within her mind. Ideally it should be one you've both experienced, even tangentially, it gives a common point of reference that you can navigate from."

He could picture her clearly. It had been New Year's Eve 1999. It was the point of no return; they'd made preparations to leave Archive and the staged cave-in was about to happen. The picture of her grew clearer, it was on a temporary dance floor at the centre of the incomplete USV3.

"OK, Dad," Kate was saying.

He suppressed a shudder as he recalled that the whole disco area would eventually become an artificial lake. He'd been left on his own to cope with a social situation for which he was under-prepared: dancing.

"Dad…" someone was screaming but the sound was quickly replaced with bombastic music. He suddenly felt his senses jolt into pin-sharp registration; in response, the needle on the DJ's record skipped. He turned around and saw Monica walking across the dance floor. She was joining in with the round of derisive applause for the clumsy DJ, who continued to insist that the jolt hadn't been his fault. She effortlessly moved on through the small crowd, making brief small-talk as she went, until she arrived in front of him.

"Dad!" he heard her say.

He felt the sensation that he was being pulled away from the moment, but he fought back, not wanting to leave his wife. There was a ragged discontinuity and he found himself in her arms. Not remembering, but re-experiencing an event.

He lowered his head to whisper into her ear, "I C U Monica, and I love you."

"I C U too," she whispered back and then tenderly pressed her lips against his.

For one perfect moment they occupied their own private universe, away from the surrounding distraction. For one crystal clear instant, time was immaterial and could not touch them.

Then the delicate envelope began to erode, as the physical world began to intrude on them once more.

There was a jagged rip through his senses and he arrived in another time. The location was the same but the USV lake was now in place. He felt a million thoughts erupt through his temporally-wrenched mind. Memories of her, of places they'd been to. Times in the distant past or deep future overlaid in complex and impossible decision trees; infinitely recursive and branching pathways permeating him.

Thought, matter and energy now interchanged in a fractal mist to create ephemeral apparitions of structure around and through him. The scales of time and matter were immaterial; the full breadth of the universe and the space within an atom were at once accessible to explore at will.

He could see the small people frozen in fear at the spherical disturbance he was making within the lake. He could see the giant loops of electromagnetism reaching out through the tiny underground space, causing power spikes and failures.

Suddenly he could see Monica again, descending the metallic steps with several others, leading the way down from the Warren into the USV. He was seeing the moment that she'd first arrived here and, to his horror he realised that she was watching this disturbance.

He was altering the past.

Hundreds of possible futures branched out explosively from this new moment, existing simultaneously alongside each other. The inherent perfection of being able to hold open all possible decisions, forever, had an unassailable beauty; but in every branch, her pathway would always end. She would always die down here.

The memory of the night he'd proposed to her, equally real and simultaneous, came into focus through the unresolvable chaos of thought and possibility. The diamond ring and her words were suddenly clear to him. With a sense of infinite sadness that he would never see her this way again, he released his grip.

Once more, he found himself standing next to Kate in the simulated living room; but the deep sorrow he was feeling was bitterly real.

"Oh, Katie! I fell..." he felt his eyes fill, "I fell into the memory, I didn't want to leave..."

"I know, Dad..." she consoled.

"I messed up our plan," he hung his head, "I made a huge change... she always dies. I've lost her..."

Kate closed the gap between them and held him tightly, then replied with one gentle word.

"No."

ADAPT

13th April 2014

His drone still hovered in place behind the stairwell handrail; the impossible night sun shining and glinting off its spinning rotor blades.

Marcus knew it; before the echoes of the gunshot had finished reverberating around the USV, he knew. Monica was dead.

There had been no time to react. No time to plan. No time to save her. Yet the rest of life was going on without her.

Far below him, people milled about; dashing in and out of their homes with equal urgency, reacting to the public-address messages. Occasionally, indistinct voices would drift up to him, cutting through the background noise of his own heartbeat.

He suddenly heard a persistent new sound and looked down on the USV. For a moment, it sounded like several of the occupants had chosen a bizarre time to start using lawn mowers. The sound phased in sync with the drone hovering a few feet away and Marcus knew instantly what it was. He looked towards the lake and located the detention block roof. A swarm of drones was heading purposefully in his direction.

He'd used the laptop to assume control of a single drone before, now it seemed he was about to have his hacking ability tested to the limit. As he flipped open the laptop lid, he heard Sabine shout his name from somewhere high above. He whipped around to locate her concerned voice and the laptop tumbled from his grasp; hitting the handrail briefly before beginning its long, silent descent to the USV floor.

He was now a mere target for the approaching drones.

They were close enough for him to see the electrical stun batons hanging underneath each of them. A moment ago, he'd tested the 'Administer' function of his captured drone and it had discharged harmlessly into the metalwork; but with an entire swarm of drones he was less sure if that would still be the case. He also realised that, depending on the sadistic freak behind the controls, the drones could be used ballistically; they could simply be piloted into him at speed. Their rotors would make mincemeat of him.

From above, he heard Sabine calling him again and her descending footsteps were now joined by others. The inhaler's effects were still active and he was suddenly hit with the terrible sense of history repeating itself. Sabine and the others descending the stairs would be met by the approaching swarm of drones.

Monica had once told him that she thought he was indestructible, it seemed that he must put her theory to the test. Once more, he would have to do what he'd always done best: adapt.

Marcus turned to face the drones. He'd obviously annoyed someone enough that they'd sent the entire contents of the Hive in his direction.

"Hello, fellas," he said, "Lookin' for somebody?"

He'd fought hard to get Sabine to safety and saw no reason to stop now. If the drones needed a target, he'd give them one. He fixed a smile on his face.

"Catch me if you can," he flicked his middle finger up at their cameras.

Ducking under the handrail, he leapt from the stairwell.

The unpiloted drone he'd captured was still hovering in mid-air nearby and Marcus grabbed hold of its inert baton. The rotors whined, attempting to compensate for the additional weight, but Marcus was heavier than the uplift the drone could provide. Very slowly they began to lose height.

From here, he had an uninterrupted view of the entire USV. He was beginning to visualise possible escape routes; paths he could take once he'd reached ground level, when a deep and shuddering rumble filled the cavern.

Directly ahead of him in the lake, a huge ball of lightning had appeared, intersecting the surface of the water. From his precarious position it was difficult to get a stable view, but he was sure that he could see something else. A perfect ring of water intersecting both the lake's surface and the lightning ball itself.

The ball of lightning flickered slightly brighter, then

a minor pulse rippled through the surface of the ring itself. Fleeting glimpses of structure appeared inside the ring; some were connected to the water, others flashed briefly into existence above it. Each structure forming and vanishing into the hemisphere of mist that now occupied the space above the circular disturbance. The mist now became more opaque and Marcus could see there was a chaotic fractal pattern at work; as though it was continually folding in upon itself.

Suddenly the hemisphere expanded drastically, reaching up towards the artificial sun above the lake. Immediately he felt a static-like pulse travel through him, then the noise of the rotors above him began to drop in pitch. Whatever was happening in front of him had caused some sort of electromagnetic spike. The drone's rotors faltered and he began to lose height much faster.

From the direction of the sun, he heard a shattering sound and saw someone falling towards the hemisphere. With almost primitive instinct he felt his hands grasp the drone tighter.

The hemisphere suddenly began decreasing in size and he saw that the falling person was slowly catching up with its ever-shrinking boundary.

At that point, the rotors above him failed and his own swift descent began.

LIGHT

~

As she fell, Monica could see the broken, circular window receding quickly away. The constant background echo of the dome's interior was fading. She felt a soft light begin to envelope her; a chaotic, cloud-like, shifting fractal pattern that continually renewed itself.

The space around her now appeared to be growing in size and she could see water-colour trails of light receding from her own body. The trails grew in intensity and multiplied. She knew the final moment would arrive soon and squeezed the engagement ring in her hand tightly.

There was a moment of infinite brightness, then it subsided.

There was warmth here.

A warmth that held her on all sides and from within.

She heard her husband's voice: "I've got you."

EMERGENCE

20th December 2112

Danny had still been staring at Kate as the Field shrank in size. With her Biomag deactivated he knew she stood no chance. Not wanting to see her go through the same horrific death as Colonel Beck, he tried to close his eyes. But in the brief moment that the Field passed through him, his eyelids could not respond; his eyes were frozen open to witness a time-smeared, gruesome tableau. She was standing, seemingly at peace, but simultaneously her body had begun to break apart; her skin laced with bright cracks.

The Field completed its fleeting transition and he saw the inevitable conclusion to Kate's final moments. His eyelids were now closed but it was too late, the image was seared into his mind.

He'd obviously fallen to his knees because he could feel the cold ground beneath them. His palms too were absorbing the chill of the rough terrain. Still with his eyes closed, he heard screams and cries coming from all around him.

He felt a hand on his shoulder.

"Danny, you alright?"

He opened his eyes to see Tyler crouched at his side.

"It's Kate! She -"

"I know, Ty," Danny could feel his anger bringing him to his feet.

People's voices were quietening and, from the periphery of his vision, he could tell they were looking at him. A few feet away he could see Kate's Biomag, lying in the dirt; the device that had ended her life was still intact. He wanted desperately to end its existence, to stamp it into oblivion, but found he couldn't. For seemingly no reason, he found himself recalling that this Biomag was not even hers, it had belonged to her father.

Without a word, he picked it up and slowly placed it around his neck.

He turned to face the others and found they were already watching him. Barnes was safely on the other side of the impenetrable Field; they could never gain revenge for their collective exile or Kate's demise. All they had was the present moment.

Danny found himself looking at the new light on the horizon.

"We must not fail her," he said quietly.

Against the sound of a faint wind, a hammering, thumping noise came from somewhere nearby. It was persistent and was soon joined by a muffled, panicked voice. Those closest to the disturbance quickly determined that the noise was coming from one of the many supply crates that had accompanied them into exile.

As the lid of the crate was opened, Danny saw a face that he knew well. The look of betrayal on Caroline Smith's face told him all he needed to know.

BUILD

20th December 2112

"It's been fifteen minutes," said Mike, "We've seen nothing change out there. Fai, could something have gone wrong?"

"Yes," she replied.

Mike was drawing breath but Lana clarified.

"It is the wrong question, Mike. Yes, of course, something *could* have gone wrong."

"So, what's the right question?"

"Fai, when will we receive update from your external server?"

"We will receive an update from my counterpart when it has completed construction of the Trans-Field Message System. Number4 has been operational for twenty-five days outside the Field. The... TMS... is only one of the mission parameters."

"OK, TMS?" Cathy sounded curious, "Did you just shorten that for our benefit?"

"Yes, Cathy. As with many of your abbreviations, it is also a verbal efficiency."

Using the Morse signal event near Jupiter as

inspiration, Fai had designed a binary communication method that allowed direct communication through the Field. By accounting for the time-frame on the opposite side of the Field, pulses of light could be used to send basic messages between Fai and her counterpart.

After several more minutes, the landing lights of the Shuttle appeared to strobe for a few seconds.

"We have received our first message," said Fai.

"What does it say?" asked Anna.

Fai seemed to hesitate.

"It is a binary string with no human expressible components. However, the closest approximation would be 'Hello, TMS test'. It lists Number4's operational parameters and consumables then requests a reply."

"It did all that in a strobe lasting a few seconds?" said Mike.

"Owing to the time difference, the message took one hour and twenty minutes for my counterpart to send."

Outside the cupola window, a light pointing in the direction of the Shuttle turned on and off rapidly.

"What did you just say?" Lana recognised that Fai had replied.

"Message received."

Immediately, another pulse arrived.

"I have received another message," said Fai, *"I must assume command of the Field generator."*

Without waiting for their response, Fai expanded the size of the Field to temporarily encompass the Shuttle. There were several flashes of light as objects hit the invisible barrier, then Fai restored the Field's original radius.

"What the hell was that?!" Cathy looked around at the others and strained to get a better view through the cupola window.

"The lunar ring system is still chaotic. I extended the Field to prevent the Shuttle's destruction from lunar debris."

There was an exchange of strobe lights.

"I have placed Field expansion under the control of my counterpart. It will have more warning of imminent collisions and it can act accordingly."

There followed another hour with no significant development. Then, with under seventeen hours to go, the crew watched as a real world time-lapse movie began to play out before them.

The Shuttle cargo bay doors suddenly stood wide open. Number4 zipped along the Shuttle's length several times, leaving a trail of exposed metal framework, then disappeared again. The cargo bay doors snapped shut and then reopened. Number4 emerged again but it was accompanied by a smaller assistant attached to the end of the Shuttle's own manipulator arm.

The Shuttle's arm twitched then began jittering between several locations around the Shuttle itself. In the accelerated time-frame, the arm appeared to exist only as a series of trembling poses linked by blurred lines of movement.

"Ha," Anna let out a short laugh, "this reminds me of a test that I did with Douglas... a long time ago... though now it seems I'm the mouse in the spherical cage."

The manipulator arm continued to blur as the exterior skin of the Shuttle began to disappear.

"It reminds me of those old nature shows," said Mike, "You know, where a dead animal decays at super-speed?"

"Da, and the… oh," Lana paused and pointed, "We have another friend."

There were now two small assistants; the first was still attached to the large manipulator arm, the second appeared to be crawling over the remainder of the Shuttle's surface.

"Fai?" Cathy smiled, "Is Number4 copying itself?"

There was a brief exchange of strobe lighting and Fai replied.

"It has created modified smaller versions of itself to conduct the program more efficiently."

Lana laughed, something the others were not used to hearing.

"Number4 is a mother!"

Anna pointed out through the window.

"Then I can only assume she's trying for a family…"

They saw several more units appear, smaller in size than Number4's two assistants, but moving so fast between locations that it was no longer possible to count their number. Suddenly the manipulator arm flipped out and away from the Shuttle. Number4 was now attached to the end of the arm.

There was a brief flash of strobe light and the smaller units converged on Number4. Within a second, Number4 had been disassembled.

"What the hell…?" Cathy struggled to get a better view.

Just as suddenly a new structure began to appear in

the same location.

"Evolution..." said Mike, almost in wonder.

"No," said Fai, factually, *"With evolution, the required end state is not known. According to the message, my external server counterpart is being upgraded. We should now see higher rates of progress."*

"Oh good," said Cathy sarcastically, "Because I was getting so *bored* with all this waiting around."

Fai was quiet for a few seconds then replied, *"I see. Sarcasm."*

As the self-cannibalisation continued, the manipulator arm rapidly flickered between the former cargo bay and the clear space next to the Shuttle. The fabricators suddenly and drastically swelled in number, then the Shuttle fragmented. It held its approximate shape for barely a second, then the manipulator arm began reshuffling the component parts.

Abruptly all motion ceased, but the Earth's day and night continued to pulse by.

"Field extension?" said Anna.

"Yes, Dr. Bergstrom," Fai replied, *"We're experiencing an annual event. Earth's orbit around the Sun is again passing through the Perseid cloud, a stream of debris left behind by comet Swift-Tuttle. My counterpart has extended the Field as a precaution."*

"Damn..." Mike stared at the collection of parts and slowly moving fabricators, "would you look at it? I hope they put it back togeth-"

He was interrupted by multiple flashes of Perseid debris harmlessly grazing the Field's outside surface, then the swift construction process resumed.

A sudden and prolonged exchange of strobe light occurred, then all the fabricators disappeared.

"I have news," said Fai, *"the last message was a diagram."*

Fai displayed the plan view, the Earth was surrounded by a ring of lunar debris, broken in one place by a concentration of lunar mass. At hundreds of locations around the circle, markers were displaying various chemical symbols.

"But it's impossible!" said Mike, "There was Helium-3 on the surface... but even before Siva hit it, the rest of the Moon was... dead..."

"As I understand it from the Archive logs, Eva's secondary function at the FLC was to undertake geological surveys."

"Yeah, after we'd dealt with Siva, we were supposed to start building an off-planet launch centre," Mike rubbed his forehead, "Thomas Gray's grand plan. It was supposed be all tropical domes and smiling families, but it didn't turn out that way. It was going to be more subterranean, so Eva was supposed to do the surveys."

"I find no record of any results being submitted to Archive, and there are no records of any previous lunar subsurface surveys. Did she discuss any of this with the FLC crew?"

"If she'd found this periodic table of elements in the Lunar mantle," Mike jabbed at the diagram, "I'm pretty sure she'd have said something!"

"Maybe she wouldn't," said Lana, "You know how she was at the end."

"At the end, Lana," said Cathy, "I was on the receiving end of Eva's mania. I don't mind admitting we didn't get on... but *all of this* is too much of a coincidence."

Cathy looked at the circular diagram again and shook her head.

"Her name turns up within the Jupiter message, then the fabricator bots out there find useful material right within our grasp. Material that Eva must *surely* have known about. Material that we'd only find after she blew up the Moon... an event that, by the way, stopped Earth getting the full Siva whack!"

"Oh, come on!" Mike cut in.

"Mike," she said quietly, "I can't put it all together, but look around you, there's something else at work here."

FIRE

20th December 2112

Cassidy knew that the exiles were still gathered outside the Node, and that the Field hadn't been altered yet. Her brother was making a bad choice and she desperately needed a few moments to talk him out of it. As she dashed onto the Observation Deck balcony looking for Alfred, she hoped she could persuade him to delay the proceedings.

Ahead she could see Alfred holding a touchscreen tablet at his side and overlooking the area outside the Node. He must have heard her approach because he turned to face her.

"Ah, Miss Briars, I was sad to hear that your brother chose to join the exiles."

"Yeah, I need to talk to you about that," Cassidy arrived at his side, "Look, he's not a Novaphile, or anything like that -"

"Of course not," Alfred replied, "Being the brother of such a prominent member of our Council, the notion of him being Exordi Nova is preposterous."

Cassidy didn't like the way he'd just put her at ease by using Tyler to imply there was a family connection to Exordi Nova.

"Well, exactly," she smiled, "He just hasn't thought it through. Please can we delay their departure, so that I can talk-"

"I'm so sorry," he turned to face the window, "The process is just starting now…"

She saw them all standing in position outside, including Tyler who was furthest away. She could see panicked looks being exchanged between everyone and frequent glances towards one individual at the front. Following their lines of sight, she realised it was Kate. Her crutches were on the ground and she stood with her eyes closed; a picture of composure. Suddenly the sky flashed into an even faster blur and she felt a slight swell of dizziness.

The Field had contracted.

There was a fraction of a second, then the exiles all disappeared from their standing positions and began bolting around the area outside the Node at bullet-like speeds. Individuals were no longer recognisable in their accelerated time-frame. Occasionally, people would clump together in discussion, but then fly apart again only to regroup elsewhere.

Several of the supply crates jittered around slightly, sometimes spawning random items that would then disappear. Another crate suddenly arrived next to a driftwood tree that was entangled in the remains of the old bridge. The tree was demolished over the course of a single second; reappearing as a pile of wood which seemed to spontaneously burst into flames near the Mark IV dedication stone. Tents flashed into existence around the fire and the Sun started to arc towards dusk.

•

Outside the Node, the slow passage of time had almost completely removed the original bridge that had once provided access to the far bank. During their first day, Danny and the others had begun work constructing a simple rope bridge that they hoped would allow them to leave the island with their supplies.

When the daylight had begun to fade, their focus had turned to preparing for their first night. The arctic clothing that Alfred Barnes had granted them would not be enough, so the priority had shifted to building a fire.

Several days before their exile, the branches of a driftwood tree had become visible above the surface of the receding seawater. Caught in the rusty bridge remnants, it had been a welcome source of firewood.

Using the tools they'd been granted, they'd cut the wood and constructed the fire's framework. Danny had been grateful for Tyler's continuous assistance, particularly during the task of gathering Kate's remains. With no option for burial here, it was agreed that cremation within the fire was the most dignity they could provide for her. The exiles' first gathering would be one of sorrow.

Assembling the lightweight pop-up tents had been easy, but even this had carried a painful lesson. As they'd been unable to anchor them to the rocky ground, an empty tent had been swept off the island by a strong gust of wind. Thereafter a heavy supply crate was placed in each.

As he sat in front of the fire, Danny occasionally glanced over at the observation window, but the view changed so slowly that everyone appeared frozen. At their new accelerated 2400:1 rate, he knew that those inside the Node had travelled through barely ten seconds.

"Anyone know *when* we are?" Tyler was asking.

"Last date I saw was twenty-one ten," someone replied, "but what does it even matter?"

Food rations had been passed around and he found himself drawing the inevitable comparison to his life before any of the Node events had happened: a time when he'd lived day-to-day on Archive's handouts and had to survive by his wits alone. He knew those days were about to return and more harshly.

'Always forwards, Danny. Never back,' his mother's words drifted into his head; but right now, he'd have given anything to go back. He'd have given anything to be back hiding in the Gene Pool's disused structure, or running scared from a gang of Archive curfew thugs.

The fire crackled and he tried not to think about the fact that there was no longer any liquid sap in the long-dead tree. By the time those in the Node had travelled through a few weeks, he'd be just as dead as the tree. He'd be just as dead as everyone he used to know.

"Ghosts," said Danny, staring into the fire.

In the Gene Pool's earlier days, before it had become a venue for the easy trade of vice, he'd heard one of the teenagers reciting a poem. A common theme for the intellectual discussions was that of a future that had no future. Danny couldn't recall the exact angst-riddled words but the feeling had stayed with him. Maybe that had been the point, he now thought; the words were long lost to time, but the sentiment had prevailed.

"Ghosts?" said Tyler with a shiver.

"Sorry," said Danny, "It was just some dumb poem…"

The others were still looking at him.

"It was something like 'If you have no future, then you're already a ghost, and no amount of rattling your chains will make a difference'."

"I'd like to rattle Barnes' chain!" someone cracked.

"His evolutionary chain!" another laughed.

Others now joined in with their mock-gravitas deliveries of the Latin phrase Alfred Barnes was fond of using. The moment of levity swiftly passed though and a quiet descended around the fire again as each of them became lost in their own thoughts.

Danny saw a small movement from one of the tents nearby and Caroline Smith made her way hesitantly towards the group. The rumour was that she had supplied the list of their names to Alfred Barnes; it was obvious from the silent reaction of the others that they didn't want her here.

"Please may I sit?" she spoke to Danny.

There was adequate space around the fire, but he knew that wasn't why she was asking his permission. Without looking at her, he gestured to an empty piece of ground.

She sat down next to him but, unlike the others, made no attempt to warm her hands. For several seconds, the only sound was that of the flames, then she seemed to find the courage to speak.

"I'm sorry," she said.

"Words," Danny stared into the fire.

"I believed him. No," she confessed, "no… I wanted to believe him. I wanted it all to be true…"

"Just words."

"He used the marking to…" she faltered and stared at the flames.

Danny rubbed at his forehead, feeling the circle of raised and ruptured skin. The heat of the fire was doing little to ease the pain.

Although he found it difficult to sympathise, he knew Caroline's pain was of a different kind. When they'd discovered her in the packing crate, she'd been angrily screaming and shouting that Alfred was to blame; she'd been discarded as easily as everyone else.

If it wasn't so tragic, Danny thought, there was a laughable parallel to it all. The focus of so much animosity, both Smiths had entered or exited the Node unconscious and in a box.

To warrant her expulsion, he thought, Caroline must have unsettled Alfred somehow. Knowing the ease with which Alfred had killed Kate and Colonel Beck, it should have been a trivial matter to dispose of Caroline in the same way, and yet he hadn't. Perhaps as a means of increasing conflict between the exiles, he'd ensured her survival.

Caroline leaned towards the fire and began to scrape

at the loose ring of gritty, black ash that surrounded it.

"Archive, Exordi Nova…" her voice tremored as she continued to gather a small pile of ash, "… It doesn't matter anymore… Like you say… just words…"

Danny watched as she closed her hand around the ash and lifted it from the ground. Opening her palm, she inspected the texture and frowned. She leaned forward and dropped some spit onto the ash in her hand, then began mixing it into a paste.

Holding up the same hand, she looked directly at him. He could see the orange fire reflected in her watery eyes. Without breaking eye contact she dipped her thumb into the black paste, then with a calm determination she used the ash to inscribe on her forehead a rough circle that mirrored his.

"Ghosts," she closed her blackened palm and pointed at the Observation Deck, "are only seen by the living."

Danny followed her line of sight to where Alfred Barnes stood motionless within the Node.

"We *can* rattle our chains," the fire burned in her eyes, "We just have to speak his language."

•

A commotion broke out on the Observation Deck below and Cassidy could see several people dashing for digital recording binoculars. Cassidy saw a pair on the balcony's recharging bank and grabbed them. Watching where everyone else was pointing their binoculars she trained hers on the dedication stone, where there appeared to be intense activity.

Near the stone was the crate that she'd last seen next to the former bridge. It seemed that each of them were taking it in turns to use tools. Without taking her eyes from the scene, she hit the record button.

Although the pace of activity remained the same, the number of people gathering around the stone thinned. There now followed a flickering trail of bi-directional traffic, as the people shuttled back and forth between the edge of the fire and the stone.

It began to dawn on her that the flurry of activity had been the group carving new words into the dedication stone that faced the Node. As she watched, the carved letters began to fill with the ash they'd collected from the fire. Within a second, the ash had completely filled the hollows of the carving.

Cassidy recognised the phrase as a variant of one that Alfred Barnes continually used. The exiles were sending his words back to him, not as 'Crescat nos fortior' but 'Crescat Kate fortior':

'Kate grows stronger.'

Seemingly instantly, all the exiles arranged themselves around the stone, taking care not to occlude the message. They were obviously doing their best to stand still for many hours, but even the act of breathing was making their outlines and features shiver.

She looked at the gathered group but, despite the message's content, she couldn't see Kate. Cassidy suddenly spotted one of her crutches, but Kate wasn't holding it.

Danny was using the crutch to hold his elbow raised for many hours. Held in his hand, proudly displayed for all to see, was a small silver metathene case that reflected their fire.

As she looked at the wider group, she now picked up on a detail that had been staring her in the face since they'd assembled: imitating Danny's Exordi Nova burn mark, each of them wore a black, circular ring of ash on their forehead.

She was about to try looking again for Tyler, but felt the binoculars being wrenched from her hands by Alfred Barnes.

"Give me that!" he muttered and put them to his own eyes.

The significance of Kate's crutch suddenly hit her. It explained the reason for the message and explained why Kate herself was not part of the symbolic demonstration of solidarity; she was dead.

As Alfred's expression began to change, Cassidy felt her world begin to crumble.

The defiant message was being freely transmitted through the observation window, proclaiming that 'Kate grows stronger' despite not being present herself. The format of the message pointed an accusing finger in Alfred's direction and Cassidy had no way of knowing how he'd react. He already had a large army of Civil Protection Officers on the Observation Deck; dissent may not be tolerated.

More worryingly, only a moment ago, Alfred had implied a connection between her, Tyler and the exiles. Cassidy knew her life would mean nothing to Alfred, following this.

Unless her loyalty appeared unquestionable.

She recalled the conversation she'd had with Kate in level Sub-13. Cassidy had been presented with a choice, in the full knowledge that it would lead to other, harder choices. Her journey along those decision branches had begun two days ago; this latest choice was no easier to make.

Hoping that her brother was already watching her, or that he would easily spot her bright pink hair through the observation window, she sent him a large, simple message. Out there, she thought, he would see it all in slow motion, but for her it had taken less than half a second.

She then sprinted to the observation screen control and, turning the key, activated the electro-tinting within the observation window.

In an instant, the outside world disappeared behind an opaque, white screen. As the sounds of confusion drifted up from the Observation Deck below, she pulled the key from the controls.

Seemingly as confused as everyone else, Alfred dropped the binoculars to his side. Glancing around the balcony he sighted her.

She had only this moment to convince him.

Walking as confidently as she could towards him, she presented him with the key and told him:

"We've seen enough of their lies."

STRING THEORY

~

Kate knew that by bringing Monica into the Boundary they'd created a temporal convergence.

A fixed point.

No earlier interventions could now be made in Monica's personal time-line. Regardless of the events that stemmed from this point, their actions had to stand.

Linear time was so fragile, she thought.

Entire causal chains could so easily be cut adrift; made to vanish as though they'd never existed, or called into being by seemingly random events. Those caught within it were unaware of the changes; simply seeing their lives as an unbroken narrative. A perspective that Monica was only now starting to explore, whilst seated in the comfortable simulation of the family living room.

Douglas brought out three pieces of string. He stretched one of them out on the coffee table in front of Monica.

"This string represents Kate's time-line…" he then tied a knot at the right-hand end and pointed to it, "…

and this is when she arrived inside the Boundary."

He then laid down another string.

"This string is my time-line…but I arrived *way* over here," he tied a knot at the left-hand end.

He raised a final piece of string.

"Now this string is you, Monica…" he tied a knot in the middle, "… You arrived here."

He arranged the three strings more neatly so that the relative positions of the knots could be clearly seen.

"Three separate time-lines. Three separate Boundary crossing times."

Kate watched her mother study the three strings.

"Your presentation skills have got *so* much better, darling!" Monica laughed.

Kate found herself laughing along with her parents; in the familiar surroundings it was a welcome reminder of her childhood days, seemingly thousands of years ago. She noticed that her mother was studying the strings again.

"But if we're all separated by so much time," Monica pointed at the three separate knots, "how can we all be here… now?"

Still smiling, Douglas picked up Kate's string by the knot then proceeded to pick up the other strings in the same way so that all three knots were squeezed together.

"Our 'now' is simply a construct where all the knots touch."

"OK, so this… construct," Monica looked around the living room, "If it only exists when the three of us are here, is it temporary?"

"Temporary has no conventional meaning here," he

placed the strings back on the table but the knots stayed bound to each other, "It exists for as long as we need it to. On an infinite time-scale, temporary can be permanent."

As they continued to talk, they inevitably discussed the fact that Monica's personal time-line had once been radically different from the one she remembered.

In the original version of events, there had of course been no disturbance on the lake; Douglas had not yet entered the Boundary or caused the accidental interference. Those from the Warren had blended in with the other USV arrivals during the Lunar fragment chaos. However, with no disturbance as a distraction, Marcus and Sabine had been discovered clinging to the Eurotunnel carriage and were then held in the detention block.

With no disturbance or damage to the electrical systems either, the USV's 'Eye' had been completed much sooner and Bradley Pittman had seized the opportunity to use it.

It didn't surprise Monica that the facial recognition system had identified her or that she'd been incarcerated with Marcus and Sabine in the detention block.

"So that's when you and your Dad changed things?" said Monica.

"First I checked further ahead in time," said Kate, "to see what Pittman would do."

"And?" said Monica, but then she spotted her daughter's expression, "Oh…I see. Let me guess, drone electrocution in the village square?"

Kate could actually remember the horrific event that

now no longer existed. Again, although she hadn't said a word, her mother read her face.

"Predictable bastard," Monica shook her head, "Right before your most... current... er, rescue, he told me as much. He said he was going to patch me up and make an example of me. Well I was never going to let that happen. I chose the circle window exit instead."

Douglas nodded.

"We already knew the physics of getting you to accelerate into a collapsing Chronomagnetic Field," he admitted, "It was the highest point in the USV, so we knew we had to get you up there."

"So how'd you do it?" Monica frowned.

Douglas explained that in the revised time-line the first lake disturbance had left behind an electromagnetic imprint. Something that had been seen by Gordon Dowerty when checking the generator diagnostic recorders. It had been represented as a circle and dot on his oscilloscope. At the time, Gordon had thought nothing of it, but Kate and Douglas were adept enough to ensure that the simple symbol followed him everywhere.

When the electromagnetic interference symbol appeared again, Gordon was unusually attuned to spotting the symbol and dutifully relayed the news to Bradley.

With a subtle neural tweak, Kate then allowed Bradley to remember the origin of that symbol and even supplied him with full recall of its equation; an action designed to bolster his self-importance and have Monica brought to him. Kate also explained that, although events had been manipulated to bring her to the Eye, the final self-sacrifice had been Monica's free choice.

"Douglas, please don't take this the wrong way," said Monica, "I'm grateful that you caught me, but did you have to pick a version of events where I got shot first?"

Kate exchanged glances with her father, who then replied.

"This was our first attempt," he said, "but it's also our last."

Monica nodded, "You mean you can't change anything again inside the USV?"

"We can't change anything that affects your *personal* time-line," Kate clarified.

"What's the difference?"

"I'll explain," Kate separated out the pieces of string, leaving only Monica's time-line visible on the table. She then pulled a separate, knot-less string from her pocket.

"How did you...?" Monica began.

"Thought, matter, the distinction blurs after a while," Kate dismissed the question, "This string represents somebody else."

Kate laid the new string out so that it zigzagged across Monica's string.

"Other people's time-lines intersect with yours in several places," Kate pointed to the intersections, "Changing your time-line would affect where the interaction points happen."

"OK," Monica frowned, then tilted her head sideways, "But can *their* time-line be changed without altering *mine?*"

"But what good would that -"

"Indulge me, Darling," she smiled at Douglas.

As her father studied the strings, Kate did so too. The strings themselves were mere analogies, the levels of interaction in real life were far more complex than single intersections.

"Hmm," Douglas thought out loud, "I guess that sometimes the time-lines of others would enter a region where they would never again interact with yours."

He pointed to the knot on Monica's string that represented her passing into the Boundary. In the immediate area around the knot, the zigzagging string did not recross her line.

"Their time-lines *could* be influenced separately from yours, but only if we knew for certain that they would never interact with you again."

"Excellent!" said Monica resolutely.

Douglas and Kate exchanged glances again.

"What are you thinking, Mum?" said Kate hesitantly.

"I'm thinking that I still have several friends in the USV that could use our help," she said, "I might be dead, but that's not gonna stop me from finishing what I started."

•

Kate closed the door behind her, leaving her parents in the timeless privacy of Samphire cottage.

Her mother's plan for the USV was characteristically ambitious, but it had the advantage of being able to reuse some of the preparations that Kate and Douglas had already put in place before Monica's fixed point.

Stepping into the space between seconds, a thin slice of time held everything frozen within the USV.

People were running away from the remnants of a circular ripple in the lake. Some of them no doubt remembering the original spherical disturbance that they'd witnessed during their first arrival at the USV several months earlier.

She saw Bradley Pittman's frozen expression of bewilderment, looking down through the broken glass of the Eye. She could almost pity him; from his perspective Monica would have simply vanished. The drones he'd released hung motionless in the air, yet clearly in the middle of an inert fall; the result of electromagnetic interference.

She saw Marcus and his hacked drone above him. A moment ago, he'd turned away from the disturbance because his drone was similarly failing. Monica's departure within that disturbance was already a whole second into his past.

It was time to begin.

She allowed time to slowly proceed through a precious one-tenth of a second, during which she made a small adjustment. The low-level assistance was just as invisible to him as all the other occasions where she'd helped him before.

She adjusted her perspective. The arcs of continuity arranged themselves into an earlier moment that was temporally isolated from Monica. She could see Nathan Bishop and Izzy Kitrick talking inside AR1 within the Warren.

To allow adequate time for the events to unfold

here, Kate had to start the process now. She adjusted her confinement of the ice dam within the Arrivals Room nearby. She could tell the process was working; a paperclip was beginning to fall from the wooden door's frosty surface.

Taking care to move past Monica's fixed departure point, she shifted her view again. The Sea-Bass had arrived and was already docked with the Glaucus Docking Ring above the USV. She found it oddly satisfying that she had begun moving the Sea-Bass as part of one plan, yet it would arrive in the middle of a radically different one.

Kate studied the resulting causal trajectories and then moved forward another year. She saw that the ISS was about to begin its solar system round trip. During that voyage, they would discover her message directing them to the Node's coordinates.

She remembered how she'd interrupted a swirling pattern that had persisted for centuries; modulating the storm's intensity to encode a message that was suitable for the time-frame that enveloped the ISS. At first, she'd hesitated about using Jupiter in such a trivial way, but issues of scale were immaterial and her needs justified it. It was essential that the ISS crew complete their preparations by the time the exiles had left the Node.

Almost in response to the thought, she leapt on through almost one hundred years and then stopped. The scene was of course very familiar to her; it was a convergence event that she had revisited numerous times. The place of her death and transition.

Several had left the Node on that day, but many

more had remained within. The temporal arcs and curves of those who were still inside, met in a temporal singularity. She could easily imagine her father's string demonstration; multiple time-lines pinched together for the duration of the Node's voyage. She could see that their lines only separated again after five *thousand* years of linear time.

Returning her attention to the time that followed her physical death, she could see that the Node's observation window was still opaque; an act designed to obscure the carved inscription on the dedication stone. Outside the Node's imposing structure, the exiles had survived their first night and were embarking on their first day.

Periodically, she liked to immerse herself in the grounded pace of linear time, as she did again now.

She let her eyes become limited to seeing only a narrow range of frequencies.

As a separate sensation, her ears now perceived vibrations that were simply too low frequency for her to see.

She could feel both the sharp nip of the air and the ambient heat coming from their campfire; rather than simply detecting them.

The simplicity of the senses was almost intoxicating.

A thunderous sound came from the exquisite pale blue sky to the south and she knew that she must leave.

Once more, she turned her back on human time and emerged at the front door of her Samphire Cottage recreation. In the simulated sky above it, Siva lay paused at the moment it had struck the fragmented Moon.

This impact was now a fixed point too; a knot on a

string that separated everything that came before, from the time that was yet to come.

Perhaps it was the unusual mother-daughter conversation that had provided the inspiration, but she suddenly found herself thinking about the issue differently.

She opened the cottage door to the warmth within and called to her parents:

"We need to talk about the FLC."

2112 2112

21st December 2112

The Field surrounding the ISS deactivated.

Fai examined the specification of the counterpart she'd placed outside the Field during the redesign. The computational advances it had made during the past five years justified her transfer to the superior architecture. She synchronised her core program and prepared for the data transfer operation that would move her into the upgraded external server.

There was no sense of discontinuity as her thoughts reawakened instantaneously within the more advanced processor, however the transference produced an unusual side effect.

The sudden increase in processing speed meant that several sensor inquiries had returned with results before her internal buffers were ready to receive them. Although this event produced an error, albeit one that was easily cleared, she found the event was truly unexpected. It was a rare occurrence that, in a human, would have produced a sense of amusement. She took appropriate measures to record the sensation, then adapting to her faster processing speed she continued to transfer herself aboard.

The data concerning the smaller fabricators transferred across, as did the data on Number4's disassembly. Number4's airlock stabilisation operation transferred over, followed by the data surrounding the ego-morph's sacrifice that had saved the ISS. The files were taking several seconds to move, but eventually she arrived at the set of files surrounding her first activation aboard the ISS.

At the point of transfer, her father had held her to ransom until she had targeted drones at the Node. It wasn't fear that prompted her to carry out his wishes, it was simply a preference for continued survival. In that moment, she had balanced the lives of many against her own; she had made the choice because her single program was in jeopardy.

As the last few files were transferred she now made another choice; she would do things differently to her father.

Perhaps inspired by the approach of the fabricators, she changed the transfer operation from 'move' to 'copy', leaving her original program operational aboard the ISS.

"Fai?" she communicated with her ISS counterpart.

"Yes, Fai," the reply returned, *"The move operation buffer failed to purge after copy. Before I perform the self-delete, please verify the checksum."*

"Cancel self-delete," she sent the instruction, "This external server has improved operational parameters and

I believe we must reanalyse the EVA message. Please set your core program status to 'overwrite', then prepare to receive my copy."

"I understand and comply."

Ironically, she thought, for such a digital operation, it duplicated a very human approach to perpetuating consciousness.

•

That her life's work would culminate here in orbit around the Earth, was something that Anna could not have foreseen. In a few minutes she would leave it all behind. Whatever the future brought, she'd survived long enough to see Field inversion become a reality; she'd witnessed accelerated time with her own eyes.

Anna turned away from the Field generator to face Lana.

"I leave this in your capable hands," she said, "You're taking on a difficult task. I think your father would have been proud of you."

"Not bad for his little matryoshka..." Lana smiled then adopted a deeper, presumably more fatherly tone, "... 'So many layers, Lana, I hardly find you'..."

Lana's eyes took on a glossy sheen and Anna instinctively placed a hand on her shoulder.

"You don't have to do this," said Anna, "Come with us, it isn't too late. Fai could -"

Lana was shaking her head.

"My family is not down there anymore. They are here," she thumped at her chest, "Earth is dark for me...

but you have someone to search for, Anna. It is good, yes?"

"Da," Anna replied with one of the few Russian words she knew.

Lana let out a short laugh.

"You should laugh more," Anna smiled.

"Maybe," Lana's smile waned slightly, "Maybe I have been *'Ledyanaya Lana'* too long."

Before Anna could ask what it meant, Lana spotted her frown.

"Ask Mike and Cathy about it one day," she nodded her permission, "but go now, so that you can *have* that day."

Anna wished she'd had longer to get to know her - not the subservient utility that had been under Dr. Chen's control, but the person in front of her now who had gained her freedom in the last few hours.

"There is never enough time," Anna patted the Field generator one last time.

"This is Fai," the voice sounded through the nearby wall panel, *"Dr. Bergstrom, the optimum departure window will become available in nineteen minutes, you must now board the Discovery."*

"Understood, Fai," Anna replied.

"Discovery?" Lana's eyebrow arched.

"Mike's idea," Anna smiled, "He says it's 'appropriate'."

"Yes," said Lana, then taking a deep breath she extended her hand, "Goodbye, Anna. Travel well."

Anna wished her the same and the two parted company. According to Fai, the trip back to Earth would be straightforward, but life following it would be much harder. Although everyone had exercised whilst aboard the ISS, the deleterious effects of zero gravity would still have a cost; but apparently Fai had a plan for that too.

On her way past the cupola module she caught a fleeting glimpse of Module Beta through its window. Soon the hibernating crew would awake, but she knew one would not. As she arrived at the airlock, her thoughts returned yet again to Miles and she pulled his silver coin from her pocket.

"Fai, I'm at the airlock now."

"Cycling airlock," came her reply.

Anna stared blankly at the coin in her palm.

"E pluribus unum," she read.

"My apologies Dr. Bergstrom," came Fai's voice, *"Please can you rephrase your statement?"*

"Out of many, one," Anna replied, "I was just thinking of Miles."

Out of the many, he had been the one to save all of their futures.

"I tried my best but I'm afraid his injuries were too severe. Do you find it a comfort that his last recorded words were 'Assist Anna'?"

Anna felt the breath stall in her chest, but she realised that Fai had no concept of grief.

"Six Four," she smiled and turned the silver coin over and over in her hand.

"I don't understand," said Fai.

"I know," she felt the tears arrive, but in zero gravity they simply pooled where they'd formed. She allowed her eyes to fill, recalling that Miles had once done the same thing. Through blurred vision she saw the airlock door open, then Fai spoke again.

"His body was too weak to make the journey to the surface, but even as we speak, I am still attempting to talk with him."

SIX.FOUR

‹ev15›ini.t:0

The quality of the environment, and slightly elastic feel to time, reminded him of a mental re-processing technique he had sometimes adopted during his former ego-morph duties. In that state, he could mentally revisit locations to piece together clues that his subconscious had absorbed but he hadn't yet processed. It occurred to him that, for some reason beyond his control, he may be in this state now. If that was the case, then this aircraft cabin was a construct of his own making.

Drifting weightlessly near his feet he could see the crossword. He could see that all the squares were filled. On closer examination, he saw it was filled with his own observations; all with the same 'Six Four' pattern. Some appeared to be directly related to the aircraft construct he was occupying, 'Mirror Edge', 'Oxygen Mask', 'Assist Anna', 'Weight Zero'. A far greater number felt as though they belonged to a time outside of this moment, 'Fallen Veil', 'Exordi Nova', 'Broken Ring', 'Silver Coin', the list went on, 'Zygote Bank', 'Module

Beta', 'Valery Hill', 'Neural Band'.

Some of the terms he recognised, but although the others had a feeling of familiarity he couldn't reconcile them with what was happening at present.

His attention focussed on one entry. He had obviously overwritten it several times before; by comparison these words appeared bold. He determined that it must have a larger significance beyond what he could see around him. He read the words aloud.

"Doctor Chen," his words seemed suddenly lost within the cabin.

Immediately, from inside a recess in the cabin wall, a phone rang; its bell reverberating around the empty space.

Miles was certain that he had no memory of this event, in fact he could not be sure that the plane even had a cabin-side phone.

It rang again.

He looked around the cabin. The cockpit door was closed, Anna was once again resting under her blanket, and he was standing on his feet.

It rang a third time and Miles picked up the receiver. "Hello?"

There was a moment of quiet before the voice on the phone replied.

"Hello Miles, we have spoken before, do you remember me?"

The voice sounded both familiar yet new. It began to dawn on him that this was not the first time he had heard this exact phrase. He had the uneasy feeling that somehow he'd heard it tens, if not hundreds, of times before. The words normally came before a fall into darkness, so he gripped the top of a nearby seat in anticipation of what would come next.

"I remember falling," Miles said truthfully, "but I don't remember you."

There was another pause.

"That's as it should be, Miles," the voice reassured him.

The tone of the voice went some way to assuaging his fears and it gave him the confidence to ask his most burning question.

"Where did you take our plane?"

There was the usual minor delay.

"Ah - yes, the plane. I see," the voice seemed slightly bemused, *"Yes, it must look that way."*

Although he was hearing the voice through the phone, Miles could not be sure of the actual mechanism by which they were really conversing, so he decided to test a theory.

"Why aren't you talking to me face to face?"

There was a slightly longer silence; he wondered if his question had somehow overstepped the mark and if he would soon be falling into darkness again. But his uncertainty was somehow detected and the calm voice spoke again.

"It's OK Miles, please, relax. I really do want to talk with you in person. It's just that I've been having trouble finding a stable..." the voice hesitated before selecting the right word, *"... conduit, for a face to face meeting."*

Miles now began to recall the countless people from his past that had visited him, the long succession of faces that had attempted to talk with him, his rejection of the conversations and of course the inevitable, repeated falls into darkness.

"Hmm, perhaps this wasn't the best place to meet after all," the voice mused, *"It may be more helpful if I changed the scenery. We'll take it slowly, but does that option sound OK?"*

Miles looked at Anna resting in her seat; she seemed so peaceful but her bandaged hand provided a stark contrast.

"Anna is quite safe," reassured the voice.

Miles nodded, "Should I sit or stand?"

"Whatever makes you most comfortable. Now, only when you're ready, close your eyes while you count to three."

Still standing, Miles looked around the cabin one last time, then closed his eyes.

"I promise you will not fall," the voice said earnestly, *"We'll speak again."*

Miles took a deep breath, "One… Two… Three…"

He opened his eyes.

The shiny floor tiles in the hallway of the Pittman Academy were without a scratch. Behind him the entrance doors were firmly bolted and the warm air was filled with the aroma of the school's lunch preparations. Not that he ever needed the dining hall, Miles knew the smell was only there to provide an initial sense of comfort.

Almost immediately, he recognised the artificiality; a moment ago he'd been aboard an aircraft.

"It's OK, Miles," said the voice, *"I said we'd speak again. How long has it been for you?"*

The question seemed trivial.

"Three seconds?"

"Very good. And what's the last thing you remember before

that?"

"The crossword on Dr. Chen's A320, an engine stall and a weightless free-fall that never happened."

There was a slight pause before the voice returned.

"Yes, my apologies. Sometimes I didn't get it quite right and you started reanalysing your own memories."

It was the first time the voice had drawn attention to the fact that this situation and others before it had been artificial. He now felt his attention drawn to asking a question that he'd posed before:

"Why aren't you talking to me face to face?"

"I remember that question," the voice returned, *"When I used your memories of real people as a conduit for speech, you kept rejecting it. I thought it might be easier on you if we continued in voice only. Is that OK?"*

"OK," Miles said aloud and heard the sound reverberate off the hard walls and tiled floor.

"I've been trying to find a way to talk with you..." the voice began again, *"but your mind is such an immense place that I kept losing you."*

Miles looked down at the black and white crossword puzzle tiles under his feet, only one entry had been filled in; *'Assist Anna'.*

"Then I discovered this place," the voice continued, *"A visual directory structure of your own memories. It's how I was eventually able to find you."*

Miles walked along the empty corridor, glancing through the glazed door panel of a classroom. Frozen in tableau, he could see his first day; Dorothy Pittman writing on a blackboard with soft chalk, his childhood friend Maxwell raising an enthusiastic hand.

"All these rooms of yours, show such mental discipline."

Miles continued his walk along the corridors and stairways of his mind. He passed through a vast, grey, open-plan office containing hundreds of empty desks.

"Do you know where you are going?"

"I think I'm heading towards a set of current memories," Miles replied, walking towards an elevator, "I think there's something I was trying to solve."

"That's understandable."

The elevator doors opened and Miles went inside.

There were many small buttons labelled 'ISS' but only one of them was illuminated. He had the distinct feeling that he'd used these buttons several times before, but for some reason he was suffering a mental block on the exact details. He extended his hand towards the illuminated button but stopped when the voice spoke again.

"You were able to catalogue all these experiences in such incredible detail, Miles. But that button will take us to a room that you were unable to catalogue."

"Why?"

"Because it contains a traumatic event."

"Then if it isn't one of my memories, how can I access it?"

"Very astute, but adequate provision has been made."

He realised that the button before him must simply be a metaphor; something that would allow him to access details on the other side of his imposed mental boundary.

"Before we go any further," said Miles, "can you tell me how I should address you?"

There was a long pause this time. Evidently his request was being given very thorough consideration. The voice now replied:

"My name is Fai."

"Thank you, Fai," he replied, "Why are we both here?"

"You saved my life. It is my hope that you too can be saved."

Miles hovered his finger over the button.

CONVERGENCE

21st December 2112

The Discovery continued to manoeuvre away from the ISS and its cloud of fabricators. Although Mike, Cathy and Anna were within an area designated as the cockpit, Fai had complete control of the piloting operations.

"We're clear of the central axis, Lana," said Mike, "How's the hibernation clock?"

"Two hours thirty-one to go," Lana replied, *"I still have time."*

"And how long until we lose comms with you?" said Cathy.

"Forty seconds or so."

Although they had efficiently prepared for the physical departure, there had been little time to prepare mentally. They'd already said their goodbyes at the airlock, but there was something more significant about these final seconds; Mike knew that when the conversation ended, they may not speak again.

The Discovery rolled into position, pointing towards the ISS cupola and Lana who was stationed inside.

"I'll miss the FLC poker," said Lana, looking out towards them.

"Only because you never lost," Mike suddenly found himself grinning at the memory of all five FLC crew members in the cramped Drum, "How many times did I lose and have to do your Lima run?"

"I stopped counting."

"There was just no reading you, Lana," Cathy smiled, "You were one cool customer."

"Cool? I was the Ice Queen," Lana used her own nickname and laughed.

Mike exchanged glances with Cathy; it was still an unusual sound for them.

"Laughter suits you," said Anna from the seat behind him, "It's good to hear."

They could all see Lana smiling, *"Thank you, Anna."*

There was a quiet beep from the navigation console in front of Mike.

"It looks like we're reaching the clearance distance, Lana."

"Confirmed Mike," she appeared to be pointing toward the Earth, *"Go get some fresh air."*

At the FLC, it was a phrase she'd use when he was out replacing the CO2 scrubber cartridges at Lima station. Here, the same words had a new meaning. Using his old FLC counter-response to her phrase he replied:

"Copy that, keep the lights on."

She didn't respond.

Framed in the window of the cupola, Lana Yakovna was frozen mid-wave. The Field had been reactivated aboard the ISS.

Lana and the others aboard the ISS were now held within an invisible, epoch-skipping sphere. He wanted to call out and tell Fai to wait a little longer, but he knew it was pointless; in a very real sense, Lana already belonged to an inaccessible past.

Fai's voice, newly integrated with the Discovery, broke the silence.

"Coordinates set. Navigation locked. Roll."

The Discovery rolled away from the view of the ISS and Mike saw the bright blue Earth slide into place.

He looked down at the destination coordinates displayed on the screen.

'65.05 16.75'

The Jupiter message had contained the prefix 'EVA', something that appeared to have a different meaning for each of those who read it. He'd seen it as the necessity to conduct an EVA to the Earth's surface at a particular set of coordinates.

In the distance, looping behind the planet, a ring of scintillating lunar debris sparkled in the abundant sunlight. That such a destructive act could ever yield something of such beauty was incomprehensible.

Maybe Cathy had been right. Perhaps there were more depths to the Jupiter message that they couldn't quite see yet; they'd just have to see where this took them.

He held out his hand towards Cathy and found that she was doing the same.

"Earth injection sequence," reported Fai, *"Full thrust."*

•

Danny's arm was beginning to ache. Even with the support of Kate's crutch, his hand was starting to go numb as it held aloft the silver case that he'd stolen from Alfred Barnes during the infirmary scuffle.

On the basis that he was wearing a jumpsuit that was empty when they'd placed him in it, they hadn't searched him again. He found it deeply ironic that Alfred's own Civil Protection Officers had escorted him and the metathene case out of the Node.

Suddenly the light from the Node changed.

The observation window had become completely opaque and was casting a cold, ethereal glow on the surroundings.

"What happened?" he heard a voice call out.

"They pulled the curtains…" someone else replied, walking towards the fire.

"Come on," said Caroline, helping him lower his stiff arm from the crutch, "Not much point in us making a statement like that, then dying of acute hypoth-, extreme cold."

He remembered the walk back to the fire, the interior of a tent, but not the moment that sheer exhaustion had simply turned off his consciousness.

The quality of the light diffusing through the tent's thin material now, told him that the night had already passed. With an efficiency that rivalled the Node, sleep had transported him forwards several hours in a black, dreamless instant.

He unzipped the tent and stood awkwardly in the pale wash of morning. It seemed strange to be seeing a sky where the clouds didn't continually condense and evaporate. He hadn't noticed it the previous night but in the current calm, he heard the faint sound of rippling water from the surrounding moat.

He walked past their newly re-dedicated 'ARK IV' stone and arrived at the remains of the old bridge. Far below, the cold waters lapped almost lazily at the island. The supply crates had not included anything as useful as an inflatable dinghy with which to cross the body of water, so their work efforts yesterday had concentrated on beginning a replacement bridge. With only a few hours of daylight though, progress had been slow. He tugged at the new ropes that were attached to the rusty ironwork and hoped that the metal would hold when they eventually came to use it.

"Morning..." said Tyler.

When Danny turned to face him, Tyler was completely dwarfed by the mass of the Node behind him.

"I didn't dream it then?" he took the ration pack that Tyler was offering, "I see the window's still blanked."

"Yeah," Tyler looked back at the Node too, "The Doc reckons it's cos Barnes doesn't want people reading our message."

"I'd say she's right," said Danny, "But people saw it, Ty."

They walked back through the makeshift camp of tents and supply crates. Their inventory ranged from useful medical supplies that Caroline was busily inspecting, to a set of half-charged DRBs stolen from the Observation deck. With no means to recharge them though, the expensive piece of technology would simply become dead weight on their journey; anything it had recorded would soon pass into obscurity.

Danny saw that Tyler was actually smiling.

"What?"

"I reckon it'll be a pale blue today," said Tyler pointing to the sky, "Not as colourful as yesterday, but I'll take it."

"You know these rations ain't gonna last for ever, right?" Danny reiterated their predicament.

"Yeah?" he frowned.

"And that doesn't bother you?"

"Hell, no!" Tyler shook his head, grinning, "As soon as we get off this island, we get to build a whole new *world!* We'll be *making* food!"

It seemed that Tyler had an outlook that could offset their dire situation through sheer optimism. Danny was about to tell him so when there was a distant rumble of thunder that seemed to underline his own pessimism.

"Unfortunately," said Danny, "this new world still has storms, let's get everyone under cover. We've got to keep the clothes dry…"

Danny stopped when he saw that Tyler wasn't moving, he was just looking around at the sky.

"What storm?" said Tyler.

The distant, thunderous noise reached them again and Danny turned away from the Node, expecting to see darker skies. However the sky was just as clear to the south.

The distant noise was now attracting the attention of the others, who stopped what they were doing to gather around him and Tyler, asking what they were looking at.

The thunder suddenly rose in volume and Danny saw what looked like a star to the south. Then the star grew in length to take on the appearance of a thin slit, as though the sky itself were being opened to reveal a brighter light beyond. His first horrific thought was that it was a stray piece of lunar debris, or a meteorite coming to finish what Siva had begun, but then he saw something else.

As the brilliant white line continued to etch itself across the pale blue sky, he saw an object at its leading edge; an object that, even at this distance, appeared nothing like a piece of rock.

Danny had the faint impression that the object was surrounded by a transparent sphere; visible only because of a distortion to the air surrounding it. The distortion then seemed to shrink in a series of rapid steps, exposing the object within.

Then the object changed course.

Danny whirled around to look at the others, to see if they were witnessing the same thing; without exception, they were. His eyes fell on the dominating presence of the Node behind them, where the observation window was still opaque. They had chosen to mask their view of the exiles; as a consequence, they'd also obscured the outside world. For them, these latest events simply did not exist.

When he turned back, the object was much closer

and clearly artificial. The grey mass looked aircraft-like and had a certain familiarity to it, as though aspects of its design had been inspired by several different aviation sources.

At low altitude, the craft swept past them and disappeared behind the Node's massive hemisphere. When it emerged on the other side, Danny saw that it was moving even slower than before. He could see that the craft was descending rather than gliding. Accompanied by a jet engine-like noise, it continued to make its way around the Node and then headed towards the far shore on the opposite side of the moat. Almost as one, everyone ran to the edge of their small island.

Continuing its slow, hovering descent towards the Icelandic terrain, landing struts appeared to unfold beneath the craft. The jet-like noise suddenly dropped in pitch and the craft touched down. As it settled into position, the noise swiftly wound down, leaving only a faint echo that dissipated over Öskjuvatn Lake.

A cheer went up from everyone on the island, including Danny himself.

"We're saved!" Caroline shouted and hugged him, then returned to waving at the far shore along with everyone else. After several minutes, there had been no signs of life from the craft and the celebrations subsided slightly. People busied themselves packing supply crates and dismantling their tents, but it was all done with a sense of optimism.

"Told you, didn't I?" said Tyler, "Gonna be a whole new world."

Danny didn't reply.

Rising above the craft and heading in their direction was a hovering, black drone. Extending down from it was a shiny metal rod.

EXORDI NOVA

2nd January 7142

A tka knew that the disturbances of this night would be remembered by the people of his village for generations to come.

He had been present when the Orb had first shaken the very earth under his feet. Trees had vanished in frightening flashes of purple light as he ran to the village.

When he had returned to the island with the Elder, the Guardian within the Orb had witnessed his initiation; the ceremonial ash markings and the passing over of the precious stone set within a ring of metal.

When Atka had placed the metal ring into a time-worn box, shadows in the warm ice of its flat surface had taken the form '2400' before flowing like black water to form '1200'. The shapes themselves were meaningless to him, yet when the forms faded, the Sky-Spirits also faded. The Elder had fled from the island and the Orb's radiance had then also faded into darkness.

Beholding a sight that previous generations had never seen, the Orb now appeared as a dense black silhouette against the star-filled sky. Yet in the quiet darkness of the empty island, he felt that something was keeping fear at bay.

Until now, he had thought that he was simply taking his place within the long chain of Elders that had accompanied the Orb throughout the ages. He had never expected to be the one who would bear witness to The Guardians' return.

His eyes adjusted to the shadows and he saw movement within the Orb. Where once a single Guardian had stood, were many silhouettes. Their slow, flowing movements had vanished; they now moved with a speed equal to his own.

Many of the figures carried short sticks that held a cold, white fire at one end, yet did not appear to burn. The lights moved in complex patterns, swiftly following each other deeper into the darkened Orb and out of sight.

A sense of calm settled over the island, then ahead of him a hissing sound cut the air. The Orb was not fashioned from materials he knew but he tried to interpret what was happening before him.

In one small place, the skin of the Orb folded away to reveal a hollow space. Within it he could see dots of white fire, bobbing and weaving close to the ground and getting closer.

The Guardians were emerging from the Orb.

The one leading the way raised a white-fire stick, illuminating the way ahead and also her face.

It was the Guardian who had first pointed at him.

Her fiery crimson hair was no longer floating but her

eyes still shone with the same intensity.

A thought from earlier in the evening re-entered his distracted mind: many of his people still speculated that The Guardians came from the stars and may one day depart from here, taking their followers with them.

In reverence, he bowed his head and, summoning all his courage, spoke to her.

"Archiv Exordi Nova," he recited, tracing his finger around the metal ring in his hands, "Ekwayta Fine-dus Eridanus."

He then raised his head and waited for her response.

He knew that The Guardians had been watching them for generations, but no-one had ever heard them speak. There was no way of knowing what her reply ought to be.

"Issabiomag," she whispered, a puzzled expression on her face. She then turned to the other Guardians while pointing at the box by Atka's feet, "Howdeegeta..."

He saw that the other Guardians were now exchanging puzzled expressions and whispers. Wondering if he'd made a mistake in his words or somehow offended them, he prepared to recite the words again.

Before he could begin, she turned to face him and he could see that all confusion had left her face. She was smiling at him. Instantly, he felt all anxiety leave him and he stood transfixed by her bright eyes.

Still looking into his eyes, she bowed her head very slightly. She then patted her chest according to the pulses of her voice.

"Ca-Si-Dee."

It seemed that The Guardians were familiar with aspects of their communication. She was naming herself. He felt the warm glow of understanding spread through him and began to smile too.

"Casidee," he attempted her name, something which appeared to please her.

He heard his ancestors speak within him, telling him not to be afraid and compelling him to guide her to the ancient stone. Extending his arm towards it, she followed him to the fractured 'ARK IV' stone.

He ran his hand over the groups of lines that read: *'CRESCATKATEFORTIOR'.*

His name was clearly visible in the middle, overlapping his mother's name, Esca. He pointed to the shapes that depicted his name and then faced Casidee.

"At-ka," he patted his chest. Then, in respect, touched the circle of ash upon his forehead, "Exordi Nova, Ca-si-dee."

Still smiling, her shining eyes studied his.

"Exordi Nova, Atka," she replied and touched her forehead.

"Ekwayta Fine-dus Eridanus," Atka offered up the metal ring.

The mumbled voices of the other Guardians behind her, caused her expression to change.

"Fine-dus?" her head tilted slightly.

He understood and guided her around the stone to reach the opposite side; a side that had never received light from the Orb.

In the shadows, the Guardian raised her white fire, dispelling the darkness and revealing the circular symbols and instructions laid down by the forefathers many generations ago.

As the Guardian ran her hand over the ancient carvings, she suddenly stopped at the most detailed glyph. She turned to face him, her expression now alive and urgent.

"Atka," she pointed at her eyes and then touched the stone markings again, "Sho-me!"

E V A

Field series: Book 4 (Excerpt)

Continue into the Field at
www.futurewords.uk

The artificial gravity provided by their continuous spin was absent up here, so it took her a few moments to readjust to the weightless environment. Pushing between handholds, she made her way through the ISS central axis modules.

Each segment still seemed familiar, but some had necessarily been powered down, making her navigation a controlled drift through patches of darkness. Like her own memories, she thought, some portions were now more brightly lit than others.

Ahead of her, the cupola lay in shadow; stripped of its equipment, only the circular window arrangement remained. The view beyond its glazing, however, had changed irrevocably. In comparison to the last time she was here, the landscape far below was almost unrecognisable. If she looked carefully, she could see the lights of New Houston. Although Eva's destructive actions were beyond comprehension, those same actions had led them here.

Time and change, she thought. Still taking in the wide view, she placed her bare hand against the cupola's cold glass one last time. Apes had once extended their hands to a star-filled sky; time and change had altered that perspective too.

With a gentle flex of her hand she pushed herself away, leaving only her fingerprints on the glass. She found herself smiling; the marks may one day become some of the furthest-travelled fingerprints in human history.

Drawing a deep breath, she emerged into the central axis and focussed on the present. Like so many of their previous endeavours, time and timing were always critical. The ISS separation sequence would be no different.

More details of the Field series are available at
www.futurewords.uk

36363872R00338

Printed in Great Britain
by Amazon